CRIMES OF REDEMPTION

A NOVEL

LINDA McDONALD

THE ROADRUNNER PRESS
OKLAHOMA CITY, OKLAHOMA

Published by The RoadRunner Press
Oklahoma City
www.TheRoadRunnerPress.com

Published October 16, 2012

Library of Congress Control Number: 2012939716

Publisher's Cataloging-In-Publication Data
(Prepared by The Donohue Group, Inc.)

McDonald, Linda, 1943-
    Crimes of redemption : a novel / Linda McDonald. -- 1st ed.

    p. ; cm.

    ISBN: 978-1-937054-25-0 (hardcover)

    1. Murder--Investigation--Oklahoma--Fiction. 2. Sheriffs--Oklahoma--Fiction. I.
Title.

PS3613.C366 C75 2012
813/.6   2012939716

For Gwynedene and Jack

Crimes of Redemption

CHAPTER 1

NOT MUCH WAS left of his face. One gray eye lay frozen half open. The other swam in what was left of his jaw. Leaning over him, Gayla held her breath, gripping a raised two-by-four so hard her fingers had turned blue-white.

The bottom half of the man looked curiously normal in the fading light — given the businessman he had been: Expensive Italian loafers, nylon trouser socks, pleated dress pants, all barely splashed by the dark red wave spreading over his silk shirt. Gayla stood but had to steady herself as the cinder block basement started to swirl, sinking in on itself.

Damp silence weighted the cellar air. She could feel pressure building in her eardrums and, for a moment, thought she might faint. Oh no, not now, she thought.

Relief came in the swoosh of a cardinal past the ground-level basement window, a blurred red streak, barely visible through the nailed wooden slats. She sucked in air, breaking the room's quiet with a wet rattle. Sounds started back up. First, the brittle buzz of cicadas. Then distant barking, cutting in and out like a haywire radio signal.

Limping to the window, she peered through where the two-by-four had just minutes before blocked off the outside world, but all she could see was a bit of lawn and a wooden fence.

"No, no, no," Gayla cried.

She slid down the wall and sat there. Legs splayed. She had nothing else to give. It had taken everything she had just to get to here. Oh no, she thought, not another wall. She glanced at his dead body and remembered what was certainly in one of his pockets. For the first time in a long time, her eyes closed and her breath slowed at the thought. Pop one of those babies, and nothing else would matter . . .

"Stop it." The sound of her own voice made her jump and jarred her back into the moment. She inhaled sharply. The pungent smell of his pooling blood turned her stomach, but she could not give up now. There had to be another way out.

Gayla pulled herself up, rubbing her aching leg. He must have fallen on it in their struggle. It hurt to put her weight on it. She limped towards the pine staircase at the far end of the room, a feature she had never been able to examine up close. She knew this end of the room only through sounds — the heavy grind of hinges on his arrivals.

With an effort, she lumbered up the stairs, noticing their still like-new smell. They stopped at a ceiling trapdoor. It was too dark to see the details of the square metal cover, but she gave it a push with her shoulder. There was no give. Then she saw the glint of metal locks. Two of them, one hanging on each corner.

For a moment, her heart beat faster. The keys would be in his pants pocket. In the darkness she grabbed one of the big locks, feeling its surface, like a blind person translating braille. Her fingertips read the cruel truth. Not a key lock but a combination. She shuffled back down the stairs before recalling what he had promised from the start: "You will never outsmart me. If anything happens to me down here, you are dead, dead, dead, sweetie."

Until now the reason for his confidence had never been clear. He could lock us both in without worrying, she realized now, because he was the only one who could get us both out. She knew without checking there would be no combinations neatly hidden in his billfold.

Tears threatened. Don't you dare, a voice in her head warned: If you go there, you are done — do something, do anything. She picked up the piece of two-by-four she had dropped at the bottom of the stairs and started at a limping gallop across the cellar floor to the window. She swung the board against the window's slats.

"Son of a bitch," she screamed.

She directed the epithet partly at the dead man and partly at the resilience of the boards covering her one and only escape route. Her frustration mounting, she swung again at the window, her hands bleeding more with each contact.

There was an odd newness to these concrete block walls and floor. Clean. Sterile — save for the blood from the enormous dead man seeping onto the floor. Everything else was gray. She stared down at the man, sprawled on his back before her. Her breath quickened.

What remained of his mouth twisted to the far right. More unnerving yet had been the air he gargled into the room after the first few blows. Her surprise at his childlike bleeps of pain and his helplessness when he finally went down had nearly undone her resolve. For a moment she had been afraid she could not finish it. But then her repulsion for him returned, more visceral than ever. It was too late for this thick, pale-skinned man to cry for her sympathy now.

She could not believe she had survived him, any more than she could believe he was dead. Her eyes finally adjusted to the sunlight, she looked out the window. The cedar fence just beyond blocked a full view of the outside, but at least there was the warmth of light. And sky. And a tangerine sun sinking into the rusty earth.

She felt better, then saw his blood darkening the seams of the concrete floor. Everything started to swirl together again. Outside, the sky began melting into a pale lilac. She shook her head, trying to clear the fog. Now that it was over, everything felt heightened, yet blurry, unreal. The sting of her cut, bleeding hands. The chill on her neck where her damp hair clung. His grotesque corpse in the middle of a room that now smelled like death. Even lifeless, he could still cause a familiar sour taste to rise in her throat: Almost metallic . . . the taste of fear.

A breeze ushered in the sweet smell of wood burning somewhere, perhaps a nearby campfire. The scent pushed into her fragile consciousness. She dropped the two-by-four with a clatter and hugged her own nakedness. She gasped.

"Where are my clothes?"

She looked down at Albert Raeder as though he might answer.

CHAPTER 2

SHERIFF TOMMY MAYNARD TOOK a final drag off his joint, then dropped the roach into an Altoid tin. It was another mile to the Raeder cabin, plenty of time to douse a cotton ball in the aftershave he kept in the glove compartment for times like this. Stick it in one of the air vents and turn on the interior fan full blast. If anyone ever did catch a whiff of pot, he figured the person would probably never dare mention it. Still, he was meticulous with his little ritual. He stuck a piece of Dentyne in his mouth and rolled towards what promised to be a lousy way to start the week.

The frantic call had come in as soon as he hit the station.

"Now, ma'am, you're all excited. Just slow down."

"You don't understand. I've been looking for days now. I'm sure he's in the shed. Oh sheriff, I'm so afraid."

With that, the tinsel female voice on the phone had shifted into high pitched sobs. Tommy had turned on his steadiest law enforcement voice, the one proven best at breaking through a wall of fear and inducing calm in the hysterical.

"Can you actually see him in the shed, ma'am?"

"No, no, no. That's where the smell is coming from. The shed."

That news had seriously cut into his morning buzz. By the time he had taken her name, a Mrs. Albert Raeder, and the location, the couple's getaway cabin on the east side of the local lake, it would have taken a dozen tokes just to get him back on maintenance.

It did not sit well with him that his morning would now be spent breaking into some reeking storage shed. In rural Oklahoma, that never boded well. The hysteric on the phone said she had no key to the out building, but even if she had she would have been afraid to look inside. That was how scary the odor was.

By the time he had found a crowbar and bolt cutter, his Monday was officially headed south. Probably the gal's husband was in Las Vegas, whoring it up, he thought, as he pushed his fingers through a thick crop of salt-and-pepper hair, and he would be stuck hauling out the family's dead dog or something worse. He shuddered at the thought. Decomposing anything could set him gagging.

He craved a few more of what he felt anyone in the same situation would certainly consider to be medicinal tokes, but he was already pulling up to the cabin. A woman stood in the driveway, waving wildly, as he pulled in.

"Finally you're here," she screamed, running alongside the cruiser as fast as three-inch, slingback pumps would allow.

Sheriff Maynard took in what had to be the caller: Blonde color job. Subtle. Expensive, he thought. Ditto the teal satin blouse and short skirt. She was eating-disorder-thin, which turned him off. There was nothing to hold onto with women like that, not their bodies or their minds. Mascara streaked her cheeks, looking curiously like dried blood splatter. And her cherry mouth was long and twisted, reminding him of those Scream masks all the kids used to wear for Halloween.

No way this call ended well. High-maintenance society-types, like this woman, were never satisfied. No matter the outcome. He saw stacks of paperwork in his near future. Sheriff Maynard sighed. Without even trying, Mrs. Albert Raeder had completely crashed his carefully constructed high.

CHAPTER 3

WILLIE MORRIS FIXED THE same breakfast every morning. She fried bacon, then scrambled eggs in the leftover grease, spackling them with black cast iron. It was treacherous for her varicose veins and hardening arteries, but she believed it was a pleasant way to grow her soul. Some people pray, she thought. I fry bacon.

Maxine, her ancient poodle crippled with arthritis and cataracts, stayed close, hugging the leg that would soon bend so Willie could offer her some soft eggs, one of the few foods the dog could gum down.

"Hold on, sweetie, it's comin'," Willie reassured her. "They have to cool down a little first."

Maxine licked the thick toes jutting out of knock-off Birkenstocks. Willie giggled at the sensation.

"You better quit it now. You're gonna get Willie all excited."

Such playfulness in the Morris kitchen would have shocked most people in the town of Luckau, Oklahoma. They believed Willie to be a loner, a curmudgeon. Her isolation in this tiny cabin five miles outside the limits of the town had earned her spook status among the local teenagers. Not that Willie Morris gave a rat's ass what anybody thought about her.

She blew on the hot eggs to hurry the cooling along and glanced out the kitchen window towards the road. A peripheral movement startled her. She looked again and almost dropped the pan of eggs.

A hunched human shape limped into her front yard, only to collapse against the gate. Willie squinted her seventy-year-old eyes for better focus. A stained blanket barely covered the body. Willie caught gasps of nakedness as white as the underside of a snake. Several minutes passed and whatever it was stayed in a pile of limbs and blanket.

As she hurried to the door, Willie debated whether she should grab her gun. She only kept it for rabid skunks or thieving coyotes. Trespassers were rarely an issue in these parts. Unnerved, she hoped whatever was there in the yard would not need killing.

Before she could decide, the lump gave a moan that raised prickles on her arms. A deep guttural sound. Not entirely human. More like the last hopeless howl of a dying critter, the kind she heard from the woods now and again. Willie pressed against the window and saw the shape drop to the grass, groaning now . . . obviously in pain. Oblivious to the drama unfolding outside, Maxine barked, a raspy demand for eggs.

"In a minute, baby. We got company." Willie grabbed her shotgun and headed out the door.

An hour later Willie Morris sat at her kitchen table, staring at the human wreck scarfing down a second skillet of eggs across from her. The dirt-encrusted woman made her think of those zombies so popular with the young people. Matted, oily auburn hair hiding the whitest face she had ever seen. Even spookier, the poor thing seemed unaware of where she was or what she was doing there. At least she had a good appetite. Willie watched the woman dip her face to the plate, using her fork as a shovel — eyes darting back and forth like a skittish dog guarding its bowl.

It had taken all of Willie's strength to pull her up and half-walk, half-carry her into the house. Not only was she nearly naked under that filthy blanket, but her hands and feet were shredded and covered in mud and blood.

Maxine had quickly set up shop at the stranger's feet, busy cataloging this unexpected feast of nasty odors. Willie had caught the old poodle enough times rolling in some fresh dung pile in the back pasture to know that Maxine was rejoicing in the outstanding stink of their guest.

The young woman finished her bacon and eggs and downed an entire glass of milk without taking a breath. Willie decided it was time to find out a few things.

"You look like you been through a war zone," she said, keeping her tone casual.

Her guest jumped at the sound of Willie's voice but gave no response.
"Your hands and feet are cut pretty bad. Anything else hurt?"
Blank greenish eyes stared back.
"My name is Willie Morris. I live here. What's your name?"
Her guest retreated deeper into the blanket.
"I'm not going to hurt you, honey. You're safe here. You understand?"
The stranger gave a tentative nod.
"Now, not being inquisitive — Lord knows I don't like folks prying into my business — but how long since you had a good bath? I could run you some nice, hot water. Might even have some bubble bath from Dollar General. Have a bunch of old clothes in there that don't fit anymore, bein' as how I'm gettin' big as the broad side of a barn. Probably got five or six different sizes. Whadda ya say? A hot bath and some clean clothes?"
The creature looked up at her, so desperate and lost, Willie had to swallow at the sight. Not more than thirty-five, Willie guessed, but her face seemed much older. Used. Finally, a tired nod.
"Alrighty then." Willie struggled to sound positive.
"Thank you," the woman said. Tears swam in her eyes.
"Ah, she speaks. That's a beginning," Willie said.
The creature nodded and pointed to herself.
"Gayla."
"Well, Gayla, let's get you cleaned up."
Willie lightly touched the pale woman's shoulder, caught off guard by a slight catch in her own throat.
"Then I'll take a look at those wounds."

CHAPTER 4

SHERIFF TOMMY MAYNARD wondered how they were gonna get their victim to the nearest medical examiner, sixty miles away in Elk City. Raeder's stocky German build came in at more than three hundred pounds and he had been dead several days. If only the examiner would arrive. Not enough weed in the world to kill this smell, he thought.

At least the screaming wife was gone. He was ready to whack her himself. Over the years he had built up a tolerance, even coping skills, for the meltdowns at accident scenes, but this one had made his ears hurt. Now she was her parents' problem; he wondered how fast the elderly couple would be flooring it home to Tulsa.

Not his concern.

The body she left behind, however, was. He figured Mrs. Albert Raeder must feel pretty guilty about something, or else why put on the big soap-opera act. By the time he had sifted through her shrill answers, the only facts that remained were that she had not seen her husband for the last two weeks, spent precious little time with him in general, and traveled more times without the man than with him.

Tommy dunked a couple cotton balls in aftershave and crammed them back up his nostrils. The sharp sweetness of the macho spice burned into soft tissues that shot all the way back into his throat. He stifled a desire to gag. Maybe he would have a chance to grab some fresh joints out of his stash back in his trailer. Pick up some whiskey before he had to help move the body. He could use that for the cotton balls instead of this nauseating spice tonic. Throw back a couple of shots, too, he thought, because I did not hire on for this circus.

For now, he was stuck waiting for the assistance he had requested from Elk City to arrive. He considered a run to the cruiser for a quick buzz, but he knew his little cow-patty town. Word of the murder would have spread like an airborne virus. Everybody and his dog would be snooping around soon.

He took in the nearly new basement before him. He had used a crowbar to pry open the locked trapdoor in the middle of the garage — or shed, as the wife had referred to it — after he had found broken glass and blood around back, where someone had slipped either in or out through a ground-level window. It was hard to tell which. The wooden slats on the window had been battered away, and someone a lot smaller than him had slid through the narrow opening. Whoever it was had left a blood trail that he had sicced his deputy Frankie Lee on. Tommy always trusted his deputy, an expert hunter, with any tracking duties.

It was not easy to look at Albert Raeder, but it was harder to keep his eyes off him. Tommy had seen plenty of death in 'Nam, mainly Viet Cong spread around in fields or leaned up against trees, grinning corpses designed to scare the living crap out of you. He hated remembering that. He had seen what remembering did to soldiers. When that "shitty little war," as they called it, was over, he had parted ways with his buddies and never seen most of them again. No need to make matters worse, he had reasoned. Why revisit the ugly past? At least now his occasional dreams of death were not about people he had known. Not like some of the buddies he had cut out of his life. All these decades later, too many of them were still mired in the past, aging men with photographs of their dead friends taped to their hearts.

Tommy had long ago decided he did not want to look at any more death. Instead he spent years drifting from place to place, hauling his thirty-two-foot Airstream behind his trusty Ford pickup. When he had tired of wandering, it was just as the Kiowa County sheriff's gig opened in Luckau, less than an hour from Elk City, where he grew up. Luckau was one of the few German settlements that had not Americanized its name following World War II, when fear of reprisal still hung in the air.

To this day, he was not entirely sure why he had jumped at the chance to join the small town department. It certainly was not because he enjoyed locking people up. But he had figured, correctly, that would be a minimal part of the job. Until now, it had been more baby-sitting than life and death — public intoxications, traffic ticket quotas, the occasional domestic disturbance. Easy enough for an affable stoner to hold down.

This was a whole new level, though. Raeder had been pulverized with a two-by-four that still lay in congealed blood a few feet from the body. Had to be personal, he thought. Someone had to have had some nasty shared history to get out of his system to keep bashing a head in like that.

Tommy could not find an ounce of cheer in the stark gray concrete block walls of the room, but he was also struck by how empty it was. The basement lacked the detritus of life, the leftovers and junk that usually filled attics and sheds, garages and basements. What was the deal? It was as though the Raeders had never moved in. Except for the blood, about the only thing to see was the body.

He averted his gaze to avoid the staring dead eye. A utility sink and toilet filled one corner of the room. Because the wife allowed no greasy hands in the house? He cataloged the thought. A cot was overturned close by. Why in the hell would anybody sleep down here?

"Tommy Maynard, you worthless tit."

Tommy nearly jumped out of his skin.

He swung around to see Elmo Dudgeon, the good-ol'-boy sheriff from Elk City. Elmo's gut had preceded him in a uniform that barely covered it. He huffed down the basement steps, the smell of hair tonic preserving a late-Elvis inspired haircut.

"What the hell you got up your nose, Tommy?" Dudgeon snorted.

Tommy yanked out the dangling cotton and extended his hand, hoping he had not looked too dorky to his big city counterpart from Beckham County.

"Your balls, Elmo, soaked in smell-em-good."

"Always the funny man," Elmo said to the young man in a nylon Crime Scene Unit windbreaker behind him. "Tommy Maynard, I think you know Joe Nguyen, our crime-scene man."

After perfunctory niceties, Joe offered them both paper dust masks.

"Beats those cotton balls," he said, nodding at Tommy's nose.

Grateful, Tommy put it on, while Elmo did the same. Then Elmo and Joe gloved up for a closer look at the body. Tommy avoided this unpleasantry by nosing around the cellar instead.

"This supposed to be some kind of safe room?" Elmo asked after a few minutes.

"Hell if I know." Tommy said. "Looks awful new, though. And see how it's all boarded up. Strange. Somebody sleeping down here, you think?" He pointed out the cot.

"Maybe a drifter or degenerate was crashing here, and Raeder surprised 'em," Elmo said.

Tommy nodded.

"Could be, but . . ."

He indicated the broken slats and glass.

"There's glass and blood inside and out. Can't be sure if somebody broke in or out."

Joe looked up briefly. "Maybe both. We'll take samples."

As exchanges about lividity and body temperature between Elmo and Joe faded in and out, Tommy wandered over to the cot. The legs were stained with something dark. He noticed for the first time the metal rungs embedded in the wall behind the toppled cot. A heavy chain was hooked to one of them, just long enough to reach the sink. What the hell?

It was not just the dead guy, he decided, giving him a chill. Tommy had never thought of himself as overly sensitive, but he felt a dreadful recognition, the kind of feeling that always came over him when he looked at creepy drawings in history books of the Salem witch trials or the Inquisition. For a moment the feeling cold-clamped him so hard, he had to struggle to get his next breath.

CHAPTER 5

OUTSIDE A VELVET SKY slipped through waving tree lace. Inside, Gayla woke with a start, disoriented in the darkness. Was night falling or a new day starting? Where was she? Sometimes, on waking, it took her a few moments to distinguish the quiet of the country from the silence of the basement. She lay still on the creaky rollaway in the front room of Willie's cabin, taking in the pockmarked gray room. She caught the comforting smell of flannel from Willie's old pajamas she was wearing and buried her face in a sleeve.

After she had left home (okay been booted out) Gayla had moved to Houston, where she found it tough to acclimate to the city rhythms — streets always snarling with traffic, people living stacked in humid box apartments, strangers screaming in foreign languages. Oh, how she had longed for quiet then.

But Gayla could never have imagined the dark vacuum that pressed itself into her basement prison. It was like a frequency you could never hear but could always feel. What few rustles of nature found their muffled way into the dark room could only be imagined, not seen.

Yet, as much as she had despised that soundless tension, the familiar noises that signaled his arrival were worse. The clunk as he opened the padlock to the shed. The scrape of metal as he pulled back the trapdoor latch. The dust sifting between the cracks in the wooden staircase, as his deafening footsteps marched down the stairs. And always that first moment when he came into view.

The sound of Willie moving around in the other room pulled her into the present. Through the window, the remnants of a vanilla moon spilled shadows on the table and wood stove. The smell of wood burning. When was that? She could not remember how long she had been free. Days? A week?

Everything seemed clearer, sharper in her head. She was sure of that. The grayness was peeling away. Her limp was much improved. Her feet and hands, which Willie had applied antibiotic ointment to and wrapped with gauze, were healing. Only the nasty gashes on her side, one of her hands, and her foot still ached.

A wet tongue tickled her ankle. She jerked, saw Maxine, and giggled. The ancient one could still sniff her way around.

"Good morning, Maxine."

She leaned off the bed to pet the poodle. The dog had assumed the role of her protector-in-chief, shadowing Gayla from room to room. And in spite of her crooked body, cataracts, and deafness, Maxine provided Gayla with a sense of security when she was about.

Outside the sky was turning the color of new hydrangeas. A new day for me, too. The thought just popped up. She smiled at the Hallmark flavor of it, but inside she prayed the notion was not impossible. It did seem pretty iffy. You remember what happened, she thought. You did what you had to do, fine. But who is gonna believe the likes of you?

"There you are."

Willie's voice made her jump. Gayla turned to see her, framed in the doorway in faded blue robe and slippers.

"Didn't mean to startle you," Willie said, watching Maxine lick at Gayla's toes. "Just be glad she can only work with her tongue now. In her prime, she used to hump my leg every chance she got. Whether I was sitting down or standing at the sink, here she'd come."

Willie chuckled, then looked down at Gayla.

"You look a little spooked. You okay?"

"Fine. Just . . . all the quiet."

"It can take some getting used to," Willie said, with a grin. "Especially if you've never been around the country much."

Gayla's smile froze. That was the second time Willie had brought that up. Fishing for information.

Willie was hardly ready to drop it, either.

"You know, I'm wondering if your family might not be looking for you," she said.

Don't want anybody looking for me, Gayla thought to herself. I'm in enough trouble as it is.

Gayla could barely reconstruct her last day in the basement, but she knew for sure how it had ended. She remembered tearing the broken slats off the window and scraping her side squeezing through the narrow opening to freedom. She had gathered her few clothes and layered herself up — three blouses and a couple of skirts. He had taken her underwear and shoes long before. "You're not going very far in bare feet, even if you do break out," he had said, grinning.

Before she left, she had stuck her toothbrush in a pocket and grabbed her sheet and blanket. The cedar fence outside her prison had a gate and after opening it, Gayla remembered standing frozen, staring at the outside world for the first time in what seemed a lifetime. She saw a serene lake, such a deep turquoise it made her throat tighten. On the bank, sage scrub oaks rustled. Beneath them, lanky riverbank grasses reached their long fingers into the twilight. As she watched, the lake turned itself into ripples of green.

She realized her feet were not only freezing but bleeding from the broken shards of window glass. For protection, and to keep from leaving a blood trail, she tore one of her shirts into strips to wrap her feet and hands. Along the way, she remembered ripping up more clothes, as the strips of cloth became too wet and bloody to stay on. There were other images, like finding that tube of lipstick he had made her wear in a pocket of one of the skirts and tossing it as far into the woods as she could throw, but they were blurred images, seen as through a restless dream.

She slept when she could no longer keep her eyes open, hobbled as far as she could before the pain crippled her legs. A crevice between some boulders became a haven. The smell of evergreens scented her way. It did not fit, but she kept seeing a red blur whoosh by a slatted window. Then . . . him with half a face. Something touched her hand, and Gayla almost jumped out of her skin.

"Hey, it's all right. It's just coffee," Willie said, handing her a steaming white mug. She sat across from Gayla, smiling. "Look, I don't mean to pry. I'm just trying to . . . please let me help you."

Gayla was shocked at the tears that sprang up at those words. It was

Willie's small kindnesses that made her finally lose her grip.

Willie reached down and stroked Maxine, trying to calm both the dog and the situation.

"It's okay. No pressure. It takes time."

"Yes. Takes time." Gayla nodded.

But I have to get out of here long before that, Gayla realized.

Long before.

CHAPTER 6

SITTING IN THE CHERRYWOOD booth in the Raeder kitchen, Sheriff Maynard studied Albert Raeder's file. He was impressed in spite of himself. No wonder half of Elk City had paraded through his office in the last couple of days. And no wonder Sheriff Elmo Dudgeon, who sat across from him this very minute, had glommed onto his investigation like a leech, though Tommy had only requested the help of the larger county sheriff's office because he had need of Joe Nguyen's forensic skills.

Tommy had figured once Elmo's crime scene guy finished up, he and his boss would move on. Let Tommy get back to his murder investigation. Instead Joe Nguyen headed to Elk City with the body, and Elmo took up residence in Tommy's office and the local Days Inn. Why doesn't he hump that sixty miles back and forth? Tommy wondered. The lodging was courtesy of the Elk City Chamber of Commerce. The chamber president had made it clear he would do whatever it took to guarantee the person responsible for the death of the town's favorite citizen didn't go unpunished, as Elmo had explained in a patronizing tone.

Tommy got it, loud and clear. The good citizens of Elk City wanted a round-the-clock watchdog to make sure the bumfuck Luckau country sheriff did not screw things up.

At least the file made it clear why everyone's bowels were in such an uproar. Raeder owned gobs of the most valuable real estate in the county. And it appeared he had never encountered a civic group he did not like.

He belonged to them all: Rotarians, Lions, Elk City Restoration Committee. Hell, he was past president of the Chamber of Commerce.

Apparently, every self-important little prick within a sixty-mile radius had instructed Elmo to micro-manage Tommy's every move. And he had, to the extent that Tommy had not caught a decent high in two days. How could he? Even now, Dudgeon was hunkered over the preliminary autopsy report, bestowing on it a seriousness usually reserved for brain surgery. Smoke from his cigarette burned Tommy's eyes.

"Could you hold that in your other hand?" Tommy asked.

Elmo looked up, with no comprehension.

"Your cigarette. It's in my eyes."

"Oh. Sorry," Elmo said, pressing it into his soda can. He leaned back, his hands locked behind his head, and assessed Tommy.

"So what's your plan of action?"

Tommy cleared his throat and looked up at the ceiling. Prick hasn't let me get a word in edgewise for two days, but now he wants the frigging master plan.

"Well, I've interviewed everyone in the area who was home," he said, which was true. He had combed that side of the lake without hearing anything helpful. "The Raeders got the seclusion they apparently wanted with their eight-foot-tall fence. Nobody, not even our most zealous retirees with high-powered binoculars, ever saw anything but his navy blue Lexus come and go on weekends. Which, by the way, they consider uppity. The Lexus, that is."

Elmo nodded. "Wife rarely came with him either, right?"

"She's hardly the small town fishing-type," Tommy said, remembering the suffocating perfume Mrs. Raeder had left in her wake. "They built this place . . ." He trailed off to locate the date in the folder. "Here it is. Three years ago."

He and Elmo surveyed the cabin's pristine kitchen, which glistened like a new car showroom. Elmo snorted.

"It doesn't look to me like they ever even boiled an egg in here."

The other rooms — with their hardwood floors, southwestern rugs, and fireplace — also looked rich but equally unused. Even the collection of Kachina dolls in the corner looked lonely dancing under glass.

"I haven't found a soul in Elk City that knew about the place either — much less visited," Elmo said. "Not even poker or fishing buddies."

"And we have some of the best catfish around," Tommy said.

"That you do. Maybe he had to glad-hand so much in his business, he just wanted a place to escape to, somewhere he could get away by himself and enjoy some peace and quiet."

"I hear that," Tommy muttered, the edge in his tone flying right over Elmo's head.

Elmo pursed his lips. "But in this big old cabin by himself? It doesn't compute."

"The locals consider a cabin this large a bona fide house, not a week-end getaway," Tommy said.

Its ample three bedrooms and two baths could sleep a truckload of guests, yet the Raeder cabin looked factory-delivered, unlived in.

"And most of them would kill for a workshop as equipped as that 'shed,' as the wife calls it," Tommy added.

They had hoped to find a clue as to what Raeder did there on week-ends when they searched the shed earlier. The ground level appeared, on first glance, like the proverbial garage workshop where husbands routinely disappear. But where was the stuff he tinkered on? Tommy had wondered. Clocks, or building projects, even model cars, for cryin' out loud? It had been outfitted, all right, but most of it lay covered in dust. The trapdoor leading to the basement was the only thing worn with use.

"The answers are in the basement," Tommy said. "Has your boy gotten back the labs on the samples he took?"

"No. Those state boys put about as much priority on this as road-kill," Elmo said. "They say it'll be next week and act like that's some big favor."

"Maybe some of your Elk City big shots oughta visit the capital then," Tommy grumbled, "instead of giving me grief."

"I told our prosecutor to grease some wheels. He's got pull. He'll whip 'em into shape."

Something in the folder caught Tommy's eye. He squinted to make sure he was reading it right. "Are you kidding me? You neglected to mention they found traces of lipstick on his suit coat."

"I didn't tell you that?"

"Come on, Elmo, that's —"

"Sorry." Elmo reddened a little, obviously caught. "Guess I forgot. Looks like a woman might fit in somewhere."

"That woman not being his wife, seeing as how Mrs. Raeder hadn't laid eyes on her husband for two weeks prior to the murder," Tommy said.

"We don't know that for certain — that lipstick could have been on there for ages, since the last time he took it to the cleaners," Elmo argued.

"Either way, information I might need to know, don't you think?" Tommy wanted to strangle the man.

This was the same kind of antics he had put up with for three days now. Elmo dogging his every movement, but blowing Tommy off when it came to passing on his own discoveries. This has gotta stop, Tommy thought. I have to get away from this guy for awhile. He kept his tone studiedly casual.

"There are a few cabins spread out on the valley edge, behind the Raeder place. Maybe I'll ride out there tomorrow, check 'em out," Tommy said.

It hit him belatedly that this would mean interviewing cranky old Willie Morris, who had hated his ass ever since he had to order her to quit burning her garbage in her back pasture. Oh well, he thought, she hates lots of people. More important, riding out to the valley would let him whip by his dealer's to resupply his stash.

Elmo looked up at him as if he were crazy.

"Wait a minute, wait a minute. The press is coming tomorrow."

"You called this big press conference, not me."

"We need that coverage. 'Cause as of now we got nothing."

"Come on, Elmo, I'm no good at that. If I get up there, I'll screw the pooch, sure as hell. You handle it." Tommy could see that Elmo relished the idea of taking it over, even though he harrumphed around as if it were an imposition.

"Hell, I guess I could handle it," Elmo finally agreed. "Now, where is it you're going?"

"Some isolated cabins back of the lake. Maybe somebody heard or saw something. Just in case. We don't wanna give some honcho cause to come after us later for not checking the obvious."

Elmo's head bobbed in agreement. When it came to covering your ass, he rarely missed a trick.

"Yeah, okay. I'll handle the press idiots. But you owe me one."

"Yeah. I owe you," Tommy said.

Tommy's whole demeanor perked up. He felt instantly more generous towards Elmo, just knowing he would have a day without him.

"Your motel room still okay, Elmo?"

Elmo shrugged, then grinned.

"The little night clerk's a cutie. Got that Katie Couric-thing going."

CHAPTER 7

PAUSING BY THE CHECKOUT COUNTER at the local Village Market, Willie double-checked her penciled list. She was not one to come into town any more often than necessary, so if she forgot anything, she had to do without for at least a couple of weeks.

Her eyes narrowed as she came to calamine lotion. Forgot to check if my bottle was dried up, she thought. Could not remember the last time she had bought any; it was probably several years ago, after that brush with the poison ivy. Willie had added it to the list yesterday when Gayla had come in from the outside red as a beet.

"Where you been?" Willie had asked.

"Out back." Gayla seemed unaware that her hours in the sun had turned her porcelain complexion bright pink.

"Well, you do look healthier, I guess." But she was like a sunburned infant. Better get something on that, Willie had thought to herself.

She found herself fascinated by the awkward young woman, and, like Maxine, secretly enjoyed mothering Gayla. Willie was moved by the little things that seemed to delight her strange guest — listening to squirrels dance on the roof, naming the colors of the sunset, giggling at Freddie, Willie's high-stepping rooster. Yet, so far, her name was about all Gayla had revealed.

Willie, written off by most of the town as a terminal kook, not only gave people plenty of room to keep their secrets, she absolutely preferred it. She could not understand why people had started putting everything about themselves up on websites and Facebook. She found the relentless personal details either boring or mildly offensive.

Willie looked up to see Jimmy Puckett, the rotund market owner, struggling with some vegetable crates.

"Jimmy, where's the calamine lotion?"

"Back in the corner, by the razor blades. You doin' okay?"

"Not too bad." It was her standard answer.

When she returned with the only size bottle of calamine available, teensy and obscenely overpriced, Jimmy was slicing through cardboard with his box cutter.

"Say Jimmy, did city council ever meet on the garbage collection?"

This was an old bone Willie could never quit gnawing. Even though everybody in this tiny place had to take their garbage to a local spot, the town still charged a trash disposal fee. And since Willie just burned hers in her back pasture, despite repeated warnings, it stuck in her craw that she still had to fork over the five dollars and fifty cents every month.

Jimmy paused to catch his breath. "I think it was scheduled, but everybody was running so scared after the murder, they ended up talking about metal detectors and forming neighborhood watches instead."

Willie's eyebrows raised. "What murder?"

Jimmy laughed. "You got to get into town more often, Ms. Morris."

"Not necessarily. Who got killed?"

"Guy who had a cabin on the lake. Somebody beat him to death with a two-by-four last weekend."

Stunned, Willie tried to remember a murder ever happening in the area. "Well, that's a first."

"Yep," Jimmy said, "though there was that hit-and-run ten years ago. Killed that little Smith girl. If you count that."

After a moment and no response, he continued. "Name was Albert Raeder from Elk City. He came in here a few times, I think. I recognized his picture from the paper. But he was mainly a weekender."

Jimmy rustled through some clutter in the checkout drawer and handed her the local and state papers with the original story.

"Thanks," Willie said, eyeing the thick face of the victim in the big photo under the front page, above-the-fold headline that read: "Area Businessman Murdered Near Lake Luckau."

"He was quite the big muckety-muck in Elk City," Jimmy said, "but nobody around here seems to remember him."

Willie nodded, fascinated by the man's sunken eyes and their dark circles — together they seemed to negate the civic-leader smile below.

"Well, the sheriff's gonna have his hands full then, huh?"

"Oh yeah, in over his head, I'm thinking."

As Willie loaded up her car, she noticed the sheriff's cruiser headed down the highway. She shook her head at the sight. Silly pothead.

CHAPTER 8

HEADING OUT OF TOWN, Sheriff Tommy Maynard sniffed the lake air with appreciation. It had never smelled sweeter. He felt so elated at having his privacy back for the day that he decided not to fire up a doobie right away.

Wait for it, he smiled to himself. The waiting was almost as delicious as that first ten seconds. That was how long the first rush lasted. A soft, weightless drift, a brief glimpse of heaven. Yes, for that ten seconds Tommy Maynard's life always felt worth living.

The cruiser rolled past cars parked nose to tail on the shoulder close to the fishing dock. He veered back towards State Highway 54, two narrow lanes that snaked for miles through slash pines and crowded scrub oaks. It was just him and his cruiser, not a soul in sight, only miles of tree-lined road and sky. Finally, he dug out his first joint and lit it up. Half closing his eyes, he pulled the smoke deep into his lungs. Come to Papa, he thought.

The familiar pungent taste made his head roll back in pleasure. The beginning of those heady ten seconds. He forced himself to shift his attention back to the road — too late.

His eyes snapped wide open as a deer trotted across the road in front of him. He cursed and slammed the brakes, steering hard away from Bambi's mom. Before he could even sigh with relief, another smaller deer, right behind the first, darted into his swerving path. This time his response was not quick enough.

CRIMES OF REDEMPTION

The sickening thump of the fawn meeting the fender of the car made him scream without realizing it. The animal sailed through the air, an unnatural aerial act, tumbling over itself. He heard it land with a thud somewhere off to the side of the road.

A snapshot flashed. The startled, wide-eyed expression of a Viet Cong soldier in a clearing, too frozen to move as he locked eyes with the American soldier behind enemy lines. Tommy closing the ten-foot gap between them in no more than a second. To this day, Tommy did not know where his speed, or his knife, had come from in that moment. It had been a gut-level decision, charging into that surprised, paralyzed soldier, despite the gun trained on him. Tommy had screamed as he ran at the enemy, head on, like a battering ram. Against all odds, the surprise move had saved his life.

It was only after, as the Viet Cong bled out in front of him, that he had realized it was only a boy in a too big soldier's uniform. Maybe fifteen, but with the small Asian build, he looked more like twelve. Tommy was alone when it happened, a shot-down pilot half mad with fear as he tried to make his way through enemy territory.

It would be his only eye-to-eye killing of the war, and at the time he told himself it meant nothing. He had done what he had to do. Anybody would have done the same. But for months Tommy replayed it on a loop in his head. Only after years had passed could he acknowledge to himself that the enemy he had stabbed again and again that day in the jungle had been only a child.

As he sensed the cruiser slide out of control on the loose gravel, Tommy still felt outside of himself. The car moaned as it left the shoulder and toppled down the steep embankment. Everything started to happen out of real time, everything pushing towards him in slow motion.

When the cruiser finally landed, he watched its windshield shatter into glass spider veins and the air bag finally deploy. Fumes, a funky electrical odor he could not identify, filled the car. Buried in white plastic, he thought, God help me, I just killed another baby.

And then he blacked out.

CHAPTER 9

GAYLA STOOD WITH HER head craning upwards, scanning a sky full of clouds that looked like jigsaw pieces to an all white puzzle. She closed her eyes; the sun bled a soft orange through her lids. Even with cheeks flushed from yesterday's sunburn, she could not get enough of the outdoors. Her senses felt newborn to the pine-tinted air and the breeze that tickled through Willie's baggy old dress.

Her body was evolving, almost hourly, it seemed to her. Not just the healing of the soles of her feet, though that helped her locomotion, nor her much improved hand, still partly wrapped in gauze — just for protection, according to Willie. No, another, more important, wave of healing was also under way.

There was a new lightness in her body, like weights dropping away. And she sighed all the time. Willie had even remarked on it. And there were these strange, prickling sensations Gayla had not felt in years. Sometimes it felt like specks of light actually fluttering under her skin, rushing minnows in a shallow stream. She could feel the light dart through her body, with a raw energy. Viscerally it was similar to when she used to wake with a hangover, the acute awareness of alcohol still coursing through her veins. Except this was a pleasant, healing sensation. When she closed her eyes, she imagined it as a cleansing, so powerful it could lift her off the ground. She could almost feel herself floating over the towering cedars, with their acrid incense-like smells that seemed almost holy.

She was looking straight up into that dark green canopy, when she heard the abrupt thump and squeal of brakes. Scary close. For several long moments, the sound of grinding metal continued and made her cringe. Then a heavy silence. The insects stopped their morning hum.

Gayla backed away from the cedar, ready to retreat to the safety of Willie's cabin, but a red dust cloud floated up into the clear blue sky just ahead, like a smoke signal. Something awful had happened, she just knew. Somebody needed help. Gayla understood that all too well.

She took off towards the smoke. Thoughts from the cellar flooded through her as she ran. Long after losing count of the days and weeks, she had screamed herself hoarse down there. Alone. Desperate. How many months had it been before the horrible realization dawned? How long after all her imagined scenarios of being discovered, saved, and freed? Finally, it had hit her: Nobody would be coming. No one. There would be no rescue in the night; no kind, uniformed officer to hug and assure her she was safe now, it was over. No, her story would end in shame or death, with her right where she was — at the end of a leg chain, hugging herself on a grimy cot as she stared at a boarded-up window.

She carried that fear with her as she ran towards the dust cloud, her feet in Willie's too big clogs crunching against the needled forest floor. Through a clearing, she could just make out a sedan stuck head first in the ground, its trunk in the air, its chassis half buried.

Gayla did not see the fawn until she was almost upon it. Gasping for breath, the baby lay on its side, spindly legs contorted in unnatural angles. Unable to move, yet still alive, its eyes twitched with fright. Gayla caught her breath hard. Not that much blood, she thought. But, everything is broken.

With tremendous effort, the deer shifted its head and their eyes met. The creature did not so much look at her as it locked onto her, grabbing for a lifeline, a last moment of contact.

"I'm sorry. I'm so sorry," Gayla blurted, desperate to offer the creature comfort. Do the dying always reach for a last connection, she wondered. And if they do, does anyone ever know how to help?

The fawn's shallow pants weakened, while Gayla unconsciously held her breath in sympathy. They both were caught up in the moment, each searching, holding the other's gaze. Then, with a struggle, the fawn lifted its head again. Weakly, almost delicately, its mouth stretched open towards Gayla, trying to catch a breath. It struggled for several moments more, its tongue hanging out one side of its mouth. Gayla found herself kneeling beside the poor creature, then tentatively, gently, stroking its long, delicate neck. It offered no resistance.

"Easy, you're okay," she lied. "That's it. Easy now."

She looked into the broken animal's eyes, now filled with both fear and wonder. She tried to send it whatever love and comfort she could, and the fawn did seem to relax. Then, with the last of its strength, it stretched upward, gave one last shudder, reaching for something only it could see. Then it went limp and was gone.

Gayla knelt, paralyzed in the grip of its passing, her hand still on the fawn's neck. She felt something enormous move through her. An energy shift. The enormity of what she had just witnessed — the natural flicker of a soul in transition — overwhelmed her. Its awful beauty was as impossible to describe as a rainbow.

The fawn's eyes were now dead and milky. There was no rescue for you either, she thought, though you were lost and trembling at heaven's gate. Her childhood sureness that God takes care of the sparrow had left her sometime during one of her weary cellar nights. It now seemed to her that everyone was hurting, and no one ever came to help.

Gayla clamped her hand over her mouth, as if to stop the emotional storm raging through her. She gulped air and started to sob. The pain poured out; her body shook with it. Mortality had reached out to her in this cedar forest; it had chosen her to witness this event and, in doing so, allowed her to connect with the universe's mysterious energy.

Funny, but she had felt none of this standing over Albert Raeder's body. Had there been that same kind of moment as life passed out of him? Had he attempted a last connection? She did not remember one. So why did her heart feel torn in two by the dying of a creature encountered in the woods, when Raeder's last cries had barely given her pause? She could not remember once thinking about his life or his loss. She could only remember thinking she had to be good and sure he was gone. That was all that was on her mind as she raised the two-by-four again and again, telling herself: Do not do it half way or . . .

She was wrenched back to the present by the smell of gasoline. She turned to where the car had gone off the road. She was still shaken, still blinded by a sheet of tears, so it was not until she came to the edge of the ditch that she saw it was a sheriff's cruiser. It was leaking gas and resting on its crunched roof.

She could just make out inside the man who surely had killed the fawn, hanging . . . hanging as limp as a puppet.

CHAPTER 10

WHEN TOMMY MAYNARD REGAINED consciousness, he hung face down, suspended by his seat belt. The collapsed airbag, spackled with blood, lay limply on the steering wheel. The only sound to be heard was a vacant, whistling wind as the dust cloud kicked up by the wreck drifted back over the crumpled cruiser. It feels so still, like a deserted planet, he thought.

It was spooky, alone out in the boonies, the wind making popping sounds through a crack in the window. Reddish dust obscured the landscape. Then he heard a faint wailing from somewhere close-by. Or is that just the wind, too, he wondered. After noting that his limbs seemed intact in spite of numbness in one leg, Tommy decided he had escaped any critical damage. But a lot of blood was dripping down through his hair, falling from the top of his head.

His first problem was breathing. The seat belt, which had successfully restrained his body, now cut into his chest, pushing on his lungs. He felt like someone parachuting whose rig had tangled in a tree, leaving him dangling in the wind. He grappled for the seat-belt buckle, but found that twisting his arms actually increased the pressure already caused by his dead weight. He pushed with his feet to relieve the pressure. Pain ran up his right foot, nearly taking his breath away. Maybe he had not escaped so easily.

Tommy rotated his body left and right looking for a way out, only to be astonished to see, through clouds of drifting dust, someone running towards his car. A woman with brownish-red hair in an ugly housedress and awkward-looking clogs hurried to him. This is like some B-horror movie, he thought. Strangers popping up out of nowhere. Not that he was not happy to see her.

"Help," Tommy blurted out, spending what breath he had. As she approached the driver's side of the car, he could see that her eyes were bloodshot, puffy with tears.

"Stay calm," she said.

She yanked on the door, but it was stuck. He watched helplessly as she struggled with the dented handle.

"It's going to be okay," she reassured him, though the door seemed hopelessly crushed in a closed position.

"Other side," he said, motioning with his head towards the passenger side of the car.

She ran around to that door, which had sustained less damage.

"Come on, come on," he heard her say as she worked the handle. After several tries, it opened. She leaned into the cab.

"I'm going to figure out how to get you out of here now. Okay?"

Tommy nodded. "The seat-belt buckle. See it?"

"Yeah," she said and started trying to unlatch it. No give.

"Just push the orange bar," he whispered.

"I am," she said, pushing repeatedly on the orange plastic square. "It's not budging. Any chance you could move some? Take a little tension off it?"

"Yeah." He pushed to relieve some of the tautness. "Now try it."

She grunted, poking the release bar again and again. "Dammit. It's just not working."

"Just a sec," he said, relaxing so the belt pulled taut again.

He had barely finished speaking when she gave the button a final push. This time it worked, dropping him on his head and onto the steering wheel.

"Oh, I'm so sorry," she said, reaching out for him.

"S'okay." He was just relieved to be out of the death harness.

The car groaned and shifted a few inches. The stranger's face filled with concern.

"We have to hurry. Car's leaking gas."

She leaned in and wrapped her arms around his torso, and he caught the scent of fresh cotton from her clothes and something flowery coming off her hair.

"Okay, I'm going to pull you across the seat," she said.

She pulled, while he struggled to maneuver his legs out and around the gearshift.

"Here," she said, helping him lift his boots. She pulled back a hand damp with blood. "Watch your foot now —"

He looked down to see blood oozing from where the toe of one of his boots should be. Before he could react, she spoke again.

"Put your arm on my shoulder. I can help you balance."

"I'm too heavy."

"No, I know the technique. I used to handle hospital patients. Come on."

The cruiser creaked again and shifted another inch.

She looked around and took stock of their precarious position.

"We have to hurry. That fuel leak could go any second."

He knew she was right. The smell of gas was growing thicker by the second. Awkwardly, inch by inch, she helped him edge out. He noted how strong she was, even though she was by no means that large.

With a final heave, she pulled him out and they limped away from the car, which was still shifting from its own weight. They both saw the danger at the same time.

"Farther away. It's a full tank," Tommy said.

They made it maybe forty more feet before collapsing together on the grass. Instinctively, he positioned himself between her and the wreck, covering her with his body.

"I hit a little deer. I couldn't stop, and the car just . . . "

His voice choked. He fell silent.

"I saw it in the woods."

"Did it die?"

"Yes," was all she said.

He shuddered.

CHAPTER 11

WILLIE'S RUSTED-OUT pickup almost drove itself home after so many years. That was why her mind was not on driving. It was on the murder. The murder that supposedly had happened just a few days before her houseguest showed up in the front yard.

Not that she was convinced the two were linked, but it was more than curious, she had to admit. Here the town had not had a murder in ten years, even if you counted that old hit-and-run, and it had been almost that long since Willie had had a visitor.

Yet in the space of less than a week . . .

An explosion a quarter of a mile up the road slammed her against the seat. She stomped on the brake, squealing to a stop. Willie's heart pounded as she shifted into first and coaxed the pickup forward. She was almost on it when she saw it. The unmistakable cruiser made her mouth drop open in recognition. Our pot-smoking-excuse-for-a-sheriff just did himself in, she thought.

By the time she reached the wreck, plumes of black smoke swirled around the burned-out cruiser shell. Hopping out of the pickup, Willie peered through the smoky curtain, relieved not to see a burnt body inside. That would be a tough one, even for someone like herself, who since moving to the country had been forced to deal more than once with dead animal carcasses all by her lonesome.

Then Willie saw them. Tommy Maynard and somebody else lying near the tree line, not twenty-five yards from the car. Oh God, she thought, please let him be okay, even if he is worthless.

"Hey," she hollered, waving broadly. "Hey, over here. You okay?"

No answer, but she thought Tommy moved a little.

"Stay there. I'll come to you," Willie yelled.

She grunted and groaned her way over the large rocks and down the sandy slope to reach them. As she neared, she recognized her old house dress Gayla had been wearing that morning.

What's she doing up here? With him? She could come up with no scenario that would throw the two together.

She reached the bottom of the ditch, knees trembling from the effort, and moved closer. Tommy was bleeding from the top of his head. His foot seemed damaged, too, the boot badly ripped and spilling blood.

No injuries to Gayla that could be seen, other than tiny nicks, probably from flying glass. They looked like two lost children, huddled together against a storm.

Willie kneeled over them. Tommy looked at her so blankly, she decided he barely knew where he was. Possible concussion, she thought. Gayla's eyes opened, the skin around them puffy and swollen. What the hell happened here? Willie wondered. Then loud and slow: "Don't move. I'm going to find help."

She wasn't sure how to deliver on that pronouncement. Even if it was safe to move them, could she get them up the slope to the pickup? Not with her bad knees.

"Have you got a cell phone?" she asked Tommy.

For the first time in her life, she wished she had one. Tommy gestured with his chin towards the cruiser, now a blob of blackened soot — even the steering wheel seemed to have melted.

Willie heard an approaching car. Actually, it was the music for the young-and-hearing-impaired that she heard first. But the partying teenagers in the old convertible had never been so welcome. If one of these kids doesn't have a phone, I'll eat my hat, she thought as she scrambled up the embankment, ignoring the shooting pain in her knees.

The black cloud and Willie's waving not only brought the car to a screeching stop but killed the music as well. The teens fairly tumbled out of the car, gawking at the smoking cruiser as everyone simultaneously punched numbers into cell phones.

"Call for an ambulance," Willie said unnecessarily.

Thank you, God, was all Willie could think. I will never bad-mouth the little morons again.

As she turned back to the sheriff and Gayla, for just an instant, through the smell of burning rubber and plastic and metal, she caught the slight whiff of maryjane.

CHAPTER 12

TOMMY NO SOONER WOKE UP than he wished he hadn't. Pain cut through his head, running ear to ear, like a pulsing electric circuit. The slightest turn made his eyes water. Vague shapes moved around the bed. A deep, female voice penetrated the haze.

"Possible concussion, Tommy. You may not be able to focus."

"Mary?" The name popped up from nowhere, but Tommy would have recognized that husky, sensual voice anywhere. They had tossed back many a tequila shot in their glory days, when, as a hot young nurse, she'd never found a party she didn't like. Now a responsible health care professional in Luckau's local clinic, that was all behind her. In the course of sobering up, Mary had once confided to him that she had gained the requisite thirty pounds that accompanies recovery and then some. She loved her sobriety now. Life was heavier physically, but lighter in every other way.

"It's me, all right," she said. "How are you feeling?"

"Like somebody chewed me up and spit me out."

"You got banged up pretty good, buddy."

"How long have I been out?"

"A couple of hours."

A white doctor's coat strode into the room.

"Hey, Doc," Tommy said.

He had met the ponytailed Baby Boomer "hippie doc," as the locals called him, in the course of a couple domestic calls. His name, however, escaped him, lost in his befuddled mind.

"Dr. Gordon, Sheriff. How you feeling?"

"Not much," Tommy said, his eyelids droopy from the painkillers.

Dr. Gordon pressed here and there on Tommy's torso and chest. "That hurt?"

Tommy's groans did the answering.

"Okay, a lot of tender spots. I can see that, and you'll probably see those seat-belt bruises turn scary black in a couple of days, but that's soft tissue damage and it will work itself out."

"My head," Tommy said.

"You took a big knock high on your forehead. I want to keep you overnight to watch that one. If there is a concussion, which looks likely, I want you here. My immediate concern is your foot, though."

Tommy almost grinned. "I can't even feel that."

"The x-rays we took earlier —"

"You took x-rays?" Tommy didn't remember that.

"You were groggy. Your foot is smashed pretty bad. Lucky your boot was so thick."

"My Fryes," Tommy said, even now taking joy in the gorgeous western cut boots that had cost half a month's salary.

"Well, you still have one of them."

"No . . . not my boots."

"You broke two bones in your foot, Mr. Maynard, which is going to limit your mobility for a spell, but the foot should heal fine."

Two broken bones? That's my driving foot. Suddenly he could feel it. A bomb dropping. Throbbing pain shooting from his foot to his ankle and up his calf. This pain made his headache seem a cakewalk. Dr. Gordon moved above him, and Mary assisted him on the other side. Tommy only caught snippets of what they were saying.

". . . something more for the pain."

". . . don't worry."

Something with lots of syllables. A pen scratching. It was like Tommy was in one of those action-adventure novels he favored on nights when he was stoned but couldn't quite get to sleep. It had that same almost-real-but-not-quite feel. He let himself slip into whatever they were giving him. Give me everything you got, he thought, I want it all.

He got it. He drifted in and out of reality; the white-white cool room left him clueless as to the time. He woke to white shadowed whispers.

First it was Mary with news for the doctor, making his night rounds.

"Sheriff from Elk City is here. Said it's urgent."

Dr. Gordon's voice. "Tell him tomorrow."

"He says it's 'bidness' and will only take a minute," Mary said, obviously repeating what she had been told probably more than once.

Tommy turned his head towards the voices. He could sense a fluid movement in his veins, an electric vibration under his skin.

"You say 'Elmo?' "

"Hey, careful there." Mary turned with a disapproving look.

Elmo Dudgeon had been standing close enough to Tommy's door to overhear his name being mentioned. It was all he needed. He barreled in, as if he had been invited.

"Tommy," he said, his thick face flushed with excitement, "don't worry about a thing. I'm taking over the case."

"The hell you are," he mumbled.

With that Mary and Dr. Gordon politely, then more bluntly, attempted to give Elmo the heave-ho, but Elmo was blabbering about Missing Person Reports from the entire state for the last year. Lots of leads. Had his deputy in Elk City tracking everything down. No need to worry.

It passed in a drugged blur before Tommy. Somewhere in the midst of Elmo's briefing, Tommy's fevered mind conjured up a movie from the fifties in which some poor SOB in a sweaty jungle shirt falls into a whirlpool of quicksand. Floundering, screaming, slapping the thick mud, he sinks lower and lower. The special effects were hokey, but the nauseous pit in his little boy stomach felt real. Every effort the man made to save himself pulled him down faster, and the expendable character finally just disappeared with a glunk. The quicksand smoothed. It was as if no one had ever been there.

Listening to the braying of Sheriff Dudgeon, Tommy couldn't help but identify. I am drowning in bullshit, he thought, and nobody can see.

CHAPTER 13

GAYLA WAS WARY OF BOTH the heavy, smiling nurse and the gray-haired, pony-tailed Dr. Gordon examining her. Probably a late bloomer just out of med school, she thought, paying his dues at this Podunkville clinic until he can move to the big city. She felt herself tighten up as his long, cool fingers pressed around her rib cage and tummy. Enough with the poking and prodding, for pity's sake.

"Tender?" he asked, eyeing her with concern.

She shrugged.

"I'm okay. He's the one you should be looking at, not me."

"The Sheriff is resting. We have set the bones in the broken foot. He's doing fine."

Gayla winced as Dr. Gordon touched the wound on her side, the place where she had scraped herself crawling out of the tight little basement window a week ago.

"You have a long abrasion here, but it's not new. Did you do that in the last week or so?"

"Yeah. Scraped myself."

Dr. Gordon looked at her, waiting for more. Then, giving up, "Pretty big scrape. What about these cuts on your feet and hands?"

Gayla wrinkled her forehead. She didn't like where this was going.

"They're healing up okay."

"Okay," he sighed, "you don't have to tell me how it happened. Relax. But you also have some old bruising — here on your arms — and the x-rays indicated a couple of old rib fractures. When did all that occur?"

"I don't remember." Scrambling for cover, she blurted, "I think I'm a little shook still."

Which was true enough. Not from anything that had happened today, but he didn't need to know that. Thanks to his questioning she could barely sustain a coherent thought.

Dr. Gordon set his mouth in a tight smile, like a parent who knows his child is lying but can't do much about it. For her part, Gayla felt off balance, upset by this unexpected examination, yes, but even more so by his interest in her. Be very careful here, she thought.

Dr. Gordon patted her hand.

"Okay. That's all for now. You can get dressed."

He parted the curtain and addressed Willie, who was waiting in a nearby chair. "Can we speak privately?" he asked.

Gayla could only hear bits and pieces of what they said. Something about Willie's relationship to her. Then they seemed to drift off topic.

The bright whiteness of the room and the smell of disinfectant were suffocating. Gayla felt dizzy, still sitting on the examination table. She stared at the nurse, who was cleaning up.

"He's finished. You can get dressed now — there behind the curtain," the nurse said.

Was it her imagination or did the nurse exude a kind of peace? She's all right, Gayla thought. She seems kind. Gayla caught herself. Like you would know, she thought, like you have a clue about how to read people or their motives. That smiley doc is probably in there right now telling Willie something is off about your houseguest . . . telling her "You'd better report this to the authorities."

"You okay, sweetie?" the big nurse asked, raising the back of her hand to Gayla's forehead. Clammy but no temperature. "Here, let me help you down."

"I'm in big trouble. Aren't I?" Gayla finally stammered.

The nurse gave a surprised little laugh. "No, hon, you're not in trouble. Bless your heart. This is a medical clinic."

Gayla's past life as an x-ray tech should have lent credence to what the nurse said. Clinics, like hospitals, were a little like sanctuaries. Still Gayla could not help but wonder . . . Did that cover someone who'd just bludgeoned a man?

CHAPTER 14

THIS PLACE IS GOING TO the dogs," Willie grunted, as she cut a section of chicken wire off a roll from the shed.

"You mean coyotes, don't you? Or was it foxes?" Gayla said, gawking at the dead chickens left from last night's raid.

"It was a figure of speech. Looks like coyotes. Now don't go crying over them again. What's done is done."

Willie was in no mood to baby anyone this morning, especially herself, after failing to notice where coyotes had been digging near her chickens. The whole incident with the crash and trip to the hospital had put her off stride. She was ashamed not to have checked around the coop for the past couple of days.

"I'm not going to cry," Gayla said, some defensiveness in her tone. "But I'm not going to eat them either."

Willie stopped to look at her old rooster's mangled body parts. A wave of sadness passed through her.

"No, nobody's eating Freddie. He would be too tough even if you wanted to. Give me a hand here, huh?"

Gayla hurried over, eager to help, but clueless as to what to do. Not so Maxine, who blindly nosed around the battlefield, luxuriating in the rich odors of fresh kill.

"Hold this," Willie said, handing Gayla a section of the wire, "and help me bury the bottom couple of inches in this fresh trench."

She was grateful to have work to do with her hands. They worked together in a comfortable silence. One of the things Willie liked about Gayla was that she wasn't nosy. Like a child, she rarely pressed for details. When she had asked about the picture of Jack at a grinning, mischievous eight years, Willie had only had to say, "That's my son." Not "That was my son." It made all the difference.

It had to have been the trip to the Luckau clinic that had triggered this rush of anxiety, Willie realized. The too familiar smells of the place clung to you for hours after you left, and it was hard to ignore the whispered exchanges between people in the waiting rooms. But even worse were the looks of pity, spotlights bearing down on anxious relatives. The polite staring, the pats on the shoulder, the gripping of arms, all measuring the enormity of their loss before their hearts had been able to even grasp it. God, she hated hospitals.

"Willie, are you okay?" Gayla asked.

Willie started. "Fine. Fine." She was glad for the interruption. "Just thinking about the other day."

"Don't like hospitals, huh?"

"Was it that obvious?"

"You just seemed in a bigger hurry than any of us to get out of there."

"I moved out here to the country . . . push the edge of that wire in a little deeper. That's right. I don't want to have to do this again for awhile."

"What did you do before you moved out here?" Gayla asked.

Willie smiled to herself. "It seems like the Dark Ages now."

"What do you mean?"

"In a nutshell, I got a fairly worthless diversified arts degree — got caught up in the sixties. Communes, psychedelic vans, the whole nine yards. Married a musician with long hair, who later turned out to be a corporate lawyer vampire in disguise."

Gayla laughed. "You're kidding?"

"Nope." Willie gauged her a moment. "Your turn."

A shadow passed over Gayla's face, as though a cloud had drifted between her and the sun. Willie was sure she had overstepped.

"I used to work in a hospital. Eons ago." Gayla pushed her lips tight together in thought.

Willie perked up. "Where was that?"

"Here and there."

Willie waited, hoping for more. When nothing else came, she ventured another question.

"I was wondering if we shouldn't be looking for your family or friends?"

"Listen, I was going to talk to you today about . . . I appreciate everything you've done for me, but I've imposed on you enough."

"Not at all. You're no trouble. Really."

"I just think I need to move on."

The new chicken wire successfully buried, Willie took the opportunity to segue as she thought this over.

"Could you hand me those tin snips?"

Gayla handed them over. Willie began to snip the end from the roll, and as she worked, she reached out in a way she rarely did.

"I like having you here, Gayla. And you're going to need some money and clothes if you're leaving. I'd like to help you with that."

"Oh, I couldn't let you do that."

"The vampire left me enough to live on. Don't worry about setting me back. If you're going to go, let me help you figure out how to do that. You can't just walk away with empty pockets. Nothing good can come of that."

"I couldn't ask you to . . ."

"Silly girl, I'm offering. But I can't help but think there are family or friends who are probably worried sick about you."

"There's nobody like that."

"You don't have any family?"

"Nope. I'm just like you. On my own."

"I find it hard to believe there isn't someone."

Gayla cocked her head at Willie.

"Really? Who would look for you if you were gone?" She nodded towards the cabin. "That son of yours? Where's he?"

Willie felt like she'd been kicked. Maxine broke the moment by rubbing up against her leg and displaying a set of teeth now holding Freddie's bloody remains.

"Maxine, you little dickens. Don't eat Freddie." But when Willie tried to retrieve the dog's prize, Maxine clamped down even harder.

Gayla smiled grimly. "She's not going to let go."

Willie felt her throat constrict with emotion.

"My son — Jack was his name — is gone. And maybe you're right. Maybe nobody would know I was missing until I started to stink. I was just trying to say that if you're afraid of people still holding a grudge for something that happened in the past. People change. Time heals. You must know people would be so glad to see you . . . that . . ."

"That what?"

"What?"

"People will be so glad to see me that . . . what?"

"That, well, that no matter what, they'd want to know where you are. They would probably . . . forgive you anything." Willie prayed it was the right thing to say.

A hardness crept into Gayla's face.

"Do you really think that's what people are like?" The sun cut a dark shadow under Gayla's eyes, giving her facial bones an almost skeletal look for a moment. "Do you find people to be forgiving?"

Willie's chest tightened. It seemed Gayla had sensed her weakness.

Gayla chuckled drily. "Yeah, forgiveness is real big on Sunday morning, isn't it? Everybody's all for it during the hymn singing. But as soon as they have to stretch themselves . . . or exercise a little of that compassion themselves. . . " She snorted. "Then you're on your own."

"Point taken."

"Don't worry. I'll leave soon as I can."

"That's not why I brought it up," Willie said, but she could feel the girl slipping away from her.

Gayla headed for the cabin door, forcing Willie to address her back. The words tumbled out.

"You're right. People aren't particularly forgiving."

Gayla turned back. "What?"

"They didn't forgive me either."

Gayla walked slowly back to Willie. They studied one another for a moment, sensing a kinship that neither had recognized before. Willie did a quiet double take when Gayla hugged her. Didn't ask any questions, just patted her on the shoulder, as a child comforts an adult. They stood there by the chicken pen under an Oklahoma sun, arms around one another. Nothing was spoken, yet everything seemed clear.

CHAPTER 15

THE IRONY OF HIS SITUATION had not escaped Tommy Maynard. Finally he had the fire in his belly to go out and do something, and he couldn't drive. And, adding to his misery, his mechanic still had not gotten the fuel pump fixed on his inherited push-button transmission Dodge. It was literally an old lady's car, left to him by his aunt when she died. He had always planned to sell it, but it had broken down before he could get around to it. Now he was grateful for the huge front seat and the hand-controlled transmission. It was his only hope for mobility.

As for Elmo Dudgeon, gnawing on takeout fried chicken across the table from him, the man was worthless, Tommy decided, as he popped another half of a Lortab. He had always thought of Dudgeon as a bit of a prick, but one you could glad hand in the interest of having a connection with the nearest big law enforcement agency. With a population of fifty thousand, Elk City had more resources, better computers, and more personnel — everything that could help a small county, like his, when it got overloaded.

But after more than a week with him, familiarity had bred not only contempt but the urge to kill. Dudgeon, Tommy now realized, was nothing more than an incompetent political hack, undoubtedly cousin to some uppity-up. It was the only explanation that made any sense.

Dudgeon had actually started to believe that it was not his skilled staff — Joe Nguyen or any of the other professionals — who were making him look good. No, Dudgeon had made a categorical shift into thinking he knew what he was doing. It was the kind of jug-headed assumption that led to Elmo talking the case to death between crunches of an extra crispy drumstick, instead of actually doing something.

"I have my boy in Records chasing down the last loose ends on parole violators and missing persons," Dudgeon said, as he shuffled piles of loose papers on the table. "So far, nothing."

Maynard swallowed his annoyance.

"What about the blood and DNA reports?"

"There's Raeder's and somebody else's. That's all we know." Elmo was looking at Nguyen's report. "Oh, some tow chains did have blood on them."

"The ones in the corner? That I asked to be tested?"

"Was that you? Huh." Elmo grunted in surprise, the possibility that Tommy had noticed something important incomprehensible to him.

"Was there a match?"

"Nope, it's not Raeder's."

Tommy was actually quite impressed with the Albert Raeder profile, assembled by a deputy named Dixie in the Elk City office. He had only met her as a low pitched southern drawl on the occasional official phone call, but that didn't stop him from briefly wondering if she was as sexy as she sounded.

Besides being Mr. Do-Gooder Restoration Leader and Real Estate Magnate, Raeder had a few lifestyle patterns that Tommy found noteworthy. The man loved conventions, as far away from home as possible, with a special lust for Vegas. A margin note in purple ink, undoubtedly Dixie's, asked: "Gambling debts?"

More interesting to Tommy was the analysis of the hotel bills, enhanced by Dixie's several calls to hotel employees. It had been pretty clear, at least to her, that Mr. Raeder was enamored of escort services. The restaurant bills on his trips were often for two. But the note that raised a red flag for Tommy, and left it flapping sharply in the breeze, was a minor police report. Seems a prostitute known as "Big Momma Earth" had reported that Raeder, under an assumed name, had asked for some serious sadomasochism action. S&M, huh. Not Big Momma's normal style, but the price was apparently right, because the problem was not that he had failed to pay for her services but that he had chewed half her nipple off and left her tied up in a motel room.

Unfazed by Raeder's phony I.D., Big Momma had left the hospital a few hours later and marched down to the hotel hosting the convention he had said he was attending. Unfortunately for him, he had not lied about that. Within an hour, she had spotted him across the lobby.

Despite Big Momma's obvious outrage, Tommy was hardly surprised to see that the charges were eventually dropped. Probably was not the only time Raeder had paid big time to get out of a potentially embarrassing situation. And the incident showed a mean streak that bothered Tommy.

"What do you think about this Vegas complaint?" Tommy asked.

Elmo looked up from a chicken leg, trying to figure out what he was talking about. When he remembered, it was almost with a shrug.

"Probably drunk out of his mind."

"At least." Tommy studied the clueless lump across from him. "You don't think it could be a sign of, say, sick, perverted interactions with women? Say, an ugly pattern?"

Elmo's grinned, conspiratorial. "Hey, if it wasn't for my uncle the cop, God only knows what might be on my rap sheet."

Tommy laughed with him, but he was thinking, so you did copy that swagger from your cop relatives, who, probably like you, don't have a clue about what they do. He made a mental note to ask Dixie to find out anything else the arresting officer might have said.

Elmo sighed and leaned back in his chair, studying Tommy with an annoying look of pity.

"Looks like I'm going to have to turn my paperwork over to you, Tommy. What with you immobile —"

"Not after today," Tommy interrupted. "My old Dodge will be up and running."

Tommy had reiterated in no uncertain terms that he was still in charge of this murder investigation, yet Elmo was still strutting around, horning in every chance he got. With an effort that took willpower he did not know he had, Tommy put on his best statesmanlike face.

"I'm grateful for the manpower and resources your department has provided for this investigation, especially Joe and Dixie. I appreciate it no end, but I'm back in the saddle on this, so —"

"I thought the doc said you needed to rest," Elmo said, his annoyance barely contained.

"I've got a clean bill of health and I'm raring to go." Tommy noted with a sly grin. "Got some grease there on your chin, Sheriff."

Flustered, Elmo's eyes narrowed as he stood and pulled the paper napkins out of his uniform collar. He started for the bathroom, then stopped and turned back.

"I'll tell you what, Tommy. I'm not sure if you can tell your friends from your enemies."

He let the charged silence between them sit for a moment, then just shook his head and lumbered away.

Tommy allowed himself a self-congratulatory grin, but he also realized it was not the first time someone had made this observation about him. But so what?

"Still doesn't mean you're not out to get me," Tommy mumbled.

CHAPTER 16

GAYLA SAT ON A LOG, watching the leaves beginning to fall from the trees and gather in little piles. A low lying haze covered the valley, blocking the clouds as well as the breeze. She came to this clearing to try and clear her head. But every time she tried to project forward, she managed, instead, to step back in time.

Albert Raeder had started to pop up several times a day now. His awkward bulk came at her in quick flashes, like a scene from one of those movie trailers filmed with a handheld camera. One moment, gregarious, mixing drinks in the basement, flashing diamond rings. Next looming over her, talking dirty as he pumped away at her on the floor, his face dripping sweat. Cut to him in a dark room holding a scary looking shotgun. Though the flashes were only her mind playing tricks, the images often felt more real than what she saw in the here and now.

How long ago had it been? She could still remember that October night, when it all went bad, slowly moving behind Randy's thin frame through the dark cabin, how cold the place had felt. She recalled damp slits of moonlight cutting through slashes in the drapes. She could just make out the Southwest decor, the Navajo area rugs, the overstuffed leather chairs. Randy led the way, the skull and crossbones on the back of his biker jacket glowing in the dark. "Stay the hell up," he hissed.

"I can't see," she shot back, as she ran smack into something hard and invisible in the dark. She moaned as pain from the stubbed toe ricocheted up her calf.

"Dammit," he whispered, "it's just like at the movies. Close your eyes for a second and let them adjust. When you open them, you'll be able to see."

"I already did that," she hissed, tears welling up in her eyes.

"It's simple, bitch." He walked back to her and grabbed her roughly. "You carry the bag and I fill it. You see anything I miss, you ask me if I want to take it."

He sighed and handed her a penlight.

"Here, use this. Just keep the beam low."

Her fingers trembled as the tiny flashlight cast a halo over Randy's weathered face. His wiry frame had fooled many an enemy over the years, most of whom had reason later to wonder where his quick muscle strength had come from. But Gayla knew enough to be afraid.

"Sorry, Randy. Thanks."

Randy pointed to a small mahogany sculpture of a Comanche chief in full headdress.

"Throw that in. I like it."

She added it to her canvas bag. Randy looked around in irritation.

"So where's all this good stuff we heard about, huh? The safe loaded with money? I don't see no damn safe."

"Maybe we should just go. This doesn't feel right."

"You pussy. We drove four and a half hours. I ain't leavin' empty." His eyes looked like black BBs. "Now you get your go at the jewelry. Back to the bedroom. Just the good stuff."

She hesitated, and he whirled accusingly on her.

"You did say you knew about jewelry."

That had been one of the ways she had gotten him to agree to trade out her debt. He had wanted his money. Money owed him. But as he had repeated ad nauseam, "Never trust a crackhead. Get what you can out of them while they're still alive."

She could feel him eyeballing her.

"Yeah. I know enough. My mom sold jewelry on the side."

At that, he coldcocked her, his fist cracking her jaw. The whisper that followed was ragged.

"Which is it, bitch? You said you knew how to tell the good stuff. Don't play me. I will cut your throat here and now."

Her head was swimming, but fear jolted her into hyperawareness.

She mentally danced as she tried to stay on her feet.

"No, I can tell what's real." She nearly backed off at his look. "I can. I didn't mean that. I just can't say what it's worth."

"I ain't getting what it's worth, anyway. Come on."

Gayla regained her equilibrium and steeled herself to finish this nightmare, swearing to herself she would never let herself get into such a position again, never let it go this far again. Ever. Truth was it was not Randy or Randy's fist that had her so shaken up. No, it was the sense of urgency in her body, a feeling that something was not right here. She tried to tell herself it was just nerves — first real robbery in a strange house far from home. But one thought kept repeating like a mantra in her head: Get out while you can.

"Do not dally," Randy growled, as they headed down the hall to the bedroom for the jewels.

She couldn't help it. Her legs and feet were lead, her entire body underwater, making each move and step an enormous effort. By now she was convinced that whatever was spooking her was bigger than the knee-shaking terror of pulling a robbery.

"Please, let's take what we have and go," she said.

"Now why the hell would I do that? This is the good stuff."

"Something's wrong here. I can feel these things sometimes." It sounded ridiculous, even as she said it.

"Get a grip. Since when are you such a pussy?"

"No, believe me. We need to leave," she pleaded.

He pulled back his hand to slap her. She winced and a bright light cut across Randy's face. Headlights. From the driveway.

"What the . . . ?" Randy's face nearly receded in the darkness. He grabbed the penlight out of Gayla's hand.

"I thought no one was supposed to be here during the week." Gayla's voice had a tremolo she had never heard in it before.

"Shut up," Randy hissed. "They aren't."

Outside, a car door closed. Footsteps crunched on the walk. Gayla bolted down the hall, looking for a back door exit, but Randy scrambled around her and got there first.

A key turned in the lock. And in the silence that choked the moment, Gayla was sure she had taken her last free breath.

CHAPTER 17

WHAT ARE YOU DOING?" Tommy Maynard asked himself, as he steered his aunt's old Dodge down the dirt road to Willie's cabin. It had taken almost an hour to get himself out of the house. Not being able to shower or bathe yet made long work of his cleanup these days. In the midst of struggling to get his trouser leg past the air cast on his foot, he had lost his temper, which just made matters worse. He finally had to sit down and unclench his teeth. Okay, he thought, so you are not back to normal. Just take it easy. One foot, then the other. Slowly.

Even minor exertion could bring on cold sweats, and when his energy left, it didn't fade but collapsed. Yesterday, waiting in the Village Market for Jimmy to check him out, he had found himself clutching the counter to stay on his feet. Jimmy had noticed, too.

"You okay there, Sheriff?"

Tommy had nodded, as a fresh wave of perspiration rolled out of his hair and onto his forehead.

"It's only been — what? A little over a week? Maybe you should sit a minute. Take a load off."

Tommy had wanted to storm out; instead, he found himself sitting in an old Formica chair in the corner of the store for a full ten minutes. And grateful for it.

"Must be these painkillers," he had lamely offered.

Jimmy nodded in sympathy. "Yeah. You sure don't want to get hooked on them. My mother-in-law did. After her wreck. God help us all, that was over a year ago. We thought she would never get back to normal."

Yeah, God help us all, Tommy had thought at the time.

Truth was his body felt so out of whack he was not sure which end was up. The prescribed Lortabs helped the pain, but made him so nauseous that after the first day he had cut the dosage in half. He could not understand how people got hooked on pain meds. When he tried smoking his only remaining joint for some relief from the nausea, he had ended up even more unsteady on his feet. All I need, he had whined to himself, is to take a tumble and screw up the other foot. As a last resort, he had glommed onto the television, staring at it for hours, without a clue as to what he was watching.

He had subsequently noticed that things he had kept at bay by staying stoned were seeping back in. When had it started? After the accident? Or before, when he felt his first shudder of recognition in the Raeder basement? Flashes of his own, dank cell in Hanoi, gray snapshots in his head of sweating interrogators with their electric batons, the crackle of the electrodes . . .

This morning had been better, thank goodness. No cold sweats in the night, no dreams of fawns or boy soldiers or worse. The only thing on his mind had been the woman, his savior, from the day of the wreck. She was the reason why Tommy steeled himself against the agony of getting dressed. He felt desperate to see her. Her face had floated past him so often since then, he no longer trusted that he remembered her right. Given his out-of-body experience that day, he could be forgiven for wondering if he had simply conjured her up.

Then there she was. Standing by Willie's porch in a big, ugly flowered dress that threatened to swallow her whole. Her sunburnt arms stuck out like matchsticks through huge sleeves. A "Luckau Feed Store" ball cap covered her reddish brown hair and shaded her face, where her mouth was dropped open wide, watching his approach up the drive.

A strange sensation came over him on seeing her again. A feeling of calm. Even peace. He was studying her so hard it took him a second to notice Willie Morris had come out of the cabin, pointing her rifle right at his windshield.

"Holy crap."

His jerry-rigged driving style was not conducive to sudden stops.

Shifting his good foot from the accelerator to the brake, he brushed the top of his injured right foot. He moaned and grabbed his knee, as the Dodge rolled to a stop.

"Well, I'll be bushwhacked," Willie said, lowering her rifle. She grinned as she gave his bleached blue car the once-over. "Didn't see who was driving. Is this an official call?"

Tommy gave a quick thank you to the powers-that-be for the breeze cooling off his damp forehead. He tried for a little levity.

"No, Willie. You can go back to burning anything you like in that back field of yours."

He knew to get that out of the way right off the bat. Personally, Tommy did not give a hoot how much trash anybody burned, much less how they burned it, but Willie had accused him of quashing her God-given rights. Sure enough, the council finally had to back off from giving any actual citations thanks to the pubic outcry, but by then he had already become the symbol of "the man" overstepping.

"That's good," Willie said with an annoying air of triumph, "because I do."

"Well, good for you." Tommy said. His toe had started to throb.

"So what does bring you out this way?"

Tommy looked at Gayla, who was eyeing him with shy curiosity. A smile played around her lips.

"I came to thank this lady over here," he said, managing to extricate himself from the driver's seat without moaning. "That is, if you're going to put that shotgun down."

He pulled out the bouquet of carnations, daisies, and baby's breath he had picked up at the Village Market on the way out of town and held them out to her.

"Oh my gosh," she said. "For me?"

She walked towards him awkwardly. Her fingers brushed against his hand as she took them.

"I love flowers."

It was such an innocent, corny thing for her to say that Tommy was momentarily relieved of his own fears of foolishness. It had been so long since a spontaneous urge had grabbed him, like had happened at the Market in front of the floral display, that he didn't know if he could trust his instincts anymore.

"Thing is, ma'am, I never did get your name."

"It's Gayla." She said with a shy smile.

"Well I wanted to come out and thank you, Gayla. You probably saved my life."

Willie, her lips pursed in a wry grin, broke the moment.

"If I didn't know any better, I'd say somebody had come a courtin'."

Tommy stammered, feeling his face redden.

"No, I was . . . "

He glanced at Gayla, who had hidden her nose in the bouquet.

"They're just from the Village Market," he said, immediately sorry he had added the last part. He felt a breeze hit the perspiration trails on his lips and forehead. "I don't suppose I could get a drink of water."

He saw Willie hesitate. It made him recall her unwillingness to allow him inside her home last year, when he had come by about the burning ban. But before Willie answered, Gayla jumped in.

"We can do better than that. I made fresh limeade this morning."

Gayla took his arm and led him towards the porch.

"You?" A schoolboy shyness overtook him, making his face go crimson. She didn't appear to notice.

"With maraschino cherry juice, no less."

"Wow."

His lameness seemed to have afflicted him with one word answers.

"I hope you like it sweet. How's your foot?"

"Better." There I go again, he thought. Man, I wish I was high.

Tommy could not pinpoint what it was about her that rendered him witless. She was appealing enough. The pale green eyes, thick auburn hair with a mind of its own, and her astonishingly white skin, now blistery pink from the sun. Yet she did not exude a sexual vibe. As she led him towards the house, her bony hand grasping his lightly for support, the connection between them felt more like childhood friends.

Gayla paused at the cabin door and they both looked at Willie, who raised her eyebrows and shook her head in what Tommy would have sworn was disbelief.

"Well, looks like we're all gonna have some," Willie said.

Later, after the best limeade he'd ever tasted, complete with a cherry on top, Tommy finally got around to business. "I guess you know we're looking into this beating death? Over in that big cabin by the lake?"

He noticed a flicker of discomfort from Gayla. Willie's face took on a studied neutrality. When neither responded, he continued cautiously.

"I'm making a swing through all the outbackers to see if anybody heard or saw anything."

"When was that now?" Willie asked.

"Ten days ago. Businessman from Elk City. Somebody went after him with a two-by-four."

Gayla shuddered so violently that Tommy reached out and touched her hand. "Sorry, ma'am."

"We wouldn't know anything about that," Willie said, swelling up like a mother hen.

Tommy tried to defuse the rising tension.

"I'm talking to everybody in the area, ma'am. Not suggesting a thing. Just trying to figure out what happened."

"Good." Willie was apparently going to be their mouthpiece.

"So you haven't noticed any strangers on the road? Or heard anything unusual?"

"Not a thing."

Tommy was tempted to leave it at that, but he could not ignore the elephant on the table.

"So how do you and Gayla know each other?"

The question hung in the air for an awkward moment. Gayla opened her mouth to answer . . .

"She's my niece," Willie blurted.

"Mmm," Tommy hummed. Then to Gayla, "Where from?"

"Kansas." Still Willie, handling the answers.

Tommy noticed Willie's eyes dart to the left on both responses, and wondered why she needed to lie. He directed the next question directly to Gayla. "Where in Kansas, Gayla?"

Her eyes dropped down when she answered. "Kansas City."

Tommy would have been pissed off if a couple of drunks had done such a half-assed job of trying to deceive him, but this felt more like two kids lying about shoplifting candy. Neither of these women was a natural deceiver. There was too much earnest desperation about them. Still, this was his job. And somebody was dead.

"Somebody steal your luggage?"

Gayla's eyes widened. "What?"

Tommy smiled wryly. "Even your shoes are too big. Not to mention every dress I've seen you in."

No answer. He pressed on, making a mental note that Willie's rifle was now propped behind the door.

"In fact, I could swear Willie was wearing that very dress in Jimmy's Market a few months back."

This was no wild guess. He had seen Willie in the dress and had, at the time, voted it possibly the ugliest dress he had ever seen. Of course, that honor quickly passed to whatever Willie was wearing the next time he saw her. Gayla seemed dumbstruck, but Willie was back in the driver's seat.

"Her house burned in Kansas City," she said, sitting back comfortably. "That's how she got here with nothing to her name."

"I'm sorry to hear that," Tommy said. He couldn't help noticing Gayla's surprise at this new story twist. It endeared her to him in a curious way. "What caused it?"

Even though he knew Willie would probably pick up the ball, he kept his gaze on Gayla.

"Faulty heater," Willie said, now anxious to end the conversation.

"And when did you arrive, Miss . . . it is Miss, isn't it?"

Gayla met his eyes. "Yes. Miss. Miss Gayla Rose Early."

"Really?" Tommy let it soak in for a moment. "Nice name. And when did you arrive?"

"Do you have to grill her like this?" Willie sat forward.

"These are not difficult questions, Ms. Morris."

"Is this an official interview?" Willie shot back.

"Does it need to be?" Tommy's sharp response got her attention, although he could feel his strength starting to wane. "I'm just getting information, so I can eliminate people."

"I'd have to check my calendar," Willie said, rising to head to the kitchen.

Gayla spoke up. "About a week ago."

"Just after the murder."

Tommy's attention had shifted to Willie, though, who had detoured from the kitchen to the front door. When he looked around, she was holding her rifle.

"Just a few days before you killed the deer, Sheriff. You remember, right before you careened off the road and my niece saved your life."

Tommy felt himself flush again, a cold but sweaty sensation familiar to those still not at full strength. Willie moved towards him, and he felt the hair prickle on the back of his neck.

Then, just as he thought he might have to draw his weapon, Willie picked up a can of gun oil from the end table and sat down, cleaning the gun, slowly, meticulously. Her coldness chilled the room.

"Here's what I think, Sheriff. You didn't come out here to say 'thank you.' Not really. The flowers were just a ruse to check on the stranger in town."

Her flare-up seemed to Tommy more filled with fear than outrage. She turned to Gayla.

"You do understand that, don't you, dear?"

Tommy pulled himself up from the uncomfortable kitchen chair.

"I am sorry if I offended you, ma'am. It was nice to officially meet you, Miss Early. I appreciate the delicious limeade. And the flowers were a poor attempt, but a genuine one, to show my gratitude, whether your aunt thinks so or not."

Moments later, as he headed for the Dodge, he hoped it was only Willie's eyes bearing down on his back and not her rifle scope. I may be just a small town sheriff, he thought, and a pothead to boot, but I am a better liar than the two of them put together.

He made a mental note to check on house fires in Kansas City in the last month.

CHAPTER 18

SHERIFF MAYNARD WAS barely out of sight when Gayla secretly slipped an Oklahoma state map she had seen on Willie's desk under her sheets. It was time, as they said in the Old West, to get the heck out of Dodge. The sheriff's questions had spooked her. Figured, just as she was feeling a bit safe, the world had closed in again. He knows, she thought. Or if he doesn't, he will in no time.

Gayla realized she was in a double bind. She not only had to get out of Luckau, but she also had to find out exactly where Luckau was. She had never been to Oklahoma before, much less this little dot of a town, until she and Randy had pulled in after dark to do the job. That was some two years ago. They had driven more than three hundred miles to get there, on a tip from one of Randy's buddies. It was supposed to be a sure thing, far enough away from Dallas that no one would ever link it to them if they were careful.

Stoned for most of the trip, she had barely listened to Randy rattle on about how quick and easy the job was going to be. He had directions to this real estate magnate's weekend cabin and assurances that the wife's jewelry alone was worth thousands. Gayla had all but ignored him until she started to lose her buzz; about that same time Randy announced they were there. It seemed a lifetime ago. And, of course, much later she had realized from Albert's chatter that his wife never came to the cabin, much less stored her jewelry there.

She studied the map after Willie left, surprised to see how far north of Dallas the town and lake sat. They were smack in the western plains. Might as well have been surrounded by desert. Did Greyhound even come through here? What am I going to do, she wondered, when I don't even know how to get out of town.

Part of her said to stay put. Willie had protected her, had even spontaneously lied for her. And there was something about the sheriff that made her feel safe.

Don't be dumb, she told herself. He is the very one who will end up cuffing you. She reminded herself that she had felt safe with Randy, too. Scared, but at least safe. Randy might have been unforgiving when she started coming up short on the drug money, but he had never hit her before that night in the cabin. He was a nickel-and-dime thief who played it safe and never carried a weapon when he pulled a job.

"Not worth the risk if you get caught," he had told her. "I can always find a hammer or kitchen knife if some asshole wants to act like Schwarzenegger. I swung a lawn chair into this gangbanger once, nearly crippled him."

Gayla remembered how she had prayed that night at the Raeder cabin that Randy could improvise their way out of this one. That never happened. Before they had a chance to regroup, they heard the front door open and close, then someone opening a cabinet and the rumble of footsteps coming through the living room and down the hall. Randy was ahead of her in the kitchen, jiggling the handle on the backdoor to no avail.

It seemed impossible in hindsight, but she could swear that night she actually felt the heat emanate off the person headed towards them. She could recall no hesitation. The massive silhouette strode straight for the kitchen. By a dim backyard light, she saw Randy finally get the door open. She hurried to him. The unmistakable sound of the pump action engaging on a shotgun stopped her cold.

"Stop right there or you're dead," the hall shadow said.

She stood paralyzed by fear.

The voice was deep, without a shred of fear.

"You at the door, put your hands up and step back in."

Gayla saw Randy hesitate.

"I can cut you in half from here. Make no mistake."

The cold confidence of the man in the darkness was scary. Wasn't it usually the other way around? Shouldn't he be nervous? Wary of them and wondering if they had accomplices? Or weapons?

Randy stopped, raised his arms in the air, and stepped back into the kitchen.

"Okay, no problem," Randy said.

"That's it. Now. You, too." The shadow motioned with the shotgun barrel for Gayla to move further into the kitchen. Her knees shook so much, she felt like she was going to faint.

The lights snapped on. A large man, about forty-five, stood in the kitchen doorway with a shiny new shotgun trained on Gayla and Randy. Were it not for his expensive gold rings, his thick features and close-cropped hair would have cast him as former military. But the custom-tailored suit and air of assurance indicated money. Lots of it.

"You." He motioned to Randy. "Empty your pockets so I can see them. Slowly."

Randy emptied out his jeans pockets on the counter next to the back door. Then he started on his shirt pockets.

Gayla had never seen a crack of fear from Randy before now. She noticed him eyeing the kitchen counters, searching for a weapon or anything that could be turned into a weapon. She had been doing the same, but the kitchen looked anything but used, much less stocked with bottles or utensils. Not even a household cleaner in sight (Randy had told her they were as good as mace if you sprayed them in the eyes right).

So that was that. There was nothing between them and a pissed-off homeowner with a shotgun. Gayla realized she was still gripping the bag with the goods in it. She felt a hysterical urge to laugh. For the first time she knew what "holding the bag" meant. She offered the bag to the man with the shotgun.

"Here it all is."

He looked her up and down, then motioned for her to put the bag down on the kitchen floor and go stand by Randy.

"Where are you two assholes from?"

It struck Gayla as an odd question. She looked at Randy.

"Simple question. You from around here?" The man carefully set his shotgun down on the kitchen table and removed his jacket.

"We're from Dallas," Gayla blurted, unable to stand the silence any longer.

"Shut up," Randy hissed at her.

"That's a long way. You drive all the way here?"

"What's it to you?" It was the usual Randy tough guy remark, but honestly, he looked helpless — bluffing, stalling. "Look, maybe we could work something out, instead of calling the cops."

"I was wondering the same thing. This your girlfriend?" The man seemed relaxed. He could have been interviewing someone for a job.

"What? No," Randy said.

The man turned to Gayla. "I bet you have family to get back to."

"What's with the twenty questions?" Randy demanded.

Gayla would never know why she answered him. Sheer nerves had taken over. She might as well have taken truth serum.

"My family disowned me a long time ago."

"That's too bad," the man said, picking up the shotgun again.

Randy turned white.

"Hey, man, it was just a robbery. Here, here's all your stuff. We were just —"

The shotgun exploded. It was so loud, Gayla screamed, sure she was hit. She turned to see Randy, blown off his feet. He was dead before he hit the floor. She turned to look at the man, positive she was next.

Instead, he grinned at her and winked.

CHAPTER 19

TOMMY MAYNARD COULD SEE right off that Elmo Dudgeon looked quite pleased with himself. Something was up. Elmo put off a certain smug glow when he felt like he was a step ahead. He had commandeered Tommy's office chair and was holding court with Joe Nguyen and Dixie Willis, the Elk City deputy who had done the nice Vegas background work on Raeder.

Joe looked bored without latex gloves on and no crime scene to work, but Dixie was clearly thrilled to be included in such a powwow. Tommy liked her. She had good energy and a sweetness about her, although her physical presence was not all her sultry voice promised it might be. He wondered if her parents had chosen her name to add some pizzazz to the mousy brown hair and split-tooth smile, which had not been blessed with childhood orthodontia.

Elmo was working up to something, but determined to prolong the drama by droning on about every last exhausting detail that Tommy might have missed doing his run of the outback locals. Like a little prick accountant milking every number at the executive staff meeting. Funny, Tommy thought, how he figures since he called the meeting, he gets to run it from my chair. This infraction alone irked Tommy so much, he could barely concentrate on what was being said.

The reason for the meeting, as far as he knew, was to get everybody up to speed on what they knew about the murder, and then decide how they would proceed. But it looked to him as though Elmo had already decided the next move — either that or he had something big he was failing to share with the rest of them. Instinctively, Tommy decided it was time to shake things up.

"So, what do you think?" Elmo asked him, as he ended another string of repetitive information. He flicked an ash from his cigarette into a gold tin ashtray.

"I think I'm not feeling so good," Tommy said.

Dixie jumped up, anxious to help out. "Do you need some of your medication, Sheriff?"

"No," Tommy said. "But thanks."

"Or a cushion?"

"No." Tommy said and stood up. "I need my chair back."

Elmo's face flushed. "Why, sure, Tommy. I wasn't thinking."

He lifted his large frame from the comfortable stuffed armchair and looked forlornly at the metal folding chairs the others occupied. Tommy tried not to enjoy Elmo's discomfort too much, as he slid back into his swivel fake leather special with casters. Elmo overlapped a metal chair. Tommy swore it gasped a little as Dudgeon dropped himself onto it.

Ah, Tommy thought, a much better point of view. "Now, Joe, you started earlier telling us what else you found in the basement."

"I was just getting to that," Elmo said quickly.

"Yes, about the fingerprints that weren't Albert Raeder's." Joe came out of his half slumber. "We ran them through the Justice databank but didn't get a hit. Then Dixie . . ."

But Elmo wasn't about to give anybody else the glory. "Then we decided to run it through some other national databanks."

"Like what?" Tommy asked.

Dixie jumped in. "State employees, medical personnel, pharmacists, among others."

Elmo could not resist a dig.

"You got to stay up with this stuff, Tommy."

Dixie shot Elmo a lethal sideways look. It was a good bet that Elmo had never heard of any of this before yesterday either.

"And?" Tommy said.

Elmo beamed, beating Dixie to the punch. "Got a hit."

"That's terrific," Tommy said, letting the one-upsmanship fall by the wayside. "Good work. Do we know who he was?"

Dixie handed him a piece of paper with a mugshot on it.

"It's a she, and we know who she is, but not where she is."

Joe tried to jump in, but Elmo cut him off: "We got her from the medical database in — where was that, Joe?"

Nguyen struggled not to roll his eyes. "Irving, Texas. She used to be an x-ray tech at Dallas Memorial. She got fired three years ago."

Tommy studied the mugshot, at first perplexed as to why it looked so familiar. Dixie's briefing faded into the background.

"After she left, nobody seems to know anything about what happened to her. Gave up her apartment. Just vanished," Dixie said.

Tommy blinked, not believing what he was seeing. In the picture, her hair was blond and streaked, she had a healthy tan and a few more pounds on her. She was grinning like it was a snapshot at one of those carnival photo booths, rather than for a work I.D. It was only when he stared into the eyes that he had to admit to himself that it was her.

"Name is Gayla Rose Early," Elmo announced. "We've already put out the word statewide."

Elmo looked closely at Tommy. "You okay?"

"Fine," Tommy lied. He looked for a date on the paper. "Didn't anyone file a Missing Person?"

Dixie shook her head. "Nope. I phoned a couple of her neighbors. They said she was definitely on drugs and going downhill fast before she moved out of her place. The 'move' pretty much amounted to a suitcase. Not a lot else left. Landlady said the place was bare. She'd sold everything for drugs."

Elmo pulled his pants up over his belly and leaned back. "Probably been wandering around the country doing whatever these dope fiends do to get their stuff. Then ran into trouble with Raeder. She could be several states away by now."

Tommy turned to Joe. "But didn't you find prints all over the place?"

Joe cocked his head. "Yep, they were everywhere. Curiously."

Elmo harrumphed. "You didn't tell me that."

Dixie jumped in. "Yeah, don't you remember? He said it was like whoever it was had practically lived there."

"As opposed to someone who had just committed a crime there," Tommy noted.

"Could she have been living there?" Dixie suggested.

"That's — what — several hundred miles from Dallas?" Tommy said. "How did she get to the Raeders' lake retreat from there?"

He thumped the photograph. "And what the hell was she doing for two years in between?"

Dixie looked at another report. "I checked what was listed as her parents' address, but they no longer live there. Military. When I tracked them down, they said there'd been no contact with her for years, and they wanted to keep it that way."

"You seen her around here, Tommy?" Elmo asked.

Tommy looked up at Dixie.

"You know, maybe I do need some of that medication. It's in my satchel."

"You seen her around?" Elmo wasn't going to let this go. "Tommy?"

Tommy carefully constructed his answer.

"I don't recognize the person in this picture at all."

CHAPTER 20

RUSHING HOME WILLIE SIMPLY could not grasp what some would have said was the obvious. Instead, she kept asking herself what was a barely recognizable Gayla — not so skinny, different hair color — doing on a "Wanted" flyer posted in the Village Market. She needed time to make sense of things, but the only other person in town who knew where to find Gayla was the worst one possible: the sheriff.

Willie maintained her nerves long enough to buy her few items and race out of the store. Speeding home in the pickup, she chewed over the developments. She could not imagine a situation in which Gayla would kill. She doubted the skittish young thing could do such a deed even in self-defense. Somebody had to have goofed.

As she pulled into the long, red dirt driveway, Willie already sensed an emptiness about the cabin. She knew before going inside that Gayla was gone. Nothing was missing, which only confirmed it. After all, nothing had belonged to the girl. No suitcases, no emptied closets. But more than that, the house felt empty.

She hurried outside, called out to all the places Gayla usually went, all within hearing distance. No response.

Back inside, Maxine wandered in circles, croaking out pitiful barks. Going from room to room and back again, Willie found herself crying. She had been here before. Someone suddenly gone. Too late. Too late.

She picked up the photo of eight-year-old Jack and sat by the window staring at it for some kind of answer. She could not say why.

By the age he was in the portrait, her boy had already earned nicknames, like "Six-Shooter" and "Crazy Jack" — or "Cracker Jack." Since the day he had clawed his way out of her and entered the world screaming, there had been no putting the brakes on Jack. You had to love him on the run. If the other kids stole one piece of candy, Jack took two. If everyone else took a dare, Jack would go for the double-dog dare. He was like a cartoon whirling dervish, no break, no relief.

Willie and her son had watched a cowboy movie the night before he died. While her husband worked on legal briefs in his study, she sat, smiling, sipping vodka and Coke (her not-so-secret remedy for the stress of mothering a lovable but impossibly high-strung boy), and watching a movie with Jack.

When the townspeople in the movie strung up the cattle rustler, letting him hang for taking their cattle, Jack had screamed and pummeled her with questions. Exhausted and slurring a little, she had half-assed explained how it was done.

"But how do they die, Mommy?" He could not fathom how swinging from a rope could do any harm.

"They just do," she said. "Now go get on your jammies."

"But I wanna know." Jack's tone had that petulant warning that he might pitch a fit if more attention were not soon paid.

"You don't need to know." She answered sharply, hoping to block his inquiring mind. "You're too young."

Her husband's voice boomed from the other room. "What are you letting him watch, anyway?"

"Just some silly old shoot-em-up. James Garner and somebody."

"With lynching in it?" The accusatory undertone in his voice annoyed her. He never helped with Jack, not with discipline, not with guidance, in spite of her pleading. Her suggestion that they have the boy evaluated for hyperactivity had been met with derision. No son of his could have such a pedestrian weakness.

Oh, he could find plenty of fault with her supervision and choices. It seemed easy for him to be critical of her as a mother. He never seemed to notice that she was the one who could not have so much as a cup of coffee alone in peace, who could not take a shower without being interrupted. Truth told, she had found motherhood to be more relentlessly demanding and wearing than her wildest imaginings.

The next morning, it was she who had found him. She had let him outside to run in the backyard while she dressed and fixed a quick vodka chaser with her coffee, something to take off the edge. She was looking forward to dropping him off for Vacation Bible School and relaxing for a couple of hours in peace before anyone came home.

Industrious to the last of his barely lived life, Jack managed to scare up a length of old clothesline in the garage and climb to the lower branch of one of the smaller pecan trees. He tied one end of the rope around the branch, the other end around his neck. And jumped.

Willie saw him through the patio door on her way to the kitchen; she screamed all the way to him. She grabbed him by the knees — one was scabbed from an earlier scrape — and lifted his small body up so the rope would relax its grip. Though she knew immediately he was dead, she held him aloft and refused to let him go, screaming even after the neighbors heard and someone called for an ambulance.

After the paramedics and the ambulance and her husband came, they had had to pry her hands from his dead limbs. She knew her life was finished, and she could not stop screaming. But she could also no longer tell if anyone heard her.

Willie and her husband never spoke of the incident. In fact, barely a meaningful sentence passed between them from the time of Jack's death to their divorce a few months later. After years of living inside liquor bottles, she had halfheartedly reentered the work world, limping along in routine jobs. Not until she bought the cabin with some of her divorce settlement had she felt parts of the old, encrusted grief actually start to move through and out her body.

The guilt was still known to rear its ugly head. And today, seeing Gayla Rose's picture on the flyer, not catching her before she fled in fear, it swooped back over Willie — that shame of abandoning a child in need. Only now she could no longer distinguish whether it was Jack or Gayla who pushed the tears back up from a well she had assumed had long since gone dry.

This realization was what gripped Willie when she saw Tommy Maynard's old Dodge rattler kicking up the dust as it rushed towards her house. She barely had time to splash cold water on her face before he had jumped out of the car and limped up the porch.

Willie's instinct was to reach for her rifle, but the look on Maynard's face was not that of an arresting officer. He seemed more a distraught little boy, one who feared he had been abandoned. His face asked the question.

Willie bit her lip, unable to stop the tears, and shook her head.

"Gone," was all she could get out. "Gone."

The sheriff nodded as if he had known all along what she would say. She told him she had searched the house and all of Gayla's favorite haunts. He took it upon himself to check the outside area again more thoroughly but came up with nothing. They sat down with some iced tea at Willie's Formica kitchen table.

This time Willie was completely honest but had scant to offer.

"To tell you the truth, she didn't want to talk about the past. The only time she got out of sorts was if I pressed her. Whatever she did, she didn't think the folks she came from would forgive her. I got the idea she'd been on her own for awhile."

"Tell me more about these bruises and cuts she had when she showed up," Tommy said.

Willie gave him a rundown on Gayla's lacerated hands and feet, and the long wound down her side.

"She was a wreck. Incoherent. Coloring almost gray, washed-out eyes. Somebody had done a number on her. That's why I lied about all this before. I'm sorry, but it just didn't jibe. She didn't look strong enough to take down a squirrel to me."

"And Raeder was no squirrel. That's for sure."

"So why isn't she telling anyone what happened, Sheriff?"

"I've seen that hollowed-out look before on people who are lost and filled with fear."

Willie nodded. "She was working her way back, but I know what you mean. Sometimes she was . . . way out there."

"Maybe whatever happened is so shameful she'd do almost anything not to talk about it."

Willie had never seen this side of the sheriff. Sensitive, sympathetic, even empathetic.

"What would she have need to be ashamed of?"

His eyes were intense when he turned to her.

"Probably nothing."

CHAPTER 21

TOMMY MAYNARD'S DODGE groaned as the needle pushed into the shaded territory of the speedometer. Since he had no idea where he was headed, the idea of getting there faster seemed ridiculous, but it made him feel he was doing something to help.

It was little comfort that Willie had admitted to lying about Gayla. He already knew that. But she had few other details to offer. Where would Gayla go? With no one to turn to, how would she start out?

His foot throbbed from all his running around, and his head beat with its own drum set, but he could not let it go. Finding Gayla was all that mattered to him. *She saved me.* The thought lodged in his head and wouldn't leave. *She saved me.*

He also knew that at this very moment Elmo Dudgeon was securing a warrant for Gayla's arrest. They had nearly brawled over it. Even Joe and Dixie had chimed in on Tommy's side, saying maybe they shouldn't jump in so quickly. Maybe bring her in first as a material witness.

But Elmo was adamant. He could smell the glory, and knew the citizens of Elk City were unlikely to carp over details when she was found guilty, which he considered a foregone conclusion.

"What is wrong with you, Tommy?" Elmo asked with a questioning shrug. "We got her prints everywhere, even on the murder weapon and his clothes. We have to start a search over a multiple state area. I've already called a news conference for four this afternoon to release her picture nationwide. Get with the program."

"What's her motive?" Tommy asked.

"Drugs, love, pure meanness . . . how the hell would I know? She beat his head in with a two-by-four, Tommy. A pillar of the community. One of our city fathers. I don't know why we're even debating this."

Tommy had not been able to muster a good rebuttal. Except that it could not be. It was not possible that this young woman with the tiny hands and the gentle soul could kill. Crush in faces. Leave a man to bleed out. Tommy had stormed out of the station like a little boy running from a bully.

Now having exhausted the hiding places on Willie's acreage, he found himself pushing down country roads, praying that if Gayla was wandering out here, he would somehow find her, despite the impossible odds. Unaware of exactly where the winding roads were taking him, he realized with a start that he was on his way to the Raeder cabin. Surely she would not go back there. He was swimming farther from shore and he knew it, but he could not stop.

He used the key Mrs. Raeder had given him to open the cabin. Could that have been less than two weeks ago? Inside, the twilight gave the stillness an odd blue glow. The cabin looked completely different to him now. Murky, suspect, mysterious.

Okay, Tommy, you say you're such a big man, he chided himself, why don't you prove it? Why don't you quit chewing on Elmo and do some investigating on your own?

The answer surprised him. Because you know where that might end up. The basement. That scary gray basement. His forehead popped a sweat, but he steeled himself. The basement could come later. For now, just start at the cabin's front door.

Everything seemed in order. Immaculate wood floors, a fireplace that had never seen ashes, spanking new furniture. That was the whole problem. Everything was too pristine. No scuff marks anywhere. This was like a show model cabin for prospective customers, with the customary high end furnishings.

It wasn't until he worked his way through the kitchen with its immaculate counters and shiny stainless steel sinks, until he was staring at the back door, that he felt a prickle on his neck. On closer examination, the door looked like a replacement. For a door that had been brand new? Why? Had the wife not liked the original door and insisted on a different one? The hinges were slightly different and a piece of the door frame appeared to have been repaired with new wood. He knelt to check the floor, a pricey tile design. In the seams, he saw something dark and dried mixed in with the off-white grout.

He took out his cell phone and dialed his office.

"Luckau County Sheriff's Office." It was Dixie, still there. Maybe he hadn't used up all his luck. "Dixie, it's Tommy. Is Joe still around?"

Her voice dropped to a whisper. "Tommy, where are you? Sheriff Dudgeon is about to have a conniption."

"Did he have the press conference?"

"Oh yeah. The photo's out to everyone now."

"What about Joe?"

"He was just about to leave," Dixie said.

"Ask him if he has that ultraviolet doodad that can detect old blood."

"Shall I use that technical verbiage, Sheriff?" She was flirting with him now, enjoying this opening.

"Only if you have to," Tommy said, warming his voice a little.

"Just a sec." He heard her talking to Joe, though something muffled the sound. After a moment she came back on. "Yeah, he carries it with him in the truck."

"Tell him to meet me at the Raeder cabin."

"When?"

"Now?"

He heard her relay the message to Joe before she came back on.

"Okay. He said it's on the way back to Elk City, so he'll drop by on his way home."

"Thanks, Dixie. And, Dixie, there's no need to bring Sheriff Dudgeon into this. It's just some clean-up stuff."

"You got it. 'Night, Sheriff."

Tommy leaned against the counter, relishing the first real accomplishment of the day. A sharp knock on the door interrupted the thought.

"Anybody in there?" It was an older woman's voice.

Tommy turned on the lights in the living room and opened the storm door to a neatly coiffed lady in a velour sweat suit.

"Hello, can I help you?" he said.

"I'm Mabel Thorpe from next door. I just got back into town and heard about Mr. Raeder. I saw the gate to his house open, which it never

ever is. I just thought I should check it out."

Nose around is more like it, Tommy thought.

"It's okay. I'm Sheriff Maynard from Luckau."

She checked out the living room and furnishings as she and Tommy spoke. "Oh, I know who you are. It's a fancier place than I thought," she offered.

"You ever been inside?"

"Oh, no. Mr. Raeder wasn't exactly friendly that way."

"Oh? You ever talk to him?"

"Oh, sure. Well, I tried, but he didn't want to hear about it."

"Hear about what?" Tommy asked, sensing a chattering neighbor's need to be part of the drama.

"The screaming," Mabel said, folding her arms over her chest.

A chill settled over Tommy. Mabel needed no urging to continue.

"I told him I thought a child had been hurt. Maybe fallen or stuck in a tree and couldn't get out."

"What did he say?" Tommy asked.

"He said it must be the stray cat he'd been having trouble with, but I never saw a cat around here. Then the screaming stopped. I guess he took care of it."

"And where were these screams coming from?"

"Near as I could tell, the garage out back behind the house."

"How long ago was this?"

Mabel's eyes narrowed. "Oh, sometime last year. Maybe earlier."

Tommy opened the door wide, inviting her in.

"Do you have time for a few questions?" he asked.

As she came inside, Joe showed up. Tommy excused himself for a minute so he could point out the tile grout where he wanted Joe to take the sample.

"Will do," Joe said, as he popped on latex gloves. "Oh, and Sheriff Dudgeon was coming in just as I was leaving. Wanting all the details. Don't be surprised if he doesn't drop by nosing around."

"Thanks for the heads up."

CHAPTER 22

GAYLA ROSE EARLY DID NOT let herself think about why she was back in this place. It made no sense, and it certainly had not been her destination. She had tossed the map, a couple of Willie's hand-me-downs, and a new three-pack of cotton panties from the Village Market into a paper sack and walked away, down the red dirt drive to the road. All she knew was she had to get out of the way. Willie had already lied for her. Gayla would ask her for nothing more.

Once Raeder's grisly death had hit replay in Gayla's head, it was more urgent than ever that she move on. The initial numbness that had settled in after the murder was gone. So was the haze that filtered out the hideous details of what she had done. Now she could not escape it. Albert's dying stalked her daily in angry red flashes, rending her nerves raw. She could not escape his stunned, horrified face, his grabbing paws, and his animal cries. She saw his arms extended as he tried to block her blows and she heard her own grunts amplified as she punched him until her hands bled.

Finally, that gray eye, staring from his death mask in disbelief. She no longer could defend or explain exactly how it had all happened, but whatever they ended up doing to her, Gayla decided, she couldn't pull good people, like Willie, down with her.

A tender good-bye to Maxine, and she headed for the nearest county road. Each vehicle that rolled by scared her more than the last. She ended up sticking to the narrow dirt shoulders, so she could scamper into the bushes or trees when she heard the motor of a car coming.

Then she had wandered, and practically stumbled onto them – the nest of boulders that had sheltered her for two nights after she ran from the Raeder cabin. They were all of seventy feet from the road. I was so close to the traffic, she thought. Yet she could not remember hearing a single car or truck pass by in the day and two nights of her delirium.

From the boulders, Gayla felt compelled, pulled to retrace her steps. She was unsure of the exact path; nonetheless, she felt a keen sense of where her bleeding feet had dragged her from before.

She caught the smell of lake water, slightly sour as it blended with rotted fish heads thrown into the weeds. Her heart beat faster as the lake came into view, its turquoise hue contradicting the dark wall of clouds that promised rain soon. And then there she was, sneaking through the side gate, the same one she had used to escape.

The yellow ribbon around the garage startled but did not stop her. Of course, she thought, it's a crime scene. But it is safe here now. He is no longer here. She was uncertain as to whether she believed that, of course. Despite the nightmares that assured her he would never walk this earth again. And maybe that was why she was here. Seeing is believing, she thought. Is that why people return to the scene of the crime? To confirm that the unspeakable things they'd done did in fact happen?

She found a new padlock on the garage door, but it barely slowed her down. She easily broke a pane in a window and slipped inside. Gayla looked around the workshop with a detached curiosity. How nicely he had laid it all out, she thought with grudging admiration. If anyone had walked in, they would have thought he was quite the handyman husband. There were hammers, screwdrivers, tool chests, even a table saw.

She could not remember hearing him working up here a single time. And she knew she would have recognized the sounds. Her own father was always making a racket in their family garage, sharpening kitchen knives for her mother or fixing a bicycle for Gayla. Going out to the garage had always been her father's escape hatch from evenings of sitcoms and dull, female conversation.

Her heart thumped as she pried open the trapdoor to the basement. It was anchored by three heavy-duty hinges, strong enough to hang a church door, she realized with a start. She had not known until she saw it from the outside that he had also installed two slide locks on each side, in addition to the enormous main clasp lock. This would have contained a den of tigers, she thought to herself.

She started down the stairs, trying to control her shaking, which made negotiating the steps difficult. Not until Gayla reached the basement floor did her legs stop wobbling. For a moment, the rush of smells and sense of place were so cloying and claustrophobic she nearly ran. But a fragile stillness in the room stopped her. The only living sound was the chirp of a cricket, hidden somewhere in the dark recesses of the basement.

That was how Gayla got to this point, squatting by the dried puddle of crackled blood in the middle of the room. It had turned a deep red-brown. Dust already had begun to settle on it. Why had nobody cleaned this up? Gayla wondered.

She had expected the dreadful images to confront her again. His pink shirt darkening with blood, his lurching around the room in awkward circles, clutching his chest. Instead, the energy was curiously neutral. She looked around, half expecting to see the bloodied two-by-four. Of course it was gone. But her cot was still there, overturned in the corner, as was the chain he had locked around her ankle. She marveled now at the planning. The chain was just long enough to allow her to reach the cot, the industrial sink, the apartment-sized fridge, and the toilet — but nothing else.

A lightning strike lit the basement through the thin cracked window. Thunder rumbled in the distance. A cool breeze blew through the broken window pane, bringing with it a sense of déjà vu. It was like she had never left. The routines of captivity took hold again. Normally, she compulsively controlled that small space in whatever way she could. The toilet, sink, and fridge she kept spotless. The floor . . . What had happened to its piney smell, she wondered. A bottle of Pine-Sol stood on the floor by the sink, near her mop, bucket, and scrub brush.

This has to be cleaned up, she thought. Moving slowly, like a sleepwalker, she drew a bucket of water at the sink and poured it over the dried blood. She began to hum as she filled the sink with the hot, soapy mopping solution. She could feel that old sense of order and control coming back, as she hummed and cleaned the basement floor. A ritual that blessedly marked time, that took the stench of his body from the room, and that always made her feel a little less filthy.

Outside, the rain started.

She was scrubbing the floor so hard when Sheriff Tommy Maynard came down the stairs that she did not hear him. She had retreated into the mind-set that kept her alive for those two long, depraved years. She was back in survival mode — detached emotionally from what she knew she had to do when the trapdoor opened.

At that moment, whether it was morning or night, weekday or weekend, the basement became her stage. Her survival depended on her ability to play act, to fake that she was glad to see and ready to seduce her jailer, the man who in turn would proceed to invade any orifice in her body that he felt like for whatever time lay ahead.

Tommy's arrival was out of context. Her mind blurred, unsure who he was. Her thoughts slurred backwards, to what she needed to do to survive a man's arrival in this place. After all, it was a different world down here where the rats play.

So Gayla did what she knew she had to . . . what she had learned was best to always do. She stood and rubbed her wet hands on her too big dress. Once more she was the cunning victim, playing for her captor like a movie star to a camera.

She unbuttoned her dress and let it fall to the floor.

CHAPTER 23

TOMMY MAYNARD WAS SO taken aback by Gayla stripping in front of him, he could only stand there in shock. He had spent another ten minutes or so in the house with Mabel, the neighbor, and had only come down for a quick look around the basement before he headed out again. He had no more stepped off the last step and into the room than Gayla was standing in front of him, wearing only white cotton panties.

His first impression was she didn't recognize him. Distant and blank-eyed, she clearly was not herself.

His second made him blanch. Scars crisscrossed her breasts. His mind flashed back to the whore from Las Vegas who had lost part of a breast to Raeder. The bastard, he nearly did the same to her.

"Gayla, it's me. Sheriff Maynard. Tommy." He kept his tone soft, gentle.

"I know what you want," she said, making no effort to cover herself.

"I don't think you do, Gayla."

"It's okay. I don't mind."

He stepped slowly towards her, his hands raised in the universal sign of surrender, trying to signal he wasn't going to touch or harm her.

"Put on your dress, Gayla." He picked it up and held it out to her.

"What?" She frowned in confusion.

Tommy smelled the Pine-Sol and saw where she had scrubbed the blood stains. He was torn between the need to hurry — who knew how close behind him Dudgeon was — and the desire to handle this the right way, as gently as possible. He feared to do otherwise might break this poor woman into more pieces than he could ever put back together. His gut told him he was right to be wary . . . cautious. Everything about Gayla seemed off: her expression, her posture, her voice. How could she sound like a complete stranger, he wondered.

"How did you get in here, Gayla?"

"I know what you're here for."

"What are you doing? Cleaning up?"

Gayla looked blank, then at the floor. "Nobody mopped up. It shouldn't be left like that. It needs to be neat."

"You're right. Sorry. I thought they had a crew coming to do that." He couldn't actually remember if they did or not.

"Somebody needed to see to it," she said.

"And now you've cleaned it up. Thank you. That's more than anyone could ask." He tried again to hand her the dress. "Here. You need to get dressed now."

"What do you want today?" It was like she hadn't even heard him.

"First, put your dress on. Then we can talk."

Nothing registered.

"Now, Gayla."

For a moment, her eyes went somewhere far off. He needed her to stay with him . . . but how to bring her back.

"Listen, there may be people on their way here," he said. "Right now. I don't want them to find you like this."

She looked up, seeming to finally comprehend what he was saying.

"They're coming for me," she whispered.

He cleared his throat roughly to cover his emotions.

"I'm afraid so. I couldn't stop them. But —"

Frantic, she dropped to her knees in front of him and fumbled for the zipper on his pants.

"Please. Let me —"

"Oh no, Gayla, no," Tommy cried, humiliated for her. He already felt an illogical sense of perversion, though he knew this was not about him. He grabbed her shoulders to try and lift her up.

A lightning flash illuminated both the rain outside, now making rumbling noises as it pounded the shed roof, and Gayla on her knees inside, clinging to Tommy as he reached for her.

A chuckle, low and insinuating, made Tommy freeze. Sheriff Elmo Dudgeon could not have timed his entrance better if he'd been a Las Vegas showgirl.

Before Tommy could utter a sound, Elmo snickered, then made an apologetic face.

"Terribly sorry to interrupt, Sheriff Maynard. I see you fellows here in Kiowa County have a lot more fun making an arrest than we do."

CHAPTER 24

WILLIE PUSHED THE TRUCK to its limit as she careened down the wet, winding road. Dark smoke shot out the back in protest. She had gotten Sheriff Maynard's call less than an hour ago. Gayla had been arrested, and he was holding her in the county jail for now. The Elk City sheriff, however, wanted a "parade perp walk," as Tommy called it, to Gayla's hearing. He muttered something cryptic about the other sheriff having to leave suddenly. Willie was not clear just why.

Maynard had started talking the minute Willie answered the phone. He promised to keep things as low profile as he could, but he needed Willie's help. Court was in session that day — hearings on everything from traffic fines to assault. Tommy had gotten Gayla on the docket for late in the afternoon. The Elk City folks were calling for everyone in the whole damn state to cover it — from the wire service to the network news shows — but for once, Luckau's size and off-the-beaten-path location might be an asset and slow the response. While Oklahoma reporters pored over state maps to locate the town, Tommy hoped to get Gayla in and out of the hearing and back on his own turf.

No matter how well they sheltered Gayla, the perp walk would be like crossing the length of a football field. It could not help but give the inevitable local crowd a good look at the first accused killer in the town's history. Okay, it had to happen. But that did not mean Willie had to like it. She could only imagine how traumatic being pushed through a pool of reporters and flashing lights would be for Gayla.

CRIMES OF REDEMPTION

To Sheriff Maynard's credit, there had been no beating about the bush with his instructions. Willie was to commence acting like next of kin. If the Elk City sheriff showed back up, she was to make a fuss, scream for a lawyer, and accuse anyone and everyone of bias and press-baiting.

Willie couldn't help but grin at the idea. It summoned the old sixties protestor in her. Since Jack's death, whenever she felt like spreading stink around the democratic way, she always took a moment to seriously weigh the possible consequences of getting involved. It was always a judgment call, whether she could talk loudly enough to get something achieved, while keeping it low profile enough to stay off the public radar. But she had no illusions about keeping any involvement in this quiet. This mess with Gayla was huge. It scared her, but could there be a more righteous cause to hook onto — or a better person to help? She could feel her energy start to bubble.

She had immediately known Gayla would need a lawyer. Several thousand dollars in an old Folger's coffee can now sat beside her on the seat. It would be enough to retain someone, surely. Willie just hoped it was enough to retain someone competent. But where to even look? Most of the local lawyers were useless when it came to criminal work.

As she hit the town limits, Willie was surprised to feel a warm joy, a sense of purpose. In a life specifically designed to take on no commitments, this should have been a bother, an annoyance. Instead she felt a part of something again. A cocky smile crept across her face as she addressed the woman in the pickup's rearview mirror.

"You want trouble. Well, it's coming right at you. Get ready."

The face staring back was not so threatening. Gray, stringy hair, double chin, eyes hooded with age. Her old elastic-waist mommy jeans and frayed seersucker shirt didn't exactly go with the tough talk. Yet had someone overheard her words and taken the time to look into her eyes, they might have reserved judgment. There in lay a steely twinkle that recalled the piss and vinegar of her youth.

Willie glared into the rearview mirror again, bolstering her courage.

"You have no idea who you're dealing with," she hollered at her reflection.

A horn blast knocked her eyes back to the road. Her pickup had drifted over the median line, and now a truck of construction workers was headed right at her. The other driver swerved, laid on his horn again, and yelled something profane as he passed. Willie yanked the pickup back into her lane and trembled at her foolishness. What are you doing, she asked herself. An old bitch screaming affirmations at herself while driving. What were you thinking?

She took a deep breath and patted the Folger's coffee can still beside her on the seat. Its cool, rusted sides comforted her. Just get your head in the game. You will go into town, bail out Gayla, and . . . then what?

Willie did not like playing it by ear. She liked things settled, planned, clean. What the hell was she doing? She chided herself again. Why are you acting like such a big wienie? Maybe it was because she knew what the accusatory spotlight felt like. It was, after all, what had driven her to buy a remote cabin in the boonies of Oklahoma. The endless prying eyes had gotten to her all those years ago, when she was dragged through the legal jungle following Jack's death.

Despite it eventually being ruled an accident, there seemed no end to the probing, the relentless scrutiny. What if all that happened again? She could hear them now: "Who's the old bag? That the recluse from the country? Why's the old lady with the killer?"

Her hands tightened on the steering wheel. Yes they could ask questions. Yes they could speculate. But what could they do to her? Not a damn thing, she assured herself.

She looked again into the rearview mirror.

Shot it her best Clint Eastwood grimace.

"Think you scare me?" she growled.

Her eyes narrowed into thick slits.

But she was scared. She surely was.

CHAPTER 25

SHE MIGHT AS WELL be sleepwalking, Tommy Maynard thought. With Gayla's first step into the cell, he noticed the change in her. The withdrawal was so complete, he would have sworn she couldn't see what was right in front of her. Now, several hours later, she still had yet to sit down on the bunk. Blank-eyed and listless, she paced from one wall to the other.

Sitting at his desk, Tommy tried to take stock of his own state of mind. The incident in the Raeder basement had been unnerving. He had been arresting drunk women for years. The M.O. for many of them was to offer sex to avoid arrest. But he had never had one just drop her clothes that way. Sexless. Perfunctory. Not inviting, just complying. She could have been a patient in an exam room.

He was beginning to grasp how much Raeder must have messed her up. He was not sure if this was classic Stockholm Syndrome, but that acquiescence had been burned into her. There was nothing natural about what she had offered him.

That worthless prick, Elmo. If he had shown him just an ounce of faith, or even inquired first as to what was going on, anything but assuming the worst. No, instead, Elmo had strutted around, ogling Gayla, who had suddenly looked so lost, as if she was wondering if she was supposed to do both of them. And instead of seeing how helpless and vulnerable the woman in front of him was, Elmo had leered at Tommy with a conspiratorial grin.

"This isn't what you think," Tommy said, his voice full of warning.

"Of course not," Elmo smirked.

"I'm serious. You can see my pants are still zipped, asshole."

"I didn't mean to cut short the fun."

"Hey! Stop it right now." Then in Elmo's face, almost whispering so Gayla wouldn't hear. "For God's sake, she's a sick woman."

All the while, Gayla had stood there, looking stunned and puzzled.

Finally, Elmo had put his hands up, seeming to acknowledge that maybe he was off base. Still, he couldn't leave well enough alone. After they had gotten her dressed again and all three were headed to the cruisers, Elmo had given him a nudge with his elbow and said with a low laugh, "I didn't mean nothing back there. Lots of guys like making it with a crazy."

That was when Tommy broke Elmo's jaw. His fist was on its way before he knew it. Pure instinct, an animal reaction, backed by years of evolution and more recently the regular use of a punching bag to let off steam.

Elmo's face morphed grotesquely as Tommy landed the punch. And now, with Tommy's hand swelling up like a pumpkin, he regretted losing his temper. Well, at least he was working on regretting it.

Tommy sat now in his office, crafting the inevitable apology he would have to deliver to Elmo, while he watched over Gayla in her cell. Elmo, cruiser lights flashing, had sped off to the Elk City hospital for x-rays and who knows what other tests on his face, all of which his ample county health insurance would cover.

When the wronged Elmo returned, groveling would be expected of Tommy, and he was willing to do it for Gayla's sake. Still. Too bad for him if he did not know when to shut up, Tommy thought. Never yet met a bully who knew when to zip it, but his thoughts turned to the woman behind the punch.

Gayla looked pale, even through her sunburn. Dixie had gotten her into orange prison scrubs and bagged Gayla's ugly green dress as evidence. Dixie had then volunteered to drive Elmo, although the forlorn look she had shot back at Tommy as she crawled into Elmo's cruiser said she would rather be going anywhere else.

Meanwhile the center of all the ruckus remained a study in panicked, perpetual motion. Her green eyes darted nervously; her hands opened and closed compulsively; her fingers pawed her neck; her palms slid up and down the sides of her pants. From time to time, she stopped, as though she might speak, only to renew pacing — from one side of her ten-foot cell and back again.

Tommy watched her, and as he did, he found himself thinking back to Hanoi. He did not consciously go there often, but watching Gayla pace the same way he had so many years ago transported him back to The Zoo. One foot in front of the other. Keep shuffling. Only way to stay alive. That is, on the days when you were able to stay on your feet.

Vicious beatings were routine at The Zoo, and they went on for months on end. Even though it was '72, after the People's Army of Viet Nam's use of torture had long been outed internationally, Ho Chi Minh's diehard interrogators apparently had not gotten the cease-and-desist memo. The eyes of the world may have been on North Vietnam, but the worst of the PAVN torture had yet to stop in The Zoo, even if it was never as well staffed as the Hanoi Hilton. Located across town from the infamous Hilton, The Zoo had been a Hanoi film studio before Ho Chi Minh commandeered it to house prisoners.

Tommy had been grateful when he first landed there. Captured by the VC while napping in the jungle, after somehow staying alive on his own several weeks in enemy territory, Tommy had been prepared to be executed on the spot. He never knew why his captors did not shoot him that first day, only that their omission eventually landed him at The Zoo, home to at least fifty other prisoners of war.

The Zoo was the kind of place no one ever completely adjusted to. Watery soup and bug-infested bread, he could take. He could even tolerate the endless dank stench and perpetually wet concrete walls. But when it became common knowledge that their torturers, who were mainly Cuban, were trying to outdo the Hilton, he began to wonder if dying upon capture would not have been a better way to go.

How the Cubans came to run torture at The Zoo — was it an invitation between fellow communist regimes? — was never explained. Some POWs later pressed the question with Washington, but for whatever reason the Cuban presence in Hanoi was never publicly acknowledged by the U.S. government, even years after the war ended. But their nicknames — and native tongue — left no doubt where they were from.

Tommy's assigned torturer was code-named "Fidel," a slight, hairy guy who overcompensated for his lack of stature by wielding an electro-shock baton like a weapon.

More than thirty years later, Tommy could feel a bitter taste rise in his throat at the memory of Fidel and how he toyed with you, twirling his baton like a western six-shooter, before zapping you where you least expected. With everyone stripped naked for the interrogations, there was nothing Fidel could not get to — especially when he decided to tie your hands to a bar bolted into the ceiling.

Tommy had never been able to talk about those sessions. Not right after it happened, not ever since. How do you talk about having your balls swell up like grapefruit after getting zapped? Or having your dick juiced so many times you were ready to beg them to cut it off? And as if the torture sessions themselves were not bad enough, there were the cruel head games the guards played with the prisoners afterwards.

Tommy might have barely been able to walk back to his cell, but no signs of what had been inflicted on him showed physically — at least where any of the other prisoners could see. This was a ploy to create suspicion among the POWs, suggesting this guy must be cooperating, right? If not, where were the marks?

And Tommy couldn't blame them. He had seen other prisoners return after being beaten with truck motor belts, skin from their backs hanging like bloodied racks of meat. They would stare at him and a few others, who appeared to have been purposely left untouched, like what kind of sweet deal are you working? Fidel found that game funny.

Tommy could still picture the little Cuban's crooked smile after any of the many barrage of shocks to his privates. Fidel would throw his hands in the air, all innocent, like, What did I do? "Why you cry, American boy? You lucky you only get burn on your dick. I put you with Pablo, he gonna cut it all the way off and make your buddy eat it, eh?"

The relentless emasculation, the gleeful perversion, not only left his privates badly scarred but also opened a gaping hole inside him. After awhile, all he did was try to figure out how to keep Fidel happy. He started identifying with his captor. Trying to think from the other side of the game, like this oily-eyed keeper of his fate might.

But eventually it was Fidel, himself, who told him what he wanted.

"We do different today. Open your mouth, pretty boy."

And Tommy thought, this is it: He's gonna make me suck his cock.

And he did not hesitate. If it will save me getting my privates torched, Tommy thought, you betcha I'll do it. He felt like throwing up, but he would do it.

But Fidel surprised him. Giving him directions as he opened his fly, "Okay, on your knees. No, mouth open little wider. No, get back — two more meter."

What the hell is he doing? Tommy thought, backing away on his knees, mouth open, panic making him sweat even more in the dark, filthy interrogation room. Is he going to run it into my mouth?

"There. Right there."

Then, giggling, Fidel whipped out his penis and started to pee, aiming the stream right at Tommy's open mouth. Tommy turned his face, an automatic response, a reflex really. Immediately he heard electricity snap as Fidel's baton zapped his cheek. A burning smell mixed with the stinking fear exuded by his own body. Of all the stories that had circulated The Zoo, and there were a million of them, Tommy had never heard of this trick. He could barely stay on his knees. The room was swimming.

"Bad move, little boy." Fidel laughed in his face, one of his hands still holding his cock; the other, his baton. "Oh, poor Capitano Thomas James Maynard, you blow it. Yeah, now you blow it."

He turned the baton on, the zap of electrodes crackled. Fidel raised an index finger in warning: "You hurt Fidel, Mr. Flash be very mad."

Mr. Flash was his nickname for the baton, which was now inches from Tommy's skull.

"Now come here, closer," Fidel's breath thick and turned on. "You do it good for Fidel and he not gonna hurt you today."

Snot running from his nose, eyes stinging from urine and tears, inching forward on his knees towards Fidel's erect penis, Tommy knew that somehow he had to do this. There would be no macho moves on his part, no sudden revolt, because as disgusting as this might be, others had had it far worse. You do what you have to, to survive.

"Come on, flyboy, you suck my prick now."

Tommy could barely breathe through the mucus rising in his nose and throat. Small groaning sounds crawled up through his chest. They seemed to come from some other animal. He hesitated just long enough to feel the rush of air as the baton headed for him again.

The clank of an opening metal door jolted them apart. Boots marched down the hall towards the cell. Fidel jumped to attention. In one move, he zipped up, motioned Tommy to his feet, and began yelling at him in Cuban Spanish. Although there were surely no rules as to what they could do to a prisoner, Fidel apparently was not about to get caught by his coworkers with his johnson hanging out.

A PAVN officer and two other Cubans appeared outside the interrogation room door and motioned Fidel to come out. There was an animated, then heated conversation — in a mishmash of Vietnamese and Spanish — among the men that ended with the Cubans looking none too happy. A few minutes later, Fidel turned, shot Tommy a nasty look, and left.

Tommy never saw him again. The Cubans were gone. From then until the war ended a few months later, he would endure beatings and more zapping, but a session never got that twisted again. The North saw the end in sight as surely as the rest of the world did.

It all left Tommy feeling not only devastated but utterly alone. Even flying reconnaissance, a job essentially done alone, there are fellow soldiers on base providing support. But since he ejected that fateful day, his plane hit by a surface-to-air, hand-guided missile, he had been alone. First in the jungle. Then here as well. Could anyone be any more isolated, he had often wondered. The empty hole in his heart told him no.

For Tommy, there would be no novel written on toilet paper in his cell, no music composed in his mind, no dream house designed on a cell wall. He often grimaced at the memory of the algebra and chemistry he had struggled with in school — all of which offered him zero help in getting through his ordeal. He should had been taking drawing and writing, he decided. He envied the guys who could invent long-term projects to fill the empty hours, who could escape the tedium by making stuff up.

Tommy could not make things up. He could only look at what was. There was only one foot in front of the other for him. You don't have to move fast, he told himself. Just don't stop moving. Don't think about it too much. At least, don't think about it all the time.

So, yes, Tommy understood what Gayla was doing. The perpetual motion of a hamster on a wheel not of its own making. Don't reflect. Don't squeeze the truth. Just stay alive even though the pit in your stomach is too deep to ever be filled. Just get through it. Because you might just surprise yourself and someday find yourself on the other side.

Tommy had gotten through it. He had come home. Well, most of him had. The emptiness was still there. Sometimes good weed could knock it back, lift him to a place that felt like enough. Except he always came back down.

What was brand new for him now was how he felt after not using pot for the past week or so. Sure, he had been busy, but it was mind-boggling to him how little he missed it.

When he was watching Gayla, like he was now, he knew it wouldn't feel right if he was stoning all the time. It reminded him of the way some of his buddies who became parents started to talk after the baby had been around for awhile. "Like there just isn't time for it, man," they'd say. "I got the kid now."

And somewhere deep down, Tommy thought, I have Gayla now.

CHAPTER 26

A DULL ACHE HAD SETTLED deep in Gayla's legs after a couple of hours of shuffling back and forth across the cell floor. But she could not stop. She could not figure out how that had happened in the basement. She was so humiliated she could not look at Tommy. And she was afraid she would never be able to explain it to him.

How could he ever understand why and how she had manipulated Raeder? Albert had punched her in the face or blackened her eyes only a handful of times during her imprisonment, usually when he was blind drunk.

"I'm not gonna ruin that pretty face," he would say. "I'm not interested in fucking something with a broken nose, but wait until you get a couple of ribs crunched. You'll change your tune."

Once she accepted that she was in the basement to stay, she proved a fast learner. He would arrive for the weekend, sometimes almost giddy, dragging presents along with her week's worth of food. Gaudy lingerie or some sickly sweet perfume. Other times, he arrived with an axe to grind, jabbering madly about someone who had pissed him off, how things always went sour.

Either way, by the time he unlocked her, he usually had a hard-on, bulging beneath his shiny suit pants. If he was in a good mood, it wasn't so bad. She just lay there until he finished with her. But if he was mad, it could get rough in a hurry, as if he was following some perverse script in his head. "You love it, don't you? I'm the best you'll ever get," he might say, pounding her, not even realizing that he not only repulsed her but also often left her sore and bruised for days after these sessions.

As the months passed, she figured out how to turn his bravado declarations to her advantage. She rewrote his own lines to say back to him. She memorized them verbatim. The dirtier she talked to him, the more his natural bent towards brutishness would soften.

Gradually, she tested his responses to stripteases, undressing him, anything she could think of to manipulate him to a less brutal place. It shocked her how easy it was. She learned to apply the garish deep red lipstick he loved as soon as she heard him coming — and, almost without fail, it helped smooth the way. Eventually, she found one that nearly always worked, an act that soothed him like no other: She would drop her dress, let him look her up and down, then she fall to her knees and go down on him. It was so unnatural to her, so forced, she was amazed he could not see through it. But he never did, and she made her peace with it. It made the rest of the sex less violent, and usually less prolonged.

But what were you thinking with Sheriff Maynard, she wondered. Immediately it had felt all wrong. He had looked at her so strangely, and she had ended up confused and shamed. From the cell, she sneaked a glance at Tommy only to find him smiling at her with a gentle, curious look of concern.

"I'm sorry," she whispered.

Tommy blinked. "Excuse me?"

"I'm sorry."

"For what?"

"You know."

He shook his head, as if it was nothing, as if she was apologizing for forgetting to refill the coffee pot. "Don't worry about that."

"I didn't mean to."

"I know. I'm going to find someone, a professional, to talk to you."

"About what?"

"About what . . . happened down there before. What you must have gone through with him."

She shrank back. "I don't want to talk about that."

"It would be somebody who might help you get over it."

The noise of the gathering crowd outside suddenly pumped up in volume. Cars pulling up, doors slamming, nervous chattering.

"It's making my skin crawl being in here," she said.

He saw her glance at the front door and gave a quick nod towards it.

"Let me worry about these rubberneckers."

Both of them jumped as Willie's voice cut through the din.

"Sheriff, it's Willie Morris."

Gayla looked relieved. "Oh, thank God."

The sheriff unsnapped his holster before he opened the door a few inches for Willie.

"Come on in."

Willie slipped inside, clutching a coffee can in one hand and what looked like clothes in the other. Gayla slipped her arms through the cell bars to try and touch her. Before she could reach Gayla, Tommy stepped between them.

"Better put down your packages first. Protocol."

Willie complied and was hugging Gayla a few seconds later.

"You okay?" Willie asked.

"I'm okay," Gayla said.

Willie turned to Tommy. "There's a bunch of nuts outside."

"And growing by the minute. You're just in time. Her appearance is in fifteen minutes. Can you walk with us? Provide some interference if anybody gets too pushy? Do you mind?"

"You're the only officer?" Willie sounded a bit incredulous.

"Yeah."

"What about Dudgeon?"

Gayla piped up. "They got in a fight."

"What?" Willie looked confused.

Tommy made a just-cool-it gesture.

"Long story. No time. I'll explain later. Will you help me walk her to the courthouse?"

"Fine. Does she have to wear this crap?" Willie asked, nodding at Gayla's orange prison scrubs. "That's ugly even to me."

Tommy choked back a laugh.

"Sorry, we had to take her clothes for evidence."

"I brought her a dress I got for her the other day. She won't look like such a target. If we have time for her to change." Willie passed the dress to Gayla, along with some hose and heels.

Looks like it might actually fit, Gayla thought. As she changed behind their backs, she heard them talking about making bail. Willie showed him some big rolls of bills from the coffee can, wrinkled and soiled, but neatly coiled with a rubber band. Their voices became more distant and hushed.

"Is anybody representing her today?" Willie whispered.

"There's a public defender on duty. I haven't been able to get him on the phone yet, but he'll be okay for today. The main thing is to get her out of here so she won't have to spend the night."

Willie drew back, studied him curiously.

"Why are you taking such an interest in her? Why do you care?"

Tommy lowered his voice and took a few moments before he spoke. "I have an idea about what happened to her down in that basement. If I'm right, that wealthy widow is going to do anything to cover it up. Not to mention the founding fathers of Elk City. And I'm pretty sure I'm the only one on this side of the law who even considers it a possibility."

"I don't understand," Willie said. "What happened?"

Gayla paused in her dressing so as not to miss a word.

"Chains, a filthy cot, and a toilet in the corner, a triple-reinforced trapdoor. And a woman missing for two years?"

He looked at Willie like, You figure it out.

"Oh my god," Willie said, "I didn't know. She never told me . . ."

"It hasn't been released to the press yet. When it is, all hell is going to break loose."

Willie turned to look at Gayla, who now had her new dress on.

"You look so nice. Doesn't she, Sheriff?"

"Sure does."

The look that accompanied Tommy's words did more for Gayla's confidence than anything she could have conjured up herself. Gayla looked at her new heels, which were a decent fit, and could not remember when she had last worn pumps. She felt uncomfortable when she tried a few steps in them.

"Don't worry about a thing," Willie said. "We'll get through this first little hearing, and then we'll deal with getting you a lawyer."

"She's gonna need a good one, for sure," Tommy said, as his cell phone buzzed. He clicked it open.

"Maynard . . . Good. No, just stay put over there and keep the press out."

He closed the phone, looking relieved.

"One of my deputies is in place at the courthouse. He'll show you where to go once you get inside. Now here's how we'll do this . . ."

What the two were saying faded into the background, as Gayla watched and marveled at them — once enemies or at least not friends — now working together to figure out how to help her, a total stranger. It felt as though someone had wrapped long, warm arms around her and tucked her in for the night.

For just a moment, she wanted to cry but not with sadness.

CHAPTER 27

OKAY, READY?" SHERIFF MAYNARD asked with a raised eyebrow. Willie nodded, though she doubted there was any way that Gayla could be prepared for what waited outside. Judging from the growing chatter and sound of cameras being set up, a good many members of the media had managed to find Luckau on the map and make the drive, even on such short notice. She draped a blue bath towel over Gayla's head, as she tried to reassure her.

"Don't worry. We'll be right beside you."

Gayla's hand trembled as she grabbed Willie's.

"Good, 'cause I can barely see."

"We'll be your seeing-eye dogs," Tommy said, gripping Gayla's arm. "On three."

He counted it out, then opened the station door to a wall of flashing lights and clicking cameras. Willie gripped Gayla's hand and struggled to keep the towel in place with her other. The rush of pressing reporters followed by their boom mics and cameramen pushed against them. As they ran the gauntlet, Willie could hear Tommy repeating, "Make way, please. Step back."

It was still scary, though. The kind of scary she could remember from her own hearing decades ago. Tommy pushed back against the more aggressive reporters as they threw questions at Gayla.

"Did you beat Albert Raeder to death, Miss Early?"

"Are they treating you okay, Gayla?"

"How well did you know Mr. Raeder?"

"How long were you lovers?"

Willie could imagine Gayla's astonishment over the familiarity of the questions. And it will only get worse, she thought. They will ask you things that your own mother would not dare. What worried Willie was that if this many media types showed up for a hasty initial hearing — for a small town murder at that — the reporter ranks would only swell in the days to come. Homicide sells. And murder with sexual hijinks sells through the roof.

She could feel Gayla shaking.

"Hold on," she whispered. "We're almost across the street and then we're there."

Sheriff Maynard pushed brusquely ahead, and the camera people could see he meant business. He took his share of questions, too.

"What will the charges be, Sheriff?"

"Was it Miss Early who attacked Sheriff Dudgeon?"

"Can you tell us what happened to him?"

"How is Mrs. Raeder doing?"

After a lifetime, they arrived at the side entrance of the courthouse, a single door that enabled Willie and Gayla to slip inside but allowed the Sheriff to stay outside, temporarily blocking the reporters from entering. A lanky young deputy, who looked more farmer than law enforcement officer, was waiting for them. Their footsteps echoed as they hurried down the side hall of the circa-1930s domed courthouse. He hustled them into a conference room around the corner, where a worn oak table and chairs sat beneath portraits of long dead judges.

"That took forever. And did you hear what all they were asking?" Gayla asked.

"You did great." Willie gave her a reassuring pat.

The deputy tipped his hat. "Ms. Morris."

Willie couldn't quite place him. "I should know you."

"Frankie Lee. Goob's boy."

"Oh, of course. You live just down the way."

"Yes, ma'am."

"I didn't know you in your uniform."

Frankie grinned. "They don't need me to wear it that often."

He introduced himself to Gayla with the same tip of his hat.

"Frankie Lee Eskew."

Gayla nodded. "Nice to meet you."

"Thank goodness, it's quiet in here," Willie said.

As she steered Gayla to a chair, Sheriff Maynard came in and heaved a big sigh.

"You did great, Miss Early. Press is outside the courtroom for now, so relax."

Maynard gave an appreciative nod to Willie.

"You handled that like a champ."

Once again, Willie noticed that strange sense of belonging somewhere, of feeling part of a cause. Something bigger than herself seemed to be pulling her into this little group of misfits. She was amazed that she sort of liked the feeling. Odder yet, she, Willie Morris, was getting ready to walk voluntarily into a courtroom with someone she hadn't known a month ago.

And she was ready to put up the bond for bail.

She realized that she would put up her farm to help Gayla if she had to, and the realization stopped her short. Either I have become an utter fool, Willie thought, or . . . Or what?

She couldn't put it into words, but it made her smile.

CHAPTER 28

JUDGE GERALD BISHOP WAS a royal prick and nobody knew that better than Tommy. Through the years, Tommy had endured a gut load of the kind of blatant favoritism shown to those with either big money or big tits. It finally led him to do some digging on the good judge himself.

Come to find out Gerald Bishop had barely squeezed through law school at a small, non-picky university; practiced briefly without distinction in Elk City; then married the ugly but busty daughter of a crooked state congressman. Quickly appointed thereafter as the judge for Kiowa County, he had managed to remain ensconced in his lucrative position through tight relations with a circle of lawyers only too happy to grease his palm for referrals or verdicts. And, of course, he always kissed the right babies before each election.

Tommy had considered reporting him for a couple of blatant mind-blowing courtroom offenses. In one case he dismissed a repeat DUI defendant, who later ran over and nearly killed a bystander at the local Cock 'n' Rock highway bar. The defendant had been there drinking to celebrate her court victory. Precisely what the big-busted woman offered in exchange for Bishop's leniency would have to be grist for the ages, Tommy finally conceded. Especially since in return, the righteous judge would, no doubt, crucify him upside down for his weed-puffing habit.

Now standing before the judge, with Gayla beside him and Willie in the first row behind them, he wondered if he should had given the two women more warning about this poor excuse for a court.

For the first time, Tommy looked over at the prosecution's table, already smacking of smugness. Wes Garrison, a braying but fairly competent local prosecutor, had been joined by an expensively suited man who looked vaguely familiar. Tommy figured right off that the stranger had to be from Elk City, maybe even Oklahoma City.

Tommy tried to take all of them in, especially the judge, who looked like he had gotten a new haircut for the occasion. Judge Bishop, with his pasty-faced eagerness, had obviously spiffed himself up for all the wrong reasons, like a Hollywood-wanna-be pretending to be seeking love on *The Bachelorette*. Every last prick here sees a career-making bonanza of a case, Tommy thought, and Lord help anybody who stands in the way of their possible celebrity.

"Hear ye, hear ye, hear ye," the pimply-faced clerk announced.

And so it began. Gayla standing, pale and wide-eyed but probably no more shook up than most people about to be charged with murder. Willie, tightly poised behind them, as if she might pounce should anyone try to harm Gayla. Tommy, just wishing it was over already.

The good judge's nasal voice drew Tommy's eyes back to the bench. "Do you have legal representation, Miss Early?"

"That is being arranged, your Honor," Tommy said. "As I understand it, the public defender has been called to handle today's proceedings."

The Judge snapped his head up. "Right." Then to the clerk. "She should be here by now."

She? Tommy felt blindsided. Where was Amos Givens? Ancient, but kindly and dependable, Givens had handled these kind of hearings for decades. The courtroom doors swished open and someone Tommy had not expected to hear from for several more days burst forth.

"Your Honor," Sheriff Elmo Dudgeon announced in a distorted voice. "May it please the court, the public defender from Elk City will replace the late Mr. Givens."

Tommy's mind raced to understand what this all meant. What had happened to old Amos? Both he and Gayla turned to see Elmo wearing a medical get-up — not unlike Hannibal Lector's custom-made face guard — to protect his jaw. Next to him stood a bright-eyed woman in her thirties, whose suit made her glow like a silk tangerine.

Gayla tugged on his arm, and her eyes widened. What's happening?

He nodded as encouragingly as he could and turned back to the judge. "Am I to understand that Mr. Givens is no longer practicing?"

Judge Bishop took a long moment, already playing for the cameras that had yet to arrive. "Mr. Givens passed on two days ago."

"Nobody told me," Tommy said, angry and embarrassed.

"Nobody needed to," Judge Bishop said, relishing the chance to zing one of his well known detractors. "Sheriff Dudgeon, is this Mr. Givens' replacement?"

"I am, Your Honor," the tangerine cooed in a southern accent. "Ms. Leta O'Reilly."

With that introduction, she hustled over to Gayla's side.

"May I have a moment with my client?"

"You may not. I have a full docket and have no intention of my day dragging on into the night," the judge said.

Unperturbed, Ms. O'Reilly raised on her tiptoes and whispered into Gayla's ear.

The judge jumped back in. "How do you plead?"

Ms. O'Reilly nudged Gayla.

"Not guilty, Your Honor," Gayla said, barely above a whisper.

"Arguments for bail?"

Now the stranger from the prosecution's table sprang into action.

"Charlie Ringrose, Your Honor."

Charlie "Baby Boy" Ringrose, Tommy thought. Of course. He had not even recognized the little creep. His high-school flattop had given way to a stylish uptown cut. But no, it was something more. Tommy grinned as he realized what it was. Charlie had gone in for some serious cosmetic surgery on his receding chin, and it looked like they might have also smoothed his once bumpy nose.

They had gone to high school together. Tommy had gone off to 'Nam, while Charlie's prominent banker father managed to snag the last spot in the local National Guard unit for his son. He remembered vaguely hearing about a year ago that Charlie was Beckham County's new hotshot prosecutor, supposedly so good there was heavy speculation that he would run for attorney general next year. And now they have sicced him on Gayla. The dirty dogs. Tommy had to give the devil his due, though. If the D.A. over Beckham and Kiowa counties wanted to prosecute, that was his purview. It was what Tommy would have done in the same place. Bring in their ringer to take the lead and use the assistant D.A. who usually covered Kiowa County to take up the slack. Poor Gayla, this guy was going to make his bones with her case.

Ringrose's voice was low and already full of dramatic outrage.

"The defendant committed a heinous crime, Your Honor, beating an outstanding citizen of Elk City with a two-by-four until his face was unrecognizable."

Judge Bishop interrupted.

"Save the red meat for your closing, Mr. Ringrose. Your thoughts on bail?"

Ringrose effortlessly shifted gears.

"Defendant committed premeditated murder and is a flight risk. The prosecution asks that bail be denied."

Bishop nodded at Leta O'Reilly, who did not miss a beat.

"Unbelievable, Your Honor. The defendant has no family and no means of running away. Defense asks that bail be set at fifty thousand dollars."

"Sounds like a transient to me. It is the court's duty to make sure she stays put," the good judge declared. "If she wandered into town, she can wander out just as easily. Defendant is remanded."

Ringrose quickly moved to the next point.

"Your Honor, the Prosecution would like to request a change of venue. This has been —"

Judge Bishop almost jumped to nip this one in the bud. "Denied."

He's not about to let the most exciting case of his bench days go down the drain, Tommy smirked.

The judge nodded to Tommy that the prisoner was his. "Next!"

Tommy guided Gayla by the arm out of the courtroom.

"Don't worry," he whispered to her. "Just follow me."

They were joined by Willie, who rose out of her seat with a frown. Tommy gave her an apologetic shrug. They headed for the exit, only to find it blocked by Elmo Dudgeon. His facial expression was concealed by the Hannibal mask, but Tommy knew what was behind it. Either abject pain or drug-enhanced malice against him.

Tommy said, "Sorry, Elmo," as they waited for him to move out of their way. "Can we talk later?"

Dudgeon moved to the side, his voice lost in a cavern of mucus.

"My lawyer will be talking to you."

He flipped the door open with a flourish. With Deputy Eskew as an added body for protection, Tommy, Gayla, and Willie once more staggered through the gauntlet of cameras and shouted questions to the door of the county jail.

Safely inside, they fell silent. Tommy felt out of whack, his mind swimming, his foot throbbing again. Nothing a decent high would not cure in five minutes. No, I am not doing that anymore, he reminded himself, though with less conviction than usual.

Across from him, Willie sat stunned by the results of the hearing. Next to her, Gayla looked spent. Her eyes were faraway planets, taking everything in, but not reflecting anything back.

Finally, Tommy stood and reached for his cell keys.

"Sorry, Gayla. I have to —"

"They're liars," Gayla said.

Willie shook her head. "I'm so sorry. I really am."

"We had hoped we could get you out while you wait for trial," Tommy said, but he stopped at the angry look on Gayla's face.

"What did they call him?" Gayla asked. "The 'outstanding citizen of Elk City.' That's a good one, huh? All those city lawyers in their monkey suits, and my so-called attorney looking like a day-glo highway cone. All of them protecting that monster who . . . who experimented on me, who kept me locked up for two years."

Gayla was almost sobbing by the time she finished. Willie put an arm around her and slowly, gently stroked her hair with the other.

"Oh dear girl, dear girl."

Tommy watched the two of them, rocking together. He stood very still, locked in the same heartbeat. It occurred to him that he no longer wanted a joint.

The door to the office opened and Leta O'Reilly stepped in. She looked at her client and Willie with sympathy.

"Are you her mother?" she asked.

"No, just a friend," Willie said.

Then Leta spoke to Gayla. "What a horrible way to have to meet you. I'm so sorry about the outcome, but I doubt if God Almighty himself could have bonded you out of that hearing."

Tommy offered his hand to the petite attorney.

"I don't think we've met. Sheriff Maynard."

Her eyes fairly danced as they shook.

"So you're the one who nearly put our poor Sheriff Dudgeon in the hospital," she said.

Unsure of himself, playing it safe, Tommy stifled a grin, in case it was a trap, before answering.

"Yeah, it was what you might call a delicate situation."

"Didn't look too damn delicate to me. Can you believe he was still trying to speak, even with a wired jaw? It sounded like it was coming directly from his adenoids."

At Tommy's look of surprise, she added.

"No love lost between me and Sheriff Dudgeon, okay? He's sloppy and Dixie can't catch everything he screws up. He's handed me one too many cases in which I ended up looking like a jerk."

Tommy immediately decided she was okay. She had that competent female bluntness that gets shredded and sneered at, day in and day out, once an office of guys decides a woman's a threat. His guess was that the Ringrose dynasty was not about to share power with any gal, period. No wonder this five-foot-tall woman was wearing an astonishingly bright coral suit.

O'Reilly then moved to Gayla, who had been listening intently.

"Miss Early, I've been appointed your public defender. If you don't have anybody else, I would be honored to represent you. I know it may look as if I could be part of that enraged Elk City citizenry out for blood. Nothing could be farther from the truth. I'm going to be honest with you. I need a good case in the worst way, and trust me on this, no one knows this enemy better. I'll bust my hump for you if you want me."

Willie looked to Tommy, who clearly wasn't going to get into the middle of this. Finally, she said, "We were going to check out some possibilities, I think, and —"

"No, wait." Gayla interrupted. She was studying Leta intently. "Tell me. Did you actually know Albert Raeder?"

"We had met, yes," Leta replied without hesitation. "Anybody who worked around the courthouse knew who he was. Always in and out on legal business. Elk City may be larger than Luckau but it's still not that big of a place."

Gayla took a big breath.

"What did you think of him?"

Now Leta took a pause, and looked at each of them straight in the eyes, one by one.

"If this leaves this room . . ."

They all nodded assurances.

"I thought he was a glad-handing, self-promoting horse's ass."

"You're hired," Gayla said, as laughter erupted around her.

CHAPTER 29

TWO MONTHS LATER, Gayla was still living without the sky. From the time she escaped that hell hole of a basement to the day they had caged her here, not a day had gone by that she had not watched the rising and setting of the sun. She had been that hungry for it. Now she was stuck with three-inch-thick glass tile as her only source of outside light.

Across from her in the cell, her state psychologist studied her with nonjudgmental eyes. Probably in her sixties, her soft, oval face and blonde-streaked blunt cut suggested she had been a coquette in a previous life. But the dull old lady shoes spoke to the care with which she now walked. The fingers that shuffled through papers were twisted with arthritis.

Arlene Hudson had not pressed Gayla too hard in their first sessions. The counselor had seemed more interested in Gayla's past than her present. She had wanted Gayla to tell her about who she was before the disease — as Dr. Hudson called her addiction — took hold of Gayla's life. It turned out to be some almost forgotten years.

Yet if Dr. Hudson had expected an addict's typical litany of her parents' faults and all the people who had had it in for her, she was in for a surprise.

Two years alone with only herself for company had given Gayla plenty of time to reflect and see things with fresh eyes. She shared with Dr. Hudson a frank assessment of both what had damaged her as a child and what her own poor decisions had brought.

Gayla described a shy, introverted child whose parents moved her constantly from military base to military base, forcing her to make new friends with each reassignment, and then, without fail, tearing her away as soon as she had found a tether. It was as if the chain of command carried over to their family life, and she was the grunt at the bottom, expected to do what the brass ordered, no questions asked. It was either get with the program or get out. Nothing in between. Her mom and dad had never seemed to realize how tough that was on her.

Both heavy drinkers, her parents had made time for the military social whirl — and happy hour at the officer's club, but rarely had time for their daughter or her problems. Gayla could recall no fireside chats in the Early home.

But she told Dr. Hudson that years of contemplation while trapped in the basement had left her with more empathy for people's struggles, even those of her parents.

"They probably did the best they knew how," Gayla had told Dr. Hudson. "They both came from broken homes and didn't like to talk about their childhoods. So childhood had probably been no picnic for them either. But without brothers or sisters, I had to count on friends to listen to me, to give me . . . I don't know what . . ."

"Perhaps a way to ground yourself?"

"Yeah, maybe that was it. I was always having to say good-bye, and pen pals don't last long, I found out. I always had one foot where we had last been stationed, while I was trying to plant the other one in yet another new place."

Making new friends fast meant going along with the crowd, and Gayla had started experimenting with alcohol to keep in the good graces of some of the other military brats. That was when she had learned the limits of her parents' tolerance. Turned out it was way too low to keep dealing with a troubled, insecure teen-age daughter.

"I knew we were all pushing the limit, drunken parties, broken curfews," Gayla said. "I was acting out — isn't that what they call it — looking for attention in the worst possible ways. The first time I got in real trouble, a whole carload of us got picked up. We all flunked the breath test. My parents were beyond humiliated. 'You're no daughter of mine' stuff. So cold. Like I was some loser they'd never met who couldn't even make it out of boot camp.

"It made me more determined than ever to raise hell. Less than a year later they kicked me out." Gayla thought for a moment. "And I deserved it."

"Really?" Dr. Hudson's voice was neutral, curious. "How old were you?"

"Seventeen."

It did sound young to her now. And, for the first time, Gayla wondered, why her parents, tough soldiers that they were, had not fought harder for her. Why could they not brave her teen years? The parents of her friends had.

But Gayla could see now that a tough, long-term problem like a troubled child would have gotten in the way of their own drinking. Her parents were broken, too — and, if you believed the conventional wisdom about alcoholics, that meant they were still emotionally stunted themselves, little more than children stuck in their own damaged past. No wonder they could not help her with the broken pieces of her life.

Dr. Hudson had nodded, taking it all in.

"Well, I suppose some of that served you well when you were taken."

Gayla looked at her, appalled. "How do you figure?"

"You had to learn to adapt quickly, and look at all the people you'd had to deal with by then. Those hard lessons may have helped you survive your captivity and manage your captor."

Gayla had never looked at it like that before. Good coming from bad. It was the first of many more revelations to come in her sessions with Dr. Hudson, but the biggest breakthrough of all came the day Dr. Hudson asked her to picture a scrapbook with photographs of herself from when she was a baby up to the present.

The image Gayla immediately thought of was one of her at maybe age nine or ten, standing on a stretch of sidewalk in front of one of their apartments on the base. Thin and straight, hair in pigtails, she wore a plaid dress, shoes, and socks and grinned shyly at the camera; her head tilted slightly and her eyes bright with excitement. There seemed a purity to that little girl, a core happiness that Gayla could see in her face that had gotten lost somewhere after that.

It was the same image she had turned to down in the basement, when her world had threatened again and again to go dark for good. That little girl's open and welcoming face became the essence of who she was, and Gayla had clung to that self-image on the days when it would have been so easy just to give up. Somehow her life had gone wrong, but that little girl reminded her that she was still someone good at heart, someone worth saving, worth loving.

The snapshot became a visual mantra for her. When she sat, hugging herself, at night in the basement, it was that little girl she refused to give up on. That Gayla was who she knew she really was — had not life and herself gotten in the way.

Now, many sessions after those initial interviews, Gayla had started not only to trust herself more, but to trust that Dr. Hudson's probing into what happened while she was held captive was only so she could help her heal. But old habits aren't easily shed, and Gayla often found herself holding back about Raeder and her years in the basement.

One day Dr. Hudson leaned forward slightly, her blue eyes cool and serene. "What is it you're afraid will come out?"

"Something they'll use against me."

"Who?"

"The lawyers. The prosecutors. Who else?"

"I'm not here for them. I'm here for you." Dr. Hudson settled back in her chair. "What would be something that could come out at trial that would hurt you? Give me an example."

Gayla squirmed. "Oh, I don't know. Like I invited it? I enjoyed it?"

"But you didn't enjoy it. Did you?"

"What do you think?"

"I think, from what you've told me, it was horrific and degrading."

Gayla's eyes welled with tears. Dr. Hudson had never voiced it quite like that before. And never so accurately.

"It was humiliating, like . . ."

"Like what?" A long moment passed. Dr. Hudson waited.

Finally Gayla revealed the unspoken picture she had carried in her mind since the beginning.

"Like when I was a kid, and boys did things to . . . you know, torture pets. Dogs or cats. Sticking things in places they weren't supposed to."

Even gentler now. "Things that are unspeakable."

"Yeah, that's it. Unspeakable."

"What if you had to speak them in order to get better?"

"Then I wouldn't."

"Not even if it meant getting well?"

A silence. Gayla frowned. "No, not even then."

Dr. Hudson nodded in understanding. She leaned back.

"Have you ever wondered why I specialize in this kind of work, Gayla?"

"Because you make lots of money?"

Dr. Hudson's low laugh was unexpected.

"It's not bad for government work, but that's not why I work with clients like yourself, survivors of sexual abuse." Dr. Hudson leaned forward again. "I do it because I once suffered something similar to you."

Gayla sat up at attention. "You? I can't believe that."

"It's no respecter of persons."

"What happened to you?"

"I was held for two weeks by a very sick man."

"It was two years for me."

"I know. I'm not suggesting I understand all you went through. Not at all. But, like you, I was prepared to kill myself before I would willingly tell anybody what went on during that time."

"Then . . . you do know."

"Yes, Gayla, I know something of your nightmare. I also know that it's become a burden you carry with you that you feel you can't put down. I know how difficult it is to open up about it, but I also know that our secrets just make us sicker."

Gayla weighed that thought, still unwilling to jump in.

Dr. Hudson placed her hand over Gayla's.

"Tell you what. I'll start with a secret of mine. Then you can tell me one of yours."

"Maybe." Gayla was still wary.

"Okay, here goes. Even though I didn't want to, and even though I hated what was happening, I had orgasms during some of the things he did to me."

Gayla's head popped up. She was so stunned, she could only stare at Dr. Hudson.

"I learned later that they weren't like the orgasms we want to have, spontaneous, loving ones. It turns out that fear and trauma can produce the same result." Dr. Hudson waited to see if she had touched a nerve. "Have you ever heard of such a thing?"

Gayla shook her head; her face a portrait in conflict.

"I didn't think so. I was too ashamed to tell anyone about what I'd experienced for years. I thought it made me the sick one. Now I try to help my patients look at it earlier in their treatment. Because if that did happen to them, I know what a blessing it is to finally get it out."

A powerful relief surged through Gayla, moving so quickly up and through her that she could barely catch a breath. Like a bird caught inside a house that beats its wings against the window glass, desperate to reach the other side, when suddenly a window opens and with a whoosh, it flies into the open.

"Are you okay?" Dr. Hudson asked, leaning low to see Gayla's eyes.

"Fine," Gayla whispered.

"I'm guessing something like that was true for you, too?" Dr. Hudson had taken her hand and was squeezing it now. Gayla's eyes were all the answer she needed. "Now whenever you are ready, Gayla, there is no rush, try to tell me one of your secrets."

A full minute passed, then Gayla cleared her throat and began.

"After he came, which didn't ever take him long, it would take him a long time to get hard again. So, sometimes, he'd use . . . oh I can't —"

Dr. Hudson squeezed her hand.

"You're doing fine. In your own time. There's no hurry."

A painful pause.

"Are you talking about rape with instruments?"

"Yeah." Gayla's voice cracked. "Beer bottles . . . stuff like that."

"These things are so hard to talk about," Dr. Hudson said. "It took a lot of strength to tell me that. I can't begin to imagine how awful it must have been."

Gayla, chin up, defiant, not about to cry: "I didn't have any orgasms during that."

CHAPTER 30

WILLIE WRAPPED MAXINE'S little body in a crocheted lap shawl, one with bright rainbow-colored squares against a black background. It had been a hard two months for the poodle. More pain than there were pills in the world. Willie had always thought she would cremate her old dog, but now, left to carry it out on her own, she did not have the heart to build the fire or watch the flames.

Instead, under her prized weeping mulberry tree, she dug a grave a couple of feet deep. The ancient poodle was so emaciated, she was about the size of a doll. The grave was not much wider than a shoe box.

Willie had asked in her own will that she might be allowed a green burial like this — no chemicals pumped in the veins, no waxy mask covered in rouge for viewing. No, she wanted to return her body to where it came, food for whatever was hungry — worms, insects, coyotes, wild dogs. She expected the county would refuse her request, and she would be moved to Plan B, the crematorium. Never mind, she had comforted herself, my ashes can still give back to the land.

Willie spent most of the night whittling the bark for a cross from inch-thick cedar branches, then she crosstied them together with rough twine. This burying is so hard to do, she thought. She did not mean the physical effort, but rather the effort it placed on one's heart. She could remember it like yesterday with Jack, despite having been so sedated at the funeral that it took people on either side to keep her from sinking to her knees. How tiny his coffin had seemed that day.

It felt natural today to return Maxine to the earth. She had always preferred being outside. Willie's memories of the young Maxine would always be of her wreaking havoc in the henhouse or belly-flopping into the stream to chase a minnow.

This morning Maxine had come to her in a dream during her pre-dawn sleep. She was her bright puppy self again, not blind or hurting. She sat on top of a huge rock right outside the back door, her tail wagging her body, her bright black button eyes telling Willie she was fine but did not have time to stay. She needed to go play.

Willie had snapped awake just as Maxine bounded off.

But little Jack, no. Nothing natural about those memories. He belonged in her arms, not lying in the dark, cool earth, especially the day they buried him, when the wind had blown fiercely through freezing sunshine. After the final graveside gathering, after the crowd had left, she had stood by his grave — they would not start the backhoe until she moved out of the way — and she remembered thinking maybe if she never stepped away they would not be able to take him from her.

Eventually out of sheer good manners, she had walked away, but she remained nearby, leaning on a grave, watching until the last shovel of dirt was packed tight and the flowers put back atop the mound. Her distraught husband had long before given up and retreated to the limousine, where he remained sobbing, head in his hands, while she stared slack-jawed at the roses, and tulips, and baby's breath, still cruelly vibrant in their wired formations.

Nothing could hurt as bad as that, she told herself.

Tucking the shawl around Maxine, Willie placed her friend gently into the ground. Choking back a sob, unable to speak, her thoughts were all she could summon. Sweet girl, I will never forget you. Thank you for keeping me company all these years. With that, Willie stood and shoveled the dirt back into the hole, patted it smooth, and placed her makeshift cross on the small mound.

Out of the blue, the thought hit her that she finally understood what "doggone" meant.

She gave a bittersweet chuckle.

Then she headed to town for jury selection.

CHAPTER 31

WILLIE WAS SURPRISED that she knew at least the names of practically everyone in the small jury pool. Then again, in a place as small as Luckau, even an isolated old curmudgeon, like her, picked up the names of most locals after so many years.

She had cut herself off for so long, however, she realized she didn't know these people at all. Her interest was piqued by the arrival of a pencil-thin blonde in monochromatic beige and the highest heels Willie had ever seen. The woman's entrance was met with half smiling, appropriately sympathetic faces from all the prosecutors. Ahhh, the monster's wife, Willie surmised. Two women behind Willie perked up at the sight of the blonde as well.

"Who's that in the silk suit?" One woman asked, nudging another.

"That's his wife. Isn't it?

"You mean . . . ?"

"Mrs. Raeder. Yeah. Who else?"

"Trophy wife, I'm guessing."

"Comes from old Elk City oil money, I hear."

"And lots of it, I would say. Would you look at that handbag?"

A third woman chimed in, obviously better informed, at least in her opinion, than the first two. "Actually the family's old money pretty much dried up some years back. The dad is a gambler, I heard. That's why she married Raeder. Otherwise the family wouldn't have been caught dead with a son-in-law without Mayflower credentials, don't you know?"

The other women sucked in their breath in unison.

"Really," they gushed.

The tidbit was kindling to their gossip. They kept chattering, but Willie tuned them out.

Willie had hated Mrs. Raeder on sight, with her glued-on fingernails, too long to even properly pick one's nose. She looked like the owner of plenty of fur trappings that little harmless animals had been skinned to make. Her snooty head tilt made Willie pretty sure that Mrs. Albert Raeder had never in her life acknowledged anybody unless there was something in it for her. Willie did not need a psychiatrist to explain this woman's glamour profile: Neiman-Marcus-camouflage for a serious absence of soul.

She turned her attention back to what she had come to see.

It was a quick jury selection. After all, only a few in the jury pool had ever heard of Albert Raeder — he might be a big shot in Elk City but as a Luckau property owner, he had been invisible. And as far as Luckau locals were concerned, Elk City might as well be Dallas, so far did it exist off their radar. And, of course, nobody knew Gayla Rose Early.

For the defense, Leta, in a throbbing sunflower yellow suit and metallic gold platform pumps, tried to search out dogmatic moral views above anything else. Leta had explained to Willie and Gayla that someone who could believe that a girl with a belly-button ring was "asking for it" would require the Messiah's second coming to buy that Elk City's former Chamber president could keep a sex slave for two years.

Leta managed to bump off a couple of obviously rigid zealots, while the prosecutors successfully seated three older businessmen who Willie feared would turn out to be the worst kind of good ol' boys. She could only imagine their thoughts when the details came out. He was probably just doing what came natural, they would think, and she took it the wrong way. Everybody knows women say no first but they end up meaning yes.

The jury ended up as five women and seven men, a gender mix that Willie was sure Leta would rather have had the other way around. But with a story as salacious as these people were going to hear, who could even guess how any jury might rule?

Willie watched Gayla, eyes straight forward beside Leta, as Judge Bishop dismissed the court until nine o'clock the next morning, when opening remarks would begin. As Leta and Gayla turned from the table, Willie was finally able to catch Gayla's eye.

"Are you okay?" Willie mouthed.

Gayla managed a closed smile and a nod. She looked like a leaf ready to be crushed by the next breeze.

Willie found herself saying a little prayer.

God, if you're up there, please take care of our little sparrow.

CHAPTER 32

SITTING INSIDE HER CELL, waiting for Sheriff Maynard to come pick her up for the first day in court, Gayla felt like what she figured she must look like: Mismatched and out of her comfort zone. Leta had brought her several nice, understated outfits to wear — thank heaven she had spared Gayla her own parrot-island palette — but the very idea of concentrating on appearance seemed foreign. Almost obscene. Why should she have to impress anybody?

Leta had patiently explained that while it would come out that she was a victim, first impressions would count tremendously. After all, she was accused of murder.

"They'll think I'm a crazy crackhead no matter what I wear," Gayla had snapped back.

"Not after we present our side, Gayla." Leta had taken Gayla's hand in her own then. "That's my job. To show them how these stories the prosecutors have leaked are dead wrong."

She was referring of course to the outrageous articles about Gayla's drug use that had gotten some play in the national rags. "Rage-filled Crackhead Dealer Hacks Real Estate Magnate to Death," one headline had read. Clearly, plenty of the press had no problem getting it all wrong.

"Everybody's going to hate me. I saw how those jurors looked at me." Actually, Gayla knew this was an overdramatic exaggeration, but her fear had spiked, as it did every time she allowed herself to think about the trial and what might come afterwards. It seemed no sooner would she manage an optimistic thought, than she began sliding backwards, like a dress shoe on ice. All sense of proportion went right out the window.

Dr. Hudson had helped her to realize that, left to her own devices, Gayla would turn just about anything into a catastrophe.

"That's one of the things that depressed people often do," Dr. Hudson had told her.

Gayla looked confused. "What do you mean?"

"For most people," Dr. Hudson patiently explained, "having a plumbing problem or a car breaking down is just something that happens in life. They take care of it and it doesn't take a huge toll on them."

"I hate having to have my car fixed," Gayla had confided, unsure of how else to respond.

"Everybody does, Gayla. But for people who are depressed, it can devastate them, immobilize them from going on about their life."

"They act as if it's a catastrophe," Gayla had repeated, startled to recognize herself. "They take simple things and build them up into insurmountable obstacles . . . wow, I guess I do do that."

Dr. Hudson grinned. "I suspected as much. And now that you have a genuine catastrophic event in your life, it probably feels impossible not to be paralyzed by it."

"But why do I do it about everyday things?"

The very thought bothered Gayla terribly.

"Ah, 'there's the rub,' Shakespeare might say. Why do you do that, Gayla? How does it help you out?"

At the time, Gayla had sworn she had no idea, but in actuality the truth had dropped like a dead weight into her stomach. It was not just that she had seen her mother do the same thing countless times, although her mom had played the role of martyr like a woman born to the role. No, it was the convenience of living life as a constant victim. The truth, she saw now, was that while she did not know for sure why that was her go-to approach, she did understand how it worked for her. Her helplessness had made the drinking and using okay.

In fact, she could remember drunkenly making the case that it was the only sane response to an insane world.

Now she sat in her cell, thinking of years lost, opportunities wasted, wondering how many more chances might be left for her. Her stomach rumbled from hunger, but she did not trust it with food. The carnival is about to begin, she thought, and I am the freak sideshow. As her thoughts threatened to sink into darkness, she heard the sound of Sheriff Maynard clomping down the short hallway to her cell.

Just seeing him made her feel better. Showered and shaved, in all his uniformed neatness, he somehow made her feel calmer. In the two months since her arrest, they had become surprisingly close, falling into a morning routine of coffee and visiting if his schedule was clear. It had started the day she first revealed a little of her past. Out of the blue, it had tumbled out for no particular reason.

Over the weeks, as he listened without judgment, she admitted to using the occasional leisure drugs while she had still worked as an x-ray tech. Eventually she explained how she had become hooked on crack, along with her intern boyfriend who worked at the same hospital in Dallas. She told him about their break-up, her descent into a hopeless cycle of artificial highs and lows, the humiliation of finally losing everything — her possessions and whatever was left of her soul — as she became a runner for Randy. She even confessed to him that in the absence of deliveries to be made, she had often given Randy sex for a fix.

It became a two-way street. Gayla found his confession to her, of all people, about his own drug use incredibly brave, an act of trust that no one had extended her in a long time. He talked of Viet Nam occasionally, although she sensed there were things there he was not willing to get into yet. But it became less and less like a sheriff and his prisoner, and more like something akin to friendship.

Now that he was finally walking without pain, and, he told her, clean and sober himself for the first time in years, his skin and eyes were clearer than she could ever have imagined. She found herself pulled towards him, to his eyes that held back secrets, to his large calloused hands, to the little boy that still surfaced in his weathered face sometimes.

The sound of people jostling for seats snapped Gayla back to the present. The courtroom was exploding with people. As crowded as it had been for the jury selection, this morning was worse — the room already out of air by nine. Now all that remained were the smells and swelling anticipation of jammed observers.

Gayla didn't know anybody in the gallery. She was alone save for Leta, whose nervous smile fit right in with the blinding green suit and three-inch-hair and -heels she had donned for the day.

"You look nice, Gayla. How are you feeling?"

"Like a whore in church," Gayla whispered.

Leta suppressed a chuckle. "If I was God-fearing," she said, nodding towards the prosecution table, "I'd be much more concerned to see those guys in church."

The little joke relaxed Gayla. Leta had thrown herself into Gayla's case with abandon, leaving Gayla with the feeling that the case was in better hands than she had any right to expect. Now it was starting.

As a witness, Willie could not sit inside yet, but Tommy, whom the prosecution had waived to be inside, stood at the back of the court-room. The feel from the crowded table of the prosecution recalled a pack of wolves smacking their lips over easy prey. In her peripheral vision, Gayla could just see Mrs. Raeder, decked out in all black, complete with short gloves and hat. Leta noticed her looking at the widow and said, "Geez, all she needs is the Jackie-O funeral veil." It made Gayla smile.

"Order in the court," the pimply bailiff called. "All rise for the Honorable Judge Gerald Bishop."

The swish of his Honor's robes followed him to the bench, where he turned and, with a seriously posed face under his pompadour, started the proceedings. "You may be seated."

The formal particulars were read for the jurors, and Gayla started to feel a little spooked. Leta patted her hand. "Relax. It's going to be fine."

It certainly did not feel fine once D.A. Charlie Ringrose started his opening. With all the hateful things he was accusing her off, she found it better to fade in and out of his speech.

"The state will show that Gayla Rose Early had been living in the deceased's basement for some time before she was discovered. Imagine, ladies and gentlemen of the jury, the horror that this simple real-estate developer must have felt when he went down there . . . for what we'll never know, maybe a gardening tool or a storage box. Only to be met by a desperate and, yes, let's say it, deranged young woman who attacked him without warning, without provocation. Who hit him, not once, or twice, but again and again. And again."

With that, Ringrose began to bang on the railing in front of the jury like a drum as he repeated the words: "And again and again and again and again."

Gayla tried to retreat from the picture.

She felt Leta's steadying hand on her arm, but Raeder's dead face suddenly swam before her without warning. That gray eye frozen half open. The other sunk into the pulp of his crushed jaw. Freshly shined Italian loafers.

A surprisingly dark pool of blood spreading over his pale silk shirt.

And that cloying thick silence hanging in the dank cellar air.

CHAPTER 33

TOMMY MAYNARD STOOD IN the back of the courtroom, watching the locals fan themselves against the stuffy air. After all the hot wind Charlie Ringrose had blown at them in his opening, Tommy figured the onlookers needed it. Leta had decided to delay her opening remarks until she presented the defense, so the prosecution was back up again.

Tommy was mildly surprised that Garrison looked to be the one to question the first witness not Ringrose. Tommy had figured they would hit the ground running with their hotshot. Maybe they wanted the braying Garrison up front so his inevitable missteps might be forgotten by the time they sent Ringrose back in with Sheriff Elmo Dudgeon, guns blazing, like the cavalry in the third act.

By then I may have some unpleasant surprises for them, Tommy thought. He would never admit it to anyone, but it still rankled that he had been treated like an interloper in his own jurisdiction.

Once Ringrose decided to spearhead the prosecution, Elmo had latched onto him like a rat on cheese. No surprise there. But the two of them took to pairing up to pore over the evidence, excluding Tommy and Dixie and everybody else. Everyone except Joe Nguyen, of course, because nobody could understand him or his technical mumbo-jumbo anyway. Ringrose and Garrison both blamed the disconnect on Joe's pronounced Vietnamese accent, but Tommy didn't think it would have made any difference if Joe's English had come with a Luckau twang.

But if Ringrose and Garrison had kept a close lid on the prosecution's case, Tommy had his own air-tight seal on some information he hoped might slow them down. He had dutifully gone through regular channels, running his evidence items by the "dynamic duo," as Dixie started calling Dudgeon and Ringrose. There was the blood sample from the Raeder cabin's back door, where Gayla said Randy had been killed. Joe had salvaged some dried blood drops from under the old frame to be tested. Then there was chatty Mabel Thorpe, the neighbor who had heard Gayla screaming and had given a deposition to that effect.

Garrison and Ringrose were both so preoccupied with their prosecutorial pissing contest, they barely glanced at Tommy's stuff.

"A fart in a whirlwind," he'd heard Garrison say of his evidence, eliciting one of Ringrose's condescending, dry laughs.

Fine, Tommy had thought. You can blow off the old lady neighbor, and you can quibble over the mass of Gayla's fingerprints and what they mean, but if that blood evidence from the back door comes back as dead Randy's, it is a whole new ball game. The only catch was the state crime lab had apparently put the blood analysis so far back on the burner that when he called for the umpteenth time to check on its place in the queue, he gave up after half an hour on hold. Tommy was still pissed about that.

The first witness up for the prosecution was Joe Nguyen, who had traded his CSU windbreaker for a navy blue suit. As they swore him in, Gayla turned in her seat to give Tommy a sidelong glance. He nodded slightly to acknowledge her without drawing attention.

During a talk the night before Gayla had confessed it made her almost sick to her stomach to think of the rows of strangers sitting behind her in the courtroom.

"My back starts to feel hot from them staring at me," she had said. "It's like they're judging my every move."

"Don't worry about that. I will always be right there behind you, keeping an eye out."

"I'm scared to look at them."

"I know," he said, "but you don't have to. Relax. I have your back, no matter how hot it gets."

That promise had coaxed a smile out of her.

Nguyen used a dollhouse-sized mock-up of the Raeder basement to show the jury the location of the blood pools and smears. Tommy noticed Gayla seemed uncomfortable with the miniature. Damn, it even has the chalk outline of the body close to the drain. It has to be creepy to see a model of the dungeon you were tortured in, he thought.

Wes Garrison questioned Joe on the hundreds of fingerprints at the scene. Nguyen recounted the general outlay of print trails.

"So would you say these are the prints of someone who was hiding out in that basement?" Garrison asked.

"Objection. Leading the witness," Leta interjected.

"Sustained."

"I'll rephrase, your Honor." Garrison offered a grin. He knew he had gotten the thought in for the jury.

"How would you interpret so many fingerprints?"

"Miss Early had spent a lot of time in the basement. She would have been quite familiar with the south end of the room anyway."

Garrison seemed caught off guard.

"The south . . ." His voice trailed off as he bent to consult papers on the prosecution table. Ringrose took the opportunity to say something low to him. Garrison nodded and continued. "That would be the other end of the basement, situated away from the entrance?"

"Correct," Nguyen said.

"Where someone might be less apt to be discovered."

Leta audibly sighed. "Objection. Leading the witness."

"Your Honor." Garrison's hands spread in innocence. "What's the harm here?"

Leta jumped back in. "The side of the space where someone could also be kept locked out of sight, Your Honor."

Way to go, Tommy thought. Maybe this O'Reilly had some brains behind that Caribbean-hued wardrobe of hers. He took heart from Judge Gerald Bishop's annoyed response to her objection.

"Miss O'Reilly, the bench hardly needs your explanations to make its rulings."

"My apologies, Your Honor."

"The objection is sustained," Judge Bishop crowed. "Witness is not in a position to draw that kind of conclusion."

Garrison continued. "What, if anything, did you find lying near the body?"

"An approximately thirty-inch length of two-by-four, a couple of feet from the body."

Garrison entered a photo of the two-by-four into evidence. "And what, in your opinion, was the significance of that piece of wood?"

"It was covered with blood and had particles of human tissue on it. There were bloody fingerprints on one end. It appeared to be the murder weapon."

Garrison's volume rose, like a preacher bringing home the message of the day's sermon. "Were you able to determine whose fingerprints were on the grip?"

"They were a match for Gayla Early's."

Tommy saw Gayla shudder as Garrison pointed to identify her for the jury. "The defendant Gayla Rose Early?"

"That's correct."

After savoring the moment, Garrison segued back to the basement model, a white balsa wood job, tapping it with his finger, before bleating: "So you are saying this chalk outline near the center was where Albert Raeder died."

"Yes, sir."

Garrison cast a dramatic sidelong look to the jury as he continued. "And though it is not depicted here, there was quite a large pool of blood by the body, wasn't there?"

"Not really."

"Huh?"

Tommy suppressed a smile. This was the second time Garrison had stepped into it. He sure wasn't ready for that answer. Garrison unbuttoned his suit coat as if it was time to get to work. "But if a man bled out there, wouldn't there be such a pool?"

"Yes, sir, if he bled out. But Mr. Raeder didn't."

"He didn't bleed out?" Garrison looked stunned.

"No."

"Can you explain that to the jury?" Garrison said, fumbling.

You mean, can he explain it to you, don't you? Tommy thought.

"This was not like a stab wound, or even a gunshot wound, both of which can cause a lot of bleeding. This was blunt force trauma, and with such an injury the amount of bleeding can vary greatly, depending on the type of impact and how quickly the victim dies," Nguyen said.

Now Garrison, clearly off stride, whipped out the crime scene photos to introduce into evidence. Displayed on a plasma screen turned towards the jury, they were enough to distract anybody from his earlier missteps. They showed Albert Raeder's face as half-dead stare, half-hamburger meat. Tommy glanced at Gayla, who looked down. After entering them, Garrison got right to the point.

"And what was your expert opinion as to the cause of death here?"

"An acute cardiac event," Nguyen said.

"In laymen's terms, please?"

"What is commonly called a heart attack."

A stunned silence, then whispers ran through the audience, like electricity down a wire. Gayla's head popped up. She and Leta both stared at Joe Nguyen with their mouths open. Tommy was stunned, too.

Is this what those bottom-feeding prosecutors and Dudgeon were in cahoots about, he wondered. Keeping this bombshell secret? Why? Obviously O'Reilly did not know about it either. He was pissed with himself for not following up more adamantly last week after being assured the final autopsy report "still had not arrived." Hell, it had never occurred to anyone that it would say anything other than beaten to death. But why had Garrison not known? Was Ringrose sabotaging his own partner in some kind of one-upmanship maneuver?

Judge Bishop banged the gavel, offended at the audience's outburst.

"Order in the court."

Leta rose to her feet, incensed.

"This is news to the defense, Your Honor. In light of it, we move for dismissal of the charges against Miss Early."

"Objection!" Ringrose rose at the prosecution table. "Your Honor, this final report was only received yesterday, and the state does not believe it changes who was responsible for his death."

The judge's eyes were angry slits. "Counselors approach."

Tommy shook his head in disgust. His so-called colleagues had been holding out on him; like hell it just came in yesterday, he thought.

It did certainly change things — no matter what Ringrose said — to know that the technical cause of death was a heart attack.

The confab with Judge Bishop broke up, and Leta, unhappy and visibly angry, returned to the table. The judge raised his voice.

"Mr. Garrison, you may continue."

Garrison's mouth was a thin smile as he leaned in low to the witness chair, but he almost ruined his own dramatic gesture by practically shouting into Joe's ear. "Are you saying, Mr. Nguyen, that blunt force trauma was not the direct cause of death?"

"Technically, no," Nguyen said.

"Then can you explain for us what caused Albert Raeder's acute cardiac event?" Garrison watched the jury as he asked the question.

"There can be lots of reasons why a heart might fail."

"What about this instance? Could the heart attack have been caused by the stress of being assaulted?" Garrison was now openly playing to the jury.

"Objection. Leading the witness," O'Reilly said.

"I'll allow it," the judge said.

Leta frowned in disbelief.

"It's possible," Nguyen said.

"So the assault itself, this vicious beating —"

"Objection. Inflammatory." Leta sounded exasperated.

"Sustained. Watch it, Mr. Garrison."

Garrison, fawning. "Pardon me, Your Honor." Then still in the same breath, "so, Mr. Nguyen, just to conclude, it's a logical theory that the assault itself could have brought on Mr. Raeder's heart attack?"

"That's a reasonable possibility."

"Then Mr. Raeder could have laid dying or been already dead while he was still being beaten with the two-by-four?"

"That is possible."

Garrison beamed. "No further questions. Your witness."

Leta took a moment. Tommy knew what she must be thinking. Even though the defense had possibly gained an advantage with this cause of death, the picture of a man being driven to a heart attack, then beaten while he suffered it, put her client in a terrible light. She could just as easily be convicted of causing his death either way. It did explain, however, why they were not asking for the death penalty. Apparently, Ringrose either had not filled Garrison in, or Garrison was so inept he had not double-checked his own evidence.

Leta began. "Good morning, Mr. Nguyen. Now explain, if you would, how one can tell if someone has died from blunt force trauma."

At last a question he can warm up to, Tommy thought.

"The typical signs of blunt force trauma might be a lacerated aorta or other major vessel, causing massive internal bleeding," Nguyen began.

"But that was not the case with Mr. Raeder?"

"No, there was little internal bleeding."

"Go on."

"There might be a lacerated organ, or hematoma, or contusions, even a crushed or severed spinal cord. Those are the major signs."

"I see," Leta said, "and were any of these found to be present in Mr. Raeder's body?"

"There were some contusions, but none considered to be the cause of death. His larynx, commonly referred to as the Adam's apple, was crushed, but that was done postmortem."

"So Mr. Raeder was beaten, badly, but those injuries were not the cause of his death."

"That's correct."

"So tell me, is it possible that Mr. Raeder might have been dead for some time before being beaten?"

Tommy wondered where O'Reilly was headed with this. It looked like a dangerous road to go down.

Nguyen took a moment to consider. "Judging from the amount of blood, he was still alive when some of the first blows were struck."

Leta considered her next question. "Would you say the majority of the blows were delivered before or after his death?"

The entire courtroom imperceptibly leaned forward.

"I would say postmortem, after death."

The spectators leaned back, taking this in.

"Now let's talk some more about these fingerprints found all over the basement." Leta leafed through a folder from the defense table. "You lifted Gayla Rose Early's fingerprints from the walls, the cot, the sink, and the floor?"

"Correct. And from the two-by-four."

"Any by the stairs?"

"Uh," Nguyen checked his own folder now, "we lifted only two of her prints from the area around the stairs."

"You say you found her prints on the walls. Any on the chains that were attached to the wall?"

A collective hush from the spectators.

"We found only partials on the chain links."

"How thick were those chains, Mr. Nguyen?"

Garrison leapt up. "Objection. Witness is not an expert in that area."

Judge Bishop had to agree but seemed a bit perturbed with the prosecutor's high drama.

Leta jumped at the chance to play the reasonable one. "Your Honor, these chains were measured for his lab report. Surely we don't have to call a specialist in just to confirm the size of the chain link."

Tommy smiled as the attorneys were asked to approach the bench again to fight it out. He knew why they did not want this little detail flaunted for the jury. Those chains were thick enough to hold down an elephant. He remembered thinking that even a bolt cutter would have a hard time sawing through them.

Suddenly, the sight of Gayla's ducked head and small back filled Tommy with a surprising sadness. He found himself struggling with a catch in his throat. He knew the fear and the shame that were moving through her. She looked so detached, so frail, sitting alone at the table.

He must have looked much the same upon coming home from Viet Nam. He had thought he would be filled with relief and joy at his return, but instead he felt more empty than ever. Who could ever understand the humiliation he carried home with him from The Zoo? It had not followed Fidel out the door that day the Cuban guards left. It had not disappeared when his cell was finally unlocked for good. More than thirty years later, something deep inside him still felt shattered. Lost. A part of him, forever trampled to death. No matter how hard he worked on it, the part of him that could trust another person unconditionally was broken. Gone. Locked away in the outskirts of his soul.

After he took the sheriff's position in Luckau, he had had a difficult time at first locking people up. He even began to wonder why — since it was so repugnant to him and called up demons from his POW days — he had taken the job at all. It was only after a few years that he understood that he was exactly the person who should be holding the key, because he knew what it was like on the other side.

If there had to be a jailer, he finally decided, at least let him be human. He had heard of the Oklahoma sheriffs who helped themselves to their female prisoners. He had seen firsthand prisoners treated like pieces of meat, had experienced it himself. Neither would ever, ever happen on his watch. And now, more than ever, he wondered if he'd been put there by some unknown power to watch over Gayla. How else could he explain the pain he went through, locking the cell door each night on such a gentle, innocent soul? He wondered if any of his jailers in The Zoo had secretly suffered with the same knowledge. If so, he had never seen it in their eyes. But for now, for better or worse, he had the key. If he had bent the rules a little too much with Gayla, so be it. He would choose to err on that side every time.

With a start, he realized Leta and Garrison were returning to their places. Judge Bishop addressed the jury. "Both parties agree to stipulate that the chain consisted of two-inch links that were three-eighths-of-an-inch thick, as indicated in Mr. Nguyen's report."

Leta tried to pick it back up. "So, whose partial prints did you find on the chains?"

"Those prints were from Miss Early and Albert Raeder."

"So there were numerous partial prints on the chains anchored in the walls, but only a few prints around the stairs? Is that correct?"

"Only a couple of prints around the stairs that belonged to Miss Early," Nguyen said. "There were many prints around the stairs."

"And whose prints were those?"

"The rest belonged to Albert Raeder."

"So, if someone was moving freely in and out of the basement, it would stand to reason that person would have left multiple prints around the stairs, which was the only way in and out of the basement. Correct?"

"That's correct."

"Based on the fingerprint evidence, then, who would you judge was leaving and entering the basement the most?"

"Mr. Raeder, of course."

"One last question for now, Mr. Nguyen. Can you tell by somebody's fingerprints whether they were left by someone living there as opposed to someone who was being held there against her will?"

Leta was already headed back to the table when Garrison screamed his objection.

Judge Bishop pursed his lips at her retiring figure in displeasure. "Sustained. We'll have none of those theatrics in my court, little lady." He barely got out the "lady" before he caught himself. His face flushed.

Oh no, he didn't, Tommy thought, grinning.

Leta turned, innocent as Little Bo Peep, and smiled at the now red-faced judge.

"I'm so sorry, Your Honor. The question is withdrawn."

She sat, her face a studied attempt to avoid looking too pleased with herself.

Judge Bishop rapped his gavel. "We'll break for lunch. Court will reconvene in two hours."

It looked like he had ruined his appetite.

CHAPTER 34

WILLIE'S KNEES SHOOK AS she walked to the witness stand. Though her legs were still strong enough to walk several miles without tiring, at the moment she didn't know if they would get her to the front of the courtroom, especially with a roomful of eyes following every step. Charlie Ringrose, the hotshot Elk City prosecutor, would take over questioning now for the state, starting with her, their second witness. It shocked Willie that the prosecution had called her as a witness, but Leta explained they needed someone to place Gayla in the lake vicinity right after the murder. Willie was uniquely qualified to do that.

Wes Garrison, the local Luckau prosecutor, had finished with Joe Nguyen quickly after lunch, and Willie had heard her name called just in time to launch a bout of heartburn. Willie had debated at length what to wear — pants and Hush Puppies or a tailored dress. After arguing with herself for a ridiculous length of time about it, she had split the difference: The dark pantsuit she wore had been bought for a neighbor's funeral and the Mary Janes, dressy enough to pass for court, were flat and easy on the feet. Still, she was grateful when her trembling knees came to rest in the hard oak witness stand after making the long trek from the waiting room.

For the first few moments after she turned to face the courtroom, the sense of déjà vu was so stunning it justified her dread of the moment. It was one thing to walk through a crowd of probing eyes, quite another to turn around and see how many of them there were.

As hard as she tried to avoid it, she kept being yanked back in time to the hearing on little Jack's death. Then the eyes of the courtroom not only probed but accused her. She could still feel the shame. Later Willie was not sure how much of their hostility she had manufactured through the veil of her own self-loathing. The court eventually ruled her not liable for her son's death, but the grim, shaking heads of the staring spectators had stalked her conscience for years.

For all the hand-wringing, however, Ringrose's questioning was quick and straightforward, even dismissive. She had assumed he would want to know her assessment of what kind of shape Gayla was in when she had wandered nearly naked into Willie's yard. He would surely be anxious to know Gayla's first words, her demeanor in those early days. Instead, Willie found herself simply a yes-or-no cog in placing Gayla close to the murder site.

After a verbal walk-through of how Willie had looked out the window that morning and seen Gayla leaning on the gate, almost naked under a blanket — this caused a prolonged gasp from the onlookers — Ringrose quickly moved to the other subject Willie could confirm for him.

"How many miles is your house from the Raeder cabin?"

"I'm not sure. Five or six, I think."

"How long would it take you to walk it? If you had to?"

"I don't know," she said. "I've never walked it."

Ringrose paused to insert some charm into the encounter. "You look like a strong and fit woman, Ms. Morris."

He paused, assuming she would jump in, but she left him hanging.

After a beat, Leta piped up. "Is there a question here, Your Honor?"

Judge Bishop raised his eyebrows at Ringrose. "Well?"

Unflapped, Ringrose smiled. "Very well. You are fairly fit, aren't you Ms. Morris?"

"Reasonably so," Willie said, resisting the smiling contest.

"So," Ringrose continued, "given the terrain around your land, would this be a fairly easy walk?"

"There's some uphill and down," Willie said.

"Even given that, if someone set out from there at, say, four in the afternoon from the Raeder cabin, he could be having dinner with you by, say, around six?"

Willie resented his patronizing tone, and so she stepped off of the witness hamster wheel for a moment. "If I was offering dinner."

Good-natured titters filled the gallery. Leta choked back a smile.

He seemed to sense she was yanking his chain, but Ringrose continued. "Did you or did you not discover her in your yard less than seventy-two hours after the death of Albert Raeder?"

Willie leaned back. "Yes."

Ringrose dismissed her with a haughty wave. "Your witness."

Leta straightened her neon green jacket. "Ms. Morris, what was your first impression of Miss Early when you saw her in your yard that day?"

Ringrose objected. Leta jumped in; she had expected this.

"Your Honor, we are merely trying to establish the demeanor of the accused."

"Not covered in direct testimony," Ringrose protested.

Judge Bishop tapped his finger under his nose in thought. "I will allow it."

Leta turned back to Willie. "Your first impression of the accused?"

"My first thought was that it was an animal of some kind — then I saw the blanket."

"How would you describe her condition?"

"Filthy. She was covered in dirt and smelled pretty raunchy. And she looked like she was starving."

"What did she say had happened? How did she come to be there?"

"Oh, she didn't say a word for the first two days, I don't think. She was hungry enough to scarf down some food, but she seemed afraid to even clean up."

"And why was that?" Leta asked.

"She was scared to death." Willie's last answer was spoken over Ringrose's objection.

"Objection. Pure speculation, your Honor."

The judge scolded Leta with a look. "Sustained. Careful, Counsel."

Leta nodded, continuing quickly. "But you were successful in getting her to take a bath?"

"Finally, yes."

"And, Ms. Morris, did you discover anything else about her physically after she cleaned up?"

"You bet I did," Willie said, her voice escalating at the memory of

Gayla's lifeless pale skin contrasting with the purplish red masses on her arms and legs. "She was dead white, and it looked like someone had manhandled her —"

"Objection." Ringrose flew out of his seat. "The witness has no idea how the defendant —"

"Sustained."

Leta regrouped. "Could you describe the marks you saw on Miss Early's body for the jury?"

Willie concentrated, remembering all they had gone over in the practice session. "There were blotches of bruises up and down her arms, and lots of small cuts just about everywhere, but especially on her hands and feet. Patches of dried blood caked her body."

"And did you notice any marks around her ankles and feet?"

"Her feet were raw. All bloody and swollen. And there was a —"

Without even meaning to, Willie glanced at Gayla, who sat, red-faced, eyes cast down. Willie felt choked by a rush of emotion. It wasn't right to have to say these things out loud, things so personal to Gayla, things that should never have to be anybody else's business. Yet here she was reciting them to a sea of curious faces, people who could barely contain their mounting excitement.

Willie fought an urge to scream. For a moment, she slid back to her questioning about Jack. How she had had to confess the humiliating details of her drunken life, things that tore the heart out of her. The way the righteous prosecutor assumed that Willie was the mastermind of some insidious plan that awful morning, that Jack's death somehow had not been a terrible accident, had somehow not bothered her. Did he not know Willie still could not look at her face in the morning when she brushed her teeth? If she could find the energy to brush them at all. That seeing a young boy on the street could trigger a panic attack. That Jack's death mask, shocked and twisted by the noose, appeared in her mind's eye every single day back then, sometimes every few minutes.

"Ms. Morris?" Leta's leaned in towards her, and Willie realized she had gone away for a moment. The charged silence in the room unsettled her, and her heart thumped wildly. "Are you all right, ma'am?"

Willie exhaled, a long release after holding her breath. Then, as abruptly as it left, the picture of Gayla's ankle popped back into her head, and she remembered what she had been about to say.

"I apologize. I was going to say that Miss Early's left ankle had a thick black-and-blue mark, like a ring, all the way around it."

"Only on the left ankle?"

"Yes." Willie felt her head start to throb. "I'm sorry. It makes me sick to remember it."

"Objection, Your Honor." Ringrose was annoyed. He didn't like where this was headed.

"Please stick to what you saw, Ms. Morris," the judge said.

But Leta fed the momentum. "Did Miss Early tell you what had caused that bruise?"

"She didn't have to," Willie said.

Through Ringrose's cries of objection and over the sound of nervous movement in the gallery, Willie spoke out loud and clear.

"It was obvious she'd been chained up."

Metal clanked on the defense table as Leta produced a chain the size of the one found in the basement. Then quickly, over the sudden gasps of the spectators, she nearly shouted, "By something like this?"

Through the gavel rapping and the outraged cries of the lawyers, Gayla looked up and Willie made eye contact with both her and Tommy, who leaned against the back wall of the courtroom.

For the first time Willie realized, though not a one of them had ever talked about it, that a kind of silent conspiracy somehow bound the three of them together. Like orphans at a Thanksgiving meal or stray dogs huddling on a cold night, they had an unspoken pact.

They had circled their stubborn little wagons and were waiting for a lemon slice of new moon to guide them through the night.

CHAPTER 35

COURT WAS DISMISSED FOR the rest of the day, which Leta happily spent in a cell for contempt of court. Judge Bishop was pissed big time, actually humiliated that such a stunt had been pulled in his court, but Leta dismissed it as a risky but necessary move. She considered her punishment a badge of honor.

"What's a night in the clinker compared to that being branded on the jury's mind. Well worth it," Leta had said, treating herself and Gayla and Tommy to takeout Mexican food.

Gayla thought it funny that Leta was locked up right across from her client in the tiny county jail. Looking a little like a Girl Scout on a campout, Leta leaned back in her bunk, still in her shocking green suit, reading through the next day's notes long after Gayla nodded off.

The next morning, Dixie miraculously appeared with a toothbrush and change of clothes for Leta, and off they went to court. Leta entered the courtroom like a chastized but still conquering heroine.

Leta had prepared Gayla for the appearance of her old hospital supervisor, who would testify for the prosecution. It was still shocking, however, to see her boss again after nearly three years. It was like someone stepping out of a fog. Janie Whitman had changed little since Gayla had last seen her. Same charming, full-figured woman with flashing blue eyes. Another decent person I screwed over big time, Gayla thought. But Janie made it a point to glance at Gayla and smile a small acknowledgment as she took the witness chair.

Gayla did not know what to expect. Leta had reminded her that Garrison would not be paying Whitman's travel from Dallas unless she could help the prosecution, so she should be prepared for the worse. Gayla figured Whitman had witnessed her descent into Crackville, and so there was little doubt as to where Garrison would be steering her testimony.

After establishing that Ms. Whitman headed the x-ray department at Dallas Memorial and had held that position for five years, Garrison jumped right into Gayla's time under her supervision.

"When did you first meet Miss Early?"

"She applied for a job as an x-ray tech at the hospital about five years ago. Actually, Gayla was one of the first people I hired in my position."

"Was it her first job?"

"Oh no, she had worked for seven or eight years after high school, waiting tables, I believe, and other odd jobs. Then as a receptionist for a doctor's office. That was where she became interested in returning to school and training for a medical skill that would afford her a better living."

It was like poring over a dark scrapbook for Gayla to recall who she was then. She might have presented herself to Whitman as eager and innocent but that had only been part of the story. She was looking to climb out of dead-end jobs, yes, but only after her parents had finally, in despair, washed their hands of her. She had rented an apartment with a couple of other waitresses, who proved even more irresponsible than her, so after a few years the only thing she could afford was a room at the YWCA. After a second DUI arrest, she had briefly straightened up and taken out student loans to go back to school.

"And why did you consider her a potentially good employee?" the prosecutor asked.

"She had excellent grades and came with good recommendations from her training institution. And I liked her. She was eager to further herself. And she was personable and seemed to be a team player."

"But that turned out not to be the case. Isn't that correct?" Garrison said, jacking up his volume so that anyone within a block of the courthouse could have heard him.

"Objection, your Honor. Leading the —"

Leta hadn't even finished her sentence before the judge weighed in.

"Sustained. Watch it, Counsel."

"Sorry, your Honor. So Ms. Whitman, tell us how Miss Early worked out as an employee."

"Excellent at first. For the first year or so, she related well with the patients and received strong evaluations. Then gradually, there was some slacking off. Being late, occasionally snapping at her coworkers, and then even at the patients."

"To what, if anything, did you attribute this change in behavior?"

"I believed she had started using drugs," Ms. Whitman said. "There was no other way I could explain her pivot from being well-liked and outgoing to becoming withdrawn and, well, defensive."

Gayla thought, wow, she was aware of a lot more than I thought. It surprised Gayla that her boss could have seen so much, when she herself had been blind to her own slide into drug addiction. What had started as drinks after work with coworkers had escalated into something Gayla never saw coming. Within six months of starting at Dallas Memorial, Gayla had been introduced by her fellow techies to more cunning drugs, the kind you could not smell on someone's breath in the morning, the kind that kept you honking as long as you needed to be up. It was a deadly turning point in her relentless search to fill up something empty at the core of her being.

"Were there other things you observed that made you think she was using drugs?" Garrison asked, as if he were about to get to the good part.

"I would notice nervous mannerisms with her mouth, a light twitch that looked like the classic dry mouth that comes with speed use, and on several occasions I observed that her eyes were dilated."

"Did you confront Miss Early about this?"

"I gave her two warnings, which procedure requires us to do, and told her I would have to let her go if there was a third. Those are the hospital's employment guidelines, but personally I was concerned about her, as well. I liked Gayla, and I believed she would be throwing her life away if she didn't own up to what was happening to her."

I was six months past hearing that, Gayla thought. It was already pissed away by the time she tried to help.

"And did she own up to her drug use problem?" Garrison asked.

"No, she refused to listen to me and became belligerent when I tried to bring it up."

"So did you eventually fire her?"

"There had been drugs missing from the storeroom, and while I had no proof who might have stolen them, I caught her high the same day. I gave her the third warning and told her I was required to dismiss her."

As her former boss finished her testimony, testimony that obviously pained her to give, Gayla could not help but think, *I wonder where would I be now if they had thrown me in jail right then.*

The answer that flitted through her thoughts made her sit up straight.

Why, I would be dead for sure. Overdosed or worse. Nothing, certainly not jail, would have stopped me using except exactly what happened to me. A shocking thought occurred to her.

In his own sick way, Raeder saved my life.

CHAPTER 36

TOMMY HAD THOUGHT he was prepared for the parade of character witnesses by the prosecution, but it was such overkill even the jury seemed in danger of dozing. He had to give the devil his due though. Albert Raeder had apparently schmoozed with everybody in a three-state area who could possibly advance his career, and it was starting to look like every single one of them was going to come up to the witness stand and hold forth with his praises. If nothing else, the man had paid his dues as a civic do-gooder. The result was a local hero.

Friday morning's testimony brought the Rotarians, Lions, Elk City Restoration Committee chairwoman, local arts council, even a hunting club, and, of course, the local Chamber of Commerce. So it was more than a welcome relief at lunch when Gayla offered a way out.

"Annoying and tedious, huh?" she said, as they ate turkey subs.

Tommy rolled his eyes, stuck an index finger to his temple, and pulled the trigger.

"Boom."

She laughed. "Leta was willing to stipulate that he walked on water, but they thought the jury deserved the full parade."

A moment hung between them.

"Hey, we both know that's not the real him. Don't we?"

Gayla gave him a grateful nod, but he could not help noticing her ghostly tone. Pacing in her cell was keeping her too thin and being inside had erased the little color she had acquired while living at Willie's.

"I'm worried about you, Gayla."

"I'm hanging in there. You're the one that looks like crap."

It was true Tommy had not been sleeping, but he shook his head, trying to take the attention off him.

"I'm fine."

"Why don't you take off early today?" Gayla suggested. "Deputy Frankie Lee is already here for his weekend duty. It's going to just be more of the same annoying drivel all afternoon. You could get a head-start on your weekend."

"Like I have a life," Tommy said, with a laugh, but then he turned serious. "There are some loose ends regarding Randy I'd like to tie up. Reports that should have come in by now."

"Like what?" Gayla asked.

"A few requests I put in the works some time ago. I wouldn't mind driving over to Elk City. Talk to Dixie face to face — without Dudgeon breathing down our necks."

"Go on then. I'll be fine. Really."

"You sure?"

"Yes. You worry about me too much, Tommy."

The first names were only for when they were alone, but he liked it when she used his. Mundane exchanges such as this were when his feelings for Gayla surprised him the most. It was like back in junior high when the girl you had a crush on turned and grinned at you from her locker or dropped her head shyly when you got too close . . . and you could feel electric currents passing between the two of you.

Tommy took Gayla's hand. She looked up at him. Whatever he had wanted to say vanished at the question in her sea-green gaze. He settled for a squeeze of her hand.

An hour later, Tommy was lucky enough to find Dixie, smelling like talcum powder and cinnamon gum, all but alone in the Elk City Police Station. It was a lucky break. She was more than happy to drop what she was doing to accommodate him.

The ongoing unsolved puzzle of Randy ate at Tommy, but with no last name to work from, Gayla's description fit a thousand speed-freaks. Dixie was his last hope in narrowing the field. Though Dudgeon rarely acknowledged her, nobody was faster at pulling up records through the Beckham County sheriff's office's new computer system. But this time

Dudgeon had only asked her for a cursory search, then dropped it, Dixie told him.

"He said he had you doing everything you could." Tommy was almost shouting.

"Man, I hate being caught in the middle," Dixie confessed, "but he's pulled me off everything in regards to Randy. Called it a dead end."

"Is it?"

"Might be. But I had barely gotten warmed up when he pulled me off the search. I know that for sure."

Worried now about what else Sheriff Dudgeon might think was not necessary to pursue, Tommy jumped to the most important evidence he wanted to check on.

"I don't suppose that blood sample from the cabin's back door has come in? It's been at least six weeks."

Dixie bit her lip. "Oh, dear. I thought he told you."

"Told me what?"

"Sorry, Tommy. It won't be coming back. I thought you knew."

"What are you talking about?" Tommy felt his face heat to a flush.

"Dudgeon canceled that lab order."

"What the hell —"

"It wasn't the only one, I will say that. We've had budget cuts just like everyone else in the county."

"That's bull. He knew that one was mine. That's why he did it." Tommy was shaking. "Dammit, it was important."

She sighed, confirming his suspicion. "I'm sorry. The wife said she used cleaning women to keep the cabin. That was all Dudgeon had to hear to throw it out."

"Sonuvabitch," Tommy said. "Is he enjoying making me pay for that punch or what?"

"It's not just that. You can't imagine how these Elk City folks are dogging him. They're after blood."

"I should have apologized better to him."

"Over the jaw? Like he would have accepted it."

"But I could have tried harder. He knew I was just going through the motions."

"Don't beat yourself up. There's plenty of blame to go around. Look, you got me now. What do you need?"

"Well, Cyber Queen, you want to take another pass at finding this drug dealer? He has to be in somebody's records."

Within ten minutes, Dixie had a whole new search humming.

"So, staying with your theory that two junkies wouldn't travel farther than say, a few hundred miles to pull off this robbery," Dixie said over the blur of a scrolling computer screen, "I've lengthened the search back to five years and generated this list."

She scrolled down the beginning pages.

"There's got to be a hundred of them."

"Don't worry," Dixie said, "we're about to narrow it down."

She clicked around the keyboard. "I'm eliminating everyone except those with first names 'Randy,' 'Randolph,' or 'Randall.' "

"And you're leaving in Gayla's name?" Tommy asked.

Dixie gave him a look like, you are so far behind.

"Done and printed up forever ago."

"I didn't know that."

"Dudgeon hasn't exactly kept you in the loop." Dixie lowered her voice, though no one else was within hearing distance. "Believe me, if Gayla had been arrested previously as an adult, he'd have hung a banner across Main Street announcing it."

"She was suspected at the hospital of stealing drugs."

"Yeah, but she disappeared into the woodwork before they could pursue that." Dixie leaned into the computer screen with interest. "Here we go. There's more than twenty. Let's have a look."

They came up with three possibilities of guys who were white, skinny, and fit the age range. Tommy felt a rush.

"Now we're cookin'."

"Okay, first one is . . . oops, still in jail at Leavenworth, serving a seven-year sentence. Next one . . . crap, he's dead, killed in a high-speed car chase."

"Come on, come on," Tommy said, like he was willing a winner in a horse race.

"Third one owns a carpet-cleaning company. Still alive, I'm afraid." Dixie turned to him with sympathy.

"Dammit." Tommy said, rubbing his eyes.

"I know."

"I hate dead ends."

"Welcome to my world." Dixie didn't know what else to say. "Can you think of anything else I could try?"

Tommy rose to go.

"Not unless you can find other victims Raeder did this to."

"Aren't Gayla and that prostitute from Vegas enough to count? Geez, you would think after the number he did on them."

"Afraid not. How could he leave no trail? Except for the Vegas problem, there's nothing."

"I have searched a lot of databases, believe me. If he did stir up trouble somewhere else, he must have paid off a bunch of judges. You know that Vegas file was corrupted to all hell, don't you?" Dixie asked.

"What do you mean, corrupted?"

"Somebody had blacked out the original witness statements. If I hadn't been lucky enough to talk to the arresting officer, who had no idea who had tampered with it, the file would suggest Raeder had just gotten into a little drunk roughhouse."

"Okay, so say, in his travels he liked skating on the edge but was able to buy his way out of any mess he got into. But here locally, he was a Boy Scout. The Vegas incident hints that other victims could be out there, but the only one we have is Gayla. What if she was a fluke? The first and only one here? I mean, if what she says is true, he just walked into an opportunity too perfect to pass up."

Dixie nodded in agreement.

"The unluckiest crackhead in the world? Wrong place, wrong time. Could be. Wow, smack down the rabbit hole." She grimaced. "If it happened like that, God almighty may not be able to help her."

"Why can't we find any of her friends from before?"

"Oh, we have. You're not hearing about them from the prosecution, because they all said she was great before she got hooked on crack. Then she vanished — just like her boyfriend."

"Have you got anything more on him?" Tommy asked. "She doesn't talk much about him."

"I tracked him down. He's a doctor in Houston now. It's in the file here somewhere." Dixie shuffled through a sheaf of papers in a background folder. "Didn't want to get involved, and Ringrose said he didn't have anything to add. Gave him a pass. Here he is. Donnie Walkabout."

Tommy looked at the old hospital employee I.D. photo staring back at him of a dark-complected intern in green scrubs with spiked hair. While he berated himself for stupidly assuming Dudgeon would keep him abreast of things, he skimmed the boyfriend's information.

"Did he finish his internship?"

"Not at Dallas. He dropped out," Dixie said. "He went back and completed it later in Houston, where he's now a doctor on staff at a local hospital."

"Where was he right after he left the Dallas internship?"

"No record of him in school or at the hospital."

"So that would have been . . . almost three years ago?"

Dixie ran her finger down the page. "I don't see any job info during that period. Definitely an off-the-grid spell."

Tommy perked up. "If he and Gayla were still together, I doubt that she was using and he wasn't. Maybe they were scoring from the same Randy."

Dixie was still speed-reading the file.

"No mention of his drug use here."

"No, I'm sure not. That would be something Dudgeon and Ringrose wouldn't be anxious to pursue."

Dixie's eyes fairly danced as she caught Tommy's drift.

"What airline do you prefer?"

CHAPTER 37

WILLIE COULD NOT SAY when she decided to put her acreage up for sale. Certainly it was after they had arrested Gayla, but it was not like she had not been thinking of it for awhile. In the last year, it had crept up on her — what a lot of land it was for her old bones to keep up with. Things she had always done herself without thinking had become taxing. She had started to weigh the danger of injuring herself when away from the cabin. It could literally be weeks before anyone might find her if something happened in the woods or down by the creek.

And in the last couple of weeks, with Maxine gone, it hurt to go home. The little cabin seemed empty without her shrill bark, the click of tiny dog nails on the linoleum. She missed dividing the scrambled eggs between them each morning.

Gayla had cried when Willie told her about Maxine.

"We have to get a new dog for you, Willie," Gayla had said.

She'd gone on and on about it, but Willie knew her own heart wasn't in it. Not yet.

What had pushed her into finally listing the farm, oddly enough, were the curiosity-seekers, the carloads of kids and adults, who had started driving by after the arrest. Some of them had brazenly driven up the long dirt driveway to the cabin itself to see the strange woman who had let the killer stay with her.

Since the trial started, a number of reporters had also found their way to her door. Her first instinct was to give them a scare with her rifle, but she could just imagine the grainy photograph of her that would follow in the National Enquirer, not to mention how the headline would read: "Rural Hermit Shoots at Curious Crowds."

Her anonymity, the thing she had cultivated and which gave her some modicum of peace, was gone. Through a fluke, she was once again a dot on the radar of human activity. Perhaps this feeling she had of being too exposed would pass; almost surely it would. But it also felt like something whose time had come. It was time to think about moving on, but to where, she had no idea.

So when the local realtor, a man named Gib Farris, one of the few souls of discretion in the area, tapped her on the shoulder as she left the courtroom for lunch that Friday, she knew an offer had been made.

CHAPTER 38

GAYLA SAT QUIETLY, WHILE Mrs. Albert Raeder held the court spellbound with testimony about the passionate and loving relationship she had enjoyed with her now-murdered husband. Sleek and long-legged, in monochromatic off-white, only her witch-length false nails, painted a soft rose, belied her near virginal look.

So this is the one he called his "rich bitch," Gayla thought. How many beatings did she take for this fashion plate? How many tongue lashings did she endure while Albert Raeder worked out his wrath over some condescending comment his "high-dollar whore" had tossed over her shoulder at him as she left for Houston with the girls?

Mrs. Raeder took to her role of grieving widow easily, Gayla decided. Her effortless descriptions of their devotion to one another played with the proper pace of a demure tennis match.

"So your life with Mr. Raeder was satisfying to you in every way?"

A nice clean serve from Ringrose.

Mrs. Raeder returned it easily. "Albert was my life. Everyone said we were too different, but we were a classic case of opposites attracting."

If I have to listen to this all day I am going to scream, Gayla thought, as the widow droned on, each fabrication more outrageous than the last.

"We used to love to spend weekends at the cabin." She tipped her head in wistful sadness. "Cooking out, getting away from it all."

Ringrose lobbed another soft serve. "And, in the more than two years you had the cabin, did you ever have a break-in or robbery?"

"Never, Albert had insisted on the extra tall security fence."

"Were you ever aware of anyone staying in the basement of the garage?"

"Of course not." She acted offended that the question even had to be asked. "We had guest rooms in the house, and I certainly would have known it if someone had stayed there, with or without Albert's permission."

Ringrose smiled, pleased with her performance. "Thank you. Your witness, Counselor."

Leta stood, ready for battle in Pepto-pink but almost offhand in her first question for the witness. The spectators could have been forgiven for mistaking it for a soft lob.

"Mrs. Raeder, could you please describe the layout of the cabin's basement for the jury?"

The witness was obviously surprised by the question. She took a moment to gather her thoughts before answering.

"It's a big rectangular room under the garage."

"What were the walls and windows like?"

"It was a concrete floor, tiny windows . . ."

"How many windows?"

"Two, I believe. Or was it just one?"

"What did it smell like?"

"The windows?"

"No, the room. What did it smell like?"

Mrs. Raeder looked to Ringrose for help, and Leta picked up on it.

"You don't need to look at Mr. Ringrose to tell me what your own basement smells like, do you?" A quick beat. "I withdraw that question. What kind of charcoaler did you have at the cabin?"

Ringrose jumped into the fray. "Objection. She's trying to confuse the witness."

Judge Bishop frowned over Leta's semantic leapfrog but apparently could not fault it technically. "Overruled."

Mrs. Raeder seemed slightly ruffled.

"The what?"

"You said the two of you cooked steaks at the cabin. What kind of charcoal grill do you have there?" Leta asked.

Gayla loved the next moment. She had never thought it possible that Mrs. Raeder might be anything but calm, cool, and poised, but this simple question, seemingly out of the blue, had stumped her. There was a universal moment of clarity in the courtroom when it became obvious the witness was not only out of her element but had no idea if Leta knew the answer.

Leta waited another moment, then looked at the judge.

"Answer the question, Mrs. Raeder."

She spoke in a lower tone. "I believe it was a gas grill. Berto took care of all that."

Berto? Berto??? Gayla thought she might puke.

"And where would that grill have been located?"

"In the back."

"The backyard, yes. Where, exactly?"

"Just off the back deck, if I recall correctly."

"I see. And that was where you and your husband cooked out, steaks and so forth."

Mrs. Raeder looked annoyed, as if she had stepped in something stinky. "That's what I said. Isn't it?"

Leta grabbed some photographs sealed in clear plastic from the defense table. She turned to the judge.

"This is Defense Exhibit A, if it pleases Your Honor."

The judge nodded permission.

"May I approach the witness?" Leta inquired. Judge Bishop nodded again, and Leta handed a photograph to Mrs. Raeder.

"Now, Mrs. Raeder, these are photographs of the crime scene, and that one on top is of the backyard. Is that the backyard in which you spent time with your husband?"

Mrs. Raeder nodded.

"Could you please state 'yes' or 'no' for the record?"

Mrs. Raeder glared at Leta. "Yes."

Leta, unfazed, then pointed at the photo in her hand.

"And what is that in the foreground here?"

"It's a grill."

"The one you and Mr. Raeder cooked out on?"

"That's what I said."

"Yes, yes you did. And what is that hanging off the side of the grill?"

"What?"

"What is the white item hanging off the side of the grill?"

When Mrs. Raeder finally realized what Leta was referring to, her eyes turned steely. She looked sullenly up at Leta.

A long moment passed.

"Could you please tell the court what it is?" Leta asked.

Mrs. Raeder's face contorted. "I can't tell."

Leta grabbed a poster-sized picture from the defense table and plopped it on the easel facing the jury. She stood beside it, pointing to a white square.

"May the record please show that there is a sales tag and a warranty card hanging in plastic from the side of the grill." She gave the jury a second for her words to sink in before capping the moment. "Please tell me, how does one charcoal meat with the price tag still on the grill?"

Gayla closed her eyes, savoring the fullness of a moment of truth. Leta's obsession with minutiae, which had driven everyone nuts during preparation, had just resulted in a home run. Leta could never have convinced a jury that this lying widow spent no time with her husband — at least not with the defense's budget constraints. But every good German in Luckau knew you could not cook steaks on a grill that had never been fired up.

Gayla stole a look at Willie, now excused and sitting in the gallery, then over at Ringrose, who was now head to head with Garrison, scrambling for their next move.

Leta stood unperturbed.

"Nothing further, Your Honor."

When she sat back down at the table, Gayla could see Leta's little hands trembling. She had been more nervous than her cool exterior let on to the courtroom.

"You are good," Gayla whispered.

Leta placed her own shaking hand lightly over Gayla's and grinned. "That'll teach them not to underestimate me."

CHAPTER 39

THE FIRST FLIGHT OUT OF Elk City's tiny airport got Tommy into Houston late Saturday. The smell of the tarmac in the thick humidity made him think of the war. Heat rose in vaporous waves as planes taxied in and out and handlers in bright safety vests guided the massive passenger planes through the maze of landing gates.

He could not remember a time he had not wanted to fly. His favorite ride at the county fair was always the tinny-looking plane for kids. You sat in the pilot's seat, and as the thick center pole holding six or eight planes started rotating, you soared high into the sky all by your lonesome, commanding your plane as it flew tethered to a chain that lifted higher and higher off the ground. Even into adulthood he had recurring dreams of flying those same tin planes over his childhood haunts. Sweet and exhilarating, so much so that in his dreams he could feel the jump in his stomach when the plane changed altitudes.

As a consequence, joining the United States Air Force had seemed as natural as breathing, though he dutifully finished two years in community college first. He had not been drafted to go to Vietnam. He volunteered. He saw it as a chance to see some real action. He had loved flying missions in his L19 Cessna Bird Dog, a light recon plane used in the war to identify military targets and send coordinates back for air strikes.

After six months, a lucky anti-aircraft gun manned from a small village had shot him out of the sky. His flying career abruptly ended. He had not piloted a plane since, despite the V.A. counselors who had urged him to give it another go when he felt ready. For Tommy, that time never came. He figured it was like a bad acid trip. Once you have one, Mr. Sunshine will never tempt you again.

But now the pungent oily smell made him long for it again. He wondered if climbing back into a cockpit would be like riding a bike. You can always get back on if you want to, he thought, as he climbed into a compact rental. Maybe it was finally time, after the trial was over.

It was a Saturday night, so the only thing he expected to accomplish was a quick run to Houston General where Dr. Donald Walkabout worked. He kept telling himself not to get his hopes up. This would probably be a closed door, like the rest of this case. He had to be prepared to go back home with nothing.

Still, a feeling was building that this could be something. He had read Walkabout's carefully worded statement to the prosecutors and decided it sounded like a doctor who had pulled himself up out of a horrific habit and didn't want anyone to know. Little wonder.

Houston General was lit up like a necklace of lights against a fading sky. Tommy parked the rental and headed inside.

A smiling white-haired woman in a sunflower dress greeted him at the reception desk. Her name tag read "Binkie Tillman."

"Good evening, sir. What can I help you with?"

Tommy flashed his badge. "Mrs. Tillman, is it?"

She grinned. "Please, call me Binkie."

He obliged, then explained that he was attempting to reach a certain doctor and needed to know if he was on duty. Talking with a policeman was apparently something new for Binkie. Her lips twitched nervously at the request.

"Well, we could take a look at the schedule. What was his name?"

"Donald Walkabout," Tommy said.

"Oh, Donnie. Sure. You're in luck. He's on tonight."

Tommy tamped down his growing excitement with a quick follow-up question.

"That's what department now?"

"He works emergency. I suppose I could page him for you."

"No, I wouldn't want to interrupt him in the middle of something. I'll mosey down that way and wait for him."

A few minutes later, using Binkie's directions, Tommy drifted into the E.R. waiting room. He took a seat in the corner of the green-and-white-tiled room and watched a bloody Saturday night in Houston descend on the emergency room. The distinctive smell of blood mixed with perspiration was intensified by the city's infamous humidity — even in the air-conditioned room, sweat poured off the waiting patients.

When, after an hour, there was still no sign of Dr. Donnie Walkabout, Tommy decided to see how much cruising the halls might produce and went in search of a men's room. Halfway down a hall crowded with stored gurneys, he saw his man, wearing blue scrubs and a badge that read "Donald Walkabout, M.D."

Walkabout was coming out of an examination room. He looked less wild than in the photo on his three-year-old driver's license. The spiked hair had given way to a slick John Edwards cut. All of which made his Native American features less prominent.

Tommy raised a finger in the air to draw his attention.

"Excuse me? Doctor?"

Donnie looked puzzled and pointed to himself. "Me?"

"Yes, Dr. Walkabout? I'm Sheriff Tommy Maynard." By now Tommy had his badge out and open. "I need to talk with you."

Walkabout hesitated only for a moment.

"I'm waiting on some x-rays. Guess I have a few minutes."

"Buy you a cup of coffee?" Tommy wasn't doing this in the hall.

A few minutes later they were in a surprisingly cheerful cafeteria, where the coffee was fresh and strong. After formal introductions, Donnie started off.

"I only have a few minutes. Is this about a patient?"

"It's about Gayla Early."

Donnie's eyes flashed, then darted around the room. It took him several moments to reply. When he did, his voice sounded flat, resigned.

"The prosecutors already talked to me on the phone. They said she'd killed someone." A pause. "When they first called, I assumed it was because she was dead."

"Why would you think that?"

"The drugs. The last time I saw her, she was heavy into them. A disaster waiting to happen."

"When was the last time you saw her?"

"Nearly three years ago. I tried to get her to enter rehab with me.

I even looked her up after I got out and tried to talk to her again about cleaning up her act. She was too far gone."

"How long ago was that?"

"A little more than two years ago, I think. Look, it's like I told that guy from — where was it? Elk City or somewhere. I have a whole new life now. A wife, a kid on the way. I do not want to get dragged into anything."

"I can understand that."

"They took a chance on me here, but their goodwill might disappear if my past got splattered all over the papers."

Tommy liked the feel from this guy. Donnie was trying to protect himself, sure, but he seemed genuine enough. At least he was not copping an attitude. Tommy decided to take a chance.

"Okay, look, here's the deal. Unlike the prosecutors you spoke with, I happen to think Miss Early's case is not so cut-and-dried."

Donnie sat back, surprised. "They said she was a drifter and a crackhead, and she ended up killing some bigwig in the community."

"She tells it different."

Donnie took a deep breath. "Was she still using when she said that?"

Tommy did not answer. And he tried to look neutral.

"Because druggies will say anything, do anything, for a fix," Donnie said.

"You're right, but she was past that point, I think. Her medical exam the day after she was arrested didn't show any drugs in her bloodstream."

"Wow. Well, good for her."

"What I need from you is corroboration about a dealer that I'm betting both of you used."

"Oh, no . . . "

"You don't have to get dragged into it . . . the trial or even the investigation. But right now, there's no one but her to say he ever existed."

Donnie listened, but he looked skeptical.

"She says he was killed in the middle of a B&E," Tommy said.

"A what?"

"Breaking and entering."

"Man, I can't believe she sank that low."

"Apparently, she was doing it to work off a drug debt. They were interrupted by the owner, and she claims the owner shot the guy."

Walkabout shook his head. "Oh, poor Gayla, always in the wrong place at the wrong time. What did this guy look like?"

"Wiry, white guy. Tattoos. Forties. Not a big guy. But he never was reported missing, much less killed."

"I believe that. Druggies don't even want their families to know where they are."

"Exactly. So I'm trying to chase this guy down. Can you think of anybody in your former circle who might fit that description?"

"Man, that was a long ago. Skinny? Tats? You're describing half the druggies I knew."

"She said his name was Randy."

Donnie squinted his eyes. Tommy could not tell if he was trying to remember or trying to cover himself.

"Randy. Randy. Sorry, maybe he was after I left."

"Where in Dallas did the two of you score?"

"Downtown, mainly. Close to the hospital. Industrial area. Lots of shelters around and boarded-up buildings. Easy access but dealers could move on a dime when the cops got nasty."

"I can't come up with anybody right now." Donnie's phone beeped and he grabbed it, punched in some numbers, and listened for a moment before responding. "Okay, I'm on my way."

He hung up. "Sorry."

Tommy stood up with him. "Anything you can remember. We can't get a bead on this guy. It's like he never existed."

"Man, I'm sorry. I have to go back on duty."

Tommy fumbled for a card. "Would you mind giving me a number?" He handed his to Walkabout. "Here. If you remember anything, please call me. Please — this could turn the case."

Donnie hesitated but took out his wallet and handed Tommy a business card. "Here. I'll call if I think of anybody. I am sorry to hear about Gayla. You know, at one time, I thought she was the most incredible person. I mean, she could light up a room. Sorry, got to run." And then he was gone.

Tommy sat there, piddling with his coffee cup, thinking how the only thing Gayla was lighting up these days was a ten-foot jail cell. And why in the name of heaven had he not thought to get a sketch of Randy for Donnie to look at? He had been so dead set on lowering the boom on

Dudgeon's incompetence, he had screwed the pooch himself at the most basic level. Had not even called in a police artist.

At least I confirmed where she was three years ago, he thought. Gayla had described the same neighborhood that Walkabout had, but given that she had been constantly stoned at the time, Tommy had not been sure how reliable her information was. Now he knew her memory was good.

The rough side of downtown Dallas was a lot of territory to cover. What were his odds of locating somebody who was there that long ago and sober enough to remember anything? But first things first.

It was time to get some help.

Back at the airport, he made a quick call to Dixie to have her bring in the sketch artist to work with Gayla on Sunday. Then he arranged to stay another night at his hotel by the airport and reticketed his return flight to include a Monday morning stop in Dallas.

He wanted to be sure when he walked into that Dallas police station on Monday that he not only knew who he was looking for but he could also show the police what the guy looked like.

He only hoped it would be enough.

CHAPTER 40

WILLIE WOULD NEVER BE ABLE to put her finger on the exact moment she first thought Gayla would be found guilty. She only knew that when it hit her, it seemed so straight-on inevitable that she could not talk herself out of it. Now that she could watch the trial from the vantage of a courtroom seat, the chilly attitude and bored complacency of the male jurors scared her. She tried to remind herself that this was still the prosecution's part of the case — of course, the stuff being fed to them put Gayla in the harshest possible light.

But Willie realized that during her own testimony, her words had not connected with the jurors in their banistered cage. When Willie had sneaked in her belief that Gayla had been routinely chained up in the Raeder basement, their expressions had not changed one iota. There were no sounds of sympathy or clucks of compassion — the women had only raised their carefully plucked eyebrows in distasteful disbelief.

Now the prosecution's final witness, Sheriff Elmo Dudgeon, was in the witness box, testifying without the face mask that had made him look as if he was headed behind the plate to catch pitches. The only thing he had been catching today was sympathy from the courtroom, Willie grumbled to herself.

Ringrose was doing the honors, treating the Elk City sheriff with a mawkish deference that cast Elmo as the injured victim. Rumors had followed the injury, and the prosecution choosing not to call to the stand the arresting officer, Sheriff Maynard, had fed the flames of speculation.

Yep, Tommy had good reason to avoid the courtroom today, Willie thought, but if they were going to damn him for the incident in the basement, she thought his physical presence might have offered a counter to what would surely be some sleazy testimony from Dudgeon.

In an adenoid-riddled voice that made Willie shudder, Dudgeon recited Maynard's involvement in the case — summarizing police reports and casting himself as the lead sheriff in the investigation. Maynard had not needed to warn Willie or Gayla about the direction Dudgeon's testimony was likely to go. They all realized the prosecution was bound to try and exploit the incident with Gayla and Tommy in the basement, and that Dudgeon would only be too happy to help.

"In the course of your investigation, did there come a point when you returned to the scene of the crime, Sheriff Dudgeon?"

"Yes," Dudgeon said, "I suggested our crime-scene expert return there to examine several things again."

Yeah, right, Willie thought. You were sneaking around trying to see what Tommy was up to.

"I arrived just after he left with his samples." At this point Dudgeon lifted a finger in an excuse-me gesture, took a cloth handkerchief from his pocket, and blew his nose with a painful snort.

"And what, if anything, did you find upon your arrival at the cabin?"

"Nothing in the house, so I went around to the garage, where I heard voices coming from the basement below."

Ringrose paused, drawing out the dramatic tension, coaxing those present to the edge of their seats.

"Whose voices were they?"

"I identified one of the voices as belonging to Sheriff Maynard of Luckau and a second female voice that I didn't recognize."

"And did you discover to whom that second voice belonged?"

"After I went down into the basement, yes, sir."

"Tell us about what you saw there."

"Well, I drew my gun and quietly went down the steps."

"Did you feel it was necessary to draw your gun?"

"That's SOP in a situation like that," said Dudgeon, who then made a quick aside to the jury. "Standard Operating Procedure. And I didn't know if Sheriff Maynard might be in some kind of danger down there."

Willie was astonished. The jury was lapping this up like cream.

"And was Sheriff Maynard in danger?" Ringrose asked.

"I would say, No."

"Describe what you observed in the basement."

Willie saw Gayla duck her head and close her eyes, readying herself for the embarrassing onslaught she knew was coming. Dudgeon shifted in his chair and leaned closer to the mic.

"Sheriff Maynard was standing in the middle of the room and the defendant over there was on her knees in front of him."

"You mean kneeling in front of him?"

"Correct."

"Could you see what they were doing?"

"Well, her hand was on his zipper, and she didn't have nothing on but her panties." He sat back in the box. "You be the judge."

The collective gasp in the courtroom was followed by an expectant hush, then the buzz of locusts descending. Gayla was white as a sheet.

The judge's gavel could barely be heard over Leta's protests and the crowd's murmurs. Thankfully Dudgeon was the prosecution's last witness.

Willie had been sickened in general by the Raeder woman, but Dudgeon's mucus-infested testimony had left a vile taste in her mouth. Leta powered through the setback with a skillful cross of Dudgeon, but it was obvious to Willie that she was hurrying through her time with the Elk City sheriff, as if she knew the damage had already been done. That left little for her to do but get Dudgeon off the stand — fast — with the hope that time and the defense's witnesses could eventually squeeze the bile out of his words. Preening with pleasure at his own performance and the state of his case, Charlie Ringrose practically purred his final words: "Your Honor, the Prosecution rests."

As Leta O'Reilly, in a resplendent white-on-white suit and four-inch patent heels, stepped up to give her opening statement, Willie tried to set aside her foreboding thoughts. Willie knew it had been a tactic to delay the defense's opening until after the prosecution made its case. She just prayed it was still possible for O'Reilly to close the gap.

"Your Honor, ladies and gentlemen of the jury, you have been led through a maze of information with regards to the death of Mr. Albert Raeder. The prosecution has painted a portrait of the deceased as a civic leader and successful businessman. And, as we heard only yesterday from his wife, a loving and wonderful husband. The defense will not dispute these things.

"Mazes, however, can be confusingly elaborate and complicated, and they can lead us down many surprising paths, often to stunningly different destinations, depending on what turns we take. The defense will show that there was also a darker side to Mr. Albert Raeder, a man capable of imprisoning a young defenseless woman for almost two years. You will hear from his victim, Miss Early, as to the cruel, sadistic nature of this man, and her testimony will be confirmed by medical and psychiatric experts."

As Leta continued her opening, Willie let her eyes wander over to the jury. Were they buying this tiny woman? Or was she too diminutive for anyone to take that seriously? Willie was stunned to see one of the men yawn. The women appeared to be listening more intently, but Willie sensed no compassion in their demeanor. Okay, so jurors were supposed to be impartial and withhold judgment until they had all the facs, and she knew from her own ex-husband lawyer that most did exactly what they had been admonished by the judge to do, keep an open mind.

But Willie was not so sure minds were open here. Unless you believed in the innate goodness of Albert Raeder. The jury's rapt attention during that part of the trial had confirmed they were definitely open to that.

One more reason to get the hell out of this place, Willie thought. The first offer on her land was decent enough that she had almost taken it as is, but Farris suggested they counteroffer, play a little hard to get. Willie had been happy to leave it in his hands.

Leta, too, seemed to sense the jury's lack of curiosity, because she brought her opening to a quicker-than-expected close.

"The prosecution would have you believe that how this crime happened is set in stone. But the defense will show a completely different interpretation of these facts.

"Michelangelo once said, 'I saw the angel in the marble, and carved until I set him free.' By the time you see all sides of this case, when we have chipped away at the enormous wall covering up the truth, you will not only see what Michelangelo meant but also believe that your only reasonable action is to set Miss Gayla Rose Early free."

As Leta returned to her seat, Willie prayed that the Michelangelo reference had not been too abstract for this small-town jury. She worried some jurors might label Leta uppity for using hoity-toity quotes.

As for herself, well, Willie thought Leta's opening had been grand, and she tried to remember that when allowed to go down her natural path, Willie usually assumed the worst about people. No matter the years she had spent trying to unlearn it, that tendency still popped up regularly with knee-jerking regularity.

Maybe the jury had eaten up O'Reilly's brilliant analogy. Who was she to say? Still, she could not help but notice that all the men's eyes were slit, like snapping turtles all in a row.

CHAPTER 41

GAYLA WAS RELIEVED THAT Arlene Hudson, the state psychiatrist, would be up first for the defense. Gayla's stomach had been on a steady burn since Dudgeon had dropped his bomb about the basement encounter between her and the sheriff, but Dr. Hudson could always calm her demons with that soft, steady voice of hers.

Leta led Dr. Hudson through a perfunctory review of her credentials, then moved quickly into the psychological effects associated with Gayla's experience. "Dr. Hudson, could you please explain how you recognized the extent of Gayla's emotional damage?"

By now, the courtroom had grown hushed, expectant.

"When I first interviewed Miss Early, she said she believed that she was the cause of what had happened to her. That she somehow deserved to be taken prisoner and degraded. This is, unfortunately, how hostages often respond to such a situation."

"How long does it take for the victim to start thinking this way?"

"Such a mindset can begin to surface almost immediately after the capture. That was what happened with the bank robbery hostages in Stockholm, from which this syndrome got its name. But when the subject is imprisoned for months or, in Miss Early's case, years, the transfer of guilt becomes deep rooted and pervasive."

"Could you explain why?" Leta asked.

"It's a basic survival instinct. In an odd way, by shifting the blame to themselves, victims gain a small bit of control over their situation.

There's a sense that if they helped get themselves in this mess, maybe they can find ways to help themselves get out of it as well."

What is she saying, Gayla wondered. I can't understand her and I am the one she's talking about.

O'Reilly may have sensed the same thing or she had anticipated losing some of her listeners at this point, because she gave her head a little shake as though puzzled.

"Can you explain how the victim could take control, Dr. Hudson?"

"In small ways. The prisoner will automatically begin to concentrate on anything she might be able to control, even if it doesn't make logical sense. By blaming herself instead of the perpetrator for what has happened, the victim can then try to 'atone' for the supposed wrongdoings. The victim might find ways to serve or please her captor, anything that will make the victim's life a little easier. Without that, the victim can only see the torture as senseless, or cruelty for its own sake, which feeds her feeling of hopelessness — that there is absolutely nothing the victim can do about the situation. If that's the case, the victim truly is powerless."

Gayla watched the jurors' wrinkled brows as they first concentrated on Dr. Hudson, then slowly, one by one, drifted away from the difficult material. She remembered one of the jurors from the O.J. Simpson trial saying afterwards, without a hint of irony, "Boy, that DNA stuff was way out there." Gayla hoped this jury was not thinking . . . Boy, that shrink was way out there, huh?

Quickly, Leta guided her witness towards the crucial point the jurors had to get: how the victim grows to identify with the captor.

Dr. Hudson was explaining that a prisoner will try to please the interrogator or torturer, by pro-actively offering what she believes he desires.

"Miss Early offered herself sexually as a way to establish a non-combative relationship. In doing so, she could maintain some control over him — allowing him what he wanted, and still getting what she needed, which was to survive her predicament while minimizing his anger and rage and the chance of being tortured."

"Isn't that an extreme reaction to such a situation?"

"I would say not. It's not that different from many situations in which we all find ourselves under someone's thumb, so to speak. Someone is in a position of authority; most of us will do a lot to make our relationship with that person go smoothly."

"Such as . . .?"

"Doing special favors, making sure our good works are noted, flattering the person, even pandering to the authority we're trying to impress."

"And how does that compare to what the defendant had to do?"

"The stakes were much higher. In normal life, we may adapt to keep a job, a spouse, or a relationship in the family. In the case of Miss Early, it was, in her mind, not only a matter of minimizing physical injury to herself but literally a matter of life and death."

"But the incident in the basement with Sheriff Maynard was not about life or death, was it? How do you explain Miss Early's actions in that instance?"

"I believe she was confused about her reality at that point. She was still emotionally unstable from her time in the basement and coming back into that dungeon, the place of her confinement, she automatically began to repeat — think of it as being on auto-pilot — what she had always done to maintain some small control there. First, by mopping the floor of the dried blood, which probably pulled her back into that captive mindset again, and then again with the sheriff's arrival — Sheriff Maynard's, I mean. She greeted him no doubt as she had greeted her captor many times before. I doubt she was sure who she was even talking to until Sheriff Dudgeon arrived on the scene."

Gayla could see the prosecution's unhappiness with the testimony, but they were not objecting. Still, they trotted out their big gun for the cross. Ringrose rose from behind the table, straightening his steel-blue tie, and approached as close to the witness stand as protocol allowed, his manner that of a patronizing, doubting scholar.

"I have this problem, Miss Hudson. I am not sure how you can tell the difference between a client who has gone through a horrible situation, such as you describe, and one who is inventing one to save herself."

If his condescending air bothered Dr. Hudson, she did not show it.

"It is very difficult to fake having gone through such an experience. Miss Early exhibits all the classic symptoms: she does not sleep well and appears quite traumatized at being stuck in a cell smaller than the basement she spent two years in."

"So she says. Correct?"

"So I have also observed. She has hand tremors, a nervous stomach, and difficulty concentrating. She is under medication for panic attacks, and her emotional state is volatile."

"Isn't that something you could say about most guilty inmates?"

"Surprisingly, the guilty usually sleep fine once they are caught. The chase for them is over. The innocent become more distraught as their incarceration goes along. They have been known to scream for days until they have no voice left. Others have injured themselves by banging their heads repeatedly against their cell wall in frustration."

Ringrose's facial expression said he did not like where this testimony was going. His discomfort made Gayla smile.

"All right, Doctor, we get the picture."

He glanced down at his open files. "Now, changing direction here a bit, did you also counsel the defendant on how to deal with the enjoyment she got from this alleged forced sex?"

O'Reilly rocketed a loud objection.

Judge Bishop's eyes reprimanded Ringrose as he motioned both lawyers to his bench for a heated exchange. Gayla smelled a rat, but when she looked towards Dr. Hudson for comfort, the doctor was staring down into her lap.

The sidebar concluded with no one happy, but O'Reilly patted Gayla's hand reassuringly as she sat back down.

"What's going on?" Gayla whispered.

"Just hang on" was all O'Reilly said.

Ringrose pulled his suit-coat lapels and drew himself up. "Rephrasing, Your Honor. Miss Hudson, did the defendant talk about her response to the many sexual encounters she had with Mr. Raeder?"

Dr. Hudson eyed him suspiciously.

"To the extent she was able, yes."

"How did she describe it?"

"She was frightened and repulsed. The act was often violent and degrading."

"Did she ever indicate that she likes rough sex?"

Dr. Hudson's answer was clipped. "She indicated no such thing."

Ringrose opened Dr. Hudson's report and studied it with a frown. He looked up at the doctor and then looked pointedly at Gayla.

Judge Bishop cleared his throat loudly. "Question, Mr. Ringrose?"

"I'm sorry, Your Honor. I will address that later, I believe."

Ringrose's head tilted forward, like a cobra slipping out of a basket. He closed the folder and patted it. "Now, moving on, who paid for all this psychiatric care you were providing for the defendant?"

Gayla found the pointed segue suspicious, but she couldn't see exactly where he was going with this new line of questions.

Dr. Hudson answered. "At first I was appointed by the state to do a mental competency evaluation of Miss Early."

"And what was your finding?"

"That the defendant was mentally competent."

"But your job hardly ended there, did it?"

"No, it didn't," Dr. Hudson said, glancing at Gayla. "Sheriff Maynard asked me if I would consider continuing sessions with the defendant."

"Now why would a sheriff of a little county, like Kiowa, want you to meet with a defendant he was holding on a murder charge?"

Ringrose's side glance to the jury oozed innocent curiosity.

"He thought she might be suffering from a form of post-traumatic stress and felt we had established a bond — that she would talk to me."

His eyes widened under a dramatically furrowed brow.

"So he paid you personally to continue sessions with the defendant?"

Gayla's head swirled. That was not possible. Yet she realized she had no idea how the finances of the arrangement had worked. She had not given it a thought. What had been going on?

Dr. Hudson underplayed the answer. "The sheriff didn't say who was paying for the sessions."

"Well, who else could it be? The defense?"

"I don't know."

"Are you telling the court you didn't even know who was footing the bill?"

Leta jumped up. "Objection. Asked and answered."

"Sustained."

Then it dawned on Gayla. She did not dare look back into the gallery where Willie sat every day in the front row. But she knew it had to be her. Tommy might have chipped in a little, but given his salary, it would be Willie with her coffee can stuffed with wads of bills who would have contributed the lion's share. She wanted to turn and hug her. That anybody cared that much about her was almost too much to absorb.

Ringrose next question interrupted her thoughts.

"Miss Hudson, aren't you a full-time employee of the state? Is taking such a job even ethical?"

Leta nearly screamed her objection.

Ringrose, quickly: "Question withdrawn."

He shot Dr. Hudson a withering look. "I'm done with this witness."

"Redirect, Your Honor."

The judge nodded to Leta.

"Would you restate for the court, Dr. Hudson," Leta began, shooting a contemptuous look at the prosecution, "how you are employed by the State of Oklahoma?"

"I do contract work when called upon. Otherwise, I continue in my private practice."

"And why did Sheriff Maynard specifically ask for you to examine Miss Early?"

"I have done a lot of work in sexual abuse cases. It's become my specialty."

"Is it unusual for you to continue to treat patients you have examined for mental competency?"

"It doesn't happen all that often, but if we seem to have a connection, I'm sometimes asked to continue counseling someone."

"But there was no family to ask for help in this case, was there?"

"Unfortunately, no. The defendant has not had contact with her parents for fifteen or so years."

"How about legal funds?"

"As I understand it, you are a public defender, working with virtually no budget."

Leta allowed herself a small smile. "So true."

Across the aisle, Ringrose twitched with impatience. "Your Honor, is this going anywhere?"

Judge Bishop pursed his lips in displeasure. "You brought it up, Counsel." Then to Leta. "Go ahead."

"So who guaranteed that you would be paid to continue therapy with the patient?"

Dr. Hudson smiled at Gayla.

"Nobody. The Sheriff said a friend of the defendant who wished to remain anonymous had promised to pay as much as possible, but there was no guarantee I would receive my full fee."

"So why," Leta moving closer to the jury box, "would a professional such as yourself agree to such an arrangement?"

"Because I was the victim of a sexual predator many years ago. I know the shame and isolation that comes with such an experience. The truth is, after seeing Miss Early's emotional state, I would have treated her pro bono if necessary."

The courtroom floated on a long silence, as though a child had spoken a simple, unexpected truth for which there was no comeback.

Charlie Ringrose wisely declined to jump back in. His retreating neck could have been a snake sinking back into its basket. But Gayla knew he had set up something earlier, an ugly surprise just waiting for the light of day.

When that day came, he would be back, coiled for the kill.

CHAPTER 42

THE DALLAS MORNING AIR was a thick smear of gray, heavy enough to trigger Tommy's allergies and make his injured foot throb. He exited the plane with his nose dripping and his aching leg forecasting more rain on the way. Stiffened by the prison of a zero-leg-room coach seat, his gait through the terminal resembled his grandfather's, after decades of arthritis and a bad knee. His limp was nearly gone by the time he walked the length of the long concourse to the rental car kiosk. He picked up a compact and was at the Dallas Police Station a half hour later. There he found a burly, sweating uniform manning the front desk.

"Sheriff Maynard from Luckau, Oklahoma. You should have a fax for me?"

"Oh, yeah," the uniform said, checking a messy stack of papers. "I just sent it down to Narc a little bit ago."

"I need to talk to someone there as well."

"Right," the uniform said, grabbing the phone, a finger raised to Tommy, as in "give me a second." He punched in an extension number. "Yeah, the request from Oklahoma's at the front desk. You wanted to know. Okay."

He hung up the phone and nodded Tommy towards a bench across the room. "He's on his way."

Tommy had a full view of the detective's approach as he headed towards Tommy's bench. Something — his gait or the tilt of his head — seemed familiar. What was it? Before he could put it all together, the man surprised him with, "Well, I'll be damned. I wondered if it could be you, but then I thought, hell, there have to be a million Tommy Maynards in the U. S. of A."

Tommy squinted hard at the detective, trying to place the face and vaguely familiar voice. "I'm sorry, I'm not sure where . . ." He finally made out the name tag: Det. Hugh Smart.

Hugh jabbed playfully at Tommy's shoulder. "I woulda known you anywhere, man."

With Tommy still looking confused, the detective rocked back on his heels. "Come on, Tommy Boy. Don't you remember me?"

Hearing his old flight training nickname sent Tommy into time-travel mode. The freckles had faded, but Hugh's red hair was still little boy curly.

"Holy crap, Smarty Pants, of course. AETC, San Antone."

He reached for Hugh and exchanged an awkward bear hug.

"From sweatin' our balls off at Randolph to sweatin' 'em off in 'Nam. Man, where have you been? You're like a ghost. Nobody's been able to scare you up for reunions or anything."

Tommy shook his head, remembering how hard he had dodged any connection with any of the old crew. It had been too much, too scary to revisit. The V.A. docs may have pronounced that his manhood would recover, given time and some highly recommended psych counseling, but after a few sessions of the circle jerk, he had dropped out without knowing exactly why. Except that I hated it, he thought, except that it felt petty trying to talk about not getting it up, while he was looking at guys whose faces were half melted off or vets who would never walk or feed themselves again.

Finally Tommy shrugged. "I guess I kinda dropped out of sight."

"More like off the face of the earth. Well, I'm buying you lunch, and we're going to catch up." Tommy started to protest. "Don't even think about saying, No."

"What about the files?" Tommy asked, as Hugh headed towards the exit.

Hugh turned, walked back to his old buddy, and patted his blazer chest. "Got 'em right here. Come on."

Tommy was still reeling twenty minutes later when they pulled up in front of a little diner alongside Dallas Municipal Airfield.

"What's this?" he asked.

Hugh grinned. "I didn't say I was going to spend much money on you, just that I was taking you to lunch, Texas-style."

The cozy café served chicken-fried steak to die for, crispy home fries, and Tommy's idea of green beans, straight out of a can. None of that half-cooked gourmet swill, with sprigs poking out the top.

As they ate Hugh caught him up on more of his life than Tommy would ever have asked about. But the trip back in time gave Tommy a chance to remember the guy's natural cheerfulness, which had sometimes been a bit much to take. Still Tommy could see it had served Hugh well. Here he was in Narcotics, the most hopeless assignment in a police department except for the sexual offender unit, yet he did not seem disillusioned or fazed by the sinkhole of humanity he had to deal with every day. How did he do it?

When Hugh finished bringing Tommy up to snuff on the state of his life — one ex-wife, one current (a keeper), three kids, a hot rod he was restoring, and another serious hobby he promised to show him later — he sat back and started on his own plate, by now long cold.

"So what's up with you, Tommy? Four kids and a house on the lake?" Hugh grinned as he dug into his meal.

"More like a trailer park across from the Luckau dump."

"I did try to track you down; I don't know how many times, but every time I got a line on you, I'd find out you had just left. Google hasn't caught up with you, man. Even when I read about this case in the paper, it was some other sheriff's name, not yours. Dudgeon, wasn't it?"

Tommy shrugged him off. "Ah, you know."

"No, that's the whole deal, Tommy. I don't know. I heard where you landed. Really, man, the damn Zoo? I can understand why you're not crazy about being reminded about it. But everybody asks about you at the reunions. 'What the hell ever happened to Maynard?' I never knew what to tell 'em."

"I don't know what happened to me, really," Tommy finally said.

"So, have you been at Luckau awhile?"

"A few years now. I bought a little travel trailer and scooted around for a bit, doing odd jobs. Probably why you couldn't find me. But after awhile I needed some roots."

"Nice little place, huh?"

"It's okay. Job's been pretty easy up until now."

Hugh pulled out a manila envelope. "Yeah, sounds like you drew a doozy with this Raeder fella. It's a hot story all over Dallas, too, her working here once and all."

He pulled out the police sketch of Randy that Gayla had done with the help of an Elk City artist. Dixie had faxed it down.

"Here's your guy."

He looked as Tommy had imagined him: A wide forehead dwindled down to a receding chin that a scraggly beard tried to cover. Tattoos snaked up his neck.

"You recognize him by any chance?" Tommy asked.

"Nope, but I wasn't in Narco then. His picture's everywhere now. My guys'll try to rustle up anything they can find on him."

"Good luck. He's a damn ghost." Tommy shook his head.

Hugh paused from chewing on a biscuit. "Hey, don't give up. Someone is gonna know him or hit it lucky. Oh by the way, I ran your girl through the system, too."

"Yeah? Anything?"

"One DUI, one public drunkenness. Small stuff, comparatively. Nothing to suggest she had murder potential."

"See, Hugh, I don't think she is a murderer."

Tommy watched as his old friend put down his fork so he could look him eye to eye. Hugh's face looked doubtful.

"I don't know, Bud. Her record is small time, I grant you, but that's quite a leap to buying all that tabloid sex slave junk she says happened."

Now it was Tommy's turn to become animated, as he shared his own theory of what happened in that prairie getaway. He told Hugh about the connection with Randy and Gayla, the basement that he believed had been a sex dungeon, and the findings of the state psychiatrist.

Finally Hugh nodded. "I can see that. I can."

"But if I can't substantiate this guy's existence somehow, that jury isn't going to buy the possibility," Tommy said.

"And her boyfriend doesn't recognize him?" Hugh asked.

"Not when I described him. I'll fax him this sketch. Maybe it'll shake his memory loose."

"I know some sections of the city you could hit, too. Places where I know some people, the kind of people who might have known this guy.

And we have her picture. Maybe someone will recognize her. We'll give it a shot."

A few minutes later, as they headed to the car, Hugh turned to Tommy with a conspiratorial smile. "Truth be told, Tommy, I didn't pick our lunch spot just for its ambience."

"Oh?"

"That's right. Have something I want to show you."

"Hugh, I'm sorry man, but I don't think we have the time. We need to get to work. I have to get back home tonight," Tommy said.

"It'll only take a minute. Promise."

"Okay," Tommy said, with a sigh.

A grin plastered ear to ear, Hugh opened the huge rollup door to a small hangar at the end of the airfield.

"This is that serious hobby I mentioned before."

Tommy's eyes followed Hugh's pointing finger. He whistled at the sight of a small, glistening candy-apple-red plane.

"Is that a Piper Twin?"

Hugh nodded, beaming like a new dad. "Piper Twin Comanche."

Tommy walked around her, eyes shining, admiring its perfect condition. "What year?"

"A '64. 10-320 series. Classic. You should see the kids and the wife in it, man. We go everywhere in this thing," Hugh said, rubbing away a tiny smear on its shiny wing tip.

"The whole family? Ah, that's great, Hugh. Man, she's beautiful."

"I wish it was newer, a 1990 or such, but I can't touch one of those on my salary."

"Oh no," Tommy protested, "these old engines are solid if you take care of them."

Hugh motioned Tommy up inside. "Check her out. I have a cruising permit, good for about anywhere I can get to from here."

Tommy felt a little light-headed as he climbed up into the interior, so immaculate it even smelled new. Hugh was right behind him, explaining every detail where Tommy's eyes lingered for more than a moment.

"That's leather upholstery — one of my wife's contributions — all spanking new."

"It's gorgeous, Smarty Pants."

"Good enough that I have a steady clientele for charters."

"Oh yeah?" Tommy said, curious. "Where to?"

"Houston businessmen. Fishermen headed down to the Gulf, even into Mexico." He pointed to the cockpit. "Go ahead, man. Sit in the master's chair."

Tommy climbed into the pilot's seat and surveyed the control panel, with its familiar dense forest of gauges, needles, and numbers. A wave of nostalgia swept through him. He could feel his hands shaking, his eyes start to water. Words seemed too tiny for the feelings that overran him. Tommy felt Hugh's hand on his shoulder.

"I'll be right back. Okay?" Hugh said and left.

Alone with the Piper Twin's shiny dashboard, Tommy's feelings swelled up. He could not remember the last time he had let himself roam his old dreams, much less smell them and taste them. Regret raced through his veins, exploding in fits and starts. Then finally sobs. His head dropped in despair. Where have the years gone, he thought.

Outside time passed. No Hugh. Tommy was stuck, forced to look into mirrors of memories he had sworn he would never look at again. It was only a half hour before Hugh reappeared, but it might as well have been hours. Tommy's face was raw and red.

"You okay, buddy?" Hugh asked.

Not trusting himself to speak, Tommy coughed and nodded. He was ready to leave the plane behind and get back on land, where he hoped the memories would not follow. No such luck.

"Okay, here's what's gonna happen," Hugh said. "I just received permission to take off. Move over. I'm flying you back to Luckau right now."

"What?" Tommy crashed back to the present. "I can't leave. We have work to do here."

But Hugh had already maneuvered him into the passenger seat.

"I have that covered. My guys are all over this. They'll be working the case in neighborhoods they know, and believe me they know where to look, okay? They're good."

"But —"

"No buts. If it can be confirmed he was here, we will do it. Anyway I can't resist showing you this little baby in the air. Buckle up, buddy."

Too stunned and emotional to protest, Tommy reached for his seat belt. As they taxied out of the hangar, Tommy felt that same tin-plane flutter in his stomach. Hugh's takeoff was flawless.

In the air, Tommy followed the green and sienna quilts of farmland beneath them, swept away by their grace and warm glow. It felt just like his first real plane ride.

"Feels pretty good, huh?" Hugh said.

"Yeah, it does. It really does. But why are you doing all this?"

Hugh shook his head.

"You may have tried to drop out, but I've never forgotten you. Neither have the other guys. You have to get back into the community, man. We love you, and there's not a damn thing you can do about it."

Tommy nodded, not trusting himself to speak.

"Now I want to know everything that has happened to you," Hugh said. "How you crashed, where they took you, what they did to you. I mean it, Tommy. I want you to tell me everything."

And, during the flight home, Tommy did.

CHAPTER 43

WHEN MABEL THORPE entered the courtroom Monday morning in a hot pink velour running suit and tan Rockport walking shoes, Willie thought, God help us all. She looks like a strawberry ice-cream cone. Not that Mabel hadn't laid out good money at the local style shop to transform her thin white hair into blown silver glass. Willie was willing to bet that sweat suit was the most stylish thing in Mabel's closet. Thankfully Leta went for a turquoise suit today. Dueling pink would have been too much to take.

Willie had first met Mabel years ago at a city council meeting in which they were both protesting potholes. When Sid Thorpe died ten years ago, Mabel had sold their house in Oklahoma City and returned to the plains where she grew up. Her little cabin next to the Raeder place had been her and Sid's lake getaway. Now in her eighties, Mabel had run through most of her assets and found herself squeezing to make ends meet. Willie knew the cash she had forked over for the hairdo was money she did not have, but she figured Mabel had seen it as a necessity to keep up her standing in the community. After all, she was the only other local witness besides Willie who had been called to testify.

Mabel took her seat as Willie noticed Sheriff Maynard take his regular spot at the back of the courtroom. Home from his weekend search for the mysterious Randy. She was anxious to hear if he had learned anything. Tommy nodded to her as he stood by the entrance of the packed room.

A weekend break had done nothing to cool the locals' curiosity about the case. In fact, more press had arrived, the growing number of media trailers clogging Luckau's small, two-lane arteries in and out of town.

After Mabel was sworn in, Leta established that Mrs. Thorpe lived next door to the Raeders, though she had not met either husband or wife until that day Mabel went to see him about the cries she had heard coming from their property.

"See, there had been a cat-killing earlier." Mabel was relishing the spotlight. "People thought it was just some kids being mean. Oh, the things they did to that poor kitty."

"So, Mrs. Thorpe," Leta trying to keep her witness on track, "you were afraid another cat had been hurt."

"Oh yes. The sounds would have made you cringe. Awful crying."

"And where did you believe these cries were coming from?"

"The Raeders' backyard, but inside somewhere, because the cries were kinda distant like. I thought maybe a cat or even someone's child had gotten trapped under the house or something."

"What, if anything, did you do then?" Leta asked.

"I went over and hollered through the gate, but I couldn't get anyone to answer. After a spell I gave up and went back home."

"And did you hear any more screams?"

"Lordy, yes. Off and on all night. I called the sheriff's department, not that it did me any good. I guess they were too busy catching people in speed traps to come out and look for dying animals."

"Did there come a time when you were able to speak to Mr. or Mrs. Raeder about the situation?"

"The next day. I was sitting on my porch when Mr. Raeder — all by himself — drives up in his fancy dark blue car. I hollered at him and hurried over before he could close the gate."

Leta seemed relieved to have gotten to this relevant point in the story. "Tell us about that, if you would."

"Well, I don't want to speak ill of the dead, but, honestly, he wasn't very friendly."

"Objection. Inflammatory." Ringrose sat back in his chair.

"The witness is entitled to her opinion." Leta told the judge.

"Jury will note this is the opinion of the witness, not a fact." Judge Bishop frowned at Leta.

"Just tell us what transpired, Mrs. Thorpe," Leta said.

Mabel patted her hairdo, looking a bit put upon.

"Fine. I introduced myself and he did likewise. Then I told him I thought he had a problem. Well, he didn't like that one little bit, acted as if I was insinuating something, sticking my nose in somewhere it shouldn't be."

Willie couldn't help but smile, since Mabel had been sticking herself into any place she wanted for so long nobody thought it odd any more.

"What did he say to you?" Leta asked, guiding her witness.

"He said it must have been a stray cat and started walking towards me, sorta pushing me back towards the gate. And I said shouldn't we go have a look, and he said he'd do it and I should go on home. But I noticed him glancing towards that garage a couple of times, so I said, 'That's right where it was coming from.' Then he got all businesslike, drew his shoulders up, and told me he thanked me, but he could find the cat himself and take it to the pound."

Mabel paused to take a breath before continuing. "So I said, 'I have a cat carrier if you need one,' just trying to help, of course, but he just kept moving me back towards the gate and saying he had one and he'd be taking care of it, that the cat was probably already dead if I hadn't heard it lately."

"And then what happened?"

"Then nothing. He's thanking me while he's locking the gate in my face. And I'm standing there thinking, 'Well, what's up with him?' "

"And did you ever hear that sound, the animal crying, again?"

"Sure, several times."

"And did you ever speak with Mr. Raeder about it again on any other occasions?"

"No." Mabel drew herself up, mildly indignant just recalling the encounter. "I know where I'm not wanted."

"Thank you, Mrs. Thorpe. Your witness."

Willie, who had been eyeing the jury off and on during Mabel's testimony, noticed they were intent on listening, but she could not read what they made of the story. Pertinent information or sad busybody?

Ringrose, meanwhile, took his time before rising and approaching Mabel Thorpe. When he spoke, his voice sounded normal, but his expression said to the jury, this is someone to be pitied.

"You like to be in on what's going on, don't you, Mrs. Thorpe?"

Leta sprang from her chair. "Objection."

"Sustained." Even Judge Bishop didn't appreciate this tack.

"Very well," Ringrose said, visibly annoyed as he picked up a sheet of paper. "I see you have been to the Luckau city council meetings on a number of occasions, something like fifteen times in the last couple of years — I am reading from Exhibit G, Your Honor. Now why would you need to attend so many meetings of your local city government?"

Leta started to protest, but Judge Bishop saved her the trouble.

"Is this relevant, Counselor, or a fishing expedition?"

"Your Honor, we believe there's a pattern of complaints by this witness that illustrate a tendency to exaggerate as a way of getting attention."

Willie churned inside. Sure, belittle the messenger, you smug bastard. True, it was how any good lawyer would handle such a witness, but it pissed her off nonetheless. She had attended many of those same meetings alongside Mabel, airing legitimate gripes, only to have the ne'er-do-well council members brush them off.

Judge Bishop squinted at Ringrose, not sure what to do. Finally, "I'll allow it."

What followed was a mind-numbing list of the many complaints Mabel had registered, with the sheriff, the council, even the local merchants association, over everything from the garbage fee to the city sales tax. By the time he had finished, Ringrose had accomplished the almost impossible. The audience was annoyed at the witness, never mind that it was Ringrose who had dragged out the questioning of her to a tedious hour or more.

When he finally sat down, and it was time for Leta's recross, she got right to it. "Mrs. Thorpe, did you hear what you believed was an animal or person crying from the backyard of the Raeder cabin on the days in question?"

"You bet I did," Mabel chirped, shooting Ringrose a nasty glance.

"And were you rebuffed by Mr. Raeder when you tried to bring it to his attention?"

"Yes, and rudely so at that," Mabel finished with a flourish, sticking her chin out defiantly.

"Thank you. That will be all."

But Mabel had one more thing to say to the room.

"And I can sure see now why people don't want to testify." The end of her sentence was muffled by the sound of Judge Bishop's gavel raps. "The way they drag you through the mud."

Titters from the audience. Leta ducked her head to cover her smile. Judge Bishop looked gravely at the jurors.

"The jury will disregard that last remark."

For the first time, Willie noticed that some of the women jurors seemed alert. Those gals may have to live with getting short shrift, Willie thought, but I doubt they like it pushed in their faces. She prayed Ringrose would overplay his hand again. Let those women feel in their bones the imbedded double standard operating here.

If it was true for Mabel, maybe they could see it might be true for Gayla, as well.

CHAPTER 44

WHEN TOMMY WAS FINALLY called to the witness stand, he knew what he had to do. The prosecution had tried to sidestep the arresting officer, but Leta needed the jury to hear his interpretation of what he had seen in that basement. It would have been nice to have someone who hadn't been compromised by the appearance of misconduct, but he was all she had. It made him even more determined to do a flawless, professional job on the stand.

Leta had briefly called Dr. Gordon, the doctor who had treated both Tommy and Gayla after Tommy hit the deer. Gordon described Gayla's physical injuries in detail. The scrape running the length of her body, from shimmying past the broken window pane and through the tiny basement window. The bruised ankle and wrists. The scarred breasts. The fear of being touched, even for the examination.

The jury had paid rapt attention, soaking up all the details from a bona fide medical doctor. Now Leta needed somebody to explain how these injuries could have happened.

Everyone — Leta, Gayla, Willie — had all given Tommy their blow-by-blow of Dudgeon's testimony. They had also agreed, at least in retrospect, that it was not such a bad thing that he was absent when Dudgeon was on the stand. Tommy had read the transcript of Dr. Hudson's testimony and thought she had been strong and articulate about the psychology that drove the event in the basement between him and Gayla.

Still, he could not miss the curious stares from folks he had known for years, nor the insinuating questions from the press. To hell with them, he had decided. What other people want to think is none of my business. The trial was moving into its second week, and inside the press section had only grown. Outside, it was a circus.

When he had returned to town Sunday night, he had hurried to the jail to fill Gayla in on everything. She was genuinely pleased to hear Donnie was doing well, and said she was not sure how much he had been around Randy. Maybe not at all. Randy may have come along about the time they broke up and Donnie went to rehab.

"Don't worry about it if nothing comes of it," Gayla said. "Maybe your friend in Narcotics — maybe he'll come up with something."

"He's a good guy. If there's anything to find, I think he will."

She smiled an apology at him.

"I'm sorry. I know they're going to try to crucify you up there on the stand, Tommy."

He felt that little soar again, hearing her call his first name. He did not want her worrying on his account. He had felt such a lightness on his return from Dallas, he believed there was nothing they could do to hurt him. And he told her so.

"All I have to do is tell the truth."

She gave him a quizzical look. "I think that trip was good for you."

She had read him right, Tommy thought. "The guy in Dallas Narcotics? He was a buddy of mine from Viet Nam. I hadn't seen him in years."

He fell quiet, not knowing how to explain the about-face he felt in himself. Talking to Hugh, having him coax everything out of him, putting it all out there, finally, both of them crying about it, cursing it, damning it, laughing with the relief of it, had been like the lid flying off a pressure cooker. How to explain the comfort of how they had vowed to get together again, how Tommy would come to the next reunion in a few months, how incredible it felt to know he was part of a community of like-minded souls. It had been like finally coming home from the war.

Gayla didn't push on his silence.

"It's hard to explain," he finally said.

"You don't have to," she said, patting his hand.

"But I want to. I do. I just don't know how to even start."

"I know a little how that feels," she said, smiling. "In your own time.

Whenever you're ready, you'll know how."

For goodness' sake, Tommy had thought, she's on trial for murder and she's comforting me. Now, as he took the witness chair and was sworn in, he looked out over the gallery of curious faces and said to himself, all you have to do is say the next true thing.

Leta led him through the original call from Mrs. Raeder, the discovery of the body, and how he had asked Dudgeon if he could borrow his more advanced crime scene investigator, Joe Nguyen, for the case. But Tommy knew what she was after were the other details conveniently left out in Dudgeon's testimony about the scene.

"What was your first impression of the Raeder basement, Sheriff Maynard?" Leta asked, getting down to it.

"Objection, asks for a conclusion," Ringrose shouted.

Leta turned and cocked her head at him, then back to the judge. "Surely a law enforcement officer is entitled to describe what he saw, Your Honor."

"Overruled."

"Go ahead, Sheriff Maynard," Leta said.

"The first thing I noticed was how dark it was. Some cardboard and pieces of wood were laying on the floor beneath this one little eye-level window, and it looked like they had been pulled away from it."

"You mean it looked like the window had earlier been covered?"

"Right."

"Go ahead."

"I guess the other thing that struck me was what wasn't there."

"Such as . . ."

"No shelving, no boxes. Usually, basements are crammed with stuff, even if it's just Christmas decorations or old furniture. There was nothing like that down there."

"Objection," Ringrose said. "Relevance?"

Leta, hiding her annoyance, replied, "I'm trying to determine the uses of the basement, Your Honor."

"Overruled." Judge Bishop shot Ringrose a pointed glance.

"So, Sheriff, what was there in the basement?" Leta asked Maynard.

"A couple of boxes with miscellaneous household items and some old curtains were shoved under the stairway. But the other end of the room had a corner set up that reminded me of, well, of a cell."

"Objection. Objection." Ringrose flew to his feet and shouted.

Now Judge Bishop took a dramatic pause and eyed both Leta and the prosecution table with pursed lips. "Counsels approach."

When Garrison, Ringrose, and Leta were all around the dais, the judge said: "Miss O'Reilly, you are treading on dangerous ground here. This could inflame the jury's perceptions."

"I beg the court's indulgence, Your Honor. There are two opposing interpretations of what that basement was used for."

Ringrose snorted: "One coming from a prejudiced police officer."

Leta ignored him and addressed the judge.

"The prosecution characterized it as a place that someone had broken into. I believe it was a place somebody had to break out of. Surely that viewpoint is also valid for the jury."

Judge Bishop motioned them away.

"Objection is overruled. Proceed."

"Thank you, Your Honor. Now, Sheriff Maynard, what did you see that made you think of a cell?"

"It was an isolated corner with only the bare necessities: a cot, an industrial sink, a tiny toilet, and a dorm-size fridge. And —"

Tommy was surprised to feel himself choke up a little. He cleared his throat but did not trust himself to speak yet.

"What else was there, Sheriff?"

Tommy, after a deep breath: "Chains, not quite as big as tire chains. Two sets of them. Bolted into the wall."

"And what did you believe was significant about the chains?"

"For one thing, there were dried blood drops on them. My first thought was that some animal had been chained up down there."

"Objection, Your Honor." Ringrose hollered. "Do we have to listen to this?"

Leta whirled to the judge. "He introduced the idea that a homeless person was living down there. This is just a different interpretation."

The judge is earning his money today, Tommy thought. He has probably juggled more legal arguments in the last ten minutes than he has in the last ten months.

Actually the judge seemed to be enjoying his starring role to the hilt. His furrowed brow and the thoughtful sighs accompanying each decision actually hinted at someone of far greater intellect than Judge Bishop.

"Sit down, Mr. Ringrose. I'll allow it. Continue, Miss O'Reilly."

"Very well," Leta said, trying not to show how pleased with herself she was. "Did you believe the chains, then, had been used to imprison someone?"

"I did," Tommy said. "The length of them was just long enough to reach no more than halfway across the basement. And inside that radius were the basic necessities — sink, water, toilet, and cot."

"And what, if anything, did you observe about the trapdoor entrance to the basement?"

"It was double locked from the inside with combination locks and from the outside with industrial strength hinges and two heavy duty clasps, also secured with two combination locks."

"So one would have to know multiple combinations to get into and out of the basement?" Leta said.

"Correct."

"But why would one need to be able to lock oneself inside the basement?"

"It would appear," Tommy said, "that he didn't want anyone but himself to be able to get in or out."

Ringrose shot into the air. "Objec —"

"Overruled." Judge Bishop rose to the challenge. "You'll have your chance on cross, Prosecutor."

"Did you see anything else in the basement that might have belonged to someone living down there? Any clothes or bedding?" Leta asked.

"Only a few towels, a sponge, mop, and some cleaning liquid."

"No other evidence of someone having been there?"

"There was evidence that someone had left. A blood trail leading from the window. Since the trapdoor had been locked from the inside, I assumed the perpetrator had to have left through the window."

"And did you follow that blood trail, Sheriff?"

"My deputy did. But after a mile or so, it disappeared."

"At a later date, were there other items that belonged to the defendant that were recovered?" Leta asked.

"Yes. Once the defendant was picked up, my deputy and I, along with some Elk City officers, did a search along the path we believed the defendant had taken from the Raeder cabin to Ms. Morris's cabin."

"And what did you find?" Leta looked squarely at the jury, hoping they were still with her. They seemed not only alert, but involved.

"We found a path of discarded, bloody clothes, most of them ripped and torn," Tommy said.

"Why was that?"

"Miss Early apparently had no shoes or coat when she escaped. She took the blanket and sheets for warmth, then ripped her clothes into strips to tie around her hands and bare feet for protection. As they dropped off or became too wet to walk in . . ."

"Objection, Your Honor . . ."

Tommy talked right over Ringrose. ". . . she threw them away and tore up more strips."

Ringrose talking through Tommy. "The witness wasn't there."

"Sustained." Judge Bishop shot a shaming glance at Tommy, who knew better than to continue after an objection. "Miss O'Reilly, please keep your witness under control."

"Yes, Your Honor." Leta then walked Tommy through the material they had reviewed, including Gayla's pulling him from the car after he had hit the deer. Tommy kept his version of the encounter with Gayla in the basement low-key, confirming Dr. Hudson's testimony, because she had assessed it so accurately. Leta did her best to drive home to the jury how sexless the encounter had actually been.

"In what way did the defendant approach you?" Leta asked Tommy.

"She didn't actually approach me at first. Just stood there, dazed and lost. Even when she took her dress off, it was like she wasn't aware of what she was doing."

"It wasn't an inviting or sexual striptease?"

"No. More like someone undressing for a doctor's exam."

"So what were your feelings about the defendant during it?"

"I felt sorry for her." Tommy wanted to look at Gayla but did not dare for fear of losing his concentration.

"She disrobed completely?"

"Except for her underwear . . . her panties. When I realized what she was doing, I told her to stop. That she shouldn't do that."

"Then what happened?"

"I asked her to please put her dress back on."

"What was her reaction at that point?" Leta asked.

"She became agitated."

"At what point did the defendant approach you?"

"Right after I asked her to get dressed. She crawled to me and tried to pull down the zipper to my pants."

"Did she say anything while she was doing this?"

"No," Tommy said. "But she seemed upset that I was reacting negatively to what she was doing."

"What was your sense of what was happening in that moment?"

Tommy paused. He wanted to get this exactly right.

"It was like I wasn't even there. I thought it was something she'd done before with someone in this situation, but this time was different. And she couldn't understand why I wasn't playing along."

"Objection," Ringrose hollered. "Witness can't read Miss Early's state of mind."

Judge Bishop studied the air for a moment. "I'll allow it. He is entitled to his viewpoint, just as Sheriff Dudgeon was earlier."

"How was this personality different from the Gayla who pulled you from the wrecked car?" Leta asked.

Now Tommy did sneak a glance at Gayla. "Night and day. She didn't even seem aware during the basement incident, but when she saw me in the wrecked cruiser, she jumped right into action. Took charge. Talked me through it and helped me out of the car to safety."

"So would you describe what she did at the crash as heroic?"

"Definitely. Definitely."

"Thank you, Sheriff Maynard." Leta turned to Judge Bishop. "I believe that is all I have for this witness at this time."

The judge nodded at Ringrose, who was already straightening his tie and lapels in anticipation of taking the stage.

"Cross, Mr. Ringrose?"

"Oh, yes. Definitely."

The Prosecutor walked around the witness stand, giving it a wide berth, as though to size Maynard up.

"Sheriff Maynard," he asked, looking down his nose at Tommy, "have you had sexual relations with this defendant?"

It got exactly the reaction he wanted. The audience began to murmur loudly, with some shocked laughter. Judge Bishop banged his gavel and looked to O'Reilly for an expected objection that never came. The courtroom buzzed.

Tommy leaned back in his chair. He and Leta had talked about how to handle this inevitable question. Neither had expected it to be Ringrose's first assault, but they knew it was coming. Leta was positive he would ask it for shock value if nothing else. She and Tommy both agreed to answer it head on rather than allow a trail of innuendo.

Ringrose looked surprised. He had apparently expected to have her objection sustained, leaving the subject hanging suspiciously in the air, ripe for occasional sniping during the cross. Instead, he now struggled to look pleased with the unexpected turn of events. He looked to the judge, who was banging his gavel again.

"I will have order in this courtroom. If there is another outburst of this sort, I will have the bailiff remove all of you people," the judge threatened. "Witness will answer the question."

Tommy, his heart pounding, said directly to the jury.

"I have not."

Ringrose paused a beat for effect.

"But not for lack of her trying, huh?"

The crowd tittered. Tommy felt his face go red with rage. From the corner of his eye, he saw Gayla cover her face with her hands.

O'Reilly popped to her feet. "Objection."

Judge Bishop glared at Elk City's golden boy. "That remark will be stricken from the record. Jurors, you will disregard Mr. Ringrose's last remark." Then to Ringrose. "Try that one more time in my courtroom and you will be found in contempt."

Ringrose ducked his head in mock shame. But the offhand zinger had done the trick, and he knew it. Tommy could have choked him. He struggled to keep his emotions in check. He could not let himself get sidetracked by this weasel.

"Sorry, Your Honor," Ringrose said, his eyes gleaming. "My apologies to the court."

"Now, Sheriff Maynard, you called in Arlene Hudson to counsel Miss Early soon after her arrest. Is that right?"

"Yes."

"What prompted that call?"

"My suspicion that Miss Early had suffered sexual abuse."

Ringrose was cruising now. "Just a lawman's hunch? Is that enough to justify going to the expense of hiring outside counseling?"

Leta popped up. "Which question would he like the witness to answer first, Your Honor?"

Ringrose quickly reorganized. "I'll rephrase. What did you observe about the defendant that warranted outside counseling?"

"She seemed barely connected to reality. I observed the classic signs of abuse, the fear of being touched, the paranoia. And there were physical findings in Dr. Gordon's medical report as well: bruises over her body and scars around the breasts and —"

"Yes, yes, we've heard all that already," Ringrose said impatiently as if to a troublesome child. "Are you telling me that is the only evidence you had to suggest that Albert Raeder could have committed the heinous acts Miss Early claims?"

Tommy's head jerked up towards Ringrose, then Leta, who suddenly looked like a cat with a warm canary in her throat. He could hear Ringrose suck in his breath as he realized his misstep. After a second, he opened his mouth to speak, but Tommy beat him to it.

"No," Tommy jumped in, "there was also a prostitute in Las Vegas who accused Mr. Raeder of beating her and chewing off one of her nipples."

Gasps rose from the audience like smoke clouds from a forest fire, as Ringrose mentally reeled. Tommy tied a big ribbon on it for the jury.

"Called herself 'Big Momma Earth.' "

Ringrose screamed bloody murder. "Move to strike! That is hearsay of the most malicious sort."

Judge Bishop, still not recovered from the last outburst, pounded his gavel for order. Too late. Locusts had descended on the courtroom.

After Judge Bishop's threats finally quieted the room, Ringrose attempted to divert the course of the testimony by taking Tommy through the minutia of the basement encounter, but none of his picky questions could defuse the situation. The energy in the courtroom was palpable. Everyone at the prosecution table looked deflated. Finally limping through his cross to a quick close, Ringrose retreated to his chair.

Leta jumped back in with a re-direct, introducing the damning report from Las Vegas into evidence. She guided Maynard quickly through it. "Would you please explain the contents of this Las Vegas police report?"

"Lawanda Stanley, also known as 'Big Momma Earth,' stated that Albert Raeder hired her from in front of a casino and they then went to her room at a nearby motel," Maynard testified, struggling to keep any smugness out of his demeanor. "Raeder insisted on tying her up, for which, Ms. Stanley said, he was willing to pay extra. With her hands bound to the headboard and her feet to the end of the bed, he struck and bit her repeatedly during sexual intercourse, resulting in severe bruising and bitemarks on both breasts. She stated that minor surgery was required at the hospital emergency room on her left nipple."

"And did Ms. Stanley, or 'Big Momma Earth,' call the police at the time of the incident?"

"No, she stated that he left her there, beaten and bloody, in the motel room. Later when she managed to untie herself — he had apparently brought thigh-high hose which he used to secure her arms and legs — she tracked him down at the real estate convention he was attending at another hotel."

"And all this was then reported to the police?" Leta asked.

"It was reported that night, but the Las Vegas police reduced the charges from assault and battery to a misdemeanor," Tommy answered.

"Why would they do that?"

"We were not able to find out precisely how that happened," Tommy said. "The police report had been redacted by the time it got into our hands."

"Redacted? In what way?"

Tommy shrugged. "Large chunks had been blacked out."

"And why would that happen?"

"It would appear both parties came to a plea of some sort. Usually, that would mean . . ."

"Objection. Witness can't guess at an incident he did not observe." Ringrose had gotten his focus back.

"Sustained."

"Question withdrawn," Leta chirped. "We can imagine, I bet."

Ringrose groaned a loud objection.

Judge Bishop pounded his gavel. "That remark will be stricken from the record. The jury is instructed to disregard that remark. Careful, Miss O'Reilly, you are on thin ice."

Ringrose came back and pounded on him some more, but Tommy was now back on his game. He kept his answers crisp, stayed on point. He didn't dare look at Gayla, but instead grounded himself in his chair.

There had been plenty of mistakes and oversights in this case from him, and he was determined to make up as much as he possibly could by hanging in there to the last question.

Ringrose did not make a dent in his testimony.

When Tommy finished an hour later, relief swept through him. As he stepped down from the witness stand, it felt like an out-of-body experience. He could see himself leaving the box, but he was flying above it, the courtroom spread before him. He noticed the specks of dust in the amber light that sliced through the long windows and settled on Gayla's face as he walked towards her. Her eyes gave him a guarded smile.

God, I love her so much.

The thought came to him just like that. His breath caught, and he slowed his walk as he passed her at the table, thinking: I would do anything for her. I'm glad I did not have to lie, but I would lie for her. I would cheat for her. I love her that much.

If only this worm Ringrose knew. There could not have been sex between them, probably never would be. Only God knew when, if ever, Gayla could ever let somebody back in that close again. And Tommy, well, Tommy had not dared touch anyone in years — for fear of not being able to see it through. Fidel had taught him well. Get it up and you get a big shock from Mr. Flash. He had quit risking the inevitable humiliation years ago.

He had learned not to hope, or so he had thought.

Now he was not so sure.

The words kept swimming through his mind, as the realization spread through his heart.

God, I love her so much.

CHAPTER 45

WILLIE'S HANDS SHOOK AS she squinted at the tiny print on the legal papers. She knew Gib Farris had dotted every "i" and crossed each "t," but a part of her still hesitated. After all these years of ruling her own remote little world, she could not help but balk, looking out into the unknown. Part of her was ready to leap. Part of her was ready to panic and retreat.

Outside Farris Real Estate, a peach sun plopped down on a hilltop, unwilling to commit to its inevitable setting.

Willie knew how it felt.

She had figured she would probably resent whoever bought the cabin, but she was also old enough and self-aware enough to recognize this for the knee-jerk reaction it was, a by-product of her own stubborn petulance. Yes, she emoted a tough-as-nails hermit exterior to the world; that tough shell, however, mostly served to disguise the soft well of fear inside her, the fear that had driven most of her choices in life.

That is why Willie felt most comfortable if there were not too many elements at play. The simpler things were, the better she felt. Getting swept up into this thing with Gayla and the Sheriff had left her seesawing back and forth between exhilaration and depression.

What if the farm were the only thing anchoring her to sanity?

The young couple buying her home sat across from her, unbearably sweet and earnest. Newlyweds, they could barely keep their hands off each other. Their constant touching had no apparent reason, other than some overriding need to be as one. Willie recognized it, though as a general rule the sentiment annoyed the hell out of her.

Today was an exception. The couple's displays of affection conjured up a mental snapshot of Willie and her ex-husband, a thousand years ago, carrying backpacks and hiking through a mountain meadow. Exhausted but jubilant, they had reached their destination, a natural hot springs nestled in the curve of a steep mountainside. An enormous log, the only way across it. The joy with which they had shed their packs and their clothes, then jumped into the roiling hot water, was etched on their faces. As they clung to one another's slippery bodies, the steaming springs soothed every ache and teased every desire. A cobalt blue sky glistened above with dollops of whipped clouds dropped into place by the gods. It had been a perfect moment in time, when they were one with each other and the universe. Later they would refer to it as the day they made Jack. Yes, she knew these young kids, Willie thought; she had once been one herself. That section from the tapestry of her life, however, had lain tattered and in threads for years.

Farris smiled patiently from the end of the table.

"I believe you'll find everything is in order, Ms. Morris. Just as you wished."

Willie swam to the surface of her thoughts.

"Oh yes. You have done a fine job, Gib."

The young bride giggled.

"So we're going to do it? We'll move in next month?" Her husband leaned in towards her, then looked with a questioning smile to Willie.

"I'm sorry. What were your names again?" Willie asked.

Gib, a little embarrassed. "Jack and Allie Lowe."

"Oh, yes. Jack." Then thoughtfully. "That was my son's name."

The young husband seemed to tune into Willie's emotions.

"Ms. Morris, I want you to know that it has always been my dream to have a place in the country like this. Your land is going to be in good hands. We'll take good care of it. We plan to raise a family here."

Willie smiled at them, so giddy with hope and love. Their whole lives lay ahead of them. Recently, new thoughts about her own life had begun to intrude. Involuntary thoughts of self-forgiveness, the possibility of someday walking out of her muddy cave of recrimination. Could she see her way to quit this rending of her soul? Could she find that she might still have something left to offer the world?

Like a nudge from a heavenly finger, she felt something first move, then surge inside her. A deep thickness was breaking up, like a wall of ice calving from an iceberg. The darkness fell from her heart. It has been so hard to let go, she thought. And then, just like that, you do. A new lightness came into her. And with it, a childlike curiosity about the unknown days that lay ahead.

She looked at Jack and Allie and smiled at all the comfort her farm would feel from this innocent, foolish young couple.

"All I need is a pen," Willie whispered.

CHAPTER 46

DO YOU SOLEMNLY SWEAR to tell the whole truth, and nothing but the truth, so help you God?" The pockmarked clerk seemed nervous at being so close to the infamous siren in the witness stand.

Gayla threw back her shoulders and looked squarely at the jury, as Leta had instructed.

Her "I do," however, came out a hoarse whisper.

She straightened the jacket of her navy pantsuit. Her fingers trembled, but the oak chair felt cool against her back and legs. She had been surprised Leta had not drilled her more about her testimony, but the reason why was comforting. They had reviewed what happened many times, and that was all Leta wanted, she had told Gayla.

"When a witness tells what happened and it's the truth, the last thing you want is to look rehearsed. Win or lose, we have to get your story out and on the record. Don't overdo it, but don't fight your emotions either. That's part of giving a true accounting of what happened, too."

As Gayla looked out from the witness stand, the crowded courtroom unnerved her. It reminded her of those wide white cartoon eyes staring out from a black background on children's television shows, the kind of eyes that always sent some poor mouse screaming from the cave. She felt her heart racing and caught a whiff of the judge's pungent aftershave. The latter left her nauseated.

Then, with a sigh of relief, she spotted Tommy standing in the back of the courtroom and Willie seated on the front row, right behind Leta's table. She decided she would concentrate on them and the jury so as to keep her head about her. Yet she could not resist one good peek at the lead prosecuting attorney, Charlie Ringrose — usually the best view she had of him was limited to a profile or his backside. He looked particularly spiffy this morning, matching green silk tie and kerchief complementing his sand-colored, double-breasted suit. Greased and loaded for bear, no doubt. As for her, well, it was all she could do to contain her hand tremors and the sweat droplets forming on her forehead.

Getting to the courthouse from the jail was still like running a gauntlet. Interest in the trial had not ebbed. As the time approached for the defendant to take the stand, the vans of the television crews and the rest of the media had circled the little town square, like covered wagons around a campfire. Restaurants had run out of food, lines formed at the local diner, and the reactions of locals to the windfall ranged from capitalistic glee to absolute outrage. (The latter being the prevalent reaction of those whose morning booth at the diner was no longer available on demand.)

Tommy had deputized some members of the local National Guard to assist with crowd control, but it was still proving to be too much for such a confined space. Tommy and Frankie Lee tried to protect Gayla from the microphones jammed in her face and the cameras jostling to get closer to her, but basically they ended up resorting to a duck-and-cover maneuver to cross the lawn to the courthouse.

Leta gave a reassuring smile to Gayla, who found it touching that her lawyer had bucked her natural inclination and donned a pale rose suit — a gesture of solidarity with Gayla Rose, she had said. Leta still sported her six-inch-heels, and even with everything else she had on her mind, Gayla could not help but wonder how Leta kept from pitching forward on them.

"Please state your name for the record," Leta began.

"Gayla Rose Early." Whoa . . . that voice was not hers. It had jumped a couple of octaves. She sounded like a little girl about to burst into tears.

Leta gave her an encouraging smile and a calming nod, as if to say, You're okay, just settle down. By the time they had worked through the basics, Gayla sounded almost like herself again.

"Now, could you tell us a little about yourself?" Leta asked.

"I was born in Stuttgart, Germany, but we moved a lot. My father was an officer in the military. After living mostly in Europe when I was just a baby, he was assigned stateside again, so I also lived in Texas, New Mexico, and Alabama. We lived in a bunch of places."

"And did you graduate from high school?"

"Yes. That was in El Paso."

"Was growing up a happy time for you?"

"It was okay. Kinda of tough moving around so much. Sometimes I wouldn't stay at the same school for even a semester."

"Was it hard to adjust?"

"Yeah — I mean yes — I didn't handle it too well. I started doing a lot of stuff to show off and draw attention to myself. I thought it would help me make friends faster."

"And did it?"

"Not really. I ended up getting in trouble, drinking a lot in high school, and causing problems for my parents."

Now *that* was an understatement, Gayla thought. Images of her father screaming down the hall at her, ranting at her for missing another curfew and coming home so drunk she could barely walk. What hypocrites. Her dad was a loud lampshade-on-the-head drinker, and her mom, true to form, a ladylike fall-into-your-soup-bowl drunk.

"Did your parents also drink?"

"Oh, yes. They considered it part of the army lifestyle."

"So you started getting into trouble early on?"

"Yes, trouble at school and home. I ended up with a public intox arrest and a DUI before I got out of high school. My parents couldn't control me. And they pretty much gave up trying."

"So after your last arrest, you were put on juvenile probation for six months. How did that go?"

"It scared me to death. I even managed to stay sober for awhile after that." Gayla's face twisted with regret at an escape route missed.

"And what did you do then?"

"I waited tables and drifted. Started drinking again. My dad was transferred, and this time I didn't go with them. I knew they didn't want me to go. It was a relief for them when I stayed behind."

"Where are your parents today?" Leta asked.

"I don't know. We haven't spoken for probably fifteen years."

It surprised Gayla how fast they worked through her early life. How short and pedestrian it seemed in retrospect. And always the same pattern. Running away from reality.

When Leta moved on into the lost years, Gayla did not attempt to either diminish or exaggerate her crack use. Her story was not that original. Introduced to drugs through a party-all-night set of friends. Going from gainful employment to selling everything she had to keep the drugs flowing, first bumming off friends and eventually robbing them to sustain her habit. Finally getting kicked out of everywhere and cut loose by everybody, even her boyfriend.

Leta had reminded her it was important for the jury to see how far she had fallen in those years. It was, in fact, essential if they were to understand how she had come to arrive at that night in the Raeder cabin.

"At this point, without a job or money, your boyfriend gone, how did you manage to acquire drugs?" Leta led her along step by step.

"That's when I met Randy."

Into Gayla's mind flashed her first glimpse of Randy. He was standing at a bar, pierced and pencil thin. He exuded a vulgar confidence. If he had been a billboard it would have read: "I use and sell. You got a problem with that?"

"Where was this?"

"A bar in Dallas. I was hustling for drugs, and we hit it off. Started hanging out. At first he got me high for free. After things cooled between us, he let me run up a debt."

"And how much did that eventually total?"

"I can't remember exactly. Probably five or six hundred dollars. I know that may not sound like a lot to most people, especially someone with a job, but for me, well, it might as well have been a million. I didn't have a penny to my name."

"Where were you living at this time?"

Gayla shuddered as she remembered her places of sanctuary.

"I crashed wherever I could — sometimes at a shelter, but only for a night because you have to sober up to stay longer. I had run out of friends, so there was no crashing on a friend's couch. My boyfriend was long gone. I slept a lot in the park . . . under overpasses . . . whatever I could find."

"And did there come a time when Randy asked you to pay up?"

"Yes. Someone had ripped him off, I think, and he was pissed and desperate for cash. He demanded that I come up right then with what I owed him."

"Were you able to do that?"

"Oh no. He smacked me around, but he knew I didn't have it."

"What did you think about his smacking you around?"

"I figured I deserved it."

Leta turned a moment and looked at the jury, wanting to make sure they got that.

"Then what happened?"

"He told me he'd heard about a place in Oklahoma, in the country, where there was a safe and jewelry, and we were going to rob it."

"How did he know about this place?"

"I'm not sure about that. He never said who told him."

"Why did he want you along? Do you have experience at cracking safes?"

Gayla let a small smile slip over her face. "Hardly. But my mom dabbled in jewelry on the side to bring in extra money. She taught me some about stones and quality. I had once offhand told Randy that I knew a lot about gems, which was a stupid exaggeration, but he must have believed it, I guess. He also wanted someone to navigate on the drive. The job was almost three-hundred miles away."

"Had you ever broken in someplace and robbed it?"

"No. I had stolen from friends, I'm ashamed to say, but I had never broken into a stranger's home. But Randy said that was how I was going to work off my debt. Help him break in and assess the jewelry; identify the good stuff. It was either do that or go work the streets."

"Were you going to share in any of the proceeds?"

"Oh no, I wasn't going to make anything other than paying off what I owed him. I was just supposed to be his backup, whatever that meant."

"Did he know anything about jewelry?"

"No. That wasn't his thing."

"How did the plan proceed?"

"Randy said he was going to get us a car and told me to be ready to go at four in the afternoon, which would get us there about nine that night. That way the house would be dark and the roads quiet. I said wouldn't somebody be home that time of night, and he told me it was a lake cabin. Nobody was there during the week."

"Did he pick you up at the appointed time?"

"Yes. I don't remember the date, sometime in October, I think."

"This was a little more than two years ago."

"That's right." Gayla cleared her throat, which was drying up. She wasn't used to talking this much.

Leta was right in sync with her client's state of mind.

"Do you need some water?"

Gayla nodded and waited for Leta to pour a glass and bring it to her. She sneaked a glance at the jury; the attention of the jurors seemed pinned on her. She could not tell, however, whether it was in sympathy or more like rubber-necking drivers at a car wreck. That said, she was finally starting to feel a little comfortable.

"Can you tell us about that night?"

"The trip was uneventful. We got to the cabin about nine as planned. We parked the car a ways down the road from the cabin."

"And what kind of car was this?"

"It was a Chevy Nova, I think. Randy was annoyed it was so old and so ugly, but he said it would attract less attention being kinda beat up."

"So it wasn't Randy's own car?"

"Oh no, he had an old Harley he rode."

"A motorcycle?"

"Right, motorcycle."

"So where did the Nova come from?"

"I assumed he had stolen it. Maybe he borrowed it."

"Go ahead. You parked the car . . ."

"Randy had a bolt cutter for the lock on the fence gate, and he picked the front door lock. He knew how to do stuff like that. His rule was no weapons and no big flashlights. He had a small penlight to check out the jewelry, but he preferred to work by moonlight. He had picked a night with a full moon so we could see."

"Why the rule about not carrying a weapon?"

"In case we got caught, it would make for a lesser charge."

"And what was your job during the robbery?"

"I carried the bag for Randy. He picked out the stuff he wanted. Then we started towards the bedroom, where he said the jewelry and safe were supposed to be."

Gayla hesitated, remembering the rush of dread she had felt.

"And then what happened?"

"We saw the flash of a headlight in the front yard, and then we heard tires on gravel in the driveway, and in just a few seconds, the front door opened."

"What did you do?"

"We both panicked. Randy headed towards the kitchen and I followed him. Nobody was supposed to be there. Randy had been sure of it. And because of that, we hadn't been in any hurry. We had been taking our time, and we were caught completely off guard. By the time Randy found the back door, Raeder was already coming into the kitchen, with a gun in his hands."

"What kind of gun was it?"

"A sawed-off shotgun."

"What did he say to the two of you?"

"I don't know if he said anything to us or not. We froze. I know that. We were only a couple of feet from the door."

"Did you give yourselves up?"

"Yes, we had no choice."

"What happened next?"

"Mr. Raeder acted . . . odd. He kept asking us these strange questions, like where were we from, were we together, did we have family in the area? Stuff like that."

"Why did he want to know?"

"At the time I had no idea. It didn't make sense."

"Does it make more sense now than it did then?"

"Sure, I know now he wanted to find out if we were locals or drifters."

"Go ahead, Miss Early."

"He wanted to know if it would be safe to get rid of us."

Ringrose flew out of his seat. "Objection! Your Honor, this kind of statement is unbelievable."

Judge Bishop cut him off with a gavel pound.

"Sustained," he snapped.

After the brouhaha over the Vegas incident yesterday, the judge had been noticeably goosey, ready to head off any repeat performance.

"Okay," Leta continued, unfazed. "You were cornered at the back door of the house —"

Ringrose was on his feet again. "Your Honor, I have tried to let this pass, but she is leading —"

"Do you have an objection, Mr. Ringrose, or do you just want to strut?" Judge Bishop was getting pissy.

Ringrose flinched like he had been bitch-slapped.

"Yes, I have an objection."

"Thank you. Objection is sustained. Watch yourself, Miss O'Reilly."

"Sorry, Your Honor," Leta purred. "So you are both in the kitchen, your backs to the door, and Mr. Raeder is holding a shotgun on you. What happened next?"

"Randy said we would give it all back, no problem. We were caught red-handed. Randy was stalling, trying to think of a way out."

Ringrose rose again, a dramatic weariness tinging his words. "Objection. Miss Early has yet to convince anybody that there was a 'Randy,' much less that she knew what he was thinking."

Now it was Judge Bishop's turn to stir things up. He pursed his lips as he considered the steeple he had made with his hands.

"I'll allow it."

Leta turned back to Gayla. "And what were you doing while Randy was talking to Mr. Raeder?"

"Shaking so hard I could barely stand. My heart was pounding. He was giving us both a real once-over. I was sure I was about to die."

"What happened next, Miss Early?"

"Randy was in the middle of a sentence when —"

She choked up as the image that had haunted her for two years gripped her again. The amazement in Randy's eyes as he heard the shot then felt his body lift off the ground and fly backwards into the kitchen door. He was dead before he landed. He might as well have been a discarded teddy bear, slumped against the back door. Black eyes now like buttons. Gayla looked at Leta. Leta was not about to rush her.

Gayla cleared her throat. "Randy was mid-sentence when Raeder swung the shotgun towards him and pulled the trigger."

The crowd was talking amongst itself now, and Judge Bishop slammed the gavel on the bench to stop it. "There will be order in this court or you will all be thrown out. I mean it now."

"He shot Randy," Gayla finished.

"Where was Randy shot?"

"In the chest. It threw his whole body back against the door. The blood spattered over my shirt and my face."

"He died instantly?"

"Yes."

"And what did you do then?"

"I don't know. It was like everything stopped for a few moments. There was this dead silence. Then I think I started blubbering. I knew I was next, but I couldn't move. I figured, this is it, I'm a goner."

"But that wasn't the case, was it, Miss Early?"

"No. Mr. Raeder just stood there with the shotgun still in his hand. I think I put my hands up to shield myself, just waiting for the next shot. But instead, he lowered the gun and then, it was so unbelievable, he winked at me."

Leta repeated, with a pointed glance at the jury.

"He winked at you?"

"Yes. He had a weird smile on his face. Then he said, 'What happens next is up to you, sugar.' "

"What did you think he meant by that?"

"The way he was looking at me, there was no doubt what he meant by that. And, well, it was obvious he was turned on."

"Objection!" Ringrose said. "How could she know whether he was 'turned on' or not?"

The crowd buzzed. Someone tittered. Even Judge Bishop could not resist the easy setup. "There are ways, Mr. Ringrose."

Open laughter erupted from the audience. The judge struggled to suppress a smile. "I'll allow it. Continue Miss O'Reilly."

Leta kept her demeanor serious and on point. She knew they were stepping onto quicksand. She had to handle the next part carefully or be swallowed whole.

"Miss Early, you observed Mr. Raeder becoming physically aroused?"

"Yes. And he was touching himself, showing me as much."

"And was he still holding the shotgun?"

"Yes, with the other hand."

"What happened next?"

"I think I was holding my breath. We stood there staring at each other for what seemed like forever. I knew what he was waiting for me to say. Finally I told him, 'I'll do anything you want me to.' "

One of the female jurors gasped and covered her mouth with her hand in shock. Another audibly sucked in her breath. Most of the audience was too absorbed to do anything but lean slightly forward.

"Did he tell you what he wanted you to do?"

Gayla felt her stomach go sour. The pressure in the courtroom was palpable, and an expectant hush thickened the air. Her breath came so shallow, she struggled for it like an asthmatic.

It was a visible moment of weakness on her part, and Ringrose pounced with fake concern.

"Does the witness need a break, Your Honor?"

Leta shook him off with irritation, as Gayla expelled the air stuck in her lungs and caught a good gulp of oxygen. Leta reminded her in a whisper, "Just breathe."

"Okay," Gayla said. "I'm fine."

"Let me repeat the question, Miss Early. Did Mr. Raeder then tell you what he wanted you to do?"

"Yes. He told me to . . ." Her voice rose to a squeak. ". . . To drop to my knees and crawl to him."

A murmur went through the crowd.

"Which you did?"

"I did. When I got there I looked up at him and — I will never forget the way he grinned — then he told me to unzip his pants."

Another murmur through the courtroom. Gayla mentally withdrew from the crowd's reaction, unconsciously becoming hyperaware of simple things instead. The slight click of the overhead ceiling fan as it spun. The weathered armrest of the witness chair, its grip rubbed smooth by the anxious fingers of those who had sat there before her.

Leta waited patiently. "Are you all right, Miss Early?"

"Fine, sorry, I'm fine," she replied.

"You were saying that he told you to undo his pants. And did you do what he asked?"

"Yes. He sort of giggled then, like a little kid caught in the act, then as if he was asking for someone to pass the salt, he said, 'Now blow me.' "

Saying it aloud, the memory returned raw and ugly, like it had happened yesterday. She felt her voice become coarse as she tied to control it. She finally managed to get out: "He thought it was all so funny."

Ringrose was on his feet. "Objection. She doesn't know —"

"Sustained. Witness can't know Mr. Raeder's state of mind."

Leta carefully led Gayla on.

"After he asked you for oral sex, what happened?"

"He giggled some more. I remember thinking the giggling was so strange given the circumstances. I could see Randy's body out of the corner of my eye. The blood had made a pool around him. His eyes looked like black BBs staring at the ceiling. I couldn't stop trembling . . . but I knew what I had to do."

Leta nodded for her to continue.

Gayla struggled to keep her voice steady. "When I finished, I begged him to let me go. I told him I would never tell anyone. I was terrified. But he said he couldn't let me go until I helped him get rid of Randy. If I would do that, then he'd let me go."

"He promised he'd let you go if you helped him dispose of the body?"

"Right. And I guess I was just flat out bawling by that point, because he also said if I didn't stop crying, he would kill me right then, too."

"What was his plan for disposing of the body?"

"He was winging it, but he was pretty sharp. He asked me where our car was parked and made me walk him to it and then we drove it back to the cabin."

"During that time did you see any lights on in any of the neighboring houses or anyone who might have seen you on the road?"

"I didn't, but I would have been too scared to call out even if I had. I believe I was in shock at that point. Details got real hazy real fast."

"Go ahead."

"So Mr. Raeder loaded Randy's body into the Nova. He said I was going to drive that car and I was to follow him in his big car. And more importantly, I was to remember he still had the shotgun."

"What kind of car was he driving?"

"I don't know for sure. Dark blue, a big one, like a luxury car."

"And what about the blood in the kitchen? Was it cleaned up before the two of you left?"

"He made me do that, while he was loading Randy into the Nova. He got out a bunch of cleaning stuff from under the sink and told me to use spray cleaner and bleach all over and wipe it up good. He gave me a new roll of paper towels, I remember."

"And did you clean up the murder scene?"

Ringrose jumped up. "Objection! That has not been established —"

Judge Bishop's voice rose over his. "Sustained. Careful," now pausing to get it correctly, "Miss O'Reilly."

"My apologies, Your Honor. Miss Early, after you cleaned up the blood all over —"

Ringrose, up again, breathing fire. "Your Honor, this is ridiculous."

Leta was now indignant herself. "The defendant was covered with blood from several feet away. That's what a sawed-off does, Your Honor. Spreads blood everywhere."

Judge Bishop, now cranky himself, leaned towards Leta until he was almost out of his chair. "Enough with the dramatics. Save it for closing."

"Very well." Leta looked back at her notes, but Gayla noticed that she looked pretty pleased with herself.

"So Miss Early, after you cleaned up Randy's blood from the kitchen floor, what happened next?"

"We took off in the two cars. I didn't know where we were going."

Leta checked the courtroom clock and lifted her eyebrows at Judge Bishop. "Perhaps this might be a good stopping place for lunch, Your Honor?"

As they waited for the Judge to rule on Leta's request, Gayla noticed some of the male jurors sitting back in their chairs with their arms crossed over their chests. They looked so skeptical, it scared her. Maybe, they were just tired, she thought; maybe they were as drained as she was. Maybe they were just hungry.

It was possible, though the idea of eating turned her stomach. But then, all she could see was the entire roll of thick Bounty towels that it had taken to clean up Randy's blood that night, and how she had not remembered that blood gave off such a strong, sickening sweet smell.

All this time later, she had never been able to forget the garish brightness of the red-saturated paper towels as she stuffed them into a big black garbage bag.

CHAPTER 47

AFTER HER JITTERY START, Tommy noticed Gayla steadily developed a poise and presence on the witness stand. He had never been able to predict how the peculiar tension of a courtroom would affect a witness. Sometimes confident people could be shaken to the bone and fall apart, and sometimes the soft-spoken could stun you with their strength and clarity and discipline. Gayla seemed to belong to the latter group. Even talking about the circumstances surrounding Randy's death, she had kept her composure, only an occasional catch in her voice giving a hint as to how hard it was for her to replay that night for the jury.

"You look strong up there," Tommy told her, as they lunched in the witness room adjacent to court. Gayla shot him an appreciative look.

"It wasn't so bad. The toughest part was Randy's . . ."

"You handled it well. You found your bearings — you will be just fine when it comes to cross."

"I'd better. I can see Ringworm chomping at the bit."

Tommy laughed out loud. "Ringworm?"

"My pet nickname for him," she said.

Tommy arched his brows. "I know a juicy secret about him."

"What? Is there a Mrs. Ringworm?"

Tommy grinned. "I knew him in high school. He used to have a terrible receding chin and a twice-broke nose."

"No way," Gayla snorted.

"He has been under the knife more than Joan Rivers. Big time work on the jaw and nose. He's probably had his ears pinned back, too."

Now both of them were laughing.

"Rumor is he needed a boob job as well."

Gayla gasped.

"Yes," Tommy said, in mock seriousness, "the man breasts were said to be a problem at the country club pool parties."

Gayla laughed so hard she almost cried.

"That's all he is," Tommy told her, softer now, "just a man uncomfortable in his own skin. You're plenty tough enough to take him on. Just don't get cocky, and don't let him get to you."

Gayla nodded. "Leta says he's a rattlesnake, so I'm not to play his game and not to lie."

"She's right, and you're going to be fine," Tommy said.

After they returned to the courtroom, Tommy made sure Gayla could see him. Behind the defense table, Willie also offered Gayla a sympathetic face to seek out to counter the judging eyes of the press, the members of which had taken over a third of the room's seating. Judge Bishop was not about to leave any publicity stone unturned if he could help it. Not that the reporters had any sharper claws than the Elk City citizens' block. Or the locals, for that matter. Lately Luckau's cloistered mindset had been grating on Tommy more than anytime in recent memory. Goodness knows he had been on the receiving end of it himself.

Newcomers were treated like backward relatives, until they proved themselves worthy or produced four or five generations within the city limits. It had taken years for Tommy to be marginally accepted, and he knew a good many locals would always consider him an outsider. Now, of course, the burg's overinflated sense of importance was being fed daily by the cavalcade of media trucks on the streets. In this shuttered-tight community, Gayla would have been looked down on even if she had never met Albert Raeder. Tommy could not help but wonder if any members of the jury could hear her story with an open mind, without wincing and jumping to a guilty verdict just to wash their hands of it.

As the questioning restarted, Leta moved to the disposal of Randy's body. "So you followed Mr. Raeder's car yourself, driving the car you and Randy came in?"

"That's correct," Gayla answered.

"And where was Randy's body?"

"Right there beside me on the front seat."

"How did that affect you?"

"It freaked me out. I didn't want to look at him, but I couldn't stop myself. It all seemed so unreal."

"And where did Mr. Raeder lead you?"

"We drove for what seemed like a long time. Maybe half an hour, no more than an hour."

"Do you remember where you ended up?"

"Somewhere by water."

"Can you describe the setting? To the best of your ability."

"The water and a few trees on the shoreline were all I could see in the dark. It was a full moon, but a black sky, no clouds."

"And then what happened?"

"He told me to get in his car and wait. He got in the Nova and parked it on a slope right by the lake, pointed towards the water. It was like a boat dock, only graded, not paved. He pulled Randy's body over and into the driver's seat. He had a rock that he wedged against the accelerator. He put the car in gear, and it drove itself into the water. After a few minutes, it sank."

Tommy's mind jumped again to the geography around the area. He had puzzled over this before. Why could he not find the car or at least the lake with the car in it? The more places he looked, the more he began to realize it could be any one of so many places.

Counting both the natural lakes and manmade ones around Luckau, there were places to fish every thirty miles. Or, maybe, Raeder just circled around and returned to Luckau Lake, covering himself in case Gayla was sharp enough to keep track. Early on Tommy had checked for anything that had been pulled from local ponds or bodies of water the past few years. An old red Ford Fiesta was discovered submerged on the north side of Luckau Lake. Besides that, nothing else except a Honda 1500 from the Fort Cobb Reservoir.

Leta's voice brought him back to the courtroom. It was now softer, more careful. "And what happened after the Nova and Randy's body disappeared into the water, Miss Early?"

"I said, 'Are you going to let me go now?' And he laughed at me. He said he had meant to wait until we got back to the cabin to — his words — to fuck me, but he said he was too turned on to wait. He grabbed me and pushed me down on his car hood and yanked my pants down."

A new roar, from Garrison this time, rocked the room. "Objection. Objection." Even his prosecutorial buddy Ringrose, sitting right beside him, turned in surprise at his outburst.

Judge Bishop, exhausted, did not bother to make eye contact. "Sit down, sit down, Mr. Garrison. You are out of order."

Leta, always the voice of calm, directed all her attention to Gayla. "And what happened then?"

"He raped me, that's what. That was the first time."

Tommy turned sour inside with rage. Gayla looked so damn small up there in the witness chair. He remembered how many men it had taken to carry Raeder out of the basement. The thought of Raeder, with almost two hundred pounds on her, manhandling her with his hairy arms, throwing her onto the hood of a car, revolted him.

He knew he had to grab a hold of himself, pull his mind somewhere else so people could not read how deeply affected he was by what Gayla was having to go through. Otherwise, it could negate his entire earlier testimony. Okay, he reminded himself, you know all too well how to tune out. Fidel had taught him all those years ago. He retreated mentally, imagining himself floating over the action and watching himself below, listening, but detached from the testimony's emotional punch. He could almost hear the purr of his tin plane as Gayla described the ride back to Raeder's cabin.

"And when you arrived back there that night, that was when he took you down to the basement?"

"No," Gayla answered, "that wasn't until the next morning. The first night he handcuffed me to the bed in the cabin."

Tommy's chest tightened at her words, which cut through his emotional firewall.

"You slept in the same bed that night?" Leta asked.

"We were in the same bed, but I didn't sleep."

"Did anything else happen that night?"

"He raped me again. Three more times."

Tommy struggled to shut it out but failed. He felt so sick inside he thought he might have to sit down. For another hour, he listened to the awful details. How the next morning Raeder had put her in the basement, then cuffed and gagged her. How he returned later with a new dorm-room-sized fridge and the chains. How he had boarded up the windows with lattice slats and cardboard, shutting out the light.

Gayla described the two-year weekend routine. Raeder's nothing if not unpredictable behavior — sometimes dressing her up like a party girl, sometimes using her as a punching bag.

"But no matter what his mood was," Gayla testified, "he forced himself on me several times a day. He would bring takeout food with him — he would go out and get more over the course of the weekend — and he left boxes of food with me for the rest of the week, for fear I might turn anything else into either a weapon or a tool to escape."

"Objection, Your Honor. Even if this elaborate story were true, the witness has no way of knowing Mr. Raeder's thoughts."

"Overruled." It was obvious Judge Bishop was just curious enough to want to hear Gayla's tale in her own words.

"Did you suffer any consequences from this diet Mr. Raeder imposed on you," Ms. O'Reilly asked.

"Yes, after the first year, not ever having fruits and vegetables or milk made my hair start to fall out. I grew a lot weaker, and it affected other things."

"What happened after his visits were over?"

"He chained my ankle to the wall and left me with whatever food was left in the fridge, and my cot and blanket."

"How long would he leave you chained that way?"

"It might be more than a week before he came back."

"At this time, Your Honor," Leta said, "I'd like to ask the witness to show the jurors the scarring on her left ankle from being chained."

"Objection," Ringrose screamed.

Judge Bishop was too irritated by now to show any courtesy. "There's no need to shout, Counselor. I'm not deaf. Now, on what grounds?"

"There's no evidence any scars would be caused by these supposed chains," he told the judge.

"Not according to the doctor's report," Ms. O'Reilly snapped back. She picked up the exhibit containing the medical report as though to read from it.

"Never mind, I've read it," Judge Bishop sighed. "The jury can make up its own mind. I'll allow it."

Ringrose skulked back to his seat.

"Miss Early, if you would," O'Reilly said, pointing where she should stand. Leaning on her lawyer for support, Gayla pulled up her pants leg and showed her left ankle to the jurors, who looked gingerly at the shiny thick scarring that formed a rough circle around her ankle. One of the women jurors put a hand over her mouth in shock.

When Gayla was back in her seat, O'Reilly continued. "Now, Miss Early, was there other sexual abuse in addition to the forced intercourse?"

Tommy had never seen Gayla look the way she did at that moment. Embarrassed, shame-filled, overwhelmed with emotion. When she pulled herself together, her voice came out raspy.

"Yes, there was."

"Can you tell the court about those events?"

Gayla coughed and tried to start.

Leta waited patiently. "Take all the time you need."

"The first time, he had brought a six-pack of longneck beer with him. He was mad about some business deal that hadn't gone through. He forced me to have sex and started punching me. I complained. He said he'd give me something to complain about. He took one of the bottles . . ."

After several awkward moments, Leta offered: "You stated in your deposition that he pushed the bottle into your vagina. Is that correct?"

A thick silence dropped over the courtroom. Tommy was so stunned and nauseated he could not move. To hear the details spoken aloud was almost unbearable.

Ringrose interrupted. "Your Honor, who's testifying here, the lawyer or the defendant?"

Judge Bishop said quietly, "I'll allow it."

"Is that what happened, Miss Early?" Leta asked gently.

"Yes," Gayla said. "He did it several times over the two years."

Leta stepped closer. "And were there any other objects that Albert Raeder used to sexually violate you?"

Gayla's voice had dropped to a whisper. "Yes. A mop handle."

The room of spectators sucked in a collective breath. In the moment of silence that followed, the only sound in the room was the metallic click, click, click of the ceiling fan.

"Did Mr. Raeder ever tell you why he did that to you?"

"Yes," Gayla said, clearing her throat. "He said his older cousins had done the same thing to him when he was young. But they had done it to his . . . rear end."

Ringrose sounded hoarse. "Objection. Hearsay."

Judge Bishop took a second. "Sustained. Jury will disregard the defendant's last statement."

But neither the objection nor the ruling made any difference to the hushed, shocked courtroom. They had heard what was said. Now they were struggling to process it.

Judge Bishop coughed, then announced, "It's five o'clock. Court will be in recess until tomorrow morning."

Perspiration trickled down Tommy's face and neck.

He tried to look into Gayla's eyes. He wanted to show her it made no difference to him what hideous things had been done to her, but he never quite made eye contact — instead he rushed to the bathroom so he would not throw up in public.

CHAPTER 48

GAYLA STARED AT THE COLD pizza left from the night's takeout meal with Leta. The day's testimony had leached the life out of her. She was grateful when Leta cut short their usual end-of-day talk and left to prepare for another grueling day of court tomorrow.

Tommy was working the night shift. Gayla marveled at how he managed. He was always there for her during the day in the courtroom, yet was still pulling half the night shifts at the jail as well. Over the past months, the two had settled into their own evening rhythm of dinner and conversation before turning in.

Tonight he had yet to come around. Gayla figured she knew why. It had been too much to expect that she would not seem different, less than, in his eyes after today's testimony. She sat cross-legged on the cot, too wired to rest, but too tired to do anything else but gaze at the colors of twilight peeping through her cell window. She had just about resigned herself to a night of her own company, when she heard the familiar sound of Tommy's boots headed towards her cell.

Unlike all the nights before, he wore jeans and a cowboy shirt.

"Out of uniform tonight."

He looked strangely mischievous. "Yep."

"What's up?"

His answer was to pass her a pair of jeans and a hoodie through the cell bars with a request that she holler when dressed. At her call, he reappeared, unlocked her cell, and motioned for her to follow him.

What's going on? Gayla wondered.

Tommy sensed her puzzlement.

"Just trust me, okay?"

"Okay," Gayla said.

He led her to the back door of the county jail and peered outside.

"Just in case reporters are hovering," he explained. "Coast is clear. Follow me."

Night was fast approaching, and salmon-colored streaks pushed across the gray-blue sky. It was the first time Gayla had been outside in months when not headed either to or from court. The air blew clean with the chill of November and a ripe lake undertone.

Tommy motioned her down a shrub-lined path that curved away from the jail and into an area thick with pecan trees. His aunt's old push-button-transmission Dodge sat parked on a back street. Luck was with them. No media sniffing around. They got in.

As he put the key in the ignition, Tommy said, "Duck low in the seat until we get out of town."

A few minutes later, the smell of cedar and pine told her they must be nearing a lake. "Okay, at ease," Tommy said, "I think we made it."

Gayla sat up. She almost asked where they were headed but instead found herself content to hang her head out the side passenger window and let the cool night air rush over her face.

"This is like when I was a teenager," she said. "I loved cruising with the windows down."

"You, too?" Tommy said.

"Back then I couldn't wait to sneak out of the house at night, but once out, I rarely knew where I wanted to go."

"Just drive into the wee hours. That's what I did," Tommy said. "Sometimes I still do."

"What are we doing, anyway? Are you breaking me out of jail?" She gave a nervous little laugh.

"I thought we'd check out a few lakes tonight. See if anything looks familiar."

Of course, looking for Randy's body. Made perfect sense. He was the law. So why does a part of me feel disappointed, she wondered.

"Good idea," she said quickly. "I just hope I'll know it if I see it."

"Maybe something will feel right or kick up some memories. If we could narrow the possibilities, I could maybe get some divers down. Dudgeon would try to block it, but I could justify it if we could only pinpoint a location."

"It's worth a shot," Gayla said, "but what if somebody calls the jail?"

"I have Frankie Lee on call, and the jail phone forwards to my cell. We're safe."

The miles passed, and their chitchat slipped into a relaxed back and forth. Tommy circled Fort Cobb Lake, an unshapely body of water with dozens of boat docks, both official and unofficial. Nothing seemed familiar to Gayla, so they headed on to Foss, a prettier lake with lots of trees.

"It's strange," Gayla said. "These trees remind me of seeing this little sapling that night. It was almost ghostly, with tiny, lacy branches. It was weird to notice a tree in the middle of that hideous night, but I still remember how graceful it looked."

"I get that," Tommy said. "When you're that scared — well, terrified, really — all your senses are at full throttle. They say you are never more alive than when you know you are about to die. The air is sweeter. You notice everything."

"You say that like someone who knows."

"When I was shot down in 'Nam I spent every day expecting it to be my last. Even now, if I let myself, I can still smell the jungle, sweet and rotten at the same time; I can feel the heat that sucked away your breath; and I can recall the way green blanketed everything and the wide eyes of the kids who came to stare at the Yankee prisoner behind the bamboo stakes. Yeah, I know."

She patted his knee and let her hand linger. "Maybe we both do."

None of the Foss Lake locations seemed right to her either, so they circled back around to Lake Luckau. Here, Tommy knew all the nooks and crannies, but after another hour of driving by one spot and then another, nothing had jumped out at Gayla.

"I'm sorry. This has been a complete waste, I'm afraid."

"Oh, I wouldn't say that." He smiled at her.

They wound their way towards what Tommy said was the last spot on his list. Gayla watched the last patches of lilac bleeding off the darkening sky. Tommy stopped the car where it couldn't be seen from the road and cut the engine. Gayla looked around and said, "I don't think this is it either."

"That's okay. Let's get out, stretch our legs."

"Good idea." She climbed out of the car and looked up at the sun, which had dropped in the sky almost to the horizon. "A sunset. It's been so long."

He grinned. "I know. Be right back." Tommy went round to the trunk of the car and unloaded an armload of firewood.

"You didn't," Gayla said, little-girl-thrilled, "but what if somebody sees us?"

"Nobody knows this spot. I've been hiding out here for years. Here, help me find some rocks to make a ring."

In the dwindling light, they built a fire ring and Tommy started a tipi-style fire, like they had taught him in Boy Scouts. As the flames flickered to life, the sky dimmed into darkness. Small waves licked the shore.

"You warm enough?" Tommy asked, sitting down beside her.

"Perfect." She sensed a new energy between them, a little awkward, but nice. "You had this planned."

"You needed a sunset," he said in that brusque way men have when they want to downplay their emotions or not expose too much for fear of getting shut down. They sat quietly, lulled by the lapping water, the crackling wood, and the dangling parchment moon now just above the horizon.

"You know, I'm really not a bad girl."

Tommy leaned away and looked at her. "What?"

"No matter how all this turns out, I want you to know that."

"I never thought you were."

"But you see the way the jury and all those people look at me, especially after today. I see it. I'm not stupid."

"What do you think they're thinking?"

"The men just see a slut. They write me off as gutter trash, even though they can't help being curious at the same time. Wondering what's it like, with girls who put out."

"Unlike a lot of their wives, I bet," Tommy threw in with a chuckle.

Gayla laughed, wryly. "Yeah, probably. The women are even worse though. They write me off as a girl who uses sex to get whatever she wants."

Tommy shook his head. "Oh, come on."

"You know they do. I just want you to know that's not who I am at all. That's what kills me. Sex was hush-hush at our house. My mom taught me to be scared of it. One time when she caught me kissing some boys in the garage — I was maybe six — she went ballistic. I was like, 'Why are you spanking me? What did I do?' "

Tommy nodded, listening quietly.

"So boys, flirting — all unfamiliar territory to me. Even when I got old enough that it was okay to like boys, I always felt out of step. Like everybody knew what to do but me. I've gone most of my life trying to ignore my body — not using it. When I got lost in drugs and — well, you know what all I did then — it was never real. I was ashamed, and I sure didn't enjoy it. I don't think I even felt it. By then, pretty much anything below my neck was numb. A wasteland."

She sighed and gazed up at the indigo sky. The stars, thick and bright, cut through the darkness. She looked over at Tommy, who still stared into the fire.

"Wow, I didn't expect all that to come out. Now I've embarrassed you," Gayla said.

"No, not at all." But Tommy appeared uncomfortable.

"Sometimes I pick up these feelings from you . . . then you retreat," Gayla said, not sure if she should venture farther. "I thought maybe you were afraid you'd be touching something dirty."

"Oh, Gayla!" Tommy's voice choked. "It's not like that at all."

Gayla plunged on. "Because I would understand, really, I would. I've read about women who've been kidnapped or raped, you know. Sometimes even if they are rescued and go back to their families, their husbands consider them untouchable. Ruined. Like me."

Tommy put his arm around her and pulled her close.

"I don't think of you that way at all. Really. You are the greatest natural beauty I have ever known inside and out. It's not that I don't care about you. I do. Deeply." His voice shook. "It's me. I can't . . . It kills me, but . . ."

"It's okay, Tommy." Gayla tried to cover her embarrassment by shouldering the blame. "I would probably have freaked out if anything happened, anyway. I'm still such a mess myself."

Tommy did not say anything for a long time, but she could see he was pained, wrestling something deep inside of him. Finally, he took her hand. His fingers trembled.

"I know something about what you went through," he said. "After I was shot down in 'Nam, they took me to a place called The Zoo. Where a man, a monster, really, named Fidel. . . he was my Raeder."

Tommy's story came out in spurts at first, as he described his filthy, wet cell, then the endless sessions of sexual torture. The two bruised souls sat side by side, hands locked tight. They stared into the fire, as Tommy shared his own tales from hell: the ferocity of Fidel's electro-shock baton, the deviant mind of his captor, and the cruel way he played Tommy off against the rest of the prisoners, all but branding him as an informant.

"Today, when you talked about Raeder's cousins raping him . . ." He sighed deeply. "I know about that, too — a lot of us in the war did."

Gayla asked few questions. Instead, she listened, pained for him and what he had suffered but also relieved that someone else had been there, too . . . someone else knew what it was like to look like everyone else in the room but to feel disfigured.

Later, Tommy, looking spent, said, "By the time the war ended I felt nobody could understand. Hell, I didn't understand it. I buried myself alive. Hid out in drugs. Thought how stupid I had been to volunteer for our shitty little war, and when I got home . . . no parades, just embarrassment for us. It was the excuse I needed to run away from everything and everybody."

"What about your family? Your parents?" Gayla asked.

"My folks both died in a car accident while I was in The Zoo. I didn't find out until I came home. It all still hurts. You would think after thirty years . . ."

Gayla wrapped her arms around his waist and rocked gently against him. "Even broken lives have value," she told him. "Dr. Hudson says sometimes they're even more precious. Now I understand what she meant. That you would share all that with me. I can't tell you how much that means."

The fire flickered out. They watched as the stars blurred together in the reflection of the lake's ripples. But after a few moments, the wind quieted, and the lake's surface grew mirror-still. Then the stars reflected so sharply on the water that Tommy and Gayla could almost count them.

CHAPTER 49

ALTHOUGH WILLIE HAD a reserved seat behind the defense, it was like running the bulls of Pamplona to reach it. The reporters and curiosity-seekers had elbows of steel. She had arrived earlier today in order to visit with Gayla at the jail for a minute, in hopes of bolstering the girl's confidence.

When Gayla stepped down from the witness stand yesterday, she had been as pale as death, as if her life's blood had been drained. But this morning, she seemed to have had a transfusion. And she is going to need it, Willie thought. When the prosecution's gloves come off, they will be as relentless as zombies in a spooky movie.

But first Leta had to take Gayla through the climax of the story, the day Raeder died. With that on tap, the spectators were squished together, like they had been blown into place by a fire hose. Sheriff Dudgeon, who rarely missed a day of court, hovered in the back. Dixie and Joe Nguyen showed up, sitting close to Mrs. Raeder, who had not appeared since being a witness. Willie felt sure the prosecution had pressured the widow to show up. They wanted her to remind the court that she was the victim in this ordeal, not some stranger with a cock-and-bull story of sexual imprisonment. On the back wall, Sheriff Maynard looked snappy in his uniform.

Gayla looked pretty great herself in the new jade pantsuit Willie had brought to jail for her this morning. Willie had read somewhere that people tend to trust you more if you are wearing something the color of your eyes. And she thought the pantsuit was a perfect match.

Leta led Gayla through a brief recap as a way to build up to Raeder's death. How Raeder had made it to the cabin almost every single weekend, sometimes dropping in on her during the week if he was out showing some real estate in the area. How he had fed her downers to soften her painful withdrawal from crack, although Gayla knew she was going to die anyway, and so didn't see the point.

"How long during this two-year period did you use the Valium and other prescription drugs he brought you?" Leta asked.

"For most of the first year. He would bring pot sometimes, or Percocet or Demerol — prescription stuff — when he came for weekends. And always beer and vodka." Gayla answered, her eyes straight ahead.

"Did he ever explain how he obtained these prescriptions and illegal drugs?"

"No. Just said he knew people."

"Did Mr. Raeder ever talk about his own drug use?"

"Objection!" Ringrose jumped up. "No drug use by the victim has been established."

Judge Bishop appeared stunned; he had been handed a dramatic moment earlier in the day than he had expected. He squinted hard in thought, then pronounced, "I'll allow it."

Off Leta's nod, Gayla continued. "He said he used Oxycontin on a daily basis, and he also did whatever other drugs he brought with him."

"And did there come a time when you stopped using those drugs?"

"Yes. After I finally got off the crack, I was depressed for a long time, even though I felt better physically. For months after that, I would swallow anything — downers, painkillers, whatever — that he brought, in hopes that it would make me feel better."

"And that was when he was there with you?"

"Yes."

"How did you get through the week?"

"He left me with enough to last until he returned."

"Did you ration them out, so you could get through the week?"

"Mostly, yes. A couple of times I tried to take them all at once."

"Why did you do that?"

"Well, to kill myself."

At her response, a nervous rumble ran through the crowd. Willie's heart went out to her. She had always tried to value Gayla's privacy over Willie's own morbid curiosity, so it was a question she had never asked. But a part of Willie always knew Gayla surely had tried suicide. Had Willie not tried to do the same during her own self-imposed sentence — chugging whole fifths, hoping to saturate her organs with enough booze to reach a deadly blood alcohol level. But she had always passed out before it could kill her. She'd wake, barely able to remember what had brought her to such a state, wondering how she'd lived through it . . . who had been watching over her?

Who had watched over Gayla, she wondered, this scared, damaged soul, as she endured the unimaginable?

After she took Gayla in and grew fond of her so quickly, Willie had hoped she could help change Gayla's life for the better. It was a shock to gradually realize just the opposite was happening. Willie found it miraculous that Gayla still had love and compassion left in her. She marveled at the way the girl had cried for the lowly chickens caught by the coyotes, the wonder in her eyes at a pearly white string of stars. It had to do with what Willie's dad called a person's constitution, an elusive strength or weakness that left some lost and done for after middling challenges, and others able to go on in the face of unspeakable wrongs or tragedy. Leta's voice pulled her back to the courtroom.

"So, except for the unsuccessful suicide attempts, in the second year you gradually stopped taking the pills he brought you. What about weekends, when he brought recreational drugs for the both of you?"

"I got good at faking it. He was so used to me swallowing anything, I don't think he ever noticed that I wasn't."

"Why did you become so determined not to take the drugs?"

"It dawned on me that if I didn't do something I was going to die in that basement. Even if I had a chance to escape, I was afraid I would be too strung out to take advantage of it. I started to pray for help. I became determined to survive. So I got clean. And I started to exercise to get some of my physical strength back."

"And did a time come when an opportunity to escape did arise?"

"Yes."

"Please tell us about that, in your own words."

"That day Mr. Raeder had arrived later than usual, and he was agitated. I knew I was probably in for it," Gayla said.

"How could you tell?" Leta drew closer to the stand.

"He was cursing as he stomped down the steps to the basement, and while he was unlocking my ankle chain, he was complaining, 'That eff-ing bitch did it again.' "

"Objection," Ringrose shouted.

Willie, along with a good many of the other locals, took a good side-long look at the Widow Raeder, who had turned the color of bleached fish bones.

"Overruled," Bishop said.

"And what did he mean by that?" Leta continued.

"It meant Mrs. Raeder — he called her 'the bitch' — had set him off about something."

"Did he say what?"

"He kept saying over and over, 'She'll spread her legs for anything that moves except me.' "

Uh oh, Willie thought, watching the free fall of the widow's face. Bad day to return to court. Those legs must be jelly or else she would be scuttling out by now. Willie appreciated the *schadenfreude*.

Leta asked, "Did he explain any more than that?"

"Just rambled on about some pretty boy," Gayla said, her pitch ris-ing. "I tried to kiss him to calm him down — that usually worked — but he was too mad. He pushed me away and told me to strip. He was as furious as I had ever seen him. He was squeezing my arms so hard I was crying. He hadn't even taken his pants off he was in such a rush. I kept trying to tell him that he was hurting me, but he wouldn't listen."

"And then what happened?"

"He sort of choked, or gasped. I couldn't see his face, he was behind me. Then he sort of fell on me, groaning. I struggled out from under him, and when I turned around, he was grabbing his chest."

Gayla's face flushed as she recalled the moment.

"At that point, what went through your mind?" Leta asked.

"I realized I wasn't chained up, that this might be my chance. He was moving around in circles, choppy-like. I ran to the window and pulled at the boards and cardboard he had nailed there. I heard him grunt and come towards me. He tackled me, but I got away from him. I grabbed at a two-by-four held in place by only a few rusty nails and used all my weight to pull it off."

"Where was Mr. Raeder during this time?"

"He had fallen to his knees but was still crawling towards me, cursing me. I broke the glass behind the boards and screamed out the window for somebody to please help, but I didn't expect anybody to hear me."

"At this point, how far away from you was Mr. Raeder?"

"Only a few feet. While I was screaming for help, I felt his hand clamp on my ankle."

As though reliving every detail, Gayla was now breathing hard and trembling.

Ringrose jumped up. "Perhaps a break to allow the witness to compose herself, Your Honor?"

Yeah, Willie thought, what he wouldn't give to dilute how this might affect the jury.

Judge Bishop leaned down towards Gayla and spoke low. "Are you all right, Miss Early?"

"I'm okay," Gayla said quickly, swiping at damp cheeks.

The judge nodded at Leta, who quickly resumed her line of questioning. "So he had managed to reach you and grab your leg."

"Yes."

"What did you do then?"

"I had the piece of wood I'd pulled off the window in my hand, and I swung it at him, but he still wouldn't let go of my leg. So I hit him again. I hit him until he let go of me."

"How many times did you strike him?"

"I don't know — until he let me loose. Then he slumped back and his eyes closed. I thought he had passed out."

"And what did you do then?"

"I ran back to the window and kept trying to pry away the rest of the boards covering it. The whole time I was yelling as loud as I could in hopes that somebody would hear me and come help. I just stood there jumping up and down, screaming for someone to please help me."

"What happened next?"

"I was frantic. It all happened so fast. I started back across the room, heading up the stairs to try the trapdoor. He had always told me I would never be able to get out that way, but I had never understood what he meant. And that day I didn't know what else to try."

"And Mr. Raeder was passed out on the floor at this point?"

"I thought so, yes. But as I went by him, he grabbed my ankle again. I sprawled out on the concrete. He had this death grip. He looked weird; his face was contorted. And he croaked, 'Low life bitch.' And I grabbed the board and started hitting him again, fighting him off. I just knew if I didn't finish it, well, I knew he'd kill me if I gave him the chance."

A thick quiet descended over the courtroom, as each observer formed his own picture of the scene. The jury, which had seen the autopsy photographs of Raeder's dead, raw face, probably had the most visually accurate picture, Willie thought, but anyone who had watched the emotions racing across Gayla's face had seen the horror the scene still held for her.

Gayla, the hunted, had finally turned the table on the hunter. She had fought for her survival and won. She had survived but at a cost. Something inside was left damaged. It was almost like looking through to Gayla's skeletal face. For just an instant, Willie glimpsed that hollow spot, the deadness behind her eyes. She had seen it in the faces of old soldiers when they let down their guard. She had seen it in Tommy's face. Yes, they were all survivors, just like Gayla, and just like Gayla, they had each and every one of them left something behind in that dark valley of death, as well as something that still sat inside them like a poison seed.

As she listened to Gayla testify about the rest of her escape and her final arrival at Willie's house, Willie wondered for the first time about Albert Raeder. What had gone through his mind in those final moments? What strength had it taken to hang on to her, even as he was under attack from his own heart. What had taken over?

Willie looked over at the widow Raeder, now mummified in her courtroom chair.

Suddenly Willie realized exactly what must have gone through Raeder's mind as he lay dying: It was those women's fault.

Always those damn bitches.

CHAPTER 50

A LUNCH OF CHEESEBURGER and fries had been forced into her somehow, Gayla downing it only in the hopes that its greasy content might ground the flying monkeys in her stomach. As wrenching as the morning had been, she knew the afternoon would be worse, an endless minefield of questions meant to trip her up. When the judge called on Ringrose to proceed with cross, Gayla could smell his expensive after-shave as soon as he stood up. As she watched his large, manicured fingers opening her file, she unconsciously rubbed the calloused edges of her own neglected hands.

He looked up at her, holding her eyes for a moment.

"Good afternoon, Miss Early."

She nodded to him.

"Let's start at the beginning, shall we?"

Don't answer anything that isn't a direct question, Gayla reminded herself. Leta had warned her that he would try to take her down that old we're-just-chums-here-talking path, but she was not to fall for it. With uncharacteristic crudeness, Leta had reminded her, "Remember this douche bag is setting up his run for higher office. He will preen any way he can, but don't you assist him."

"Very well," Ringrose said, as if her lack of response was fine with him. "As a teenager, you sneaked out drinking, isn't that correct?"

Gayla counted to three before answering, as Leta had instructed her to do. "Yes."

"Without your parents' permission, correct?"

"Correct." Gayla kept her voice quiet and calm.

"So you lied to your parents?"

"Objection. He's putting words in her mouth," Leta said.

"Overruled."

Ringrose smiled at the judge, then back to Gayla. "Did you lie to your parents about those nights?"

Three seconds. "I didn't tell them, no."

"So you lied."

Leta, exasperated. "Objection. He's badgering the witness."

The judge looked grave through slit eyes. "Sustained. Move on, Mr. Ringrose." Leta sighed, glad to have nipped it in the bud.

"When you sneaked out as a teenager, did you go out with boys as well as girls?" Ringrose said, while looking to the judge as though to show how fair he was being.

"Yes."

"Were these steady boyfriends?"

"No."

"Was there sex involved in this after-hours partying?"

"Objection," Leta said. "Relevance?"

"I'll allow it," the judge said, nodding to Gayla.

"There was some playing around."

"Was there kissing?"

"Yes."

"Necking?"

"Yes."

"With how many of them did you engage in intercourse?"

Before Leta could object, Gayla jumped in. "None."

"Really?"

"Asked and answered, Your Honor," Leta said, rebounding.

"When did you first have intercourse?"

"Objection. Irrelevant."

Judge Bishop frowned at Ringrose. "Both of you, approach."

Gayla tried to hear the arguments but could not catch their whispers. Her mind flashed to her supposed first time. Stevie somebody. When it was over, she didn't think they had actually done the deed, because Stevie came before he got it in, but he was a big football jock and tried to push it on in anyway, limp and noodly as it was. She was pretty sure this did not count, but she knew better than to laugh at him. Now she could not even remember his last name. The best thing about it had been that he had sweet breath, a good boom box, and U2 had been playing.

The confab adjourned at the bench and Gayla put her game face back on. Ringrose was smiling as though things had gone splendidly, but Leta didn't seem unhappy either. She announced, "Your Honor, the defense stipulates that the defendant was sexually active before she met Mr. Raeder." Gayla wasn't fooled, she knew plenty more probing lay ahead. Leta had reminded her earlier that morning to expect it. "We knew this was coming after our motion to limit testimony on this failed."

Now it was Ringrose's turn.

"You had, in fact, traded sexual favors for drugs, is that not correct?"

"Asked and answered," Leta showing some irritation. "Is this cross or does Counsel just want to reiterate the direct testimony?"

Judge Bishop agreed. "Move along, Mr. Ringrose."

"Now, when you worked at Dallas Memorial Hospital, what percentage of the time would you say you were high on drugs?"

"I'm not sure."

"Did you ever tell your supervisors you were high while on duty?"

"No."

"So you lied to them as well."

"Objection," Leta said.

"Withdrawn," Ringrose said quickly. "Now how was it that you and this Randy fellow had come to hear about the Raeder cabin?"

"Randy had heard about it. I don't know for sure how."

"But there was no jewelry there. Was there?"

"We never made it to that part of the cabin."

"But you had told Randy you were an expert on jewelry. Was that a lie as well?"

Leta objected, but the judge overruled her.

"I never told him I was an expert. Just that I could tell what was fake and what was real."

Ringrose flipped open a file. "An inventory of the cabin after the crime shows no jewelry at all there, so had you tricked him into —"

"Your Honor, no crime was reported the night of the original robbery. Is Counsel referring to some inventory after that incident?" Leta paused, deliberately waiting for a decision from Judge Bishop.

Caught scrambling the details and timeline, Ringrose colored a little. Loftier than necessary, he said, "Your Honor, we are assuming that since there was no safe there when Mr. Raeder was brutally murdered, there never had been one."

"Strained logic, I must say," Leta responded. "But more important, he's trying to confuse the witness, Your Honor."

Gayla watched her lawyer with awe. What a pistol. Leta was a fighter who relished giving and taking the punches. She had channeled her frustrations, her petiteness, and her brains into an arena where she could not only compete but beat up someone twice her size.

Leta threw another verbal punch. "Is there a question here?"

Ringrose, as though this were all so simple if only the defense counsel could grasp it: "Well, Your Honor, we have only the defendant's word that there was jewelry at the location. For all we know, she set up this whole thing and lied about the jewelry to get him to bring her along."

"Then ask her that," Judge Bishop snapped, clearly unhappy that the afternoon had gotten off to a rocky start.

"Did you have any knowledge about the Raeder cabin and its content before you drove to Luckau?"

"Nothing specific," Gayla said.

"What kinds of items did this Randy pick out for you to put in the bag you were holding?"

"Some bronze statuettes, some sterling silver serving pieces. He wasn't happy with what we found."

"How was that?"

"The place was furnished more like a cabin. Other than a collection of Kachina dolls, there weren't many valuables."

"Where did Raeder get his supposed shotgun when he entered the cabin that night?"

"I don't know. I heard a cabinet door, or something like that, open and close after he came in, so I figured he took it from a gun rack."

"But you said there were no lights on in the house."

"That's right."

Ringrose turned to the judge — his exasperation obvious.

"Your Honor, Prosecution refers to Exhibit 22, which shows no shotgun was found on the premises, and no shotgun is listed in its inventory."

Leta jumped up. "Your Honor, that inventory was taken after Mr. Raeder's death, not after the initial robbery. Once again, Counsel is trying to scramble the dates to confuse the jury."

"Stick to the correct year, Counsel."

Ringrose turned back to Gayla. "So it was dark inside the cabin. How could Mr. Raeder even know you were there?"

"After Randy picked the front lock, we left the door ajar. He must have noticed it when he came in."

"Does violence turn you on, Miss Early?"

Gayla started at the unexpected question. Leta glared.

"Objection, Your Honor."

Judge Bishop sat there, hands tugging at his cheeks as he considered his move. Gayla felt frazzled. Ringrose was jumping all over the place. And why was the judge taking so long with this objection?

The judge finally ruled: "I'll allow it, but watch where you go with this, Mr. Ringrose."

"Of course, Your Honor," Ringrose said, with a deferential nod, then swiveling to the witness. "Does violence turn you on?"

"No." Although Gayla had to admit the thought of choking Ringrose at that moment had its appeal.

Ringrose tapped a folder on top of a stack of papers on his table. "But your psychologist, Miss Hudson, said in her report that you experienced orgasms when you had sex with Mr. Raeder."

Whispers erupted in the courtroom.

"Objection," Leta cried. "The witness can't testify about her psychologist's findings."

"Why not?" Ringrose retorted, looking at the judge. "She had the orgasms."

Gayla looked down in shame. Leta had told Gayla she was hoping to bypass these kinds of questions, which is why she had not brought it up during Dr. Hudson's testimony, but when Ringrose obliquely set it up during his cross of Dr. Hudson, Leta had known they had probably failed and to be ready for it.

Now Ringrose was going to make Gayla take it. Gayla noticed that the jurors looked at her like they had just smelled something nasty.

The spotlight returned to Judge Bishop, and everyone in the courtroom held a collective breath to hear what he would rule. With every eye on him, he savored the moment. Gayla knew this line of questioning could quickly go south. If allowed any latitude, Ringrose would brand her as a fun-loving, conniving whore.

Finally, the judge announced, "Overruled. The witness may answer."

Leta looked thunderstruck. "Your Honor, I want my objections to this line of questioning entered into the record."

Annoyed, Judge Bishop nodded his head at her. "So noted."

Ringrose, sharpening for the kill, said sweetly. "Should I repeat the question?" Then without even giving her time to respond, he asked the question again. "Very well. Does violence turn you on, Miss Early?"

Gayla felt her face reddening. "It does not."

"And yet, in your sessions with Miss Hudson, you admitted that you had orgasms during sex with Mr. Raeder, did you not?"

"What happened was because of —"

"It's a yes or no question. Did you or did you not?"

"It was explained to me that —"

Ringrose swept his hand in the air towards her, as if to say *I can't do anything with her.* "Will the witness please answer either yes or no?"

Leta intervened now. "Objection. The witness is trying to explain."

Ringrose scoffed. "Either she did have orgasms or she didn't, Your Honor. It is not a halfway deal."

Laughter sputtered from some of the spectators. Judge Bishop rapped his gavel. "Order, order. This proceeding will be orderly. Miss Early, a yes or no, please."

Leta rose to her feet. "Your Honor . . ."

"You can clarify on redirect, Counsel. But the Prosecution gets his answer."

Gayla slumped mentally. She looked at the jury. She feared there would be no overcoming this; she could envision no later explanation that could change their perception of what was said in this moment. Whatever image they had forged of her as a victim could be lost in a heartbeat. She could already see the women jurors mentally shielding themselves from her: the men, turning cool and aloof. Meanwhile Ringrose had actually expanded his arms, like a minister praying over his flock.

"Did you have orgasms with Mr. Raeder, Miss Early?"

"Some, yes," she said, defeated and angry.

She tried to remember that in one of their strategy sessions, Leta had warned her, if it came up, the only thing worse than having to admit to it was to deny it. If the jury thought she lied about that, then they could be convinced she was lying about everything else.

"Only some? That sounds strange, since you say the two of you were having sex almost every weekend, several times a day."

Leta pounced: "I don't hear a question, Your Honor."

Ringrose addressed Gayla again, almost mocking now.

"Did you or did you not say you had sex several times a day almost every weekend?"

Gayla felt like she was hanging off the side of a cliff with no safety harness, but if she was going to be left dangling, she was going to sneak in everything she could. "Forced sex, yes."

"So you say."

"Actually I would say rape."

Gayla caught a sharp glance from Leta, who did not look unhappy with her unsolicited retort but who also seemed to be cautioning her: *Careful now. Stay on track.*

Ringrose ignored her answer. "With all the sex you were having with Mr. Raeder, how was it you never got pregnant?"

"My menstrual cycles have been nonexistent for more than two years now," Gayla said, simply.

"And was that due to your crack addiction?"

"That was when my system started shutting down, yes."

"And even after, according to you, when Mr. Raeder helped wean you from the crack, you still missed your menstrual cycles?"

"Yes, I did."

"Can you understand how unbelievable that sounds to the court, Miss Early?"

"Objection."

"Sustained. Save it for close, Counselor."

But Ringrose stayed on message. "Can you offer any plausible reason as to how you could not become pregnant during two presumed years of sustained, unprotected sexual activity?"

"Objection," Leta cried out.

"Sustained," Judge Bishop shouted.

Ringrose preened and asked Gayla again.

"Can you give any plausible cause for how you avoided pregnancy over two years of regular, unprotected sex, Miss Early?"

Gayla saw her opening.

"The same state of fear that causes atypical orgasms."

There, she thought. The jury might not know what to think, but she had gotten it in. Whether they could or would connect the psychological dots was beyond her control.

It was equally difficult for her to tell what Ringrose thought of her answer, as he proceed to exhaustively take her back over her direct testimony. He questioned her for several more hours, but Gayla thought he ended up boring the jury with his constant picking at details.

When he sat down, Leta jumped back in on redirect and offered parts of Dr. Hudson's report that explained the traumatic underpinnings of atypical orgasms in rape victims, but the jury looked either confused or disbelieving, Gayla could not tell which.

And, then, just like that, it was over. The grueling questions and answers done. She could not say how the jury seemed. It was naive to believe her truth would somehow win out, anyway. Everyone clutches to their own truth, after all. Maybe hers was no more true than Raeder's.

It did occur to her that the only time she had been asked why Albert had done such things to her was when she had testified about the bottle rape. Oh, the other things she could have told them. How he had drunkenly cried into the night about his love for her, his "little sweetie girl," about his joke of a marriage. When he was way out there, he would sometimes sob about the older cousins he loathed for abusing him in the old storage shed. He had only been five when their cruel poking around at his little pecker had shifted any natural childish discovery down a darker, unnatural path.

During one crying jag that lasted into the dawn, he had confided that as a teenager, he could only get a hard on when he hurt himself . . . or hurt someone else, like the animals he had tortured as a child, or those same cousins he had systematically paid back. Yes, he had confessed to her to beating and stabbing his cousins, never saying for sure if that had resulted in only maiming or, as he hinted, perhaps death. He would be bawling so loud during these confessions, that she could not catch all of it, especially after his voice and thoughts rambled into incoherence. He had always recanted these sessions, with a gruff abruptness, the next day, but they had rung too true for her to believe his later denials. She was sure that his drunken, painful stories of abuse as a boy were absolutely the truth. In spite of herself, she had felt sympathy for him.

He was not a monster, really. He was more like a raging black energy that had never found a home. All those years later, still despising his cousins, still torturing others, still hating himself . . .

Yes, she thought, it is just as well you are gone, Albert.

Nobody in this courtroom would believe your story either.

CHAPTER 51

TOMMY SAT BURIED AMIDST unsorted piles of clothes on his couch, wrestling with an insistent urge to head down the road and score some pot. He knew from recent experience that if he could go even a few minutes without giving in to the craving, it would probably go away. That was why he had started picking up the sea of empty takeout sacks, even cleaned his kitchen. But later, as he leaned over his mobile-home-sized sink and stared out the sliver of window above it, the itch remained. The moon that stared back at him was fat and luminous. The wolves are out tonight, he thought. Hungry and on the prowl. He understood their hunger.

Twenty minutes later, when he found himself cruising through thick green moonlight in his aunt's hydromatic Dodge, he did not let himself analyze it. He just hunkered down and drove. So when he turned onto a different road headed to the most unlikely of spots, no one was more surprised than he. And even though it was after midnight, Willie Morris had let him in, without a fuss even, and made hot chocolate for them both.

"It's just instant," Willie said, handing it to him in a worn Fiestaware mug, "but it's not bad." She wore a chenille robe with a threadbare hem.

Tommy nodded his thanks. He had noticed piles of boxes, half filled, when he came in.

"Getting packed up, huh?" he asked. "I never did hear who bought the place."

"Couple of silly kids. They have no idea what they're in for."

"What are you going to do?"

She shrugged. "Don't really know yet."

Studying her face, Tommy noticed how much her frown lines and drawn demeanor had softened.

"Not knowing doesn't seem to be bothering you."

"It's not. Go figure that one, huh?" She sipped a little cocoa. "You, on the other hand, don't look so good. What's wrong?" Then, as though the thought had just dawned on her: "Oh no, is Gayla okay?"

"Yeah, everything and everyone is fine at the jail. Honestly, I'm not sure why I'm here. I was going stir-crazy at my place, so I got in the car and ended up here. Maybe it's the full moon."

"You're under a lot of pressure right now."

Tommy wrinkled his forehead. "Maybe that's it. I don't know."

"That's when I always reached for the bottle." Off his look, Willie put her hands up in gentle protest. "Don't worry, I'm not psychic. It's more like radar. You may be a stoner instead of a drunk but same difference. I knew that look as soon as I opened the door."

Tommy's shoulders dropped in relief. Somebody had recognized it without judgment. He studied his hands. "I haven't gotten high in more than two months now. Then, tonight . . ."

"It sneaks up when you least expect it."

Tommy nodded. "I probably would have ended up scoring. That's where I was headed, but for some reason I turned into your driveway instead of going on to my old dealer's."

Willie laughed. "And that's hardly a natural detour for you, is it?"

"Not hardly." Tommy glanced up at her. "Look, I know you've never liked me much, but lately it . . . we seem to be getting along."

"I like you just fine now, Sheriff. Let me say that right off. And yes, I used to not like you, but then I used to find fault with just about everybody. Hell, if I knew you, I probably hated you."

They both laughed at the truth in her words.

"I've been working on improving that. Truth is I resented you because you reminded me of myself, back when I was tearing through people's lives like a tornado."

"Well, I have to say you're not the cranky ole grouch I thought you were, either."

"Well, we got that settled. Now, what about this sudden urge to get high?" He looked up but didn't say anything, so Willie went on. "Okay, I'll start. Anybody with half a brain can see you're in love with her. If you can't own that, then you will certainly find yourself back rolling joints in no time at all."

"I didn't know it was so obvious," Tommy said, leaning back, trying to look casual.

"Oh, I get it from both of you," Willie said. "She hangs on your every word. She has it so bad I practically have to hit her over the head to get her attention nowadays."

Tommy blushed, but inside, of course, he, indeed, did know.

"Guilty as charged. I have it bad, I'm afraid. And that's not good, as the old song goes."

"No, that's great. You fit together somehow, always have — even with the age difference. I think I knew it from the second you came out here with that pitiful little bouquet after the wreck, when I acted like such a horse's ass."

After a few moments of silence, Willie studied him closely. "Have you thought about — if she doesn't get off?"

"I think about it all the time," he said, wrinkling his forehead. "All the time."

"I don't suppose . . . there's anything we could do," Willie said.

"I haven't gotten that far," Tommy said. "I'm thinking."

Willie laid her hand on his and looked him in the eyes.

"I would do anything I could. Just remember that. Anything."

"That time may come." Tommy said, easing his hand away and standing to stretch. "You know what? It's gone. I don't want that joint anymore."

"Want to keep it that way?"

"Well, yeah. I'm a lot better off than where I was a few months ago."

"Then you know what you need to do."

And that's how Tommy Maynard found himself walking into the Elk City Police Department a few minutes after eight the next morning.

"Hi, Tommy," Dixie said, unconsciously primping as he came inside. "What's up?"

"Mornin,' Dixie."

"Fresh pot of coffee. Want some?"

"Sure. Elmo around?" Dixie nodded towards Elmo's office.

Okay, Tommy thought, here goes nothing. While talking with Willie, Tommy had grudgingly come to admit Elmo was hardly the monster he had built him up to be in his head. Elmo was more like a scared kid, craving acceptance in his town's good-ol'-boy club. If he had really been a plotting mastermind, he would not be trying to people-please every asshole in Elk City. And he certainly was not worth obsessing over, which was what Tommy had been doing. How had Willie put it? "You're letting him party rent free in your head."

He raised his hand to knock on Elmo's door. Just stick to what you did to him, he told himself. Apologize for that. Forget what he did. And move on. Tommy hoped that was not too tall an order.

"Come on in," Elmo said, without bothering to see who had knocked.

The Elk City sheriff was spread out behind his enormous oak desk when Tommy walked in. He looked up, clearly surprised by his visitor. Tommy was relieved to see Elmo's broken jaw looked back to normal. Elmo coolly pointed at a chair and leaned back, waiting. He was not about to make this easy.

Tommy sat down and leaned forward. Just start, he told himself.

"Elmo, I owe you an apology. I was wrong to take a swing at you . . . and I didn't mean to break your jaw." Tommy could hear an unexpected quiver in his voice but pressed on. "Is there any thing I can do to make it up to you?"

Elmo looked stunned — and for once, speechless.

The clock ticked, while he gathered his response.

"Well, insurance has already paid for everything."

Tommy felt more at ease now that he was out of the gate.

"But I still acted like an ass, Elmo, and I'm sorry. I appreciate that you didn't take legal action."

A flicker of enjoyment crossed Elmo's face. "I could have."

"I know you could have. If it'd been me in your position, I probably would have. And I'm grateful that you didn't."

Elmo grinned. "Yeah. That infernal high road."

Tommy was caught off guard by the unexpected levity. He risked a slight smile. "Why didn't you, anyway?"

"I was just . . . let's say, a little bit out of line myself, Tommy. Shouldn't have made fun of the situation. Or the girl. I don't think I particularly deserved getting my jaw knocked down my throat for it, but truth be told, I was a tiny bit to blame, too."

Tommy reeled. Blustery Elmo, finding insight? What was the world coming to?

Elmo seemed to read his thoughts and grinned.

"At least that's what my wife's minister tells me," he confided.

Tommy chuckled, but he had to admit what he was feeling wash over him since he had entered the office was much deeper: A relief so exhilarating he was shaken. He tried to keep his voice even as he extended his hand to shake.

"Thanks, Elmo."

"Now that don't mean we agree about this trial. No sirree. She's guilty as sin."

"I know, I know."

The shrill note of Tommy's cell phone made him jump. He managed to answer it on the second ring. "Maynard."

Hugh Smart answered, sounding crisp and wide awake on the other end. "Hey, Tommy, sorry to get you up. It's Hugh."

Tommy shot out of his chair, his heart pumping.

"I'm up. Can you hold on just a sec?"

Tommy said a quick good-bye to Elmo and stepped out into the street before he spoke again.

"What's up?"

"Good news. One of my officers stumbled onto a druggie in the hospital who recognized your guy from the police sketch."

"You're kidding."

"And listen to this. Know why you couldn't find him in the system? Legal name is Terry Randolph Sewell."

Tommy shook his head. "No wonder. The middle name, and not even 'Randy' but 'Randolph.' "

"This guy knew Randy's last name. That's how we tracked him."

"Have you talked to him yet?"

"I'm on my way there right now. My gal says he is an old crackhead dying of AIDS. On his last legs, but he's articulate and sure that he knows your guy, remembers that he disappeared just before Thanksgiving two years ago. Swears he reported him missing to the police, but nobody followed through on it."

"We've got to get him here right away, Hugh." Tommy said. "The defense is ready to rest tomorrow. Gayla finished her testimony yesterday."

"It'll take his doctor's approval. He's not exactly ambulatory."

"Anything you can do?"

"I have a call in to his physician right now." Hugh said, then chuckled low. "If it's an emergency to get him up there I may have to fire up the Cub." Then playfully. "Dammit."

"I'll call the defense attorney right now. She will put things in motion on this end."

"Give her my number and I'll send her the particulars."

"This could be a lifesaver, Hugh. Thanks."

"Just make sure I have to personally fly him up there, got it?"

Tommy grinned. "You got it, buddy. Keep me posted."

As soon as he disconnected, he called Leta O'Reilly and gave her the news. After screaming for joy, Leta kicked into high gear.

"Okay, I am on my way to ask for a conference with the judge, and he is going to find himself hard put to say, No."

"Go get 'em, Tiger," Tommy said.

He gave her Hugh's cell number and after they hung up, Tommy hurried to the jail. For the first time, he noticed they were actually having an autumn in western Oklahoma this year. That was not always the case. Sometimes the dry summers just left the leaves brown and they dropped without fanfare. But today, the soft oranges and buttery yellow leaves swirled under a slight breeze, dancing around him as he walked.

He looked up into the smoky blue sky and thought of that elusive universal spirit he never quite knew how to address. Somehow today the words came easily: Thank you for the leaves, thank you for the sky, thank you for air, for the earth . . . and for my measly little wonderful life.

CHAPTER 52

IT WAS ALL HAPPENING SO DAMN FAST, Willie thought. It was she who had put the wheels in motion, granted, but she had expected it would take six months to sell her place. Instead someone had snapped it right up. She figured the closing would take another six weeks. But no, they could be ready to roll in a week. Not that they were forcing her out, they insisted — she could move out whenever — but since they were using family trust money rather than a bank loan, they could complete the legalities almost immediately, if she so desired.

She realized as she tried to organize her packing that she was actually feeling put upon. For God's sake, she laughed, what is wrong with you? Didn't you get exactly what you asked for? Yeah, she thought, just not so fast, dammit.

It was the enormity of her action that had come crashing down on her. She was grateful to have the full day of court recess, while Leta handled the legal brawling over admitting the new testimony. Gayla had insisted Willie go home, away from the madhouse. Willie had reluctantly agreed. She had not spent this much time rubbing elbows with the public for years. Getting away was like a tonic. Besides, she knew Tommy and Gayla would enjoy a little time alone. Not that they said anything, but Willie had developed pretty good instincts for their sweetly awkward ways. They might not be quite sure what they were about, but they sure did not seem to want to be apart.

Okay, okay, enough day-dreaming. She needed to get on with the moving, and it was not going to be easy. It was not a problem of quantity. She had pared her belongings to a minimum a long time ago, during one of her many pushes to make it simple for her distant cousins to clean up after she died. The thought of their strange hands touching what was left of Jack's things — special little outfits, broken toys — had made her cringe. And Willie had not wanted anybody to read her journals, the chronicles of her despair after little Jack's death, yet she also had not been able to bring herself to burn them.

As she sat on the bed looking at everything, she felt again the power of those items she couldn't bear to part with. Gripped by melancholy, Willie touched the objects in her hand: Jack's Cub Scout pin, the little rocks and stones he brought back from places they visited, and a stick drawing of "Momy & Me" holding hands. How do you say good-bye to your child's things?

Then she had a thought: This is like forgiveness. You don't do it because you're ready. You do it because you have to.

Harnessing all the energy she could find, she dragged the musty boxes out to the pasture and built a small bonfire from the brush pile. She found herself feeling almost reverent as she knelt over his sled, broken action figures, and an ancient Batman costume.

"God, help me to let go," she prayed. "Help me to move on."

When the flames were dancing high into the air, she threw it all into the fire, then one by one, she dropped her journals into the flames, too. When she was done, she couldn't tell if she was crying with regret, or gratitude for the strength to have finally finished it.

She picked up a baby blue bandanna Maxine had worn home from the groomer's. The poodle's unique smell lingered — almost too sweet to bear. Willie still teared up when she came upon a hidden bone or toy tucked away in some nook of the house.

She wondered again, Now why am I doing this? No answer came. The odd thing was it did not stop her momentum. I will know it when I get there, she thought, as she turned to go inside.

Had she not been a free spirit once, going with the flow, interested in too many things? Or so she had been told. Willie had never been able to settle down to one of those specialized majors that promised the big bucks. She had wanted to try everything. She had jumped feet first into dozens of jobs: non-profit work, art gallery assistant, landscape gardener, health food store clerk, even pastry chef. She had wanted to travel, live near the water or the mountains, practice her French or Spanish in a foreign country. What an irony, then, to have found herself trapped in a dull life with a boring man and a hyperactive child, one who left her drained and exasperated more often than not. But that was a lifetime ago. After decades of working a farm she had gotten too old to handle, now she got to be the dreamer. And Willie was not sure she knew how anymore.

As she returned to the cabin, the ring of the phone startled her out of her reverie.

"Willie!" It was Leta. "We did it. The judge is going to allow the new witness."

"That's wonderful. But what's this 'we?' You did it. You. Ms. Fire-brand Lawyer. Congratulations. Tell me everything."

"Well, they threw every legal argument known to man at me, but I hung on like a bulldog."

Willie could hear the pride in Leta's voice as she gave her the blow-by-blow. Apparently the prosecution had, indeed, poured on the histrionics, but in the end Leta, the lone gladiator, had prevailed.

"You should see Gayla," Leta said. "The jail hasn't been this happy in a long time. Sheriff Maynard even showed up with a cake."

"Give everybody my best and go have a piece of it yourself. Tell Gayla I will see her bright and early. I'm so proud of you, Leta. Thank you. Thank you for everything."

She hung up with a relieved sigh.

"Hallelujah," she said, before scrunching her nose up at the smell of cornbread burning. Uh oh, there goes lunch. As she scurried to the kitchen, a movement at the bottom of the screen door caught her eye. She ignored it in favor of getting the scorched cornbread out of the oven, then returned to the door, hot pads still in her hands. Her first thought was raccoon. Please not a skunk, she prayed. But it was neither. Only a skinny mutt of a dog scratching at the door. Oh, damn. Twenty pounds tops, red-brown and white, with muddy fur and a freckled face. What a nasty little runt, Willie thought. A collar. No tags. She was pretty sure it was not from around there. She had never seen it about, and she knew most of the neighbors' dogs.

"Get out of here. Go on home, boy." Willie said firmly and walked back into the kitchen. She was not ready to get saddled with another dog. A mewling sound came from the door. She put down the hot pads and went back to glare at the dog, hands on hips.

"No whining now. Go on home."

But as she started to slam the inside door, she noticed a red smear around the dog's back leg.

"Oh, for crying out loud."

She pinched her face into a scowl and opened the screen door to get a closer look.

"What did you get into? You little dickens."

From the looks of it, the dog had probably been nicked by one of the many traps left by hunters in the nearby woods or maybe the teeth of another critter. Willie leaned down and gingerly tried to touch the injured leg. The dog snapped at her.

"Take it easy," she said. "I'm just trying to look."

She could see some of the fur and skin was torn away, but it was nothing a little antibiotic ointment could not fix. Unfortunately, when she tried to touch the dog, he snapped at her again.

"That's no way to treat a good Samaritan, buddy."

But Willie noticed he did not run off.

"You're probably dehydrated. Crap."

She went inside and found Maxine's water bowl under the sink and filled it. She put it out outside and stepped back inside. The dog went right to it, drinking hard.

"How'd you get all the way out here? Bad owners, damn 'em."

Dropped off by someone from town, like so many whose owners lied to themselves that coyotes surely would not feast on their suddenly disposable pet. If memory served, an ancient bag of dry dog food still sat under the sink, left over from when Maxine lost her teeth and Willie started babying her with scrambled eggs. You know what will happen if you feed him, she told herself. Don't do it. Time to get back to packing. And so she turned her back on him and returned to her meal.

Afterwards, staring at the burned cornbread sticks, she couldn't help but think it was a good day to be alone, even though the packing had been etched with melancholy.

Tomorrow she would be back in court, with any luck seeing a new witness to testify for the defense. That left the rest of the afternoon and evening to watch the moon come up and to hear the night calls of the woods. Outside, her visitor whimpered through the door screen.

Still here, Willie grinned. Not such a tough customer after all.

The scorched cornbread made her think of how much Maxine always loved it with sweet milk poured over it. If I gave him just a little something, he would probably let me clean up that leg. Then I could send him on his way without guilt. So, not allowing herself to think it to death, that is what she did.

If he is back in the morning, she told herself, then I'll show him who's boss.

CHAPTER 53

GAYLA'S HEART POUNDED AS Leta announced to the court, "The defense calls Mr. Vincent Bordellini." Moments later, the double doors at the back of the courtroom opened. A wheelchair carrying a skeleton of a man maneuvered its way down the aisle, pushed by Sheriff Maynard. The hush that fell over the courtroom was broken only by the whirr of the moving wheels of the chair. The laborious process of getting Mr. Bordellini into the witness stand mesmerized everyone, even Garrison and Ringrose, although their eye slits looked less like compassion and more like hungry lions waiting to rush the Coliseum.

If Gayla had not looked directly into his eyes, she might not have recognized him at all. She had never known him as Vincent Bordellini, so she couldn't be sure who was showing up when Tommy told her his name yesterday. It turned out to be the guy everybody called "Guido," because he was relentlessly Italian, from his brassy accent to his shiny leather jackets. She had not known him well; he was just one of the regulars who hung around Randy's place. The ghost being lifted into the witness stand now, however, was barely a man, much less the lively Guido.

When he was settled in the chair, Guido nodded at Gayla, so she knew he recognized her as well. Faded jeans hung on him as if on a scarecrow, and a thick sweater could not hide his shrunken bony shoulders. Gone was the curly mop of black locks, the cigarette dangling from his lips. This creature with thin gray wisps of hair was close to death, and it made Gayla cry inside to see it.

Nobody deserved such a slow wasting away, she thought.

Leta, in a neon butterscotch suit and matching gold heels, moved into her questioning with a respectful deference to the witness's state of health. After quickly establishing that Bordellini had lived in Dallas for the past three years, working as a furniture warehouse manager until his illness, the questions got more to the point. "And how did you become acquainted with Terry Randolph Sewell?"

The voice that answered was raspy and low, which made the audience sit almost motionless, people craning forward to hear.

"I met Randy — that's what we called him — when I moved to Dallas. He was my main source for drugs."

"Did you know the defendant, Gayla Rose Early?"

"I'd met her, yeah, and seen her at Randy's place and sometimes at Muskrats, a local bar we drank at."

"Would you say she was closely associated with Mr. Sewell?"

"I'd say so, yes, for a few months anyway."

"Tell us about Terry Sewell, or Randy, as you call him."

"Randy lost his parents when he was just a kid and got knocked around from one foster home to another. He was a sharp guy, knew about a lot of stuff, fun to talk to. He liked to tinker with electronics, talk sports, politics."

"And when did you become aware that you hadn't seen him around?"

"I realized sometime before November two years ago that I hadn't seen him in awhile."

"You're sure of that time frame?" Leta asked.

"Yes. Neither one having family, we had gotten together for Thanksgiving before. With the holiday coming, I was keeping an eye out for him, but I couldn't find him. It had been several weeks."

"And had you seen Miss Early during that same time period?"

Guido looked at Gayla thoughtfully.

"No. Actually, I looked for her at the time, because I thought she might know where he was. Nobody had seen either of them."

"And did you give up then?" Leta asked.

"Not really. By then I was beginning to suspect what might be going on. See, before coming to Dallas, I was a card dealer at Caesar's Palace in Vegas for a couple of years . . ."

Leta raised her hand to interrupt him so she could remind the court.

"This was the same casino where Albert Raeder attended real estate conventions for a number of years, and how was that relevant to Mr. Sewell's having gone missing?"

Guido paused for a sip of water.

"I met Albert Raeder there when he won big at my '21' table and gave me a generous dealer's tip. This was just before I moved to Dallas. I ran into him later that same night in one of the bars at Caesar's and offered to buy him a drink. We proceeded to get drunk together and talked until almost dawn. Raeder starts telling me about his enormous real estate fortune and his new cabin on a lake near Elk City, where he said he had so many valuables he had to keep a safe. He was quite a braggart, anxious to impress me with how rich he was."

Boy, he got that right, Gayla thought. Raeder was always going on about his vast real estate empire. If he bothered bragging about it to her, she had no doubt he would have piled it on thick with a stranger, especially if he was drunk. Only this time Raeder's boasting had left him open to a sometime hustler.

"And did there come a time when you passed this information on to Randy?"

"Yes. I told him all about it one night when we were shooting the breeze. Randy got real curious and did an Internet search on Raeder and his holdings. Sure enough, he found the lake address and directions on how to get there. We figured if the guy was half as rich as he said, the cabin would be an easy mark, what with it being vacant during the week."

By this point, Guido's voice had faded to a rasp. Leta poured him another glass of water before continuing with her questions.

"When presented with a photograph of Mr. Raeder, you were sure it was the same man who befriended you in Las Vegas?" Leta asked.

"Absolutely."

"And you are sure that the cabin address where the defendant was held by Mr. Raeder is the same address that you and Randy looked up with the idea of robbing it?"

"Yes, I am."

"When did you and Randy intend to act on this information?"

"We talked about doing it together, but neither of us pushed a particular time. It wasn't really my thing — I had a job and all — but Randy was hot to do it. Then suddenly he goes missing. When I heard later through the grapevine that Randy had gone out of town, I suspected then that he'd cut me out of the job, decided he wanted it all for himself."

"Why would he do that when you were the one who brought him the information?"

"I only pulled jobs with Randy when it was convenient, really. He was the full time dealer and hustler. I usually went along as backup more than anything."

Guido's voice had grown softer as the questions continued.

"Only a few more questions, Mr. Bordellini," Leta assured him. "Did Mr. Sewell ever talk about using the defendant, Miss Early, as backup for this job?"

"No. He thought she was too nervous to stay cool, but he did mention that her drug debt was starting to get ridiculous, and he was going to have to do something."

"Do something? Like what?" Leta moved closer to the stand.

"He didn't really say. Probably cut her off, or make her fence something for him. Do something risky, for sure."

Leta walked to the defense table and picked up some papers protected by clear plastic sleeves.

"Did there come a time when you decided to make an official report about Randy having gone missing?"

"Well, yeah, after I had called the hospitals and everywhere I could think of, I finally called the police and filed a Missing Person Report."

"And on what day was that?" Leta looked down to check the date.

"The detective who found me looked it up and said it was filed two years ago on November 10th."

Leta handed the official document to the clerk.

"Exhibit 14, Your Honor. And what, Mr. Bordellini, was the outcome of that investigation?"

A hard flat tone in Guido's voice. "Nothing. Nada. Zilch."

"And do you know why that was?"

His face darkened. "Because nobody cares about a drug dealer, anymore than they care about tweakers or drunks."

Garrison sprung from his chair, for the first time.

"Objection. Inflammatory and —"

Quickly from the bench. "Sustained."

"You suffer from AIDS, is that correct, Mr. Bordellini?" Leta asked.

"Right. The last stages."

"And why, since you're obviously in pain, did you choose to come here to testify today?"

"Well, Randy and me knew the score. We made our choices, both of us. But to get gunned down, unarmed, like Miss Early said he was? Nobody deserves that."

Leta concluded. "And in the past two years have you seen either Terry Randolph Sewell or Gayla Early in Dallas, or anywhere else?"

"No, sadly, I have not."

"Thank you, Mr. Bordellini. We appreciate your making the long trip here in your condition. That's all I have for this witness at this time."

Leta stepped back and sat beside Gayla.

Garrison rose to cross examine. His voice, following Leta's, sounded like a watermelon splatting on a hot sidewalk. Guido visibly shuddered at the prosecutor's foghorn volume.

"You said you have full-blown AIDS. How many medications are you on now?"

"I take a combination of prescription medications, most of which I can't pronounce. I made a list for the court."

"Aren't you on morphine?"

Guido glanced at Leta. "Yes, that too."

Leta stood up. "May it please the court, Mr. Bordellini takes a prescribed time-release form of morphine that is markedly different in effect than the instant release version of the painkiller."

"Nevertheless, it is still a powerful narcotic," Garrison said.

"This new application of the drug is used so patients can function effectively even as their pain is managed." Leta explained to the judge and jury.

"Irregardless," Garrison barked, with a wave of his arm. "It is still morphine."

Judge Bishop barked: "We got it, Mr. Garrison. Move along."

Garrison straightened his lapels, before addressing the witness.

"Mr. Bordellini, how well did you know the defendant?"

"Like I said, she hung out with Randy some. I knew her a little."

Garrison smirked. "Did you talk with her?"

"Yes."

"Alone?" Garrison's smirk grew more suggestive.

"Alone? No, I don't recall that." Bordellini looked confused.

"You were never alone with the defendant, even though you saw her in Terry Sewell's apartment and in this Muskrats bar?"

"I guess I could have been, but I don't recall it."

"Did you ever have sex with the defendant?"

"Objection!" Leta shouted. "Relevance. And the insinuation is disgusting."

Judge Bishop bit his lip. "I'll allow it." His eyes darted to Ringrose.

Leta stood her ground, stunned.

"Your Honor, since Mr. Bordellini stated he was never alone with the defendant, is the prosecution suggesting they had sexual relations with others present?"

The judge squirmed a little, probably realizing he had missed the inference. "The jury can decide that," he said, not meeting her eyes.

Garrison squared his shoulders and tilted his head back waiting for Bordellini's answer.

"No, I did not," Guido said, barely above a scratchy whisper.

"What drugs did you observe the defendant doing?"

"Crack. Powder cocaine. Some pot."

"That's it?" Garrison exuded disbelief.

"Far as I can remember, yes."

"I'm sure with all the morphine, remembering is often a problem," Garrison slipped in.

Now it was Leta's turn to bellow. "Objection, Your Honor."

"Sustained. Save your commentary for closing, Mr. Garrison."

Garrison regrouped. "And during these evenings of cocaine trips and wild drug use, you were never intimate with the defendant?"

"Objection," Leta cried out. "These are blatant distortions. He is harassing the witness."

"Sustained. This is growing tiresome, Mr. Garrison," Judge Bishop said. Yeah, Gayla thought, and he's only been at it ten minutes.

"How many years did you work for the Dallas Furniture Warehouse, Mr. Bordellini?"

"Two and a half years all total."

"And when did you leave there?"

"Eight months ago."

Garrison grinned big. "Actually, you were let go, were you not?"

"Yes, I was."

"You were let go for excessive absences due to your drug use?" Garrison asked it as a question but was clearly reading from a report in his hand.

"Yes, my drug habit got out of control, and I fully understand why they let me go."

"Mr. Bordellini, could you explain for the jury what you mean when you say 'out of control?' "

"I had sold nearly everything I owned for drugs; I had gone from being a dependable employee to being erratic and ineffective. I no longer had friends who wanted to see me." Guido was matter-of-fact in his response, but there was real sadness in his voice.

"So if no one else trusted you, why should the jury believe you now?"

"Because I care about Randy and want to help find out what happened to him. I am here to say what I know. If the jury chooses not to believe me, that's their prerogative."

"I'm sure it wouldn't be the first time you couldn't be believed."

Before Leta could even object, Guido shot back. "Spoken like a man who knows firsthand."

Titters from the audience. Judge Bishop flushed crimson. Leta was on her feet with, "Objection. That is a cheap shot from the prosecution and beneath this court, Your Honor."

The judge jumped in. "Miss O'Reilly, control your witness."

Leta hand-signaled Guido to be quiet.

Judge Bishop turned to Garrison. "Enough. You, Mr. Garrison, are in contempt of court. Five hundred dollars by day's end or you will spend the night in jail."

Ringrose shot a get-over-here gesture to Garrison with a crook of his finger for a quick whispered consultation.

Gayla studied Guido's dark hooded eyes and hollow sockets. She liked this guy she had been too high to really remember. His smarts and his own prickly code appealed to her. It was unbearably sad that his body had almost been reduced to vapors.

It had always surprised Gayla how many charming, articulate people were also drunks and users. There were buttheads, too, of course, but she found them outnumbered by the clever, creative ones. It was only when the booze or drugs stopped working for them that the brilliance slowly shattered, exposing the personal emptiness. Charismatic railing against the world morphed into dark rumblings of doomsday. But until that twist occurred, those personalities had energized the rooms they entered.

She had never considered herself one of those bright lights, but Guido certainly was. While Gayla had listened to him testify, new memories had popped up. In Muskrats, Guido was the generous guy who would slip a few extra bucks to some down-and-outer or leave a big tip for a harried waitress, the guy who always seemed upbeat, who relished the political arguments that came with each news day.

Guido seemed to barely have any memory of her. By the time they had met, she was already sliding downhill faster than she could crawl back up. She had stopped even thinking about all the dreams she had buried, much less talking about them. She wondered if she was as much as a blip on most of her acquaintances' radars. This is all I will be remembered for, she thought, if at all . . . beating a man to death and fifteen minutes of fame in some crude tabloids. The sound of Garrison's next question interrupted her thoughts.

"So, Mr. Bordellini, you were actively involved with Mr. Sewell in a life of crime?" Garrison asked.

Guido, reluctantly. "We pulled some jobs together, yeah."

Garrison smiled. "Breaking and entering?"

"They were small jobs, smash and grab stuff."

"How many, would you say?"

"I don't know. Maybe a half dozen."

"So you have direct knowledge of what sorts of jobs Mr. Sewell committed in his criminal career?"

"I only know about the jobs we did together, and what he told me about doing on his own. It wasn't much," Guido answered, a little wary.

"So, did he do any home invasions that he told you about?"

"No."

"Assault and battery?"

"No, he wasn't a violent person."

"Really. You never saw him hit anybody in the bar or on the street?"

"I don't recall anything like that, no."

Garrison was warming up to this subject.

"He never stole money from you?"

"No."

"And you never saw him become violent with anybody?"

"Objection. Asked and answered, Your Honor," Leta said.

Judge Bishop looked perturbed.

"Where is this headed, Mr. Garrison?"

The prosecutor looked pleased with himself. "Your Honor, we'd like to enter into evidence the Dallas Police file on Terry Randolph Sewell."

Gayla glanced at Leta, who had prepared her for this. Randy's rap sheet was lengthy, and Garrison took his sweet time, presenting a man who had been busted for drugs, had spent time in youth correctional centers for brawling, and who had been listed as a suspected dealer long before he disappeared.

Yesterday Leta had explained to Gayla, "We're not claiming he was a saint, just that he was murdered. If they enter his rap sheet, they are at least acknowledging he existed, which is more than they have done up to now."

After a numbing half-hour rundown of Randy's criminal career, Garrison wheeled back on Guido, who was showing the strain.

"The defendant testified that Mr. Sewell struck her on several occasions. You never saw that?"

"Not personally, no."

"So the defendant was lying about that, too?"

Guido rolled his eyes as Leta hopped up yet again on her five-inch gold heels.

"Objection."

Judge Bishop looked annoyed. "Don't go there, Counselor. There's more citations where that earlier one came from."

"Sorry, Your Honor."

But Garrison's quick smirk and glance at the jury belied his words.

Gayla had not watched the jurors much during the questioning, but now she noticed as Garrison droned on and on, that they were staring with barely disguised disgust at Guido. Her mood shifted as she realized how differently they might be reacting to Guido. Their hooded eyes frightened her now. If they felt that way about Guido, and Randy, they could certainly feel the same disdain for her.

Yet Guido was also real — as much flesh and blood as they were — no matter how uncomfortable he made them. He is proof I am telling the truth, she thought, hope bubbling back to the surface.

Surely the jury would have to admit now that her story was real. Here was corroboration, even if they did not like the source.

CHAPTER 54

THE NEXT DAY'S CLOSING arguments packed the courthouse with folks from near and far, like gawkers at a western-style hanging. Tommy had brought in Frankie Lee and anyone else he could rustle up to help with security, and for good reason. The lines started gathering around the building by sunrise, and by eight that morning they spilled into the town square. Everyone was ready to jostle for a seat in the gallery. Ahead of the crowd, Sheriff Dudgeon, Dixie, and Joe Nguyen, who had driven in from Elk City, accompanied by a cluster of local big shots, took their seats first. Then someone ushered in Mrs. Raeder, head-to-toe black crepe, and this time she actually was wearing the Jackie-O veil, right out of JFK's funeral procession.

Tommy prowled the back of the courtroom, hoping to hear the closing arguments but ready to bolt if trouble erupted. As Willie headed towards her designated seat behind the defense table, she paused by Tommy, staring in disbelief at the widow's getup.

"Are they bringing in the riderless horse as well?" she asked him.

With the opening of the courtroom doors, it was every man for himself. Within two minutes, the place was filled to fire-code capacity, and Tommy had the doors closed. People were already sweating by the time Judge Bishop entered and called the proceedings to order.

As expected, Ringrose led the charge for the prosecution. After an exhaustive rerun of the details of their case, which took almost to the lunch hour, he served up his best stuff for last.

"Ladies and gentlemen of the jury, Mr. Raeder's good name rests in your hands. Will you choose to believe this woman's outlandish tale of kidnapping, murder, and sex slavery? This self-admitted crackhead with a history of consorting sexually with men to get what she wanted?"

"Objection, Your Honor," Leta interjected.

Tommy watched Judge Bishop barely consider her objection before hollering: "Overruled."

Leta blinked in stunned surprise.

So that's how he is going to get back in Ringrose's favor, Tommy thought. It is going to be anything goes during his closing.

"Thank you, Your Honor," Ringrose said, continuing right where he had left off. "Do you want to believe this discredited defendant and her rogue's gallery of shady characters? Or do you believe her victim, a beloved patriarch of Luckau's sister city? You see in the gallery dozens of Elk City leaders, men who knew Mr. Raeder for the civic leader he was, a man concerned with historic restoration projects and new park development and school improvements. Ask yourself, could a civic leader, nay a city father, who did all these selfless things for his community, be in reality such a Dr. Jekyll and Mr. Hyde? I think not.

"Consider the glaring holes in the defendant's story. She claims her partner in crime was killed. That the victim shot him in cold blood with a sawed-off shotgun. Yet the defense has produced no shotgun, no physical evidence, and, most importantly, no body to support her claim."

Hard to do, when that evidence goes missing or gets destroyed while in police hands, Tommy thought, his throat tightening as he remembered the microscopic blood traces from the cabin door that had disappeared somewere inside the bowels of the Elk City police station. Tommy could not help but glance around at Dixie, whose lips were pursed with disapproval. They had both beaten themselves up over that, Tommy was pretty sure.

Ringrose rammed ahead. "The defendent claims she was dragged along to commit this crime, yet we have no evidence that she didn't actually plan the original robbery herself, if there even was a robbery. And if she and this supposed partner in crime did sneak into the Raeder cabin, who's to say she didn't kill Terry Randolph Sewell herself, in a fit of anger or because the robbery went bad. As for the witness we heard from yesterday, his testimony is self-serving. Now that he is too ill to go to prison, of course, he is ready to confess his crimes."

"Objection," Leta shouted, only to be quickly overruled.

"But the charge the defendant makes that is the most cynical of all, ladies and gentlemen of the jury, is that Mr. Albert Raeder held her for two years as a sexual slave." Ringrose paused to shake his head in disbelief. "This claim insults not only the deceased but our shared history with him. It stretches the bounds of credulity. I knew Albert Raeder. To suggest that he could be capable of such a heinous act takes a twisted mind, my friends, one that is surely damaged from years of drug use."

This time Leta stood and her voice shook with outrage: "Objection! No evidence was ever —"

Judge Bishop cut her off. "Overruled."

Leta closed her eyes and sighed. So this is how it was going to be, Tommy thought. Ringrose could shovel anything to the jury he wanted, play to their most base instincts, and the judge would rubber stamp it.

Ringrose addressed the jury: "The defendant asks you to believe that this upstanding citizen kept her locked in a basement, had sex with her hundreds of times without contraception, yet managed never to be discovered or to impregnate her over the course of two years. Both are ludicrous on their very face."

Ringrose turned so he was standing only a few feet in front of Gayla and looking down his nose at her.

"Lies, lies, lies. That has been Gayla Early's modus operandi her entire life. Would she recognize the truth if it appeared in front of her, ladies and gentlemen? With her history, I say not. Consider the source."

And with that, Ringrose began to tick off the blunders of Gayla's life on his fingers: "Sneak out of your parents' home when you're young. Lie about it. Do drugs at work. Lie about it. Steal from your friends. Lie about it. Murder a man. Lie, lie, lie about it. Invent a story so outrageous, so damning that it scars an entire community. Why not? For Gayla Early, lying is a way of life."

Infuriated, Tommy squeezed his lips together and forced himself to remain still. But if the look he shot Ringrose had been a lit match, the prosecutor would have been incinerated. Ringrose has no right to stand over her like that, to browbeat her before God and man, he thought. He took comfort, however, in the fact that Gayla seemed to be handling Ringrose's barrage of charges just fine, thank you. Back straight, head tall. The damsel in distress did not appear to need rescuing.

Tommy started. Had Ringrose just inched back perceptibly from the defense table? Tommy almost smiled. In spite of the vitrol streaming from his mouth, Ringrose seemed to be losing ground. His glare was softening even as his argument rose to its crescendo.

"Her way of life is something our townspeople want no part of in this community. Drug use, promiscuity — we have no use for someone who poisons everything and everyone she touches."

Ringrose turned from Gayla's unblinking gaze back to the jury.

"Don't let her get away with this, ladies and gentlemen. She lay in wait for Mr. Albert Raeder, and when he was at his weakest, when anyone with an ounce of decency would have called for help, dialed 9-1-1, what did she do? She hit him with a splintered two-by-four, again and again and again, stopping only after half of his face was gone.

"Oh, the defense is going to hurl all kinds of unprovable, wild theories at you in an attempt to confuse and distort. Do not allow yourself to be thrown by their fabrications and lies. This hideous excuse for a human being is anything but a victim. She is a stone-cold killer. You must, and I believe you will, do your duty as sober, upstanding citizens of this great state and not only find Gayla Rose Early guilty as charged but recommend that she be punished to the fullest extent of the law. We may not be able to ask for the death penalty in this case, but Gayla Rose Early should never again see the light of day."

Tommy could feel his body relax as Ringrose walked back to the prosecution table. Gayla had not looked away from the prosecutor once. Had not broken her gaze under his relentless attack. Hers was a strength no lawyer, even one as talented as Leta, could instill in a defendant. It came from within.

Judge Bishop looked at the clock on the wall and banged his gavel.

"Lunch recess until two o'clock."

As the crowd dispersed, Tommy walked over to the defense table and spoke low to Gayla. "Congratulations. You stood toe-to-toe with him through that entire barrage of horseshit."

Gayla looked at him with a tired smile.

"Who said I didn't learn anything from being a military brat?"

Tommy nodded, with an approving grin. "Lunch is on me."

"Okay," Gayla said, with a little smile. "Make mine raw meat."

CHAPTER 55

WILLIE WONDERED WHY SO often the people with the nicest clothes were also the most unbearable: Widow Raeder lying through her teeth in custom silk. Ringrose, spouting poison in cashmere. The morning had been almost intolerable for Willie, listening to Ringrose's carefully articulated message of hate. Such rants always aggravated her acid reflux, and even though almost nothing dented her appetite, that Elk City snake had managed to kill it.

She hoped Gayla had responded inside as well to Ringrose's assault as it looked from the outside. Willie knew from experience that lots of women, herself included, could talk the talk, had the strong woman demeanor down, but could never quite get past a niggle of internal shame. It had happened to Willie when her then-husband of the Gucci loafers and custom-made suits had started the divorce negotiations by offering her one of their rent houses and a ten-year-old car. Nothing else. No cash. No alimony. Nothing. And she probably would have agreed to it, too, if she had not heard him cover the mouthpiece and share a chuckle with his lawyer at her expense on the other end of the phone. She had felt that poorly about herself. Instead her own lawyer had gotten her that first offer plus a payout that, while peanuts for her husband, she had managed to turn into a modest income for herself all these years.

Willie was relieved to see Gayla holding on well and ready for lunch. Willie's stomach still felt sour, so she skipped out for a quick run to her cabin. She told herself it was to pack a few more boxes, but she knew that was not true. The wandering mutt had not shown back up this morning. Instead of feeling relieved, she had found herself worried sick, imagining him in the clutches of a coyote. There were vicious critters out in the woods, capable of taking out a little squirt like that mutt for a mid-morning snack.

As she turned into her driveway, she saw him. He had gotten himself cornered under the porch by one of the neighbor dogs, a Rottweiler who tolerated no nonsense from trespassers. The mutt had squeezed through a small opening in the wood lattice that the Rottweiler could not get through, but in doing so Mutt Dog had also managed to trap himself.

Willie pulled up the pickup, parked, and got out. The huge dog turned to her, as if anticipating a word of praise for his efforts at patrolling the neighborhood.

"Now, Hugo, what are you doing here?" The dog's body began to wag a welcome and its attention whipped to her. "Good dog, yes, that's what you're supposed to do with strangers, but this little guy doesn't understand that."

She gave Hugo's head a good scratch, then shooed him away.

"You go on home now." The dog quickly headed back to the porch. "No," Willie laughed. "Fun's over. Go on home now."

As Hugo broke into a run across the field headed home, Willie approached the porch.

"Where are you, boy?" Two terror-filled doe eyes peeked out, so pitiful Willie did not know whether to laugh or cry. She coaxed the tiny dog towards her. "It's okay, boy. He's gone. That's it. Come on now."

When his trembling, scrawny body landed in her arms, she could feel his heart beating double time, like a little bird's. For a moment, she gave herself over to the warm feeling.

"Can't leave you alone for a minute, huh? Well, don't go getting used to it. No, sir. Don't you get used to it."

Then, of course, Willie put out more of the dry dog food. It would be cruel to let him be traumatized and go hungry, she thought.

She dragged out an old dog bed of Maxine's and put it inside the shed, in a nice dry spot. Tomorrow she would put a notice in the paper or maybe tack up some flyers around town. See who had lost this poor, little critter. Whoever had dumped him in the country should be horse-whipped, she thought sternly on the drive back into town.

Willie arrived at the courthouse and claimed her reserved front row seat. She noticed with relief, as soon as Gayla was brought in, that the weight of the morning's relentless accusations still did not show on the young woman's face. Instead, her whole being looked smoother, softer.

Leta O'Reilly, on the other hand, looked so jacked up on espresso that Willie could feel the electricity crackling from her. Maybe that was necessary, Willie thought, with the gargantuan task looming before her. Leta, rock steady on six-inch platforms, began with a short recap of Gayla's life, then moved bravely into the tricky area of her crack use and the proverbial gutter she was inhabiting when she accompanied Randy to the Raeder cabin.

"Ladies and gentlemen, the prosecution refuses to acknowledge the disappearance of Terry Randolph Sewell, even after seeing his police record, even after hearing a Missing Person Report had been filed on him. A former acquaintance testified as to the activities of these two during the same time period that Gayla Early went missing. They didn't simply fall off the earth. And Randy has never been found or seen again. If he is not dead, where is he? After two years, nobody in Dallas has seen him; no arrest record from any other town in the country has surfaced. In spite of national media coverage, no one has come forward to enlighten us as to his whereabouts. The defense has shown that he was in the Luckau area, and an investigation into his disappearance and death now becomes necessary and appropriate.

"But this proceeding is to judge the guilt or innocence of the defendant, which hinges on anything but a clear series of events. Did Gayla Rose Early strike Albert Raeder with a two-by-four numerous times that day in October? Yes, she did. But in what context? What caused her to lash out like that? And was she even responsible for the heart attack that caused his death?

"The prosecution has told you that Gayla Early was a transient, a drifter who had either broken into the basement with plans to rob the house or to use it as a place to sleep. They say Mr. Raeder surprised her there, that she turned viciously on the unarmed man and beat him to death. Well, let's compare what the prosecution says to what the physical evidence shows. Hundreds of Miss Early's prints were indeed found in the basement, but they were found on only one side of the room. And we have heard an expert testify that there were too many fingerprints to assume that she had only been in the basement a few hours, or even a few days. Her prints were found not only on the small fridge, sink, cot, and portable toilet but also on the chain that was clamped around her ankle. Dr. Gordon found deep bruising on that same ankle several days later. Her blood drops were discovered on the ankle clamp. You yourselves saw the thick scarring on her left ankle left by that same clamp.

"As for the glass from the basement window, it fell more to the outside than inside. The two-by-four used as the murder weapon was pulled from that same window while she was trying to escape, ladies and gentlemen, not breaking in. Desperately trying to get away from her two years of horror in that prison. The Raeders' neighbor Mabel Thorpe has testified to the desperate cries she heard coming from that basement.

"Make no mistake here. The only crime Miss Early committed was with Terry Randolph Sewell: breaking and entering the Raeder cabin. Her nightmare began in the kitchen of that cabin, when Albert Raeder shot Randy Sewell to death in front of her. Perhaps he had intended to shoot her as well. Then it dawned on him. Here was a perfect, unexpected prize in front of him, a gift of opportunity, as it were.

"If his ultimate intentions had not been so vile, we would call it a fluke. Albert Raeder recognized it as an opportunity. The chance of a lifetime. There she was, beautiful and vulnerable, caught red-handed in his kitchen. No one of consequence would be looking for her. She was not from the area, and she had admitted she had no close relatives.

"Ask yourself, why would a victim ever ask such questions of someone caught robbing his house? This was the ultimate random situation. Albert Raeder recognized it for what it was and jumped on it, and he succeeded beyond his wildest dreams, I imagine. He managed to keep his sex slave for almost two years, right under the nose of his wife, his family, and his community.

"We are shocked and stunned by this, as well we should be. How awful to find out such terrible things about people we think we know well. I know firsthand how angry and disbelieving all of us in Elk City felt upon hearing of these allegations. Yet the perpetrators of crimes, such as the ones that unfolded in the Raeder basement, are routinely described as ordinary people — often popular in their community.

"But Mr. Raeder had a dark side, ladies and gentlemen. In his frequent out-of-state travels, he let another, sexually hungry personality emerge. We know of his assault on a Las Vegas prostitute that he was able to keep quiet. How many more incidents might we be able to uncover if we had the time —"

Ringrose's head swung up. "Objection. There is no —"

"Sustained."

That's okay, Willie thought, she got it in. There isn't a soul in here that hasn't wondered the same thing by now.

Leta paused for a quick sip of water, then returned to her story.

"I spoke to you earlier of Michelangelo chipping away at his block of marble until the angel hidden within emerged. The defense has had the difficult job of chipping away at a high-profile and well-liked community figure. And, you may rightly argue, the defendant is no angel. She is a flawed human being, as all of us are, but she might as well have been encased in marble the way she was trapped in that underground bunker.

"The truth is, she would likely still be a chained prisoner in that dank place had Albert Raeder not suffered a heart attack in her presence. Put yourself in her position. The man who kidnapped her, imprisoned her, violated every part of her person, suddenly loses control before her. And she happens to be unchained. Stunned, she begins to scream and bang on the windows for help. Desperately, she tears away at the window coverings and yanks off a piece of wood that has kept her from the outside world. She's in a panic, running around the room for any means of escape. Yet Albert Raeder, even now, even while disabled on the floor, panting for breath, tackles her and brings her down. He fights with every ounce of strength in his three-hundred-pound body to stop her only opportunity to escape in two years. And, what a paradox — his only possibility of medical help.

"Ladies and gentlemen, even as he lies there, in the middle of an acute heart attack, he still manages to hold her back. He is willing to die to keep her from ever getting out. Why?

"There's only one thing it could be. To keep his twisted tale of depravity from finding the light of day. This was a fight to the death because Albert Raeder made it one. He crawled, fought, and tackled her. In the rage of that moment, Gayla Early knew that if she didn't stop him, she would never set foot on the earth above them again. That, my friends, is self defense. That is a justified killing.

"Do not imagine for a moment that, if found not guilty, Gayla Rose

Early will go on her merry way. Her life has been changed forever. She has lost two years in a horror story. Her life will never be carefree again. People who have endured this level of physical and sexual torture often need the rest of their lives to learn to trust, to love, to feel safe again. Things you and I take for granted.

"Only you can end Gayla Rose Early's long, grueling nightmare. Send a message that no person should be subjected to such horrors. Return to her what is left of her life. Let us close this sorry chapter of degradation and let her healing begin. Thank you."

Willie almost applauded. Leta's closing had been delivered with such passion, such clarity. And Willie was not the only one caught up in the moment. A charged stillness ran through the room. Her words had touched people. It had been a grand closing. Even the jury seemed moved.

As Leta sat back down, Willie noticed Gayla was dry-eyed, head up. She took her attorney's hand and squeezed it hard with an appreciative nod. She seemed oddly at peace, as though she had accepted that it was all out of her hands now. The only thing left was to submit to her fate.

Tommy, however, leaning against the side wall now, looked as though he was barely holding himself together. His upper back was stiff, but his head was slightly bowed, his eyes brimming with tears.

Willie knew how hard it must be for him to hide the emotions he felt for Gayla from the outside world, but she suspected what he was experiencing now went a lot deeper. The night he had come to the farm, he had seemed markedly different. Gone was the swagger of before, and in its place, humility. And what she had always read as indifference had been replaced by compassion.

Going through this ordeal with Gayla had started profound changes in both herself and Tommy, Willie felt. It was more than just a renewed ability to care for someone again. Parts of them that had been dark and shut down for years had somehow cracked open. She understood the guilt and isolation that had been illuminated and banished for her, but what switch, she wondered, had flipped on for Tommy?

She studied him as he gripped the tops of his thighs, struggling for control. Whatever it was, that stoic dam of his was threatening to break. She understood the inner battle, had experienced it herself. It was not just that Tommy was a man and dare not let himself cry. No, he was afraid if he ever let himself start crying, he would never be able to stop.

Poor Tommy, what has happened to you, she thought.

Willie glanced out a side window of the courthouse. A tiny red cardinal perched on the sill, watching the goings-on inside. The bird's black-lined eyes fluttered with attention. What are you still doing here, Willie wondered. You ought to be flying south by now.

Then a random thought floated up from out of the blue.

Maybe we all should.

CHAPTER 56

A SKY ALL BUT DEVOID OF blue peeked through the rippling curtains of clouds, signaling the threat of ice and the beginning of the transition from fall to winter. Gray tree branches stretched into the fading light, then curled back onto themselves, casting mottled shadows on the ground. Gayla had collapsed onto her cell cot, numb, exhausted. Just like that, it was over. She had expected something enormous to overcome her as the trial wound to a close. Instead, she felt like a bird dropped from the sky, hitting the ground with a splat.

She sat — hugging herself and rubbing her arms, a habit she had started during those long, dark days in the basement. Then it had been one of the only ways to comfort herself. She had talked to herself as well, as though to an injured child, telling herself over and over that it would be all right, not to worry, this will be over, you will get through this. As one month of solitude grew to two, and then to three, and then to a year, she grew to inhabit her own multiphrenic world: victim, healer, cheerleader, confidante, teacher, and, finally, in that moment when Raeder's guard dropped, bloody warrior.

She had pieced together multiple identities to survive. Now it felt odd to be alone, just her, just Gayla, especially with so much on the line.

Leta had left to change her clothes and pick up what she promised would be a dynamite takeout meal, from a real restaurant, which meant she was driving at least thirty miles away. There were no *real* restaurants in Luckau.

Willie had stepped out for a quick errand. Gayla was not sure where Tommy was. He had come in and then hurried back to his cubbyhole of an office.

She had noticed his shaky emotional state by the end of Leta's closing. It had carried an energy of its own that almost enveloped her, too. But Gayla had vowed to stay dry-eyed and strong through the closings of both sides, so she had had to shove Tommy to the back of her mind. It had worked, but now her worry for him was front and center again.

Since they had returned to the jail, there had been no chance to talk. It had all wrapped up quickly after Leta's closing. Judge Bishop gave brief instructions to the jury as to the charge of second-degree murder. Now, across the lawn inside the courthouse, they were in the jury room deliberating, and Gayla's thoughts felt like prayers. Help me to bear this, whatever it is, because I cannot live in a cage any longer.

Gayla had often contemplated lifers in prisons, speculating as to how they managed in their tiny, isolated worlds. Some with never a visitor. Only an hour a day lived outside their cell. She had summoned all her strength to fight for her life that day with Albert. But if they sent her to prison, she did not know if she had another fight in her. She rubbed her upper arms. Help me to bear it, whatever comes, she thought.

"How are you holding up?"

Tommy's words made her jump. He stood on the other side of the bars, seemingly calmer now. Gayla stood up and grabbed through the rails for his hands.

"I'm so glad to see you. I didn't dare look at you in court. I was afraid I'd lose it. Are you okay?"

Tommy squeezed her hands with reassurance, pushing his arms further through the bars and wrapping his hands around her elbows. His voice was shaky.

"I should be the one worrying about you. You're the one who —"

"Tommy . . ."

Damn, it was hard to get out. He was so close, it made her flush. Instead, she pulled his hands up to her lips and covered them with kisses. Their rough, dry calluses made them all the more dear.

"Hey," Tommy said, "What's all this?"

She looked up into his eyes and blurted it out before she could change her mind: "I have to tell you, no matter what happens, you will never know how much it means — what you've done, how you've been there for me. I love you — for that — and . . . I don't want them to take me away without telling you I love you."

His big hands gently pulled her face to his through the iron bars.

"Nobody's taking you away," Tommy said. "I promise."

Then he leaned in and kissed her, with an insistence that took her breath away. It was like he had been saving it up for years. And here it came, all at once. It flowed through her, a warm comforting river. She never wanted it to end. For a moment, she forgot all the unwanted kisses she had endured in the last two years and gave herself over to it, to him.

The sound of giggling pulled them apart. The jail door was being opened and the source of the giggles stepped into the outer office. Tommy stepped back, his eyes saying what he could not.

"We'll talk . . . later," he whispered.

"Okay," she said, with a shy smile.

Around the corner came Leta with carryout boxes and Willie with an armful of roses and a cake box. Both women paused and grinned at the two of them, sensing something had been interrupted.

Finally, Willie said, with a chuckle, "Should we go back and come in again?"

"Oh, no, please," Leta begged. "I can't run the gauntlet of reporters again today."

As Leta and Willie set the table, Tommy and Gayla continued to communicate without words, catching one another's eyes, with the delicious guilt of teenagers almost caught by their parents. Leta had brought back four filet mignons, baked potatoes, salad, and shrimp cocktail to start them off while they warmed up the rest of the food in the microwave. Willie found a plastic pitcher in which to put the long-stem roses and opened the cake box, which had a carrot cake with "We love you, Gayla" in red icing.

For the moment, time was suspended, and everyone seemed to have silently agreed to ignore the uncertainty of what lay ahead. This was not a celebration of possible victory but more a toast to their coming together, and the richness they each felt for that having happened. Gayla looked at the faces around her and smiled at her good fortune. They ate with gusto and the joy of the moment.

They were laughing and only halfway through their steaks when

Frankie Lee opened the jail door and slipped inside. He smiled, but his forehead was furrowed.

"I don't know how to tell you guys this," he said, "but the jury is already back."

Forks paused in midair; they sat frozen, as though posed for a photograph. Finally Leta looked at her watch.

"How long's it been?" Tommy asked.

"Less than three hours."

As though on cue, the jail phone rang, and Tommy jumped up to answer it.

"Yes. Yes. I'll tell her." He hung up and looked at everyone. "They're announcing the verdict in a half hour."

Gayla felt like that bird again, the one that had taken to the air once more, only to fly this time into a telephone pole.

"It's a bad sign. Isn't it?" she asked no one in particular.

"No," Leta quickly reassured her, "not necessarily. Maybe they saw through the prosecution's flimflam quicker than we thought."

Her words did not comfort Gayla.

She was barely aware of her feet as they all trudged back to the courtroom. It was a grim trek; everyone still stunned by the quickness of the jury's decision. The flash of cameras across the courthouse lawn and the white heat of the television lights left Gayla feeling light-headed. She disappeared beneath her hood and tried to ignore the questions being hurled at her by the reporters.

"Which way do you think the jury went, Miss Early?"

"Are you ready to go to prison?"

"How do you feel about the jury coming in so soon, Miss Early?"

As they waited in an antechamber ready to enter the courtroom, Tommy whispered something to Leta, who nodded and stepped out, leaving him alone with Gayla. Tommy put his arms around her and held her close.

"Listen," he whispered, "before we hear the verdict. What I didn't have time to say earlier."

She nodded, even though her head was swimming. His breath brushed against her ears.

"I love you, too, and I'm not letting you go. No matter what happens, I won't let go."

When she didn't respond, he said, "Do you understand?"

She nodded, though she was anything but sure what he meant.

As Gayla and Tommy entered the brightly lit courtroom, its windows shone like a lantern out into the dark streets of Luckau. Tommy led her to the defense table where Leta was already seated. Gayla hoped her lawyer could keep her anchored to reality.

The call to order came in slow motion and jumbled voices. Judge Bishop entered and the rustling crowd fell silent.

"The clerk will bring in the jury, please."

A pulse throbbed in Gayla's temples. The jury filed in, the shuffle of their feet the only sound. Not one person looked at her. Not the women with their pinched mouths. Not the men in their pressed suits.

Judge Bishop nodded to the jury box.

"Has the jury reached a verdict?"

The jury foreman, a smallish man in a brown suit, stood and cleared his throat.

"We have, Your Honor."

"Will the defendant please rise?"

Gayla felt Leta's hand under her elbow, lifting her up, as they stood together. Tommy moved to stand at her other side. She wanted to look at him, at Willie, at these dear people who had denied her nothing, but it was all she could do just to get to her feet.

A piece of paper passed from the foreman to the judge to the county clerk. And then, as if in a muddled dream, Gayla heard a nasal voice read the verdict.

"We the Jury find the defendant, Gayla Rose Early, guilty of murder in the second degree."

There was a moment of absolute stillness. Then Gayla felt her knees buckle. She dropped to the floor before she could take a breath.

CHAPTER 57

TOMMY GRABBED FOR Gayla too late to stop her fall. He heard the crack of her knees on the marble floor and managed to reach her before she hit her head. The courtroom erupted. Stunned, Leta fluttered, not sure how to help. Willie dashed from her seat to them. Most of the reporters fled to their outside cameras before Judge Bishop banged for order. Tommy carried Gayla into the witness room adjacent to the courtroom and tenderly laid her on a hardwood bench.

"Should we call someone?" Leta asked. "Dr. Gordon?"

"Let's see," Tommy said, as he gently shook Gayla. "It's the shock, I imagine."

Gayla's eyes opened, groggy, out of focus.

"Are you back with us?" Tommy asked.

She shook her head to clear it. "What happened?"

"You fainted dead away," Willie told her, as she emerged from an adjoining restroom with wet paper towels for Gayla's face. "Don't try to sit up yet."

Willie coaxed Gayla back down and onto the bench.

"Can you remember what happened?" Tommy asked.

"Oh yes, I remember," Gayla said, covering her face with her hands. She remained like that for a long moment, before looking up at the anxious faces surrounding her. "I can't believe I fainted."

Tommy took her hand. "I've seen it lots of times."

That was a lie — he had never seen it before, but he had watched plenty of people fall to pieces when their verdicts were read. What they usually needed most at that moment was someone to walk them through what came next, as kindly as possible.

"First, just get your bearings," Tommy said. "We're going to do one thing at a time. We stay here until you are feeling okay and we are sure you can walk. Then we go from there. Right now I have to make a quick call."

He stepped outside with his cell phone and arranged for a couple of the National Guard members who had been directing traffic around Luckau's tiny square to help with Gayla's escort back to the jail. With the extra security, as well as Frankie Lee, Leta, and Willie, they would be able to form a solid, protective circle around Gayla, like stage coaches circling before an attack.

All went according to plan, and Tommy's makeshift barrier kept the cameramen at bay and the camera lens away from Gayla's hooded face as they hustled her back to the jail. It was a small blessing. Still Tommy was glad there would be no photos of Gayla to accompany headlines blaring "Sex Slave Guilty in Speedy Verdict."

Back in the jail, the silence was charged. No one knew what to say. Everyone, Tommy included, reeled from the speed and crush of the verdict. It had drained the life out of them. Their half-eaten plates from the earlier feast looked as sad as trampled party confetti the morning after. The untouched cake's "We Love You, Gayla" inscription taunted them.

Finally, Leta sat down and took Gayla's hands in her own.

"It isn't over, you know," Leta said. "We will appeal this thing all the way to the Supreme Court if we have to."

Gayla shook her head. Tommy had never seen her so defeated.

"Do you think any jury's going to believe me, much less come to a different verdict? I don't think so. Not anymore," Gayla said.

For once, Leta had nothing to say.

Later, while Leta and Tommy cleared the half-eaten meal, Willie spent almost an hour quietly talking with Gayla in her cell. When she came out, she shook her head at Tommy and Leta.

"She's going to need some time," Willie said.

"You all go home," Tommy said. "I'll take care of the rest."

Leta, suddenly bedraggled in her neon green, sighed.

"I thought we had a shot. I really did."

"We should have," Tommy said. "You were incredible, Leta. But now I wonder if anything you could have done would have made a difference with that jury."

"Bastards," was all Willie could spit out.

They left and Tommy took out the trash, before heading back to Gayla's cell. A locomotive rumbled through his guts.

He opened the cell door and walked inside. Gayla sat on a corner of the cot, head buried in a corner of the wall. She did not look up.

"Don't feel sorry for me," she mumbled. "It'll just make it worse."

"I won't," he said. "Promise."

He sat down beside her and put an arm around her shoulders, pulling her to him. He could feel the heat from her body rise up as she leaned in to him. They sat like that for a long time, her gently crying from time to time, him stroking her hair, and both thinking about what had to come next.

When she finally dropped off to sleep, he slowly withdrew his arm, laid her down on the cot, and covered her with a blanket. He slipped away to the front office and got out his cell.

When the answer came from the other end, he kept it short.

"It's me. It's happened. We need to talk."

CHAPTER 58

THE SMUG SMILES FROM Ringrose and Garrison when the verdict was read yesterday ate at Willie. It had killed her that she could not do a damn thing to wipe those self-satisfied smirks off their faces. All she could do today was channel her fury into packing, hurrying, so she could get back to town to be with Gayla as soon as possible.

She found herself barking orders at her neighbor's son, a strong, perpetually broke seventeen-year-old, who would do anything Willie asked of him for a little more than minimum wage.

She dropped another box into his arms, when the jittery look on his face registered. Willie smiled sheepishly.

"Oh, Joe, I'm sorry. I've been yelling at you for no good reason all morning. Haven't I? I've a lot on my mind. Just ignore me."

"It's okay," Joe said. "I'm used to it."

Willie looked quizzically at him.

"My dad," he said, by way of explanation.

"Oh, right. Well, don't get me started on your father. Please put all the boxes in the bed of the pickup. The rest of this stuff is going into storage."

Done with the boxes, Joe came to the door.

"What about this?"

Willie looked through the screen door.

"What?"

"This," Joe repeated and pointed to Mutt Dog, who had assumed a sad-sack stance in response to all the hurly-burly going on at the house.

"Not mine," Willie said firmly. "Ignore it."

A few hours later, to her amazement, her house was bare — save for the appliances that had been sold with it. They'd also dropped off the boxes at the Luckau Load 'n' Lock storage unit she'd rented by the month. By the time she dropped Joe off it was past noon. She returned home to clean out the rest of her fridge by making some sandwiches to take into town. Mutt Dog was now parked on the porch.

"Don't look at me like that," she said. "I told you I am not feeding you anymore."

Her voice was firm; inside she wavered. The last few handfuls of Maxine's dry food soon found their way to the porch. The dog dug in.

When Willie arrived at the jail, Frankie Lee was on duty and Tommy was nowhere in sight.

"Where's the sheriff?" Willie asked Gayla through the bars.

"Said he had important business. I don't know."

Willie noticed Gayla's eyes were swollen from crying. It had been a long and lonely night for the girl. Willie found it difficult to make conversation that did not seem trivial in light of what Gayla was facing, but they made an effort. Willie talked about packing up the house; Gayla, about her court schedule. Every subject drifted into an awkward dead end. Her guilty sentence hung over them, like a noose. Trying to ignore it by talking news and weather was impossible.

It was a relief when Tommy joined them an hour later.

"Hi, Willie." He turned to Gayla. "How are you doing?"

Gayla nodded. "I'm okay."

"Good."

Willie sensed an air of purpose about Tommy, a turnabout from the distraught man she had seen the other day in court.

"What's up, Sheriff?" she asked.

"Willie, could I have a minute? I need to talk to you in my office."

Willie said her good-byes and ducked into the messy little area that passed for Tommy's office. After a minute, Tommy joined her. He closed the door so Frankie Lee could not hear them. He did not mince words.

"I need your help."

"Anything," she said.

CHAPTER 59

GAYLA HAD NEVER UNDERSTOOD toothaches. All through her crack use, when most people's teeth would have been decimated, hers had remained intact. When Tommy took her in for routine medical and dental checkups during the months before the trial, the Elk City dentist had marveled at how little damage had been done to her teeth despite years of neglect, poor diet, and drug use — though he had been professional enough not to mention the latter. His hygienist had cleaned Gayla's teeth and he had sent her on her way.

As a child who had never had a single cavity, Gayla knew she had a rare genetic gift. Consequently, she also had no clue as to how a toothache felt or what a person with one would look like. Was it maybe like getting socked in the jaw, she wondered. She knew how that felt. She had gone so far as to ask Tommy, "So how would I look with a toothache?"

Stunned by the question, Tommy had laughed before answering.

"Don't worry. We'll stick a cotton ball in your jaw."

"Like Marlon Brando in *The Godfather?*" This just keeps getting weirder. You want to fill me in on what's going on?"

He stared at her a moment, then shook his head.

"It's better if you don't know any details."

"Come on. I can't stand it."

"It can't be any other way. You don't have a poker face. Know what I mean?" He took her chin in his hand. "Try to trust me."

And that had been that. She promised to do whatever he asked, only to have him then clam up on the details. What on earth was he planning? This was not the Wild West, where you rode in with an extra pony, knocked out the sheriff with the butt of your gun, and emptied the jail. Then again, she thought, Tommy is the sheriff.

Leta's arrival brought her back to reality.

The sentencing date had been announced for week after next. That gave Gayla ten days to get her affairs in order. Gayla shrugged at the news. She had no possessions to store, no relations to wrap things up with. She knew if her parents hadn't surfaced by now, they never would.

Her rundown of what lay ahead done, Leta turned to go.

Gayla spontaneously grabbed and hugged her.

"Leta, you are such a wonderful spitfire, a regular gift from the gods. Thank you, thank you, thank you. You have earned points in heaven for the lengths you went to help me."

A surprised and pleased Leta hugged her back.

"Hey, it's not over. We're going to appeal."

Gayla heard the promise in the words, but she could not help feeling that it was too late. Something had ended, and something else was beginning.

Willie arrived as Leta was leaving. She wanted Gayla's sizes, for everything from jeans to walking shoes. Gayla wanted to pelt her with questions but held back. Something in Willie's eyes seemed to say, you have to trust me, too.

CHAPTER 60

THE MIDAFTERNOON SUN CAST crisp shadows through the towering pecan trees that rimmed Luckau's town square. Early that morning, Tommy had loaded everything into the trunk of his cruiser, well before any activity started around the courthouse. Gayla now paced back and forth in her cell, while Willie waited at her cabin — all empty and ready for the buyers to move in the coming week.

When Frankie Lee arrived early for his afternoon shift, Tommy took a deep breath as the plan slid into motion. He brought Frankie up to speed on the rest of the day's schedule, and was relieved when the deputy told him to leave early.

"I got it, Chief. You need to get her to the dentist for that tooth."

"Okay, Frankie," Tommy said, "that's good of you. We'll head on into Elk City and see the dentist. Don't rightly know what time I'll have her back."

"I'll hold down the fort, Boss. You get on out of here."

Tommy felt a mix of sadness and guilt at leaving this awkward farm boy, whom he had trained into a decent peace officer.

"Okay, you know how to handle things. In fact, you oughta run against me next election."

Frankie looked up at him, shyly pleased. "Awww."

"Really," Tommy said, unlocking Gayla's cell door. "You would do right well in the position."

He put the plastic tie-cuffs on Gayla and guided her to the door.

With the media circus gone, getting her into the back of the cruiser was simple. Tommy was about to get in himself, when he turned back to Frankie, still standing at the jailhouse door.

"Thanks, Deputy."

Behind him, he heard the crunch of gravel.

"Where you headed?" called out a familiar voice. Tommy winced and turned to see Sheriff Dudgeon pulling up in his Elk City cruiser.

Crap, Tommy thought, but "Elmo," was all he said.

"You on your way out?" Elmo seemed in a jolly mood. "I've come to bury the hatchet — thought we could talk about who should host next year's softball tournament." Every spring Elk City, Luckau, and the surrounding towns put on a tourney with teams comprised of city and county officials and law enforcement.

"Uh, not a good time. I'm taking Miss Early into the dentist."

"Too bad. I was going to offer to buy you lunch," Elmo said.

"Sorry to pass that up, but she has a bad toothache. Figured I had better get her in." Tommy gestured at Gayla, whose cheek was puffed out with cotton balls.

"Then you're headed to Elk City to see Dr. Olsen."

"Yep." Tommy tried to keep his tone light.

"Well, alrighty then. We'll just figure it out another time."

Relieved, Tommy went to start his engine when Elmo walked over.

"Hey, you know what? I am on my way home, too," he said. "We can talk in the dentist's office while Miss Early is getting fixed up. I'll just follow you guys."

Tommy's mind whirred, but nothing clever came to mind. What now? He did not have an appointment with the dentist, was only headed north far enough to pick up Willie, but now they were trapped.

"Sounds good," Tommy said, giving a wave and a smile to Elmo, who was already talking with someone on his car radio.

"Crap," Tommy said in a low voice, as he strapped himself in. "We're going to have to figure this out as we go."

Tommy could feel Gayla start to nervously pump her feet and legs.

"What are we going to do?" Her voice squeaked. "It's not going to work, is it. Let's go back inside. I can't let you do this. It's too risky."

Tommy stared at the dashboard for several long moments.

He took a deep breath.

"It'll be okay. Put your hands up here close to the grate."

Careful to cover his actions, he snipped the plastic tie off her wrists through the metal grid separating the front and back seat.

"As soon as we're on our way, get out that cell phone I gave you and call Willie on hers. The number's already programmed in."

Tommy gave Dudgeon a finger-wave as they pulled away from the jail. After a moment, he heard Gayla punch the buttons.

"Now what?" Gayla asked, as she waited for Willie to answer.

"Tell her we're moving to Plan B."

"What's Plan B?" Gayla asked.

Tommy frowned and shrugged.

"Don't know yet."

CHAPTER 61

WILLIE WRESTLED WITH Mutt Dog, trying to keep him from crawling into her lap, while she checked out the controls on the Jeep Cherokee, the only SUV the Elk City rental agency had had available. What she'd really wanted was a muscle car, but all of those were two-seaters now and that would not do for today. Meanwhile, she had decided she could not leave Mutt Dog to certain death in the country, but instead would drop him off near the feed store on their way through Luckau, where someone would surely take pity on him, she told herself. Well, at least his odds would be better there.

"Stay over there on your side, or I'm going to throw you out the window," she warned the dog. They were still arguing when the prepaid cell Tommy had given her buzzed.

"Get over there, Mutt. Now stay," she said, jostling for the phone in her purse. Finally, "Yeah."

"Willie, it's Gayla. We have a problem."

"Already? What happened?"

"Sheriff Dudgeon is on our tail, following us to Elk City."

"For the love of Mike, how did that happen?"

"I'll explain later. Tommy wants to know, Where are you now?"

"My place, waiting for you all."

A pause, while Gayla consulted with Tommy.

"Tommy says how fast can you get to Highway 152?"

"Five minutes, give or take."

Another pause, and Gayla came back on the line.

"Okay, we are a few minutes from your cutoff. He says when you get to 152, turn north towards Elk City. Both cruisers will be ahead of you on the road by a few minutes."

"Okay. Then what?"

"He wants you to catch up to us and pass both of us, speeding like a bat out of hell."

A smile crept across Willie's face.

"Sounds fun. But what the hell will it accomplish?"

"Knowing Dudgeon, Tommy says he won't be able to pass up giving you a ticket, which will buy us a little time. Unless you have a better idea — he's open to suggestions, but we don't have much time."

"Yeah, okay. Then what?" Willie asked, feeling her excitement rise.

"As soon as we see he has you stopped and once we're out of his sight, we'll double back to your place."

"Then we'll rendezvous at my place like we originally planned," Willie said. "Sounds good. See you in a few."

Actually Plan B did not sound all that solid, but she did not have a better plan. And any plan was better than no plan. She started the engine and grinned at Mutt Dog.

"Okay, Buddy. Time to raise some hell."

Inside her, everything had quickened — her pulse, her heartbeat, her breathing. There was even a ringing in her ears. She had not felt this exhilarated since being arrested at a peace protest in the sixties.

She practically raced the late model jeep to the highway and turned north, towards Elk City, instead of her usual route, south into Luckau. Eventually, she spotted Dudgeon's Elk City cruiser just ahead, following behind Tommy's. Willie looked over at Mutt Dog, who was panting with excitement as the scenery whizzed past; you would have thought he knew what was in the works, thought Willie. A crazy whoop rose from deep inside her.

"Okay, Super Dog, let's roll."

It was clear country road as far as the eye could see when she whipped out in front of Dudgeon's cruiser, passed Tommy's, and pushed the accelerator to seventy-five. In a sixty-mile-per-hour zone, she figured that should be bait enough.

She kept the jeep steady at seventy-five. After all, she wanted a ticket, not a night in jail. A few minutes later, sure enough, here came the whir-ring lights behind her. Willie pulled over, and before Dudgeon could open his car door, she saw Tommy and Gayla whip past them.

Clearly in a hurry, Dudgeon barked for her license, registration, and proof of insurance, which Willie was painfully slow in producing.

"I haven't got all day," he barked.

"Sorry, it's a rental, and I don't know where in this packet all the stuff is," Willie replied sweetly. "Oh, here's my license."

She handed it to him.

"Why the hurry?" Dudgeon asked as he took in the name on her license. "Ms. Morris?"

"Taking the dog into the vet."

Dudgeon squinted his eyes at Mutt Dog, who looked spectacularly perky after the whirlwind ride. "Doesn't look sick."

"He cut his leg on a hunter's trap, and it's infected."

Sure enough, the rag on Mutt Dog's leg was still there, with bits of blood on it. Willie tried to slow things down.

"He showed up at my place bleeding. I don't know why the Luckau police don't do something about the farmers who put out those traps, willy-nilly, without even —"

Dudgeon cut her off. "Ain't my jurisdiction."

Willie grasped for anything to prolong the stop. "Well, it doesn't seem like anything is anybody's job anymore. Luckau won't do any-thing about it. How do they handle such things over in Elk City? That's where you're from, isn't it?"

"Ain't much to be done if a farmer wants to trap coyotes." Now Dudgeon squinted hard at her. "Didn't I see you at the trial in Luckau?"

"Yeah. I was there like everybody else in town."

"No, you were . . . a witness. You sat in the front row, right behind the defendant."

Willie was suddenly anxious to move on.

"Anything wrong with that?"

"Just curious," he said, but Willie could have sworn something had clicked with him.

"Helluva show your Elk City prosecutor put on," she said. "I never did like that loud-mouth we have. Garrison hurts my ears."

Dudgeon looked at her for a long moment.

"Yeah, I guess somebody should've given him speech lessons." He finished writing the ticket. "You slow down now. That dog'll get to the vet a lot safer if you do."

"I'll sure do that, Sheriff," Willie said.

She watched him, with a surly face, climb back in his cruiser. She waited until he peeled out and disappeared down the road, then she hooked a U-turn and headed back towards her place. She hoped she had bought enough time for Tommy and Gayla to safely disappear on one of the back roads that led to her farm.

When Willie pulled into her place fifteen minutes later, she breathed easier seeing they were already there, unloading the cruiser. Gayla had changed out of her orange jail garb and Tommy out of his uniform. Now in jeans, boots, and jackets, they could pass for any small town couple.

Willie related the details of her conversation with Dudgeon, and there were nervous hugs all round.

"Did he recognize you?" Tommy asked.

"Yeah, sorta. I'm not sure if he bought the coincidence or not."

"It should be close to an hour before he hits Elk City. That gives us time even if he did think something was up," Tommy said.

They loaded their suitcases into the rental and Tommy parked the cruiser in Willie's garage. As he went to remove the police scanner to take with them, it squawked a message to Sheriff Maynard.

"Ten-minute delay. Still headed into Elk City right behind you." Dudgeon's voice vied with the static.

Tommy punched the receiver. "Copy that. See you there."

The three of them looked at one another for a moment. This was the last chance to back out. Nobody said a word.

"Okay," Tommy said and removed the scanner. Willie put the lock on the garage door. They planned for the cruiser to remain undiscovered until the buyers moved into the house next week. If not, at least the law would need a warrant to get to it.

As they packed themselves into the jeep, with Tommy driving, Willie realized Mutt Dog had not relinquished the passenger seat.

"Oh, sorry," she said as she grabbed the dog and got in the backseat, "I was going to drop him off at the feed store in Luckau on the way. He'll just get eaten by something if I leave his sorry ass out here in the country."

"Let's move," Tommy said. "He's the least of our problems."

Once they were on the road, Tommy turned to Willie.

"We can't risk being seen in Luckau now, Willie. I'll take County 195 around instead. It hooks up with the two-lane headed south."

"Hear that, Mutt Dog? You get a stay for the moment," Willie said. "He made for a good excuse for old Dudgeon, though. Told him I was hurrying him to the vet."

Gayla lifted the bundle of ragged fur into her arms and hugged him.

"Maybe he's our lucky rabbit's foot."

A charged energy filled the jeep as Tommy picked up speed moving towards the highway. Pumped up and breathing hard, they began winding their way down into Texas.

CHAPTER 62

IT REMINDED GAYLA OF ONE of those tense but thrilling movies in which the fugitives keep to the backroads, not sure of their next meal or when a black-and-white might roar out of a roadside hiding place. The danger put life in technicolor: the trees were vibrant greens; the earth, a richer sienna; and the sky, the silkiest of blues.

While Tommy drove, Gayla settled in beside him. After a bit, Willie gave her Mutt Dog to hold. Gayla loved the puppy's warm belly resting on her shoulder, his little breaths tickling her ear. She felt herself trembling with life, a force all the stronger for her knowing how quickly it could come to an end.

Tommy leaned forward, tensely tuned to the police scanner. Gayla wished he would settle down, but the encounter with Elmo had unnerved him, and she could tell he was still shaken. Punishing himself probably, she thought, for not thinking of every possible glitch. Nothing she or Willie had said seemed to comfort him.

Into the muddle of officer and dispatcher messages, a familiar voice suddenly screeched over the scanner.

"Be on look out for Luckau sheriff cruiser. Sheriff and prisoner gone missing. Last seen off 152, ten miles north of Luckau."

Tommy clicked his teeth. "Okay, he got to the dentist's and knows there was no appointment. So we're officially on the lam. "

"We still have a good jump on him," Willie said.

Then for the umpteenth time since they had left, Gayla said again.

"Listen, you guys, it's still not too late for you to —"

Tommy turned to her. "Enough already, okay?"

Willie grinned. "Yeah, zip it."

"Okay, okay." Gayla held her hands up in surrender, then in her best cop voice: "Copy that."

"Damn right, copy that." Tommy grinned, reaching over to squeeze her arm. "Both of us, Willie and I, are right where we want to be."

Dudgeon's voice came on the scanner again.

". . . Also be on look out for late model Jeep Cherokee . . ."

Gayla felt her stomach drop. For a moment, no one spoke.

"Oh Lord," Gayla said. "How does he know what we're driving?"

Willie was the voice of calm. "We knew they'd put two and two together on that. But so fast. Didn't count on that."

Tommy bit his lip. "Yeah, must've had someone check your farm and figured out we're all together. They may have found the cruiser by now, too. Dammit."

Willie reassured him. "Well, we're on the back roads now and they don't even know what direction we're headed."

"They'll figure that out soon enough. Don't you think?" Gayla said, looking with alarm at Tommy.

"Yeah," Tommy admitted, then to Willie. "Maybe we should have used your old pickup, after all. It would have blended in with a hundred others in this area."

Willie shrugged. "Too late now — I sold it to my seventeen-year-old neighbor for a dollar. He's probably drag racing as we speak. I don't suppose there's any way to ditch this vehicle."

"I'd sure feel safer," Tommy said.

Gayla sat back and closed her eyes, trying to quiet her nerves. She found herself praying, as she had so often in the basement. God, these people have put everything on the line to help me. Do not let them get hurt. I know this is a shameless prayer from the trenches, but that's where we are. If our plan is part of your plan, show us a sign . . . please.

Gayla had no idea how long she repeated her little appeal to the heavens. She could hear Tommy and Willie talking quietly from time to time in the front seat, but she kept praying, saying the same words over and over, while petting the dog.

Then she saw it, out in the middle of a field, just off the county road they were now on. An ancient Chevrolet Impala, paint peeling off what used to be a red exterior, with a hand-painted sign: "$3000 OBO."

"There's the answer," Gayla said.

"That beat up thing? For three thousand?" Tommy couldn't help but laugh. "I don't think so."

"Pull in," Gayla insisted. "I have a good feeling about this."

She did not say it was a sign, but she knew it to be so in her heart. Against improbable odds, that beat-up Impala with grass growing around its wheels was the answer to their prayers.

Willie turned into the drive of the nearby farmhouse.

"It can't hurt to check," she told Tommy.

"We'll lose time and risk being recognized," Tommy countered.

"No more dangerous than this car being spotted," Willie argued. She looked over at the run-down house. "They look poor as church mice. Want me to do it?"

"No, I'll go." Tommy got out and walked to the front door. A young-ish man in overalls answered his knock. Gayla kept out of sight, but both she and Willie could hear the conversation. Without enthusiasm, Tommy asked about the car.

"Yeah, hate to let her go, but the wife's been real sick . . . we got medical bills."

"How's the car run?" Tommy asked.

"Real good. That's why I'm asking so much. It was left to us by my wife's aunt. I did all the engine work on her myself, and we were saving up to get her repainted. Now we got to sell her. You can test drive her if you want, but she's solid."

Tommy and the man walked across the field and hunched over the engine together a few minutes. The engine roared to life. Willie and Gayla watched open-mouthed as the ragged-looking Impala whipped out onto the asphalt road and peeled out of sight as if it was pacing a NASCAR race.

Willie squealed with delight. "Shoot, we got us a muscle car after all. This is going to be fun. Where's my canvas bag?"

Willie unzipped her bag and set it on her lap. Gayla caught a glimpse inside and was stunned.

"Willie, what have you done?"

Willie put her hand over the bag's mouth, but it was too late to hide its contents. "Don't you worry about that."

"But . . ." Gayla did not even know where to begin.

"Just let me be the moneybags, okay? It's what I want."

A few minutes later, Tommy and the man returned. Tommy stepped out of the Impala grinning from ear to ear. He winked at Gayla and Willie, then did one last check under the hood before walking over to the jeep.

"Okay Gayla, I'm eating crow. You were right. It's just what we need. I gave him thirty-five hundred."

"But, I have cash right here," Willie protested.

"It's okay. I sold my trailer to my neighbor yesterday for five thousand cash. It'll hold us for a while, but we'll need yours soon enough."

As they switched out the bags and scanner into the Impala, Gayla asked Tommy what he planned to do with the jeep.

"Isn't it rented to Willie?"

"Yeah," Tommy said, "but the extra five hundred was so the guy wouldn't 'discover' it deserted in his field for several days."

"He didn't ask questions?" Willie asked.

"No. Just said he didn't normally break the law." Tommy grinned. "I told him, normally, neither did I."

They finished reloading and settled into the roadster. The original leather upholstery was beat to hell, but the seats were still comfortable. There was no cruise control, so Willie acquiesced to Tommy's handling the driving again. The last thing they needed was to get caught for speeding. The scanner gave up no more clues as to Sheriff Dudgeon's whereabouts. Tommy figured they knew he was listening and had gone dark.

Evening fell, like a protective shawl, around them. The sky shifted to a dark blue, with only a moon to shine on the bulbous clouds that flowed over the horizon.

The dashboard instruments became their only light, the hum of the motor their only sound. It felt as though they were floating just above the earth, as they pressed on into the night.

CHAPTER 63

IT WAS AFTER NINE WHEN they passed the Dallas city limits sign. Tommy pulled out a prepaid cell and punched in Hugh's number. After a couple of rings, he answered.

"Hey, we're here," Tommy said.

"You're late. Run into trouble?" Hugh asked.

"A couple of delays, had to take the backroads, which slowed us down, but we're clean. I hope."

"I'm already at the hangar."

"Copy that," Tommy said and clicked off.

Both Willie and Gayla were wide-eyed. Only Mutt Dog was still snoozing in Willie's lap. The Impala had run as well as the farmer had promised, and the one cash stop for gas was quick and uneventful. By sticking to the back roads, they had avoided the highway patrol and passed only a handful of local black-and-whites. As they wound through the night guided by the lights of farmhouses, Willie could not help but think it had felt like lanterns giving the all clear to a night train.

Only in the last hour or so had they allowed themselves to talk about the colony of veterans south of the border where they were headed. How Willie's money would set them up there, maybe even buy them a little house. How Tommy had been assured he would be able to find work within the community. There was always a need for security, Hugh had said, though during his numerous visits to the enclave he had found it as safe or safer than most Mexican or even American towns.

CRIMES OF REDEMPTION

Hugh thought Gayla's medical training would be a natural fit in a place that had only one doctor and nurse to serve a population of several hundred. Assurances had been given that they would be welcomed as potential assets to the colony. In any case, they would hardly be the first or last fugitives to grace its grounds. Tommy assumed, as in many towns south of the border, that a few dollars greasing the right palms would go a long way towards protecting one's anonymity.

With the Dallas skyline in their sights, the trio rode quietly, no one daring to jinx this last leg of the trip. The police scanner had broadcasted an all-points bulletin on the cruiser and the rented Cherokee, and given descriptions of the three of them, so they knew better than to take anything for granted. Still, they were nearly there, and Hugh was waiting to help them on the next step of their journey.

They sped past the airport diner, Tommy smiling at the place where the seed of this had been planted not so long ago, and pulled up to the hangar. A lone light shone through the entrance door. As they exited the car, Tommy motioned Gayla and Willie to hurry ahead of him. And they quickly slipped inside the hangar.

He breathed a sigh of relief when he saw Hugh inside alone. They hugged, and Hugh gave Tommy a couple good pats on the back before he broke away.

"You made it, man," Hugh said, then grinning at Gayla and Willie. "Hello, ladies."

"A couple of problems averted," Tommy said, "but we're here. Can we load our stuff onto the plane?"

Hugh nodded and they headed back to the Impala; he kept watch outside the hangar door as they relayed their stuff onto the Piper Cub. After everything was in place, Hugh drew Tommy to the side.

"I haven't told you everything exactly," he said.

Tommy's face fell. "Oh no, what?"

"Your sheriff from Elk City tracked me down this afternoon."

"Oh damn, is he here?"

"Not yet, but he's definitely on his way. He got my name from the court records. He figured you might be headed here to see me. I told him I didn't know anything, of course, but by now he is bound to know about the plane as well."

"Then we have to move. Now."

"Yeah, right. But, Tommy, now that he knows about me, I can't be the one to fly you down. It would mean my badge, my family, everything."

Tommy frowned and nodded in understanding.

"Then why did you let us load up? If we can't go . . ."

"I can't fly you down. You'll have to do it." Hugh handed Tommy the keys. "I'm headed home right now. The only place I can be, when and if your sheriff shows up, is my house. Understood?"

Tommy started to protest.

"Listen," Hugh said firmly, "when this plane 'disappears' from my hangar in a few minutes, I'll be home and won't know anything about it. You see now?"

"Hugh, I haven't flown in —"

"Don't remind me of that, please. I am refusing to let myself even think about that. It's a simple engine. You have flown in cockpits ten times more complicated."

Hugh dropped an envelope into Tommy's hands, then looked his friend straight in the eyes.

"You can do it, Tommy."

Hugh pulled out his car keys and headed for the door.

"It's all arranged at the other end. Someone will fly the plane back when it's safe. Maps, everything are in the envelope. They'll meet you and take you on in. Sorry, buddy, but that's all I got. Now move. I'm out of here."

"Wait," Tommy said, fishing out the keys to the Impala. "Here's a new project for you. It looks like a dud, but runs like NASCAR."

Hugh grinned. "Okay, man. Now go before I change my mind."

"I'll make it up to you," Tommy said, embracing Hugh so hard he scared himself.

"Just go be happy. I'll visit you as soon as I can. Now git."

"We're okay to take off?" Tommy asked, running up the ramp to the plane.

"You don't have to file a flight plan with a private plane. Now get out of here." And Hugh was gone.

Tommy stepped into the warmly lit Piper Cub. Willie and Gayla watched uncertainly as Hugh's car drove away. When Tommy climbed into the pilot's seat, they went wide-eyed.

"Okay, ladies, change of plan. God help us, I'm flying this baby."

He quickly checked the plane's interior, then the cockpit, sizing up the dials and gauges. For the first time in decades, Tommy readied for takeoff.

"Buckle your seat belts," he said.

The engine rumbled to life, and he guided her out the hangar door.

The Piper Cub rolled onto the runway, just as an approaching siren split the air. The little band of fugitives held their collective breath as a black-and-white screamed around the corner at the end of the row of hangars. The cruiser hurtled towards them, its bubble flashing red and blue kinetic patterns against the sides of the hangars.

Tommy's hands flew, trying to pick up the plane's acceleration. The Piper picked up speed, but the cruiser came so close they could read the Elk City logo on its side.

"It's Dudgeon," Gayla yelled over the engine noise.

"Hang on," Tommy yelled back.

"And pray," Willie added for good measure.

Gayla and Willie looked out the side windows as the cruiser screeched to a stop and Dudgeon's thick frame jumped out of the car. His hands waved wildly and he screamed after them, but the words were lost in the roar of the plane's engine. Still hollering, Dudgeon drew his sidearm and ran after the taxiing plane.

Tommy gunned the engine and took off down the runway. Behind them, Dudgeon fired warning shots into the air. He heard Dudgeon scream to no avail: "Stop, dammit. Stop in the name of the law."

In the silence that followed, Tommy realized Dudgeon had figured out that they could not hear him. He glanced back and saw the Beckham County sheriff had stopped and turned his revolver on the plane.

Tommy heard a bullet whiz over the left wing.

"Crazy bastard." Tommy pushed the engine harder.

Then, in the moment that always makes the heart skip a beat, the wheels stopped their rumbling and the Piper Cub whooshed into the air. In seconds, the only sound was the sweet hum of the engine as they left earth. The wheels rolled back into the plane's belly with a delicious, satisfying grind.

A rush of relief washed over Tommy and a little cry escaped his lips. He heard Gayla and Willie clapping their hands. As he pushed the

Piper Cub up, up, up into the sky, Dudgeon became a forlorn dot on the runway below.

No one spoke.

No one needed to.

Tommy's eyes watered as he once again felt the same youthful joy as flying the little tin plane in his dreams, climbing high above the ground, headed into the stars.

And as marvelous as the stars ahead promised to be, he thought, they were nothing compared to the way the universe sometimes conspires to bring fresh beauty into old hearts, without our knowledge, and even without our permission.

* * * * * * * * * * * * *

Willie had apologized the whole trip for Mutt Dog and had promised herself (and anyone who would listen) that she would be dropping him off somewhere along the way, long before they reached Dallas. Yet here he was sleeping in her lap. Next stop, Mexico. It seemed that everything in her life had opened back up. As a young woman, how many times had she dreamed of getting in a boat and sailing off into the horizon?

She thought of what she had brought for the trip: a few clothes, some pictures of Jack, a family heirloom or two, including a doily her great-great-grandmother had crocheted. That was it. Only a few months ago, Willie would not have been able to let go of anything. Release came, when she realized that nothing could really be left behind. Not the bad or the good. It had taken all of it to bring her to where she was tonight. She had given up her fight to change the past, and with that surrender came the beginning of self forgiveness. Now it seemed Jack was laughing as he walked through her heart. She hoped he knew he would always be welcomed there.

Mutt Dog almost had her trained. His nose nudged her hand the moment she stopped petting him and didn't stop until it returned to patting his soft fur. She had always marveled at how dogs could relentlessly ask for what they wanted. They felt no shame in going after what they needed. Neither petulant or demanding, they just were. In fact, all the dogs she had ever loved had shared a simple wish: To be good and to love you back. Willie looked down at her fuzzy, new companion.

"You think you have it made in the shade, don't you, Buster?" Then, still trying to be truculent, she announced to the plane.

"Well, I guess it's gonna need a name."

Gayla turned around from her seat beside Tommy.

"How about Navigator?"

"We might need one," Tommy quipped.

Willie smiled, pleased to see him jump into the conversation so easily. She barely recognized this man behind the controls. This new Tommy smiled and laughed and told jokes, as they glided through the cloudy night sky.

"Navigator. Nope, too many syllables."

Willie thought a moment as she studied the puppy's button bright eyes now wide awake as if he knew they were talking about him, then snapped her fingers.

"I got it. I think he's a Scout. Yeah. Scout. You like that?"

She picked up the puppy and shook him playfully like a happy baby.

"I could use a Scout."

* * * * * * * * * * * *

The purr of the engine made for a perfect lullaby, Gayla thought. She loved the up-closeness of the heavens visible through the cockpit's rounded glass. She shivered a little at how high they were in the dim space of night.

She looked over at Tommy, who was beaming like a kid on Christmas morning. After their angst-filled getaway and his initial reservation, he wore his role as their leader easily. The delight on his face was evidence that he had also again become comfortable as pilot. She reached over and touched the top of his hand.

"You handle this like a champ."

Gayla had given up on how to begin to thank Tommy and Willie. Words seemed so pitiful compared to what they had risked and left behind for her. She understood they did not see it that way. She knew they believed they were all making a second run at life.

Still, she could not help thinking: This is as close as I will ever come to unconditional love. She had lived long enough to know that this carried no guarantees. Life would continue to produce new twists and surprises down the road, and their story could still turn out differently than any of them imagined.

For now, that did not matter.

Tomorrow would be here soon enough.

For now, it was enough to be a blinking firefly in the dark skies, flying into their new life. She reached back for Willie's hand. Willie smiled, her eyes soft and peaceful.

Gayla put her other hand in Tommy's and he squeezed back. She held on tight. It was too much right now to sort out all her feelings for Tommy. We'll have all the time we need for that, she thought.

For now, being together was enough.

Gayla gazed out the window at a backdrop of celestial lights, glowing ever brighter as the sky slipped towards midnight. It seemed to her as if the heavens had lifted them up and, ever so gently, tossed them into a milky way of light that rolled under the moon like a new river.

EPILOGUE

The following summer, a drought caused the muddy red waters of Lake Luckau to drop to their lowest level in more than a decade. During a Saturday beer party in late July, four teenagers swimming in the lake discovered a rusted, sunken Chevrolet Nova. At the wheel sat the skeletal remains of a middle-aged male. A large rock weighted down the accelerator. The next day Leta O'Reilly, in a resplendent cherry red suit, announced her candidacy to unseat Charles Ringrose as district attorney for Beckham and Kiowa counties. She cited his failure to investigate the disappearance and murder of Terry Randolph Sewell as evidence of his incompetence.

ABOUT THE AUTHOR

Linda McDonald was born and reared on the western plains of Oklahoma. She holds master's degrees in theatre from the University of Kansas and in creative writing from the University of Central Oklahoma, where she also taught for many years. Active in regional theatre, she both performs and directs. Her plays have been produced in Oklahoma City, Dallas, and New York. *Crimes of Redemption* is her first novel. She makes her home in Oklahoma City, Oklahoma.

ACKNOWLEDGMENTS

Special thanks to my friend Gaylene Murphy for paving the way and to the other rocking members of my writing group: Ron Collier, Ranell Collins, Rick Lippert, and Jennifer Lindsey-McClintock, who listened, gave advice, encouraged, and supported this effort.

Thanks to John Soos, who shared what he lived.

Thanks to Jeanne Devlin for finding value in these pages and to The RoadRunner Press for its refreshing belief in both Oklahoma stories and writers.